# PERIL IN THE OLD COUNTRY

# COUNTRY

## SAM HOOKER

ISBN Print  978-0-9997423-0-3
Illustration by Lian Croft
Cover design by Najla Qamber
Edited by Melissa Ringsted
Interior Layout Design Rebecca Poole
Publication date June 5, 2018
Black Spot Books

# DEDICATION

For Jack. May your way through the world be ever lit by stars. May you always follow the brightest ones, and may they lead you to joy and wonder.

# ACKNOWLEDGEMENTS

This novel would not have been possible without the unwavering support of my amazing wife, Shelly Blair. While my talent for lining up words in clever patterns may have helped, I never could have done it without her.

She is my sunshine, my only sunshine.

Furthermore, I would be remiss in failing to mention Lindy Ryan and the exceptional team at Black Spot Books. They are the difference between a good manuscript and a book worth publishing. My thanks to all of them for their faith in, and support for, the silly nonsense I've written.

Thanks also to Lian Croft for the illustration of Sloot. Her ability to deliver brilliance with no more direction than "just make him look really, really worried" is astonishing.

# ⅊⅂THE FORGOTTEN WATCH⅊⅂

The first hues of indigo muscled their way into the sky over Salzstadt, which the inky black of night really should have seen coming. It had happened just like that every morning since the dawn of time, but nighttime is resistant to change. It's the grumpy old codger of the celestial routine, always mumbling about how great things used to be, when mornings were respectful toward their elders and gave them a few extra minutes to wrap things up.

Days were always in a hurry now. Had to be. You start letting people sleep in, and it's all downhill from there. You might find more permissive, reformist sorts of days elsewhere in the world, but not in Salzstadt. The good salts who live there have a fanatical respect for the rules. After all, rules are what keep the goblins away.

Few have ever seen a goblin, save the occasional blur in the corner of one's vision, but everyone knows they're there. Goblins are foul little spirits made of mischief, teeth, and a knack for knowing when a trouser-related mishap will cause the most embarrassment.

Salzstadt is the capital of the Old Country, which has a proper name, though it's forbidden to speak it aloud because it attracts goblins. So does swearing, which is unfortunate for the innumerable salt miners who live near the docks. Most of them know enough swear words to qualify as bilingual.

There are a few low-grade swear words, such as the one that starts with an "M" and describes the face people make right before a sneeze, which goblins find too tame for a reaction on their part. Other swear words may attract a single goblin, or an entire congress (being the preferred nomenclature for a group of goblins).

"Leave me dinner in the oven," many an old salt has said to their spouse over the years. "I've got to get me out to the crags, for I'm of a mind to say the one that rhymes with *elbow*."

There are other rules that keep the goblins at bay, but the dawn is increasingly impatient to get on with things. All the rest in due time, then.

It wasn't until the aforementioned indigo had cleared some sky for purple, then blue, and even a touch of amber, before Sloot Peril stirred from his dreamless sleep. He'd once heard something about his dreams coming true as the result of hard work. Given the frequency of the one where he's naked in the counting house again, giving up dreaming altogether seemed the safest bet.

Like every salt who had graduated from youth, found stable employment, and was counting down the decades until retirement—and the privilege of complaining at length about how much better things had been in their day—Sloot went through the motions of patriotism while he dressed in his modest woolen outfit.

When reciting the Loyalist Oath, it was traditional to square one's shoulders and speak clearly toward the mighty flag of the Old Country. Three white circles on a field of red, representing the salt that was the life's blood of the nation. The Domnitor, long may he reign, whose family had ruled over the Old Country for generations, had taken great pains to ensure that his subjects could look through virtually any window and see an enormous flag waving valiantly in the breeze, atop one building or another; however, the tiny window of Sloot's apartment above a butcher shop offered a view of nothing but a similar window. It looked into another apartment within arm's reach, which was occupied by a man who looked remarkably like Sloot. Curtains might have provided them both some amount of privacy, though they'd also have robbed them both of any natural light that managed to elbow its way between the two buildings on occasion, and into their respective apartments.

Their unspoken compromise was just to ignore each other, hence no name is available to give for this neighbor, who will probably never be mentioned again.

Fortunately, the Office of Domestic Scrutiny had made paper representations available for a modest fee, and the one pinned to the back of Sloot's front door kept him in the Domnitor's good graces, as far as he could tell.

Sloot cleared his throat, placed his hand over his heart, and recited:

"Hail to thee, oh mighty Salzstadt, capital of name redacted,

"I pledge good faith and daily strive to see justice enacted.

"And if so much as merest thought of something nearing treason,

"Should come to light within my sight,

"I'll cry out loud and form a crowd,

"With pitchforks you'll find pleasing."

There were three dozen more stanzas, all of which he recited flawlessly, and with no reduction in fervor.

While he was still in school, when the class had finished the recitation, the teachers had the children turn and slap each other across the face so they wouldn't forget. Sloot had never been sure what he was supposed to do about it now that he did his recitation on his own, so he slapped himself just to be on the safe side. He reasoned that he was far too old not to know, and didn't want to slip up if anyone were watching.

Sloot had spent his life up to that point nurturing an utter dearth of "self-confidence," a term he believed had been invented by guidance counselors who truly enjoyed lying to people. In any case, the slapping seemed to be working. He was nearly forty, and heresy had yet to creep into his mind.

The cobbles outside his building were slick with dew, so he walked carefully toward the north gate of the city. Salzstadt is the southernmost point in the Old Country, encircled by mountains except for the southern coast, where the Three Bells Shipping Company sends its ships out to trade with the rest of the world. The great road winds its way north from the city's central plaza to the massive main gate in the equally massive north wall. It's anyone's guess why they bothered building a gate into it at all, given that it never opens. Anyone coming into Salzstadt from the surrounding countryside does so through one of several smaller gates to the east and west of the main one.

The main gate stands as a symbol of protection against the Old Country's great enemy to the north, the heathen barbarians who long ago decided to unite under a very non-Old Country flag and form the nation of Carpathia.

The Carpathians are a warlike band of savages who, as far as Sloot had been informed, wore the untanned skins of the beasts they killed with their bare hands, communicated only through grunts and bloodthirsty screaming, ate fruit without washing it first, and worse.

Even as a child, Sloot was made to be so deathly afraid of a Carpathian invasion that he had nightmares. He and his mother had lived near the main gate in those days, so she took him every morning before school to place his hand on it, so he could see how genuinely mighty it was, and that it was still closed.

It now added just over a mile to his walk to work in the Three Bells counting house, but he still made the trip every day.

And so it was that on this morning in particular, just as he had on every morning before—including Sundays, which the feral Carpathians couldn't be trusted to take off—he placed his hand on the main gate and took comfort in its solidity.

"You there," said a comically muscled guard, whose head sat squarely on her shoulders. "Let's have a look at your papers."

"Certainly," said Sloot, producing a stack of papers bound in a leather wrap. He was so eager in doing so that it probably came off as suspicious, but little was more exciting to Sloot than an opportunity to comply with the law.

"I don't see a stamp from the Border Authority," she said, leafing through the pages. "What are you doing so close to the gate?"

"I've got special dispensation from the Public Health Authority." Sloot pointed to a red caduceus stamped on a medical form, right above the words "severe nervous condition."

"So you have to come touch the gate every day for ... what, nerves?"

"Yes, ma'am," said Sloot. "Every day since I can remember."

"Huh." The guard squinted one eye in confusion. "Oh well, you don't look like you could cause much trouble if you wanted to. On your way, Mister … *Peril*. What sort of name is that? Sounds Carpathian."

"I get that a lot," said Sloot. "But I'm as true a salt as you're likely to meet. A loyal subject of the Domnitor, long may he reign."

"Long may he reign. Yeah, all right." She shoved the papers back into his hands and was on her way.

Like most people whose nerves were constantly on edge, Sloot was comforted by routines, and hated deviations from them; hence the pained whimper that rose from him when he reached into his pocket for his mother's watch and came up empty.

It was an inexpensive thing, made of tin during the war when every scrap of steel went into making swords for the Domnitor's valiant troops (long may he reign). The watch clanked loudly, needed winding eleven times a day, and like the main gate was a comforting reminder that his mother was always there to provide the sort of severe patriotism in lieu of affection that he'd known as a child.

He knew it hadn't been stolen, he'd simply left it sitting atop the dresser. This presented a quandary, which caused Sloot a measure of disquiet that not even the main gate's imperviousness could assuage.

He had two options, which were one too many for his taste: go back home and get the watch, and almost certainly be late to work; or go to work without it, and let this be the first time in the nearly twenty years since his mother had given it to him that it was allowed to wind down and stop ticking.

For the most part, Sloot was only as superstitious as required by law. The rational part of his mind that didn't truck with sentimental nonsense assured him that the watch wasn't a metaphor for his mother's heart, and that she was in no mortal danger if the watch were left to wind down *one time*.

Right. It definitely wasn't.

By the time he made it back to his apartment, he needed no further reminding that he was not suited to sprinting. His physical agony paired tragically with dismay when he saw the line outside the door to the butcher shop on the ground floor. It was the only door into the building, and only wide enough for one person. Luckily, the butcher was not yet open for business, so Sloot held onto the hope that he might be able to slip past the dozen elderly salts who were waiting to buy their daily meats.

"Pardon me," said Sloot to the old gran at the head of the line, who had the grave misfortune of being the Widow Kranksi, one of the most disagreeable people Sloot had ever met.

"No cuts," the Widow Kranski stated plainly. Her arms had already been folded in grim determination about something else, but she made it a point to refold them for emphasis.

This was a delicate situation. One of the more severe breaches of Old Country etiquette was cutting in line, a universally reviled practice that was an irresistible lure for goblins.

"Right you are," said Sloot, "but I'm not here to buy anything, I live upstairs. I've got a key and everything, I just need to—"

"No cuts! Them's me final words on the matter!"

"It won't be cutting, though. I just—"

"Now you look here!" A bony finger gave a very practiced waggle in Sloot's face, the result of expertise gained over a lifetime of telling people off. "I'll not have the oldest butcher in Salzstadt infested with goblins, not while it's in my power to stop it. No cuts, and not another word!"

The other old grans in the line started murmuring and glaring in a way that couldn't end well. They were all queued very formally, the way that all salts did to make absolutely certain that lines weren't even cut by accident.

Sloot was a breath away from making another plea when he noticed that the Widow Kranski's arms had unfolded, and her fists were now planted on her hips. With a defeated sigh, Sloot hung his head and walked to the end of the line.

"Lift your feet!" shouted the Widow Kranski. "You're shuffling!"

It's very bad luck in the Old Country to throw a punch. "Punching up a goblin," they called it. That's why the preferred footwear among its citizens is hobnail boots. Fights tend to involve a lot of kicking, and no one wants to be the one sap wearing bedroom slippers when things get ugly.

Ever the follower of a good trend, Sloot was thusly outfitted for a proper row, but there was no way he was going to fight an old gran. Men hated fighting women because they could kick higher, and lacked a certain target that was handy in ending fights. Older women were especially feared, having the benefit of experience.

Sloot tapped his foot in constant agitation as the butcher took his sweet time with each of the old grans and gramps in turn, until at last he was able to dash up the stairs. At least the watch hadn't wound down before he got to it, though its clanking seemed even more labored and desperate than usual. His hands shook as he wound it, his own heart likely in more danger than his mother's.

✢┄✢┄✢┄✢┄

"Where have you *been?*" hissed Beatrice from the desk next to his, without bothering to look up from her work.

"It's a long story," said Sloot, who hoped that he wasn't shouting, but couldn't tell for the thundering of his heart in his ears. "Have the supervisors noticed?"

"Worse than that," said Beatrice. "I'd get that report checked as soon as possible and walk it in yourself!"

Sloot looked down at the report on his desk and was overcome with dread. While checking reports was generally one of his favorite parts of the job, this particular report was bound for Mrs. Knife.

Sloot had never met Mrs. Knife in person, though he'd nearly been brought to tears once upon finding himself in the same room as her reputation. Mrs. Knife was the personification of malevolence, assembled in hell by puppy-hating demons and given advanced degrees in robbing souls of joy. She had no official title within the organization but was understood to rank far above everyone except Lord Hapsgalt himself.

It wasn't yet time for lunch, and already Sloot's day had crumbled into an unmitigated disaster. His hand trembled as it reached for his quill.

"Hurry!" Beatrice hissed. "If you don't finish soon, she might come over here!"

The thought alone was enough to curdle milk. In a flash of desperate inspiration, Sloot's mathematical expertise found a way to fuel itself with sheer terror, and he channeled his very soul into correcting the report.

His horror was compounded by the fact that the report had been written by none other than Vasily Pritygud, the utter nincompoop who had graduated last in Sloot's class at the University of Salzstadt. Vasily's work was consistently abysmal, so it was reported to his father—a very affluent shareholder in the Three Bells—that his son's work was nothing if not consistent. It always fell to Sloot and his coworkers to fix everything that Vasily wrote, which took a lot of time. Time was something that Sloot, on this day in particular, did not have.

What he did have, in abundance, were ulcers. Permanent damage to his innards, the result of years of worry over the most disastrous possible conclusion to any sequence of events. They had turned him into the imminent perfectionist who was now rewriting the report with blinding speed. Time seemed to slow down as his frantic scribbling approached the speed of thought. Panic attacks hadn't reduced him to the shell of what might have turned out to be a happy and functional human being, they had prepared him for this moment.

Well, they'd done both, really, but Sloot was trying to remain positive. It rarely ever worked, but odds are beaten by persistence.

In the end, he'd rewritten the entire report himself, largely by contradicting everything that Vasily had written, probably while drunk. At least Sloot *hoped* that Vasily had been drunk. Otherwise, he could only think that the sheer number of errors had been malevolence, not stupidity.

As Sloot ran down the hallway, waving the pages in the air before him to coax the ink dry, he seriously pondered another possibility. Maybe

Vasily just longed for the sweet release of death so intently that he intentionally erred so egregiously with regard to Lord Hapsgalt's money.

Mrs. Knife's office was the one at the end of the long, gloomy hallway that raised one's hackles simply for having looked at it. The air in the hallway had an ominous, greasy feeling. Sloot did his best to ignore the impression that it was looking forward to murdering him.

Not wanting to give the hallway the (accurate) impression that he was afraid of it, Sloot slowed his sprint to a rushing walk and spent a moment failing to catch his breath before raising his hand to knock on the door.

Just as his knuckles made contact with the wood, the door slid soundlessly open, slowly enough to give him time to consider making a run for it, but quickly enough to assure that he'd fail if he tried. And just like that, with no further preamble or opportunity to steel himself, he was looking directly into the cruel and calculating gaze of Mrs. Knife.

"You're late," she said, her gaze unblinking, her fingers steepled. She sat in a high-backed leather chair behind a desk of dark polished wood, the gloomy grey sky over the harbor visible through the large window behind her. There were no other furnishings in the room, no papers on the desk, no place for Sloot to sit, not that he wanted to stay a second longer than he must.

It was hard to tell how old Mrs. Knife was. She appeared old, but as sharp as her name. Her grey hair was pulled into a bun. She wore a simple black dress and no jewelry, aside from a ring on her left forefinger that looked like two silver snakes coiled around a black stone.

Still out of breath, he walked in stiffly, attempting to maintain as much professional decorum as possible. Mrs. Knife made no motion to take the papers from him when he held them out, so he laid them upon the desk and waited.

Her eyes never left his. Sloot fought to suppress the urge to confess to crimes he'd never committed, and nearly lost before she broke the silence.

"Tell me plainly, mister …"

"Peril," Sloot squeaked. He cleared his throat. "Sloot Peril, ma'am."

"Peril," she repeated, her eyes narrowing. "What sort of name is that? It sounds Carpathian."

"Er, not that I'm aware of, ma'am. Born and raised in Salzstadt."

"We'll see about that. Give me your report."

"It's just there on the desk, ma'am."

Baleful glares do not usually growl with impatience. That was a first in Sloot's experience.

"My time is more valuable than yours, Peril. Tell me what's in it, and be brief."

"Yes! Sorry, ma'am."

"Never mind that. Does Lord Hapsgalt need to count his money or not?"

Sloot was not a rich man, but he worked for those who were. He knew enough about the very, very rich to understand that in their eyes, counting one's money was tantamount to the end of the world. A slippery slope that ended with auctioning off one's larger estates and living the rest of their lives in the relative obscurity of being merely *wealthy*.

Being *wealthy* is vastly different from being very, very rich. The wealthy are driven to unspeakable depths of depravity, such as knowing, at any given time, roughly how much money they have. The very, very rich, on the other hand, have the luxury of merely knowing that they have far more money than they and their family will ever be able to spend, and that they can simply refer to their piles of money with words like "vast" and "unfathomable."

"Absolutely not," said Sloot, speaking with confidence for the first time since having recited the Loyalist Oath that morning. "Lord Hapsgalt's holdings are as vastly immeasurable today as they've ever been."

Mrs. Knife's gaze withered a few years from his life. Sloot felt as though she were waiting for him to confess something. Fortunately, they were now in his territory. Numbers possessed no capacity to hide truth from Sloot Peril.

He'd probably saved Vasily Pritygud's life by rewriting that report. The scandal of counting of Lord Hapsgalt's fortune, to say nothing of the expense of hiring the scores of accountants who would have to say good-bye to their families for the lifetime of work they'd be undertaking, would have cast a pall over the financial landscape. Entire financial markets have crumbled over less.

"You're nervous, Mister Peril."

"Yes, ma'am."

"And you're also quite certain about your findings?"

"Quite, ma'am."

A geological epoch passed while Mrs. Knife willed Sloot to crack, but he did not.

"Very well," said Mrs. Knife, sweeping the report into the wastebasket at the end of her desk. "I have another task for you."

# ⇜⇝THE FEAST OF SAINT BERTHA⇜⇝

Bertha earned her sainthood for the discovery of the broom; or rather its application as the single most formidable weapon in the war against the goblins. Brooms had already been discovered in the most basic sense.

The Festival of St. Bertha, apart from being a handy excuse for getting drunk in public on a Thursday, reminded every salt in the city of her heroism.

Well, not everyone. Everyone who hadn't been singing goblin carols into the bottom of a beer mug all day, at least.

Children, then. It reminded children of St. Bertha's heroism.

Ages ago, thanks to a sudden influx of sailors from a far-flung island where the men wear dresses and speak no intelligible language of their own—though they insist that mumbling into ginger beards most certainly *does* count as a language—Salzstadt was plunged into one of the most vociferous periods of uninhibited swearing ever seen anywhere in the world. At one point, according to the Ministry of Obscure Historical Statistics, there were actually more swear words than proper words being uttered in the city at any given moment.

The Domnitor, long may he reign, blamed the ginger men in skirts, their "language," and the insanely potent liquor they brought over on their ships. All three have been banned in Salzstadt ever since, especially the language, which the good folk of the Old Country called "Mumbly

Crivens." Scholars recollect that it is composed mostly of swear words, alongside a few phrases meaning "pour me another," "pull the other one," and "I'll give you half my fish for a date with your sister."

By some stroke of luck, just as the goblins came to outnumber the people, an old gran named Bertha found herself surrounded by an entire congress of goblins, intent on using every part of the gran in the construction of a ghoulish beer tent.

For the record, the dismemberment of grans at the hands of goblins was not considered "lucky" by the Domnitor, long may he reign, the people of the Old Country, or any agents thereof. The aforementioned "stroke of luck" refers not to the menacing and endangerment of the elderly, but to the conclusion of said encounter, as follows.

Bertha found no weapon in her immediate grasp, only her broom. It was a good broom, long heather with a stout oaken haft. Legends say that her eyes turned a flaming red as she took it in her grip, and with chiseled biceps and throaty roaring, she swept through the shambling lot of them, sending them all evaporating into the puffs of shadow from whence they came.

She cleared her house, went next door, and bade the Widow Chiminski take up her broom as well. They cleared her house together, went to the next door down the street, and so on.

Several fires resulted from the events of that night, as many hard-of-hearing grans misunderstood that the brooms need not be doused in kerosene and set alight to achieve the desired effect. It took the better part of a week before the burning buildings were no more than smoking rubble.

In the end, it was a battle-hardened band of grans who looked out over the city, free of both goblins and ginger mumblers in dresses, whom they'd sent back to their boats with a packed lunch and a scarf in case they got cold on the way back home.

So it was that Bertha was sainted on the spot in Salzstadt's great cathedral. Every year since, the Feast of Saint Bertha has commemorated that day.

Of course, a proper story would have gone on to say that ne'er a goblin was seen again within Salzstadt's mighty walls; however, salts had become very good at swearing, second only to mumbling sailors with really good whiskey. Old habits die hard.

Sloot was across the street from Gildedhearth, Lord Constantin Hapsgalt's sprawling estate, when the tail end of the parade was walking by. Four columns of grans, walking single-file in the most orderly lines one can imagine, giving every cobble the most thorough sweep it had seen since this very same thing happened the year before. It was a rare treat indeed, seeing that many brooms in the same place all at once. It wasn't as though one could just walk into a store and buy one. In spite of their mysterious power against the goblin menace, only married people were eligible to own them. Broom making was a highly profitable cottage industry, with the premier artisans in the field spending all of their time crafting works of art to be presented at the most decadent weddings of the year.

*That's tradition for you,* Sloot thought, being careful not to do it aloud. If the people of the Old Country were more pragmatic thinkers, he'd be allowed to own a broom; then again, Sloot decided that maybe he didn't want to live in a world where that sort of wanton anarchy ran unchecked. What would be next? Could he punch who he liked, cut in lines, and say the proper name of the Old Country to his heart's content? His broom would provide a means to deal with the consequences, so why not? He shuddered at the thought.

The parade moved past, and Sloot was momentarily reticent to tread upon such clean cobbles; then again, he was far more reticent to keep Lord Hapsgalt waiting, so tread he did.

"Name?" The downward lilt, the drawn expression, and the powdered wig on the butler standing outside the gate had formed a committee for the single purpose of insinuating to Sloot that while he probably belonged somewhere, Gildedhearth was not that place.

"Peril. Sloot Peril. I've been invited to—"

"*Summoned*," said the butler. "You've been *summoned* to dine with His Lordship, *Mister* Peril."

"Right," Sloot replied. "May I go in, then?"

The butler's second chin followed his first in a righteous waggle, accompanied by his lips in a curling into a gentle sneer.

"You'll have to complete an application."

The butler may have been formidable in his use of bluster and pomp, but Sloot was an accountant. He ate standardized forms for breakfast, in triplicate (literally in one case—teenagers can be cruel, but that was well over a week ago).

Sloot was provided a walking stick and a skin of water for his walk down the main hallway, every inch of which was festooned with gilded scrollwork, marble columns, and frescoes so lifelike that art students were encouraged to walk through it. Having done so, they tended to decide they were in over their heads and take up law or medicine instead.

Sloot was surprised that he'd never heard of many of the artists whose names he read from the plaques, and reckoned that their entire lives' works may well reside in that obscenely long hallway.

It was nearly dinner time when Sloot finally reached the foyer of the main house. He was greeted there by a woman dressed in a high-collared black dress, wearing spectacles that would have been judgmental enough just sitting on a desk, much less perched upon a hawkish nose that could have looked down upon the sun.

"You're nearly late," she said.

"Then I'm on time?"

"That's your one." She took a step toward him and thrust what appeared to be a magic wand in his face. Sloot knew enough about magic to know that he didn't know the first thing about magic. Best to assume that it could go off at any moment, then.

"Sorry," replied Sloot.

"My name is Olga," said Olga. "Mrs. Knife informs me that you've never dined in a proper house before."

"I'm not sure how to answer that."

"That's all right, it wasn't a question. I'll be your mannerist for the evening, just do as I say and there's an excellent chance you'll leave here with all of your fingers. Are we clear?"

"All of my fingers?"

The wand was a blur as it went *whack* against the knuckles of Sloot's right hand.

"Ow!"

"I'm not keen on questions, Peril."

"I understand," said Sloot, who didn't quite, but wasn't keen on further instruction.

"Very well," said Olga. "Here we go then, eighth chair on the left, don't sit until Lord Hapsgalt has done."

Sloot nodded. Olga turned and rapped twice on the great oaken door with the ornate bronze door knocker that looked eerily like Sloot being eaten by a dragon. He shook his head and chalked it up to hubris, nonetheless trying to recall whether any bronzesmiths had lately been studying him.

The double doors were opened from the inside by the most enormous pair of brutes that Sloot had ever seen up close. He followed Olga quickly past them toward an enormous table, where at least twenty well-dressed people were standing beside their chairs and speaking in low tones.

Olga led Sloot to his chair and motioned for him to stand beside it.

"No time for a proper lesson on forks," said Olga. "We'll muddle through, just start from the outside and work your way in. You *do* know how to use a fork, don't you?"

Sloot smiled. "Well, I haven't had any formal training or anything, but I think—"

*Whack* went Olga's wand on Sloot's knuckles again.

"That sort of cheek might win you giggles in whatever pub you abuse with your presence, but do it again here, and I'll have your apartment burned down." There wasn't a hint of malice in her voice, just the matter-of-factness with which a waiter might recite the soup of the day.

The other attendees abruptly stopped speaking at once, causing Sloot to wonder whether his hearing had quit. The sound of footsteps from behind him assuaged that fear.

*Whack* went Olga's wand across the back of Sloot's neck. He fought the urge to cower from the blow, noticed that everyone else had turned in the direction of the footsteps, and followed suit.

The man walking toward the head of the table could have been any one of the millions of people in the world whom Sloot had never met, but he was Lord Constantin Hapsgalt. That was not the product of probability, but the inevitable result of generations of well-orchestrated plotting. Lord Hapsgalt's black suit was exquisitely brocaded in gold, and he towered over the pair of butlers walking before him. He was a tall man on his own, and the high-heeled shoes that were all the rage among the very, very rich would clear up any ambiguity that dared to hang around.

"Sit, sit," said Lord Hapsgalt, waving his hands.

"Not until everyone closer to Lord Hapsgalt has done," said Olga, her wand in a lascivious position to prevent him from sitting out of turn. She eventually withdrew it, and Sloot sat. Olga stood beside him.

Sloot looked around the table, despite the feeling of dread that came from knowing he might make eye contact with someone he didn't know. Or worse, someone that he did. And then, as proof that the worst thing that can happen usually does, Sloot found his gaze met by that of Mrs. Knife. His heart sank into his stomach, no doubt hoping that she wouldn't think to look for it there.

"Welcome," said Lord Hapsgalt, "to all of you on this auspicious occasion. I'm sure that you all know my son, Wilhelm."

Lord Hapsgalt motioned to his left and a caricature of a man, whose pencil-thin moustache strained to separate his monumental nose from the most prominent pair of eye-teeth that Sloot had ever seen, stood slightly and gave a little bow. The cavernous curls on his powdered wig made a whooshing noise as they moved through the air. His suit looked mossy, an unfortunate side effect of green velvet.

"It is a proud day in a father's life," Lord Hapsgalt continued, "when he gets to announce that his one and only son has finally decided to stop tom-catting around and settle down!"

It was then that Sloot noticed that nearly everyone at the table was wearing a ring like Mrs. Knife's on their left forefinger: two silver snakes coiled around a black stone. He couldn't help but notice because they all started clinking them against their wine glasses by way of applause.

Olga thrust a spoon into Sloot's hand and gestured toward his wine glass with her wand. Sloot tapped along with the chorus.

"And who's the lucky lady?" asked Mrs. Knife, who was sitting across from Wilhelm with an unreadable expression. The expression on the frightful figure next to her was very readable, a treatise on general disgust with all it surveyed. He was an old man with long, greasy white hair clinging to his nearly-as-white pallid face. He was holding a wine glass filled with a viscous red liquid that didn't look like any wine that Sloot had ever seen; however, considering the nightmares that would likely result from further speculation on the matter, he decided that wine was the only thing it could have been, and resolved to consider it no further.

"Greta Urmacher," answered Wilhelm, in a tone so nasal Sloot thought to offer him a hankie. "She couldn't be here tonight, something about the time."

"Isn't she the clockmaker?" asked a satin-swaddled monstrosity whose gown could easily have been worth as much as the building where Sloot lived.

"That's right," said Lord Hapsgalt. "Her grandfather built the great clock in the central square. I believe she's doing some work on it tonight."

"Work?" asked the satin gown with a person in it. "Then she's a … a—"

"A commoner," said Wilhelm with an enormous grin. "Yes, I know, it's an unusual choice for someone as fabulously wealthy as I am, but the heart wants what the heart wants."

"And you approve of this match, my lord?" croaked the greasy ghost from behind his glass of what definitely must have been wine, thank you very much.

"Well, I admit that I was as surprised as the rest of you. I always assumed that Hapsgalt stock would be so intimidating to the proletariat that this common girl would have merely fainted at the sight of Willie, but she's made of sterner stuff. Her family isn't rich, but they've been in Salzstadt from the beginning. My boy knows what he's doing! She'll make him a fine bride."

The clinking of the rings—and Sloot's spoon—started up again. Mrs. Knife and the old ghoul both seemed dour. Their applause lacked enthusiasm but attempted to make up for it with malice. The result was terrifying, like a birthday cake filled with wasps.

Lord Hapsgalt picked up a tiny bell from the table and gave it a jingle, which prompted a slew of servants carrying silver trays to flood into the room. A bowl of soup was placed in front of Sloot, who received a crack across the knuckles when the spoon in his hand moved toward it.

"Applause spoons aren't for soup," Olga hissed.

Sloot put his spoon down and picked up the one that Olga's wand indicated. The soup tasted like nothing Sloot had ever eaten before, and did so in such a nebulous way that he was unable to describe it any further than that.

A rail-thin man wearing more makeup than all of the ladies in the room combined cleared his throat. "If Willie's to be married, then doesn't the Book of Black Law indicate that—"

"We have a guest with us tonight," interrupted Lord Hapsgalt, glaring at the thin man. "A mister …"

"Peril," said Mrs. Knife. "Sloot Peril."

"Peril?" repeated Lord Hapsgalt. "Sounds Carpathian."

"He assures me it's not," said Mrs. Knife, who sounded less than convinced.

"Fine," said Lord Hapsgalt. "In any case, Mister Peril, I'm told that you've done us a great service today, is that right?"

"Y-*yes*," squeaked Sloot, jumping to his feet at the insistence of Olga's wand. "Well, that is to say, I found some issues with a report that indicated—"

"Thank you, Mister Peril." Mrs. Knife's interruption was abrupt, leaving a silence hanging in the air during which Sloot sat awkwardly back down.

"Your good work couldn't have come along at a better time, Mister Peril. You see, as Judge Heidrich was about to point out before he was so handsomely interrupted, the occasion of Willie's nuptials means that he's going to be put to a test."

"A test?" Willie's brow wrinkled in disappointment as he whined.

"It's tradition," said Lord Hapsgalt. "Now that you're getting married, you'll be eligible to take over the family business. The only thing you need to do is to render proof of your worth, by undertaking some great work."

"No thanks," said Willie. He started slurping his soup with a lack of grace so deliberate he must have taken lessons. Olga's heightened sense of etiquette was so affronted that she gave Sloot's knuckles a whack of pure indignation.

"*No thanks?*" Lord Hapsgalt glared at Willie.

"I'd rather not, but thanks all the same. Just sounds like a lot of work, that's all."

"Well, of course it's work," Lord Hapsgalt snapped. "That's the whole point! You've known this was coming."

"Yeah, I suppose. But really, I appreciate you thinking of me and all, but if running the company is going to be a lot of work ... well, it just doesn't seem like, you know, my style."

"I suppose you'd rather live out your days at your hunting club, then? Wasting your days at leisure, squandering the fortune that your forefathers have left you?"

"Well that sounds a bit shabby of me, doesn't it?" Willie paused. "There must be a more flattering way to say it. But yeah, that sounds about right."

"Listen to him, Constantin," said Mrs. Knife with a sneer. "He doesn't even want it! I'm your cousin, I can inherit—"

"And you will," Lord Hapsgalt interrupted, "if Willie fails to render proof of his worth! He's my son, and he'll be given a chance. That's where you come in, Peril."

"Me, Your Lordship?" Sloot jumped to his feet again, at the urging of Olga's wand.

"Willie's never lived outside of Gildedhearth," said Lord Hapsgalt, "and part of rendering proof of his worth means striking out on his own."

"And I'm to strike out on his own ... with him?"

*Whack.*

"Don't sass His Lordship!" hissed Olga.

"So to speak," Lord Hapsgalt continued. "I'm giving Willie Whitewood, an estate that we haven't used in a number of years. He's going to need a financier to run the place, and thanks to your good work with this report, Mrs. Knife and I are convinced that you're just the man for the job. Congratulations, Peril."

"But I don't *want* to move to Whitewood!" Willie stomped his foot with practiced petulance.

"Yes you do," Lord Hapsgalt insisted. "Do you want me to have Gregor convince you?"

Willie looked across the table at the pale old ghoul next to Mrs. Knife, who appeared to be attempting a smile for the first time in his life. It was unsettling, like he'd read books about it but had never actually seen it done. Willie stayed silent.

"That's a most gracious offer, Your Lordship," said Sloot over the clinking of rings on glasses.

"Yes," said Lord Hapsgalt, "it is. I know you won't fail me, Peril. I should warn you though, we haven't been inside Whitewood in a *very* long time. Very good chance a goblin or two will have set up in there. I hope you know someone with a broom."

"Er, not as such." Sloot was about to say something else, though Olga's wand in his ribs indicated that whatever it was could wait.

"I'm sure you'll work it out," said Lord Hapsgalt.

"He could hire Nan," Willie suggested.

Lord Hapsgalt's hands curled into fists and rested on the table. He closed his eyes, and reopening them, directed his gaze down into his lap, which must have held some reserve store of patience that he desperately needed to dip into just then.

"That would be difficult to do," said Lord Hapsgalt through clenched teeth, "given that you haven't seen her since I dismissed her on your twenty-first birthday! I *am* correct in that assumption, am I not?"

"Oh," exclaimed Willie, wide-eyed with apparent realization. "Right, right. I was speaking hypothetically, you know, if she were still around somehow."

"Even if she were," growled Lord Hapsgalt, his furious gaze fixed on Willie, "she'd never find work at Whitewood, or any other Hapsgalt estate! You hear me, Peril?" Lord Hapsgalt was standing now, and shouting in Sloot's direction. "That woman will never set foot in Whitewood, on pain of your death, and the deaths of all those you hold dear! Am I in any way indicating to you that I am anything other than completely serious?"

"Er, no sir," said Sloot. *Whack.* "I mean, yes sir," *whack,* "there will be no Nans employed at Whitewood, Your Lordship."

Another *whack.*

"What was that for?" Sloot hissed.

"You're doing fine," whispered Olga. "A little bit *too* fine, actually. I'm warning you, Peril."

"Good," said Lord Hapsgalt, his reddened face attempting to readjust to its usual pallor. "Let's get on with dinner then, Mister Peril has an early start tomorrow."

❧⚜❧⚜❧⚜❧⚜

Several courses and dozens of *whacks* later, Sloot managed to fill his belly on the most decadent and unidentifiable food he'd ever seen, grovel out a series of farewells, and make the long walk back to the front doors of Gildedhearth. He was just about to step out onto the street when a runner approached him with a note on a pewter tray.

"Message for you, Mister Peril."

"Er, thanks," said Sloot. He fished in his pocket for a coin to give the boy, who chuckled and turned away before Sloot managed to find one. His livery was likely more expensive than Sloot's entire wardrobe, not that that was saying much.

It was a simple piece of parchment, folded and sealed with a blob of red wax. The seal was a single knife over three bells. He cracked it and read.

*Don't forget who's done you this favor. You may begin to repay me by hiring a young woman by the name of Myrtle, who will apply for a position in Willie's kitchen. I've got my eye on you. —Mrs. Knife*

# ❧ GALLONS OF BLOOD ❧

A t one time or another, a person in need of help simply had to place a sign in their window saying "Help Wanted – People Not Vociferously Agreeing with Political Views of Proprietor Need Not Apply." At some point in the city's long and colorful history, one or more bureaucrats (almost certainly more) realized that their lack of interference in the process was giving people the impression that getting things done without paperwork was a perfectly viable means of conducting business. There were other matters as well, such as the operation of restaurants, the renaming of streets, and the public airing of grievances pertaining to the weather; all of which had gone unchecked since time immemorial, with neither records kept nor taxes paid.

This chaos may have been good enough for your average Carpathian heathen, but Salzstadt held itself to a higher standard. That's what happens when you're unlikely to be the blood sacrifice to some deified farm animal on any given day. This was how Central Bureaucracy came to be.

The innumerable cogs in the machine of Central Bureaucracy worked tirelessly to ensure that nothing got done too quickly, because they didn't want people getting the wrong idea. Success and prosperity, if too easily won, gave common people the impression that the same could happen to them, and that was just trouble waiting to happen.

One of the most successful means of keeping the wheels of commerce turning sensibly slow was really long lines; thus Sloot found himself standing in one of the longest lines of his life the following morning. He'd gotten to Central Bureaucracy before the sun had come up and the doors had opened, and although he was the first person through the door, he only got to walk a few feet inside before becoming the end of the line.

Scores and scores of people, some wearing powdered wigs, some with armloads of papers, and most of whom were obviously professional queuers wove a tight and orderly line that maintained itself via an intricate system of velvet ropes. Sloot had been through Central Bureaucracy several times during his career, and he knew three things about it.

First, it is generally pointless to try and understand the system of velvet ropes. Better just to stay in one's lane and wait it out. The only people who seem to know what's happening with the ropes are the lobby staff, who occasionally open a section of rope, wave a few people through, and then close it again, generally just before Sloot can make it past.

Best just to nod and smile at the staff, and at all costs avoid asking them "Isn't there anything you can do?" That phrase always seems to open the section of rope that leads to the back of the line.

Second, best not to think too hard about the professional queuers, as frustration tends to slow time down. Professional queuers are unionized. They spend their days standing in the lines, talking to people at the front desk at length, then going to the back of the line again.

While most professional queuers are contracted to queue on behalf of someone else, some are hired by Central Bureaucracy just to pad the lines. It makes standing in them seem more appealing. Rumor has it that the original Head Bureaucrat got his start in nightclubs.

Third, one should have one's forms filled out in advance. One will have to re-do them, of course, because by the time one reaches the front of the line, they'll inevitably have changed; nevertheless, the mere presence of a fresh sheaf of papers legibly filled in goes a long way toward establishing that one fits in.

The staff can smell out confusion in a person, and seem to find great amusement in opening ropes and directing them to the back of the line.

Sloot was like a fish in water here. Had anyone been counting, they'd have known that it only took him eleven hours to complete the requisite postings for Willie's staff, while eleven and a half was the standard for that sort of thing.

When he left, the sky was the same amber color it had been when he'd gone in, only coming from the other direction. The jarring *"clank, clank"* of his mother's watch in his pocket reminded him that he hadn't yet shared with her the good news of his promotion, so he set out across town. He'd bought himself an extra half hour, so why not?

Sloot's mother, Sladia Peril, lived in the same tenement building where Sloot had been born and raised. It was a vast apartment with far more room than she needed, which suited her, as bemoaning the cost of heating unused rooms is a favorite pastime of elderly salts. It chafed at Sloot's instinct for making sound financial decisions that they were both wasting money by not sharing it, but Sladia insisted that it just wasn't fitting for a man Sloot's age to live with his mother.

Of course, she'd first said that when Sloot was ten years old. That's how old she'd been when she came to the city and gotten her first "coin fetching" job in the salt mines. The mines were always looking for young children who could wriggle into severely hazardous nooks and crannies, and Sladia had managed to negotiate herself a very generous wage doing just that. That was a long time ago, before children were allowed to join the miners' union.

"Who is it?"

"It's Sloot, Mum."

Silence.

"Oh, right," said Sloot. *"They were all out of waffles down by the docks."*

The clacks of several locks sounded from the door. It eventually opened, and Sloot rushed in to appease his mother's dislike of open doors.

"Can't be too careful," she said as she reset the locks. "All of the murders that have been going on of late."

"Glad we've got the passphrase, then."

Sladia had always been hyper-vigilant, instilling more than a bit of paranoia in Sloot from a very young age. She did have a point, though—the bloodless murders had started up nearly a dozen years hence. At least three or four corpses turned up every month, without so much as a single drop of blood in or anywhere near them. The constables hadn't managed to pin the grisly spree on a culprit, though they had imprisoned dozens of people over the years who had been careless enough to look the part.

"You look thin," said Sladia, once she'd shown Sloot into the parlor and brought him some tea. Sloot knew that she didn't actually think so, but she was a traditionalist. There are certain things that mothers are expected to say to their sons, and who knew if the goblins were listening for that sort of thing?

"I'm fine," he replied dutifully. "In fact, I've got some good news. I've been promoted!"

"Well it's about time," said Sladia. "You've been in the counting house for nearly twenty years now! Supervising then, are you?"

"I'm not in the counting house anymore. I'm the personal financier to none other than Wilhelm Hapsgalt himself!"

Sladia dropped her teacup. Her eyes went wide and her jaw dropped open. Sloot even thought he felt the *"clank, clank"* of her watch speed up in his pocket.

"My son, that's wonderful! When did this happen?"

"Last night," he replied. "It's why I couldn't join you for the Feast of St. Bertha. I was in Gildedhearth, sitting at Lord Hapsgalt's table."

"You were not!"

"I was." Sloot abandoned all pretense of controlling the ridiculous grin that had spread across his face. "Vasily Pritygud had entirely botched a report, and nearly told Lord Hapsgalt that he needed to count his money."

Sladia laughed. "I'm sure His Lordship would have needed a change of trousers if he'd read that!"

"Probably. I fixed the report, and Mrs. Knife thought my work was good enough that I should fill this post! I'd have come and told you sooner, but I had to go to Central Bureaucracy to get started on hiring the younger Lord Hapsgalt's staff."

"At his table! For the Feast of St. Bertha! Oh, my son! You've made me so very proud."

"Thank you, Mother," Sloot beamed.

"Not only that, it means I finally get to retire!"

Sloot's head cocked to one side.

"Retire? Mother, you haven't worked in the salt mines in twenty years."

It occurred to Sloot that his mother may have parted with her marbles. At last! It was tradition after all, and Sloot was running out of ways to avoid answering questions about his frail and doddering mother, who was far from frail and had never once doddered. She'd never so much as called him by the wrong name or sent a card with a painfully small amount of money for his birthday.

"Right," said Sladia, speaking very slowly, the way people tend to do when they have something unpleasant to say. "That's true. And I haven't had much real work since then, but … well, there's something we need to discuss."

Sladia picked up a candlestick and walked out of the room, motioning for Sloot to join her. He followed her down a dusty old hallway that she obviously didn't use on a daily basis, or possibly even an annual one. Producing a key from the pocket of her apron, she unlocked a door. The two of them walked into the empty room and Sladia locked the door behind them.

"Never know who's listening," she said with a conspiratorial wink.

"It was just us in the parlor."

"As far as we know, but it's easier in here to be sure. Goblins like to hide under furniture. Nowhere to hide in here."

"Now you're being paranoid," said Sloot. His mother was ferocious with her broom, and he'd never seen a goblin in her house. "Besides, what could you possibly have to say that would be made worse by a goblin overhearing?"

Sladia sighed. "I'll just come out with it then, really no good way to deliver it softly. Sloot, I'm a Carpathian spy."

Sladia continued talking, but Sloot could hear nothing but a high-pitched whine. He'd expected the sound of his life as he knew it bursting into flames to be more dramatic, yet there it was. A sort of highly efficient eternity passed, during which he managed to have a mental break, lose the power of speech, and rehabilitate himself before Sladia finished speaking.

"You were doing that thing again," said Sladia with a smirk.

"I was— What thing? What?"

"The thing where you go all the way 'round the track of an existential crisis. You used to do it when I left the crusts on your sandwich. Glad to see it takes a bit more these days."

"You're a spy?"

Sladia nodded. "Okay, you remember that part. That's good. And you're able to speak, that's an improvement."

Sloot sank to the floor, his legs splayed out in front of him. Sladia shrugged, and gently lowered herself to sit across from him.

"It can't be true," said Sloot. "I'm a proper salt! I've got papers and everything!" He started rifling through his papers, looking for any inconsistencies or forgeries. He'd always heard that Uncle could tell a forgery from a mile away, so surely a good salt like Sloot could spot one from within a foot.

That wasn't a reference to an actual uncle, of course. Every salt knew that "Uncle" was the new moniker for the Ministry of Truth, following its rebranding by the Ministry of Propaganda. It had worked surprisingly well to soften up their image, though the annual rate of citizens disappearing due to affairs of state had increased significantly.

"Everything I've ever told you has been true," she began again. "Coming to the city when I was a little girl, working in the mines, all of it."

"Well, not all of it!" Sloot exclaimed. "You didn't tell me you were spying on the Domnitor, long may he reign, on behalf of our most loathed enemy!"

"That's right, I didn't. I also didn't tell you that I *wasn't* a spy, so it still works."

"Semantics."

Sladia shrugged. "Perhaps, but I can still say that I've never told you a lie. And I haven't been involved in any daring-do since before you were born."

"Born! Yes!" Sloot rifled through his papers again and brandished a yellowed and creased page in the air like a sword. "I was born right here in Salzstadt, and here's the proof! And if you hadn't done any spy work since before I was born, it's got nothing to do with me."

"Well, just a bit. The fighting had died down by then, and the cold war was on. Just a bit of message-passing, that sort of thing."

"The sort of thing you might have done while carrying your infant son around with you?"

Sladia cringed, pausing just long enough to admit to the accusation by not denying it.

"Oh, that's just perfect!"

"You were never in any danger."

"Says the woman who was committing high treason between diaper changes!"

"Neither of us ever set foot in the gulag. I was very careful."

"But there was always a chance! Tell me, Mother, what was the acceptable level of risk for bouncing me on your knee while passing secret missives to men in dark cloaks on wharfs at midnight?"

There was silence then. Between this, the scrutiny from Mrs. Knife, the physical abuse he'd endured from his dinner coach, and everything at stake with the younger Lord Hapsgalt, Sloot was having trouble wrapping his mind around the enormity of it all.

"Don't try to consider it all at once," said Sladia.

"Yes, I know, you know me better than I know myself."

"That's right!" Sladia was suddenly on her feet. It was uncharacteristic for her to weather that much conflict with her calm intact, and Sloot saw that he'd just found the limit. "I've seen bits of you that you've probably taken pains to avoid viewing yourself! You came out of me, and I got you through every skinned knee and hurt feeling since then. I know you, Sloot Gefahr Peril, and I know that you're capable of doing great things, once you've stopped whinging about the risks and applied yourself!"

Middle names are a special curse with which all mothers enchant their children, to be used when they need a good filling with dread. If there had been any goblins in the room, they'd have fled at that, wishing the child good luck in whatever fate had in store.

Sloot stood up. Sladia dusted him off, took his face in her hands, and kissed his forehead.

"I know it's hard," she said, "but it's the truth. It's not fair, but neither is life. You are more than capable of handling this. Do you believe me?"

Sloot nodded. "You're Carpathian?"

"*We're* Carpathian."

"But I was born and raised in Salzstadt!" He brandished his papers again. "I've never been outside the walls!"

"More than likely, that will continue to be true. I've not heard from the spymaster in nearly twenty years now. He may be dead, for all I know. Anyway, it's a cold war now. Nearly nothing left to it."

"But it's still there," Sloot countered. "Why do I have to be a part of it?"

"So that I can retire," said Sladia. "Your employment with Wilhelm Hapsgalt means you're in a position to be valuable to Carpathia, which means my work is done. I can live out my remaining days in peace, in the knowledge that the spymaster will never knock on my door again."

"So I'm your retirement plan."

"You might be a little bit more grateful. I've set you up with a career."

"I already have a career."

"Accounting? That's just your cover! A very clever one, too. If I were anyone else, I'd never be able to tell."

"No, Mother, I'm a real accountant. I'm good at it!"

Smiling, Sladia nodded with pride. "Brilliant. You're ready for this, Sloot."

Sloot had never performed an act of bravery in his life. Better to leave that sort of thing to soldiers, who probably had lessons in charging headlong into things, and were flush with things like grit, mettle, and moxie. But what sort of son leaves his mother—who was due to get on with doddering any day now—to spend her declining years skulking in the shadows?

Not the kind of son that Sloot Peril was going to be, by the Domnitor, long may he reign!

"I'll do it," said Sloot, surprising himself. "What do I have to do?"

Sladia threw her arms around Sloot's neck and hugged him. "There's nothing to *do*, really. The spymaster will already know who you are. If he ever needs to call on you—which, again, he probably never will—he'll ask you if you've seen the pencil that he was using on Thursday."

Sloot couldn't entirely suppress a mischievous grin. That was real cloak-and-dagger stuff there. He was more averse to danger than most, but he'd never felt more rough-and-tumble since the time he'd lied about brushing his teeth. It had made him feel guilty at the time, but he didn't agree with his mother that his teeth were strong enough to go without.

They had dinner, and then it was late. Sladia hurried him through the door and reset all of the locks behind him, having reminded him numerous times to look both ways for anyone carrying the tools necessary to make off with several gallons of blood.

By the time he'd made it back to his little apartment above the butcher, he'd found himself making significant progress on a new ulcer.

In his initial panic, Sloot had somehow entirely ignored the fact that his mother had been committing high treason the entire time she'd lived in Salzstadt. A lifetime of exposure to the clever posters and slogans of the Ministry of Propaganda told him that it was his duty to report her to Uncle immediately.

But how could he turn his own mother over to Uncle? Now that he knew about his Carpathian heritage, wouldn't he be betraying it?

It was late, and he needed to be up early in the morning to get to work on Whitewood. He got into bed, largely convinced himself that his mother was right and he'd never be called upon to commit high treason, and resolved to resume panicking over his entire life having been a lie in the morning.

He'd nearly managed to drift off to sleep when his closet door burst open, and a scruffy-looking, bug-eyed old man dressed all in black leapt onto the bed. One of his hands had pulled the front of Sloot's pajamas into a fist. The other was covering his mouth to prevent the high-pitched screams it was making from reaching the ears of his neighbors.

"Calm yourself!" the old man hissed. "I just need to know if you've seen the pencil I was using on Thursday!"

Sloot's panic was replaced with the relief that comes from knowing he wasn't going to be brutally murdered and robbed of his blood. Then he realized what the old man had said, and his panic returned to play an encore.

"No!" said Sloot. "This has to be some sort of mistake. My mother told me that she hasn't been contacted in years!"

"Well, that's true," said the old man. His eyes were enormous, and he never seemed to blink. "I've been waiting for her to retire for some time now. Your mother started getting messy, see? Blood like you wouldn't believe, hard to cover up. Got to keep things quiet nowadays. That's how cold wars work."

"You don't mean the bloodless murders!"

"Not even close. Really messy, blood everywhere. The people doing the so-called bloodless murders are much worse."

"How did you get in here?"

The old man *tsked* at Sloot. "I can see that we'll have to start by teaching you to ask the right questions. How's 'how did you get in here' going to get you out of danger when the person who's just burst from your wardrobe is an enemy operative with a big knife, instead of a dashing spymaster just saying hello? You've got to be quick if you want to be a spy."

"That's all right then. I don't want to be a spy."

"Then you shouldn't have accepted your mother's resignation."

"Well, it's not like I had a choice."

"Of course you had a choice," said the old man. "Carpathia's a constitutional monarchy. You have rights."

"I'm sorry, a what?"

Salzstadt is the seat of fascist rule in the Old Country. Fascism is a tyrannical form of government that gives the ruler absolute power over the people, which makes it very attractive to the tyrants who elect to use it. The first order of business in a new fascism is to restrict their people from learning about all of the other forms of government.

"A constitutional monarchy." The old man snapped his fingers. "That's right, you've never been outside of Salzstadt before, have you?"

"Certainly not," said Sloot, straightening his pajamas. "Nothing but wolves and Carpathian savages out there! Oh, sorry."

The old man shrugged. "It's hurtful, but you can say it if you want. You're a Carpathian after all, it's your right."

"How many rights do we have?" Sloot wasn't sure he was entirely comfortable with the concept. These "rights" sounded a lot like responsibilities to him, and he already had a great deal of those.

"I'll get you a copy of the constitution," said the old man. "But forget about that for now! We've got important work to do."

"Hang on a minute! You said I've got rights, and that I have a choice in this whole spy business."

"You do have rights, but you *had* a choice. You accepted your mother's resignation, right? So you're a Carpathian operative now." The old man's fist shot into the air. "Blood and honor!"

"Er, okay." Sloot'd missed the opportunity to not be a spy, but was mildly comforted by no longer being responsible for making a choice.

"You're supposed to say it back," said the old man with a sulk, his fist slowly withdrawing to his side. "Never mind. Tomorrow's a big day for us, so I should just give you your briefing and let you get some sleep."

"Wait, tomorrow? No, that's too soon! I have to be at Whitewood to hire the staff, and the younger Lord Hap—"

"Calm yourself," said the old man. "That's exactly how we get started. You'll hire me as the younger Lord Hapsgalt's valet."

"And then what?"

"That's all, for now. These things take time, you know."

"What things? What comes after getting hired as the valet?"

"Above your pay grade, I'm afraid. I'll tell you when the time comes."

"I get paid for being a spy?"

"Not really," the old man replied. "I mean, we in the foreign intelligence service traditionally forego our salaries, since we wind up getting paid by the enemy."

"Oh," said Sloot. His finances were already on a firm footing, but the prospect of extra income had his mind bubbling with annuities and other savvy investments. It reminded him of the giddy feeling he'd felt as a boy, when he'd sit on the steps of the bank and calculate interest rates in his head. He'd pretend he was a junior bank manager, advising his imaginary friends regarding their pensions. His mother thought it was odd, but at least he hadn't taken up with boys who knew lots of swear words.

"How much blood?" asked Sloot.

"How's that?"

"You said Mother started getting messy. Lots of blood."

"Right." sThe old man's enormous eyes deftly shifted to avoid Sloot's. "Well, a lady's got to hang onto *some* mystery, don't you think?"

"How would I know?" Sloot had never fared well in matters of the heart.

"Think it over," said the old man. "If you're sure you want to know, I'll tell you over a pint."

Sloot pondered for a moment whether he did, in fact, want to know how much Old Country blood his mother had spilled for Carpathia. He shuddered and searched the dark recesses of his mind for a spot to repress yet another terrifying thought, hopefully forever.

"I'll be there bright and early," said the old man. "If you think about it, I'll have done you a favor. One fewer people you'll need to interview."

"Do you even know how to be a valet?"

"Well, I've posed as one several times."

"Posed?"

"Yes," answered the old man, "back when the war was still hot. Of course, back then, the poor sods who'd hired me didn't live long enough to write me letters of reference."

"You murdered them?"

"Not to worry, I've been to the forger. I'll bring you letters for my file in the morning."

"That's not what I'm worried about! You're going to murder the younger Lord Hapsgalt!"

"Don't be ridiculous," said the old man. "We need him alive for the foreseeable future."

"And after that?"

"Well, it's unforeseeable, isn't it?"

"You can't murder the younger Lord Hapsgalt," said Sloot.

"That decision will be made above your pay grade, I'm afraid."

"Fine," said Sloot. "But given that we're paid by the younger Lord Hapsgalt's estate, and that I'm employed by him directly, we'll have to leave it up to him when and if he's murdered."

The old man raised a forefinger and started to speak, but Sloot cut him off.

"And since I'm hiring the staff, you work for me. That makes the decision above your pay grade, too."

The old man's eyes narrowed. "We'll see. In any case, I've no immediate need to murder him, and I'm proud to say that I've never murdered anyone without a reason."

"Oh, that's comforting."

"Get some sleep. You've got a big day tomorrow."

"One last question."

"Yes?"

"What's your name?"

The old man smiled in a way that Sloot imagined would have come across as dashing forty years ago.

"Roman," he replied.

"Roman, I've always been told that Carpathians are bloodthirsty savages who glorify violence. Is that true?"

"Glorify? No. It's a means to an end, that's all."

"So you don't take surnames that inspire terror in the hearts of your enemies?"

"No. Well, sometimes."

"What's your surname, Roman?"

Roman hesitated. "Never you mind."

"Oh come on."

"It's classified."

"Really?"

"Yes, Mister *Peril*, really! Now if you don't mind, you're not the only one who could use a good night's sleep."

## ⇜⇝CONGRESSIONAL INFESTATION⇜⇝

The Hapsgalts owned a large part of Salzstadt, including a number of mansions that were regarded as true architectural marvels. They also owned Whitewood.

It was immense, and that was probably the nicest thing that anyone could say about it. Saying anything complimentary about it would call into question whether one had ever seen a building before. It must have been grand at some point in its history, but that would have been before the goblins got to it.

The rumbling from within it made Sloot very thankful for the old stone table in the front courtyard. It would serve as a desk where he could interview the long line of applicants who must have been eager to work for a Hapsgalt, as it was well-known that no one in the family had ever laid off a servant. He hoped that someone with a broom and a penchant for danger applied soon.

Beyond Carpathia's northern border was the land of Nordheim. The Vikings who lived there believed that the sound of thunder had something to do with tantrums thrown by their many gods.

"I read that in a book once," said Myrtle, who had been first in the long line of applicants waiting to talk to Sloot at sunrise. For all of the apparent lack of efficiency in getting anything done at Central Bureaucracy, the results certainly proved that the machine was capable of functioning, once the gears could be bothered to turn.

"It's goblins," said Sloot, "not thunder. I've heard enough cackling to know that we've got our work cut out for us."

"More likely than gods throwing tantrums," said Myrtle, "though a touch less romantic."

"Aren't you awfully young to be a 'Myrtle'?" Sloot had only ever met old ladies named Myrtle, and never a Myrtle who made him feel the need to be substantially wittier than he was, to dress better, sit up straighter, and invest in some cologne.

"Oh, Mister Peril, I took you for far too sophisticated to make such an obvious joke." Smirking, she batted her eyelashes in a way that made Sloot worry less about whether he'd just been insulted, and more about whether a good tailor could coax some pectoral muscles from his coat.

"Have you ever been a housemaid, Miss Pastry?"

"I haven't," she admitted. "But I'm a quick study."

"Well, I've been asked to hire you as a favor to Mrs. Knife, so I suppose I'll have to trust that you are."

"Who's Mrs. Knife?"

"You mean you don't know?"

"IT WOULD HAVE BEEN SILLY TO ASK IF SHE KNEW HER, WOULDN'T IT? Quiet, you!" Myrtle clamped a hand over her mouth.

"I beg your pardon?"

"Sorry, Mister Peril," she said, her cheeks turning pink as she desperately scanned the ground for something, probably anything that wasn't Sloot's perplexed and wounded expression.

Sloot was no stranger to beratement. Clever boys who choose mathematics over sports must abide a measure of buffoonery from other boys, he'd always said. Perhaps if he hadn't, they'd have bullied him less severely. At any rate, the sting was especially sharp from someone asking for a favor. A very pretty someone, at that.

"Er," said Sloot, "I'd like very much to stay in Mrs. Knife's good graces, but—"

"I know," she said, "I apologize. It … that wasn't directed at you."

Sloot wasn't sure what facial expression could adequately convey the depth of confusion into which he'd just been plunged, so he didn't perform one. He managed a slow blink, which seemed minimally appropriate.

"I suppose it will come out sooner or later." Myrtle sighed. "Have you heard of possession, Mister Peril?"

"I'm an accountant," Sloot answered. "I'm familiar with the concept of ownership."

"I mean the possession of people. By the dead."

"Oh, *that!* Yes. Well, in point of fact, no."

"Well, it's something I'm all too familiar with, and sometimes the offending dead are a bit, well, offensive."

"I see," said Sloot, whose suspicious expression indicated that he did not.

"THAT WASN'T OFFENSIVE," grumbled Myrtle, "YOUR YELLING WAS MUCH WORSE."

"I didn't—"

"No," said, Myrtle, "he's talking about me."

"He?"

"Arthur," said Myrtle. "He's a philosopher."

"Ah."

"HENCE I'M ABLE TO DRAW OBVIOUS CONCLUSIONS, LIKE THE ONE CONCERNING WHETHER SHE'D ASK WHO MRS. KNIFE WAS IF SHE ALREADY KNEW!"

"She?"

"That'd be me," said Myrtle.

"Right." Sloot was torn between his desires to wrap his head around the rapidly unfolding concept of the possession of the living by the dead, appease Mrs. Knife, and watch Myrtle's hair dance in the breeze across her bare shoulders, perhaps in a sunny meadow.

"I can manage housekeepery." Myrtle leaned forward with her brow furrowed in sincerity. "Arthur tends to sulk whenever I'm working. It's the only time I really get any peace."

"Well, that's something."

"I DON'T SULK," said Myrtle. "I SIMPLY TURN MY THOUGHTS

TOWARD MORE ENLIGHTENED THINGS THAN TIDYING UP." She rolled her eyes but said nothing.

It's common knowledge that philosophers abhor the act of manual labor. The entire profession is predicated on the idea that doing things is trivial when compared with thinking about things; furthermore, thinking about *thinking about* things is the cornerstone of our ability to function as a society. It should be left to people in the trades to find a way to monetize the service that philosophers provide for the good of all people everywhere.

They're certainly *capable* of monetizing their trade on their own, of course; but ask any one of them why they don't, and they'll answer with Ignatius the Mumbler's one and only platitude: *Why?*

"Can you keep this Arthur business under control?"

"Absolutely, Mister Peril. Arthur will refrain from saying a peep while outside the servants' quarters, won't you, Arthur? I CAN'T IMAGINE WHAT I'D HAVE TO SAY TO A PAMPERED ARISTOCRAT. Arthur! OH, FINE, NOT A PEEP."

"Good," replied Sloot, who was less than convinced of her abilities as a housekeeper, but very keen to see her smile at him with that eyelashes maneuver again. There was also the matter of not vexing Mrs. Knife, though even that seemed rather less important. "We'll get you started on tidying the house as soon as we get the goblins cleared out."

"Oh, thank you, Mister Peril! Er, if I wouldn't be in the way, would it be all right if I sat on the little bench over there for a while? Arthur says he needs a ponderance."

"Er, fine," said Sloot. Myrtle stood and curtsied, then went and sat on the little stone bench and stared into the birdbath next to it. It was a mournful sort of stare. It had existentialism written all over it.

*Better her than me*, thought Sloot, who was doing his best to avoid existential thought at the moment. That would certainly have led him to consider his quandary between the life he'd led thus far as a loyalist in the Old Country and his newfound traitorism as a Carpathian spy. Could one man serve two flags?

He shook his head. Leave the ponderances to Arthur, there was real work to be done.

"Hello, Mister Peril!" Roman practically shouted. He leaned on the stone table in a way that screamed "casual" with utter disregard for subtlety. "My name is Roman, and I have never met you before! Would it be quite all right if I were the younger Lord Hapsgalt's valet, then?"

"Er, right," said Sloot, his eyes squaring in alarm at Roman's forceful winking, which seemed hell-bent on going the long way around brazenness to sneak up on subtlety when it was least expected. "Do you have any references, Roman?"

"Certainly!" Roman's trembling hand jutted forth, sending a conspicuously large stack of papers careening into Sloot's chest and scattering about the lawn. "All in order, none of them dead by my hand!"

"That's uh, good to know." Sloot couldn't imagine Roman as a spy, much less a spymaster. Was this all an elaborate ruse of his mother's, to get a friend a job?

That was a comforting thought. Perhaps he wasn't a Carpathian spy now after all! Existential crisis averted! Sloot started picking up the papers.

"Thank you, Roman, this all appears to be in order. Well, out of order, but once we've picked them up, I'm sure. I'll introduce you to Lord Hapsgalt as soon as the house is habitable."

"Is that strictly necessary?"

"What, meeting Lord Hapsgalt?"

"Yes, that."

"It'll be hard for you to valet for him otherwise."

"Yes! Right, I suppose it would be." Roman wiped a profuse accumulation of sweat from his brow, which was unusual in the chilly morning air.

"Er, that'll be all, Roman. Perhaps you'd like to go have a brandy and lie down?"

"Careful with that tongue, Peril," Roman had leaned in to whisper. "Don't forget which of us is in charge here!"

"Wouldn't that be me?" Sloot asked, in a very sincere way. He had never been in charge of anything before, and in truth, he wasn't entirely sure.

Roman paused. Realization dawned on him with such fervor that it came with its own chirping birds.

"Thank you, Mr. Peril!" said Roman as he hurried through the gate and into the street.

Most of the interviews that followed went a lot more smoothly, the way Sloot thought they should. People presented references, negotiated salaries, that sort of thing. None of them caused him any consternation until the applicant for groundskeeper, a mister Django Dirtsmith.

"Hello, Mr. Dirtsmith. And for what position are you applying?"

Mr. Dirtsmith made no attempt to conceal his shock at the question. On the contrary, he projected a wounded gasp as though the people in the cheap seats were shouting for him to speak up.

"You've never heard of me?"

"I'm afraid not," said Sloot. "Should I have?"

"I am Django Dirtsmith! The foremost gardener in the city! I'm famous for my lawns. Aristocrats the world over salivate over my floral arrangements. And by the looks of this place, you're in desperate need of my services!"

"The lawns do need some work," Sloot conceded. "Do you have any references?"

"Have you ever worked with your hands, Mr. Peril?"

"Daily," said Sloot, who pointed with his right hand to the quill in his left.

"Your hands are soft," Django sneered. "Have they ever had dirt on them?"

"Not recently," said Sloot. "I work indoors most of the time, but there are too many goblins in there at the moment."

"That's not real work. What I do, that's *work*. How dare you ask me for references, you—"

"That'll be quite enough out of you!"

"What?" squawked Django, with more of the same practiced offense. "Who is this girl who dares to challenge Django?"

Myrtle stormed right up to Django, nearly standing on his feet to waggle a stern finger in his face, which was almost two heads above her own.

"Mr. Peril is cutting you a lot of slack right now," said Myrtle from between her clenched teeth. "I'd hold my tongue if I were you!"

"You've got a lot of nerve to talk—"

"Not another word! Not one!"

There exists a certain forcefulness of tone exclusively reserved for use by mothers in need of scolding naughty children. It comes from a very primal school of magic, for which there is no formal school at all. It's as old as time itself and far more expansive. Mathematicians are loathe to try and quantify it for fear that they'll be sent to bed without supper if they succeed. Mathematicians love supper.

Django said nothing. Although Myrtle couldn't possibly have known his middle name, her tone made it clear that she could still find a way to use it against him.

"You're familiar with the rose trellises on Gildedhearth's southern lawns, are you not?"

"Of course," said Django, "I planted them myself!"

"And do you know why you should thank Mr. Peril for that?"

"I should what?"

"Thank him! Before he came to Whitewood, Mr. Peril was the estate accountant for the elder Lord Hapsgalt. He was responsible not only for funding those trellises but for deciding which gardener to hire to raise them."

"Then why did he ask for my references?"

"Most likely to see whether you're the sort of man smart enough to understand his place in the grand scheme of things, or the ignorant sort of hayseed who thinks no further than the end of his trowel! Now, if you ever want to find respectable work in Salzstadt again, you'd do well to apologize to Mr. Peril. Unless, of course, being blackballed by the entire Hapsgalt family is the sort of inspiration you've been seeking to push you into a different career!"

Django made the sort of face that pairs well with panic. Sloot knew that one all too well and could have offered him some pointers.

"I'd change my name as well," said Myrtle, "if I were you."

"Sorry, Mr. Peril," Django grumbled. "I can bring you my references tomorrow if you like."

"Th-that won't be n-necessary," Sloot stammered. "Of course I know who you are, just testing the … the hayseed thing, like Myrtle said. Can you start tomorrow, Mr. Dirtsmith?"

"Tomorrow will be fine," said Myrtle, glaring at Django.

"Tomorrow … yes, fine," replied Django with a hangdog look. He slinked off without another word.

"I suppose you'll be wanting to have a word with me in private then, Mr. Peril." Myrtle was a lot louder than she needed to be for Sloot to hear her. She strode off in the direction of the bench where she'd indulged Arthur in his pondering. Sloot stood and followed her, unable to think of anything else to do under the circumstances.

"What just happened?" Sloot was unaccustomed to walking away from beratements unberated, and as such intended the question as a simple curiosity.

"You can't let people talk to you like that," said Myrtle, in a way that confused Sloot further still. Her words were stern, but she was staring at her feet and shrinking away from him. "Especially in front of the other applicants. They'll think they can get away with the same."

"They'll all be afraid of me now. Wait, are you afraid of me, too?"

"Not at all," said Myrtle. "But they're all looking at us now, and it'll be better if it seems like you're angry with me for speaking out of turn."

She was right. Everyone in the line was gawking at them, like zoo patrons at feeding time.

"Why are you doing this?"

"You mean helping you?"

Sloot nodded.

"Arthur has been teaching me about pragmatism. Better to get on your good side. He says I should apply some flattery as well, but I don't think I have a talent for it."

"Oh," said Sloot, in a deflated sort of way. "I thought maybe, well, I don't know …"

"What?"

"Er, nothing. Sorry. I just thought … you see, men and women … oh dear. That is to say—"

"Oh, for pity's sake, he's smitten with you!"

That was how Arthur brought the conversation to a crashing halt. Myrtle's face went scarlet. Sloot was fairly certain that his had done the same, and feared his eyebrows might catch fire at any moment.

"That's … interesting," Myrtle managed to say before the silence fermented. Silence, like really expensive cheese, becomes nauseating if left to sit in the sun too long. Sloot thought there was a bit of a skip in her step as she walked away, and felt certain he'd spend the rest of the week wondering what "interesting" meant.

The rest of the applications went very smoothly, thanks in no small part to the telling off that the entire line seemed to remember Sloot doing.

Poets, most of whom live with their parents, like to think that mysterious people elude description, defying definition. They don't. Poets are just lazy. "As silent as the grave, as dark as a shadow," requires far less effort than actually describing a person. Poets cut corners so often it's a wonder poetry isn't written on round paper.

There are exactly three things that a person needs to do to qualify as mysterious, no more and no less. One must appear with one's hood drawn up, choose a scene with dramatic lighting to do so, and initially decline to give one's name. So it was that at sunset, Sloot's mysterious last applicant of the day did just that.

"Hello," said Sloot, relieved to see that the stranger was leaning on a broom. None of the other applicants had one. He'd asked. "And you are?"

"A friend," said the mysterious stranger, which you should have seen coming.

"Er, okay," said Sloot, who had no friends to speak of, and had never gotten the appeal of poetry.

"I was told that you needed a housekeeper."

"Yes," said Sloot. "Oh, right. No," he continued, upon hearing a very pointed *ahem* from Myrtle and Arthur's bench. "The housekeeper has been sorted out, but we still need someone to do the sweeping. That's your own broom you've got there, I presume?"

"It is," said the stranger, "but doesn't your housekeeper have one?"

"Not as such."

"How can you be a housekeeper without a broom? Got to have a broom to run a house. That's a rule, everybody knows it!"

"Easy," said Myrtle, who was suddenly looming. Sloot knew philosophers to be practiced at brooding, which involved many of the same muscle groups as looming. Arthur must have loaned his expertise to the undertaking.

"This can't be her," exclaimed the stranger. "She's far too young!"

"Never you mind my age," said Myrtle. "I'm the housekeeper, broom or no, and if you don't like it you can find the gate on your own!"

"No, wait!" Sloot jumped to his feet. "We are in need of some sweeping, I'm sure we can find a position for you."

"What about the nanny?" The stranger's hood flew back to reveal a gnarled old woman with a very excited look, which was hardly in keeping with the whole mysterious stranger thing. No poet auditing the scene would have approved.

"We won't be needing a nanny," said Sloot.

"But what about little Willie?"

"Little Willie? The younger Lord Hapsgalt doesn't have a son that I'm aware of."

"Well of course he hasn't," said the stranger. "He's six years old!"

"Who is? The younger Lord Hapsgalt is forty-two, or perhaps forty-three."

Sloot and the stranger showed each other their best expressions of confusion, and Myrtle joined them just for good measure.

"Right," said the stranger after a while. "Look, I don't want to argue, I just want to work for Willie."

"You mean Lord Hapsgalt," countered Myrtle.

""Yes! Of course. Whatever gets us there."

"Do you …" Sloot paused. "Do you *know* the younger Lord Hapsgalt?"

"No! Never met Willie in my life. I swear it on his wittle toesies."

"Then why do you keep calling him Willie?"

"What? No, I don't. Look, do you want my services or not? This place is crawling with goblins!"

Her point was punctuated by a suit of armor flying through a second-story window and landing in a cacophony of clanging steel and tinkling glass. A chorus of laughter erupted from within the suit. It got clumsily to its feet and ran cackling back into the house in a haphazard way that only a suit of armor full of goblins could have managed.

"No argument there," said Sloot. "We're going to need a lot more brooms if we're ever to—"

"I can do it," said the stranger.

Sloot looked her up and down. She was vital in a way that people her age tended not to be, as though she'd fought tooth and nail to give the ravages of old age the slip and succeeded; or at least come to agreeable terms following a standoff, and walked away with just the wrinkles and the enormous nose.

"It's not a one-woman job," said Sloot. "No offense intended, Mrs …"

"Never mind that. I can have that house goblin-free by sun-up, you have my oath on it!"

Sloot heard at least half a dozen distinctive "pops" of new goblins arriving in the house to join the already formidable congress. Oathbreaking was a particularly serious way of calling goblins, to the extent that even making somewhat-difficult-to-keep oaths was invitation enough for goblins with a penchant for gambling.

Sloot shrugged. "No one else is chomping at the bit to do it, no harm in giving you a chance."

"You do look like you've lived a long life," said Myrtle in agreement.

"Never you mind how old I am either," said the stranger, waggling a finger at Myrtle.

"Good luck to you." Sloot gathered up his papers. "If you manage to succeed—"

"*When* I succeed, I'll be guaranteed a permanent position in the household."

"But not as the housekeeper," said Myrtle.

"Fine," said the stranger.

"Very well," said Sloot.

"I want your oath on it." The stranger's expert finger-waggling took aim at Sloot. "Swear it on the salt, and spit in your hand!"

Sloot balked. Salt was something that the residents of Salzstadt took very seriously, and a risky oath sworn on salt and spit ran the risk of ballooning the already formidable Whitewood congress up to a bicameral parliament. He was already dubious with regard to her ability, and fortifying the goblins' numbers before going up against them seemed deranged in a way that would cause professional lunatics to draw the line.

"That won't be necessary," said Sloot. "We have an agreement, no need—"

"Swear it!" The stranger spat in her own hand and extended it toward him, causing Sloot to wonder if the gesture was intended as an enticement.

"Do it," said Myrtle.

"Why," said Sloot from the side of his mouth, "did Arthur tell you something?"

Myrtle's face grew dark, and her hands went to her hips. "I can have insights without the assistance of dead philosophers, you know."

"Right," Sloot muttered. "Sorry."

Sloot was a loyalist, a good salt through-and-through (with the singular exception of recently having become a Carpathian spy, of course). As such, he had never once brought goblins into a house by making oaths of any kind; but his natural timidity won out in the end, and he spit in his hand.

"Clear out the goblins," he warbled as though his voice had decided to crack from puberty for a second time, "and your permanent position in Whitewood is assured. I s-s-swear it on-n the s-s-salt."

Then came the most disgusting handshake of his life, to the rumbling of an entire freshman class joining the congress inside.

"I'll see you at sunrise," said the stranger. Her head tilted to the side, causing her neck to make a sound like half a hundred twigs snapping, and then she walked into the house with nothing but her broom. She turned, nodded to Sloot, and shut the door behind her.

"I've just murdered an old woman," said Sloot.

"She seemed really eager to have a go at it," Myrtle remarked. "Why not say that you gave an old woman her dying wish?"

"Her dying wish just gave us more goblins to deal with later," said Sloot, who was starting to gulp down air in anticipation of a proper panic.

"She seemed very sure of herself."

Anyone can panic, but it takes a worrier to make a real spectacle of it. Sloot was a tried and true worrier. He'd just made a sure-to-be-broken oath on salt and spit, and sent an old woman to a grisly death. He was seeing stars, clutching his chest, and sinking to his knees with aplomb. He really made it look easy.

He wasn't typically a fainter, but he was on the cusp of it when he felt hands on his cheeks. Soft hands. Ones that smelled nice.

"It's going to be all right," said Myrtle in an even voice.

His breathing started to slow. The stars faded from his vision, and there was Myrtle, her eyes locked serenely on his.

*It's going to be all right,* she'd said. It was an unusual phrase, one he thought he could vaguely remember having heard before. A magic spell, perhaps? If he was being frank, Sloot had to admit that he didn't really understand what philosophy was. It was altogether possible that *it's going to be all right* was some sort of incantation, and that the ethereal remains of a wizard were rolling around in Myrtle's head.

If it was a spell, it had worked. He wasn't sure if her smelling nice was a part of it, but it certainly helped.

"Thanks," Sloot managed after a moment.

"Don't mention it," said Myrtle. "Come on, I'll walk you home."

As he closed the courtyard gate behind him, Sloot paused to listen as thuds and screams reverberated from within the house. He hoped the screaming was the goblins, but it was hard to be sure.

# ❧☞TO THE LIBRARY☜❧

A
t the end of the day, a true worrier doesn't just hang his cloud of
lurking dread on a hook and drift peacefully off to sleep. Years
of practice have made it no trouble at all to stay awake for hours
on end, torturing themselves over trivial details. Their haunted, waxy
expressions are the result of countless wakings in cold sweats. Their
dedication to their craft can be measured by weighing the bags under
their eyes.

Sloot jolted awake, short of breath and sweating profusely, and why
wouldn't he? It was only the second time he'd awoken as a disloyal traitor to the Old Country, and he had no idea how many times he'd have
to do that before he either got used to it or gave in and reported himself
to Uncle.

His heart continued to race. He couldn't catch his breath. The human heart only beats a certain number of times before it quits for good.
Sloot worried that his heart's current pace would put him in the grave
before he'd even had a chance to do something properly disloyal. His
epitaph might read no worse than "Here Lieth Sloot Peril, Struck Down
Ere He Could Be Convicted for Possession of Heresy with Intent to
Distribute."

He took a deep breath and decided to give self-delusion a try.

"Things aren't that bad," he said aloud, forcing a smile and willing
himself not to make a rational argument to the contrary.

"That's the spirit," said Roman, who was sitting in the chair beside the bed.

Sloot shrieked. "What are you doing here?" he demanded, pulling his bedsheet up to his face with white-knuckled fists.

Roman leaned in close. "Spy stuff," he replied with a wink. "Had to make sure you're not the sort who talks in his sleep. Good news! Just a lot of whimpering noises."

"Perhaps that was just tonight. What if I talk in my sleep tomorrow night? Would that mean I'm unfit for duty?"

"Oh yes," said Roman.

"Well, don't you think you should check in again? Tomorrow night, perhaps?"

"Good idea," said Roman. "You're a smart lad. Better that we find out as soon as possible, in case we need to give you the treatment."

"Treatment?"

"I can't say too much, or you'll be expecting it. The redacted version is that I wake you up the hard way every time you make a noise in your sleep. Did you know that freezing water can cause quite a lot of bruising if applied correctly?"

"I didn't," answered Sloot, with equal parts disappointment and terror. "Probably not a problem then, forget I mentioned it."

"I know a good idea when I hear one." Roman stood and stretched. "I knew I was right about you. Improving the program already, and it's only your second day!"

Sloot groaned.

"Well, long second day ahead of us," said Roman. "I'll see myself out. See you at Whitewood, *Mister Peril*. Ha! I'm going to enjoy pretending to take orders from you!"

Roman made a bit of theatre to go along with his exit, pausing to listen to the door, peeking through the keyhole, then eventually, slowly, opening it and slipping through. Sloot initially dismissed it as ridiculous, then wondered whether he should be doing the same.

Eventually, the sun came up, and Sloot was left facing the grim reality that he did, in fact, have to get out of bed. He had to restart the

Loyalist Oath five times before he managed to get all the way through it without breaking down into tears, so he slapped himself twice as hard to make up for it. It left him a bit short on civic pride as he made his usual walk to the north gate.

There it was, as massive as ever, but it gave him no comfort to rest his hand upon it. All these years, and it had done nothing to keep the enemy out after all! Sloot himself was the proof! He turned on his heel and started off for Whitewood, secretly wishing the entire time that he'd succumb to a spontaneous fit of rage, and do to himself what every other Carpathian savage would love to do to any salt they happened to meet: drown him in the river and make balloons from his guts.

Except perhaps he'd find a quicker way to do the former, and he'd need to arrange for someone else to handle the latter.

Unfortunately, Sloot had to swallow his disappointment and walk through the front gates of Whitewood as unmurdered as ever. Also there, alive, sweaty, and smoking a pipe, was the stranger.

"Is it done?" The shock was apparent on Sloot's face.

"Aye," said the stranger. She took the pipe from her mouth, leaned to her left, and spit a glob of red onto the ground.

"But how? There must have been—"

"Never you mind how," said the stranger. "I done what I said I'd do, and now I'm owed what you swore on salt and spit."

"But where are the bodies? Are they still in the house?"

"You've never swept a goblin," the stranger surmised with a grin. "Can't say I'm surprised. No bodies, only smoke! You don't kill a goblin, you just send 'em back to the shadows whence they came."

"I never knew," said Sloot.

"You hear that?"

"Hear what?"

"Nothin'," said the stranger with a satisfied smirk. "Nothin' as far as the ear can hear. No goblins cacklin', or smashin' furniture, or commentatin' on their boulderchuck league matches. Can't beat nothin' for proof that I done what I said I'd do."

She was right. There was a stillness emanating from within the house that screamed "no goblins in here, that's for sure!" Sloot could hardly believe it, yet there was the silence.

"Sure enough," said Sloot. "Well done, friend! As promised—"

"Sworn!"

"Sorry, as *sworn*, your position in the house is guaranteed. We'll put you on the books as 'goblin sweep' for now, Missus—"

"Nan!" Sloot turned in surprise to see a burgundy satin-swaddled Wilhelm Hapsgalt running toward him with an exaggerated high step that one only sees in courtly runs designed for high-heeled shoes. Sloot didn't practice them himself, but had walked through the arts district often enough to know it was probably called something like the Ponzi Ponce or the Bishop's Trot. Unsure of what else he could do, he curled himself into the classic Coward's Defense and resolved to think happy thoughts until after the younger Lord Hapsgalt was finished colliding with him.

But the impact never came. After a moment, he looked up to see the younger Lord Hapsgalt snuggled into the lap of the stranger, who was stroking his hair.

"Wait," said Sloot, "did you say 'Nan'?"

"Well of course I did. It's her name, silly!"

"That's enough cheek, Willie," said Nan. "I hadn't given Mr. Peril my name, there was no way he'd have known."

"Oh. All right."

"Oh dear," said Sloot. His panic regarding the whole Carpathian spy bit yielded the floor, albeit briefly, to the terrifying realization that he'd just unwittingly defied the elder Lord Hapsgalt.

"Run along for a moment Willie," said Nan, ruffling Willie's hair. "Nan's got to have a talk with Mr. Peril."

"I can stay," whined Willie, his jaw jutting outward in defiance.

"If you want," said Nan, "but it'll be boring. Grown-up stuff."

"Oh." Willie appeared to weigh his options for a moment, then picked up a stick, brandished it like a sword, and ran into the house with a "tally ho!"

"Look," said Nan, "I know that Lord Hapsgalt don't want me around Willie."

"Well, in point of fact, no," said Sloot. The fact that she'd broached the subject for him did little to mollify his feeling of awkwardness, which was currently standing naked in front of a fictive classroom, unable to move.

"He says I'm keeping the boy soft." Nan paused to relight her pipe. "He's six years old! How hard were any of us at that age? Not fair to hold that against me, in any case."

"I'm sorry," said Sloot, "how old did you say Willie is?"

"Six. His birthday's not for another month. Don't worry, plenty of time to buy him a present."

"We must be talking about a different Willie. The younger Lord Hapsgalt is forty-two, unless I've got my math wrong." He hadn't. Not once in his life.

"Ha! *The younger Lord Hapsgalt!* You're a riot! I mean, that *is* his proper title, but to talk like that of a six-year-old boy!"

"I'm confused," said Sloot, who was. "The fellow who just walked into the house?"

"Aye."

"That's the younger Lord Hapsgalt."

"So formal!" said Nan with a delighted chuckle.

"In the high heels and the burgundy satin. Big nose, thin moustache."

"Yes, yes, I've eyes, ain't I?"

"You believe that he is six years old?"

"'Tis the truth! Whether I believe it or no matters not."

"And the moustache?"

Nan shrugged. "Early bloomer."

Reality and Sloot were old friends. Until recently, that friendship had been boring and predictable, much to his satisfaction. He was starting to miss that reality, and the Sloot-shaped impression he'd made in it by sitting in it the same way every day of his life.

"Listen," said Sloot, in an attempt to get the conversation back on a sensible track. Unfortunately, unaccustomed as he was to managing lunacy, that was as far as he managed to get.

"No, you listen! You've sworn an oath on salt and spit. Break it now, and there'll be no unseating the congress of goblins that moves in on Whitewood. I'm your goblin sweep until I say otherwise!"

"That's true, but—"

"But nothing!" Nan planted her fists on her hips. "I don't care what old Constantin has to say on the matter, and I don't care how old Willie is. He's only six years old, and he needs his Nan!"

Sloot was at a disadvantage. He couldn't break his oath, and he had an utter dearth of talent for dealing with irrationality. He briefly entertained the notion that she'd be more receptive to absurdity than reason, and tried to concoct some; unfortunately, all he could think of was ducks eating toast, which was a small step away from ducks eating bread, which wasn't absurd at all.

In the end, Nan agreed to keep out of sight when the elder Lord Hapsgalt or his agents turned up at the house. She said that she'd been doing just that for years.

"Where's Master Wilhelm?" asked Roman, having appeared suddenly.

"Don't call me that," said Willie, whose timing was impeccable. "Call me Willie, that's my name. Also, I have a question. Where is my house?"

"Er, this is it," Sloot replied. "The one you were just in."

"I doubt it," said Willie. "That house is all wrecked up. I'm supposed to move into Whitewood. It's very fancy."

"It will be," said Sloot. "We've only just got the goblins out. We've got workers coming in today to fix it up and bring the furniture."

Folding his arms, Willie glanced back at the house. His face showed no deference to anyone else's busy schedule, taking its sweet time in wrinkling into an expression of dissatisfaction.

"No," said Willie, shaking his head. "I've never lived in a house that needed fixing or furnituring before. That's not how fancy houses work."

"You've always lived in your father's house, Willie," said Nan.

"Right, and it's never needed fixing!" Willie rolled his eyes, exasperated for having to explain every minute detail of his point. Then he paused, and his head shot up like a deer who'd heard anything at all, or possibly not.

"Wait a minute," he said, waving a finger as a smarmy grin set up shop on his face. "Did Nipsy and the boys put you up to this?"

"Who's Nipsy?" asked Roman.

"Right," said Willie. "I'll play along. Oh, look at the dreadful hovel that I'm expected to live in! Oh, woe is me! I suppose it's just the four of us here, and there's nobody hiding … behind … here!" He clop-clopped to the other side of the little fountain as quickly as his high-heeled shoes would carry him.

"A-ha!" he exclaimed, to nothing and no one. He was crestfallen for a moment before he spied a little tree on the other side of the patchy brown lawn.

"Oh, sneaky." He pointed to the tree.

"There's no one there," said Sloot. "That tree is far too small for anyone to—"

"Ah-ha!" exclaimed Willie, jumping to the other side of the tree. He seemed genuinely perplexed again.

Roman and Sloot made eye contact. Roman raised an eyebrow in a vague "what's with him" sort of way, to which Sloot rolled his eyes and wondered how long he could keep this up.

Willie's hands went to his hips, bringing a nearly imperceptible groan from Sloot. He wasn't particularly keen to fight Willie. Aside from his vicious-looking heels, Willie was his boss. Win or lose, Sloot would lose in the end.

"I think the joke's gone far enough." Willie moved forward with a bouncy little walk that couldn't decide whether it wanted to be a saunter or a swagger when it grew up. "In fact, I'm starting to think Nipsy might not even be here."

"There's no one else here," said Sloot. "I've already told you that."

"But that was just for show." Willie was nearly pleading now. It was apparent that he wasn't accustomed to being made to wait for things.

"No, it wasn't. There's really no one else here."

"Why are you here then? And where's the real house?"

"I'm Sloot. Sloot Peril, remember? I'm your financier, and this is your house. Your real house."

Willie stared at Sloot for a long time. His brow furrowed over panicked eyes. His thin upper lip curled up over his teeth. His face nearly broke into the full-on despair of a tearful tantrum before it relaxed completely, as though he'd forgotten where he was. Then his eyes narrowed, and his greasy smile took the stage once again for an encore.

"Nearly had me there," he said, wagging his finger.

"Oh, for pity's sake, Willie," said Nan, the last vestiges of her patience having found something better to do. "No one's playing a prank on you! This is your house, it's just not finished yet!"

Willie stared at her wide-eyed for a moment, then turned his vacant stare back to Sloot. Having absolutely no idea what else he could have done, Sloot returned the stare with equal or lesser enthusiasm.

Willie's smile returned for an encore, along with its finger-wagging backup dancer.

"Almost had me again," said Willie. "I've got to keep my eye on you."

"Er, Willie," said Sloot, desperate for a change of topic, "this is Roman. I've hired him to be your valet."

"Oh," Willie's face lit up, "I know about valets! Some of the other boys at the club have them. You follow me around, hold my cape, and fight other valets when I get into disagreements with other boys."

Roman shrugged. "I suppose I could fight a child's valet for you, if that's what you wanted."

"I think he means *gentlemen* when he says boys," said Sloot. "Willie is a member of a hunting club, isn't that right?"

Willie nodded.

"No place for a six-year-old boy," Nan grumbled. "You should have some friends your own age, Willie."

"Willie has a friend at the club who's six years old?" Roman looked puzzled.

"It's a long story," said Sloot.

"All right," said Roman. "Anyway, you want me to follow you around now?"

"That'd be great," said Willie, with a toothy grin. "Oh! You can follow me to the library! Sir Wallace Scoffington is signing copies of his new book today. He's my hero, you know."

"Oh, Willie, please don't go to the library!" Nan was hugging Willie the way that certain very large snakes in very large jungles hug very large mammals, who then go to sleep. "It's a dangerous place, and that Sir Wallace is a bad influence on you!"

"The library? Dangerous?" Sloot had spent a significant portion of his youth in the library. In his experience, as long as one didn't cross the battle-hardened librarians with the giant hammers, it was one of the safest places in the city.

"But I have to go," said Willie. "Sir Wallace!"

"Perhaps when you're older."

"He's what, forty?" asked Roman.

"He's six years old!"

"I'm curious," said Sloot before Roman had another chance to weigh in, "how old will Willie be on his birthday next month?"

"I'll be—"

"I'd like Nan to work it out if you don't mind, sir."

"He'll be six," said Nan.

"No, I won't!"

"That's enough backtalk," said Nan. "Now if you'll all excuse me, I need to get Willie off to school."

"We'll handle that." Roman gave Sloot a wink and a nudge.

"Yes," said Sloot. "Yes, we can do that."

"All right then." Nan pushed Willie's head down to the height it would have been if he were six, then bent low and kissed his forehead. Then she put her hands on her knees and crouched a bit.

"Now you be good for Mister Peril, understand?"

"Yes, Nan," Willie replied with a dejected lilt.

"Off to school with you, little man! I'll have your snack waiting when you get home."

"And where will that be? Here, or at the real house?"

"Both," said Nan. "Now off with you."

Willie said a swear word. Sloot heard a faint "pop" from inside the house, and the cackle of a goblin eager to set up a new congress.

"Oh, Willie," said Nan, "I'd just gotten them all swept out!" She grabbed her broom and started stomping back into the house.

People in the Old Country avoid swearing in or near their houses to keep the goblins out. This is how hiking was invented, as a means of getting oneself a fair distance from town when one had significant swearing to do.

Willie's head bobbed from side to side in a sulk as he stomped through the gate, staring down at the ground. Sloot and Roman followed him along the cobbled avenue that wound its way past several statues of prominent statesmen who'd served in the Salzstadt legislature over the years. One such was Karl "The Stalker" Heringskraft, whose string of barehanded strangulations was overlooked for nearly thirty years, in deference to his passionate crusading for the well-being of incredibly wealthy aristocrats. It wasn't until he accidentally strangled one of *them* that he was swiftly brought to Old Country justice.

"It's not fair," said Willie after a few blocks. "I'm a big boy now, I shouldn't have to go to school anymore."

Roman gave Sloot an incredulous look. Sloot shrugged.

"Well, today's your lucky day," said Roman. "You never have to go to school, as long as you're with your pals Roman and Sloot!"

"Really?" Willie looked hopefully toward Sloot, who looked to Roman, whose bug eyes got even buggier as he nodded to Sloot knowingly.

"Of course," said Sloot. Though Willie wasn't the brightest, sending him to school would have been ridiculous. Still, he wasn't the brightest ...

"Let's go to the library," said Roman, "like you wanted. You still want to go to the library, Willie?"

"Last one there's a Carpathian savage!" Willie took off running at a full sprint, his high-heeled shoes failing to slow him in the slightest.

"Well, he won't be wrong about that, eh?" Roman elbowed Sloot's ribs.

"I suppose not," said Sloot, who hung his head and lamented everything that his life had become. "Why're you so keen to get him to the library?"

"I'm not," said Roman, his expression suddenly turning serious. "I'm keen to gain his trust, and so are you, *Mister* Peril."

"Willie's part of your secret plan, then?"

Roman's enormous eyes narrowed to the size of a normal person's. "I suppose you might be ready to know a thing or two about the plan. So, yes. He's a part of it."

They started walking in the direction Willie had run, regardless of the fact that it didn't lead toward the library.

"Look, if you'd rather leave me out of this business altogether—"

"Looking for a way out of the intelligence service, are you?"

"Yes!" said Sloot. "I thought I'd been clear about that from the beginning!"

"You won't like what happens to deserters."

"Is it anything like what happens to disloyalists here? Because that's particularly nasty on its own."

"Worse," said Roman. "Well, mostly the same, standing in the stocks and being pelted with rotten vegetables. Only in Carpathia, the vegetables are soaked in whiskey and lit first."

⧓⧓⧓⧓

The Library of Salzstadt was more than just a grand old building that housed countless thousands of books. It was also a tax haven for the Hapsgalt family. Granted, the tax laws had largely been hand-written by Constantin Hapsgalt and his forefathers to favor those whose fortunes defied counting, but that didn't mean that the Hapsgalts were frivolous. They did everything within their power to ensure that they never parted with a penny more than necessary.

Poor people would always be poor, after all. How offensive it would be indeed, to think that their problems could be solved simply by throwing money at them!

Most of the great libraries of the world did not feature golden fountains with swans in them, nor did they enforce dress codes. Nor, for that matter, were they under the totalitarian auspices of Imelda Lilellien, who had only accepted the position of Head Librarian after being told by the Domnitor himself, long may he reign, that her tactics were far too violent for the battlefield. She relented because cold wars weren't her speed anyway, and what's the use of being Field Marshall of His Excellency's Armies if you never get any blood on you?

Imelda's portrait was hung in the foyer. Sloot must have seen it thousands of times, but only just noticed the ring on her left forefinger: two silver snakes coiled around a black stone. Exactly like the ones everyone had been clinking against their glasses at Gildedhearth. It couldn't be a coincidence. How were they all connected?

"There he is!" Willie shouted. He was promptly shushed by one of the hulking librarians who was wandering around with a massive warhammer. These weren't the sort of librarians who could help one find a book, nor could many of them do a stellar job of reading one. One would want the *other* sort of librarian for that.

Of course, *they* were far too busy working whatever eldritch rites were necessary to keep all of that printed knowledge in check. While we'd all like to believe that the ideas in books simply sit there on the shelves, waiting to be read in their own contexts, the librarians know what danger looms in the silence of the stacks. Ideas are prone to leakage, and anything that leaks can pool. Some particularly nasty goblins have arisen from the commingling of ideas that were better kept to themselves.

The big librarians with no necks were hired to keep order among the patrons because the proper librarians had bigger things to worry about; plus, when the proper librarians *did* deign to shush people themselves, it was infinitely more harrowing. Better to be menaced by a thug with a hammer than shushed by a librarian who'd spent years mastering shushery.

Sir Wallace Scoffington was seated at a table, signing copies of his books for a long line of mostly older women. He smiled at them with what must have been a charming gleam in the eyes of anyone with sufficient cataracts to miss it altogether.

Finally, after nearly an hour of Sloot's practically having to restrain Willie into politely standing in line, they reached the front.

"And who shall I make it out to?" Sir Wallace's smile fell a bit as he looked up at Willie, who was clearly not his target demographic.

"Willie— *Wilhelm* Hapsgalt, if you please, Sir Wallace. I'm your biggest admirer!"

"I genuinely hope that that's not true," said Sir Wallace, chuckling to himself. Sloot thought he looked ridiculous in his light brown ensemble with the kerchief around his neck, but it did fit the persona. He was thin and aging, his long, blond hair caught up in a ponytail with a few intentionally wild strands hanging out.

"Wait," said Sir Wallace, his quill hovering over the book. "You did say *Willie Hapsgalt*, didn't you?"

"I did, yeah. But sign it to *Wilhelm* please, I'd like it to seem more grown-up."

Sir Wallace looked up at Willie for the first time, his face a kettle of amusement on the brink of boiling over.

"I've had letters from a Willie Hapsgalt, but I assumed that you were much … *much* younger."

"My boyish charm," said Willie with a smirk. "That's what Nan calls it. She says it'll make all the girls swoon when I get older."

Sloot stood rigid, desperate to suppress the mortified groan that so desperately wanted to declare to all within earshot "we're not with him, please limit the scope of your derision to the bucktoothed manchild." Unfortunately for Sloot and his chagrin, that manchild was his livelihood and, even more unfortunately, the basis of his career and reputation.

"I remember your last letter," said Sir Wallace. "I can recite it from memory. It read, and I quote: '*Your great. Love, Willie.*' I know the whole *your* and *you're* business can be tricky, but how old are you?"

"I'm a bit confused on that point, actually." Nan's nuttery had seen to that. "But the important thing is that you got my letter! Where did it reach you? On the veldt? In the jungle?"

"On my credenza," said Sir Wallace. "Listen, you seem like a nice fellow—"

"I'm glad you think so," said Willie, "because I'd very much like to be an explorer like you when I grow up!"

Sloot's composure was fighting for its life. His chagrin had the upper hand now, and he was near fainting from the exertion. Abstention from guffaws was sweaty work.

"Really," said Sir Wallace, who was in the throes of losing a similar battle with his decorum. His next exhalation was as likely as not to be accompanied by a hoot or a cackle. "And when do you think that might be?"

⁂

"It could have been worse," said Roman later, over drinks at the pub.

"I don't see how." Sloot took one of the beers that the barmaid had brought for him and placed it under his chair. That was the bargain with the goblins in this particular establishment: for half your libations, the stool under you kept all of its legs. The bartender liked his stools, so pints were only sold in pairs.

"It could have been a simple disaster from which we profited nothing."

"Oh right," said Sloot, "at least Willie got a book autographed by his hero who, coincidentally, laughed in his face!"

"Willie was none the wiser," said Roman. "But that wasn't the profit."

"I'll bite," said Sloot. "What did we gain from that?"

Roman looked left and right, then leaned in and motioned for Sloot to do the same. "Willie wants to be an explorer."

"An explorer? What good is that? He may as well have said he wants to be the Domnitor himself, long may he reign, for all his chances of succeeding. Does he know anything about exploration? I imagine it involves tying knots. I had to manage his shoelaces for him three times today!"

"You're not wrong for doubting his ability," said Roman, "but you're overlooking the most important bit."

"Which is?"

"The test! Willie's got to prove his worth, or we're both out of a job. And we need to stay close to Willie for the secret mission!"

"Oh, right," said Sloot. "In all of the embarrassment, I'd forgotten about all of the treason and heresy I've got to commit."

"Keep your voice down! Willie's got enough money to turn just about anything into a success, but he's also got the attention span of a goblin with a machete. We just need for him to focus on something—*anything*—long enough to throw a pile of money at it."

Sloot's face brightened in realization. "We only need him to impress his father."

"He's never done that before, so I imagine that's a pretty low bar."

"It's practically lying on the ground."

"So we carry out an expedition to just about anywhere—"

"And the job's as good as done!"

"Now you're getting it," said Roman with a wink. "Then Willie's so grateful to us for making him look good that getting him to help with the secret mission is no trouble at all!" He waved to the barmaid for four more beers.

"One thing at a time," said Sloot. "What's the expedition, then?"

"Somewhere outside the city." Suddenly Roman's eyes went wide, even for him. "We'll take him to Nordheim! It's perfect!"

"Nordheim?" Sloot knew little about Nordheim, other than it was north of Carpathia and full of Vikings. He reckoned it could only be worse if it were south of itself and full of Carpathians, but Carpathia had that position filled.

"I can see your gears turning." Roman guzzled his beer like it was his last.

"Hasn't Nordheim already been discovered?"

"Every place has been discovered," said Roman with a dismissive wave. "Every place worth discovering, anyway. Even the ones that haven't, I'd imagine."

"You imagine that people have discovered places that haven't been discovered."

"Not properly. You saw that Sir Wallace, didn't you? He's the sort of fussy lad who wouldn't want his bootprints associated with an uninhabited island. Wouldn't sell any books."

"But what does that have to do with Nordheim? Willie simply can't discover it. It's too popular. People won't buy it."

"He doesn't have to discover it," said Roman. "He just has to go, and bring something back."

"And that qualifies as exploration."

Roman nodded. "I looked it up. No official accreditations for explorers, no program at the university. Just a bunch of gits in khaki, writing books about where they went over the summer."

"At least he's qualified, then. Or he will be, once he's been to his tailor."

"Precisely," said Roman. "What's more, I know the way there."

"You've been to Nordheim?"

"A few times, during the war. There's a passage through the mountains, don't even have to go through Carpathia! Only takes a couple of weeks to get there. The hardest part is getting past the gates."

"Outside the city," said Sloot with a gulp. He'd never been outside the city before, and although he was now one of the bloody barbarian savages who lived beyond the wall, he had no idea if they would recognize him as one of their own. He'd been raised as a salt, after all—would they make him eat a baby, or spit on a sidewalk to prove his barbarism?

The barmaid set another round of drinks on the tall table between them.

"One above and one below," said Roman as they each put a beer under their stools. "Don't worry about the expedition, my boy. I've been beyond the wall dozens of times, you'll be as safe as the Domnitor in his bedchamber … long may he reign!"

# ⋘⋙SHOES FIT FOR A BUREAUCRAT⋘⋙

The speed with which the staff had turned the broken shell of Whitewood into a presentable manor was astounding. Using the time it took Sloot's landlord to manage simple repairs in his apartment as a reference, he'd have thought it impossible; then again, he had neither the elder Lord Hapsgalt's piles of money nor his flair for employing credible threats to accomplish his goals.

"What do you think?" asked Willie, who was now dressed entirely in light brown and wearing a pair of tall riding boots, sitting awkwardly in an overstuffed chair in front of the fire.

"Very nice," said Sloot. "I would have expected the paint to need longer to dry, but they've already hung these animal heads on the walls."

"No, the outfit! Do you think I look like an explorer?"

"Oh," said Sloot. "Yes, of course." He couldn't be sure, but it looked like the very same ensemble that Sir Wallace had worn in the library.

"But the animal heads help, don't they? There's a man at the hunting club who sells them to me and the rest of the lads. Nipsy's got a bear head just like that one."

"I believe that's a moose," said Sloot, examining the antlers on the head to which Willie was pointing.

"All right, mister expert," said Willie with a sneer, "if you're so good at identifying things, what's this sit?"

"I'm sorry, *sit?*"

"Yes! This thing that I'm doing on the chair right now, what do they call it?"

"A ... sit?"

Willie rolled his eyes. "Right, but which one?"

Sloot said nothing. He was no master tactician, but he'd worked this one out a long time ago. He couldn't think of anything that he could say that would approach being taken for correct, and reasoned that a well-placed nothing was the smart alternative to the wrong something.

"It's the Brunt of the Evening," said Willie eventually, with the haughtiest simper he could muster. "I didn't really expect you to know it, it's very new. Don't beat yourself up."

"I won't."

"I've developed a keen sense of the way the world works." Willie stood up to lean against the mantle in a pose that Sloot was sure must have been named the Pouting Hedge, or some such nonsense. "It's not something that you can pick up on the streets, mind you. It comes from spending a lot of time listening to people you pay extremely well. None of them ever contradict me, so I reckon I've got it all worked out!"

"I see," said Sloot, who'd heard more sense from the congress of goblins who'd taken up residence in the cabinets of his last apartment. They'd gotten into his stock of beans and couldn't stop laughing at the rude noises that ensued. He'd had to move out for the overpowering smell, and without his security deposit.

"Well, I suppose Nan will want me to turn in soon. Good night, Sloot."

"Good night, Willie."

Things really were coming along. They'd barely been in the house a few days, and if Sloot hadn't known first-hand that it had been a literal goblins' nest earlier the same week, he'd never have believed it.

"Are they all gone?" The voice hadn't come from behind Sloot, or from any other direction relative to where he was standing for that matter. It was just sort of *there*, as though it had come from every point in the room at once.

"Sorry," said Sloot aloud. "Who?"

Silence. Maybe Sloot was hearing things.

"The goblins," answered the voice.

Silence again. Sloot *hoped* that he was hearing things. Maybe he was just catching half a conversation from another room, one person standing too close to the flue or something.

The voice sighed. "You there, have the goblins all gone or not?"

Sloot's insides lurched as though his guts wanted to run away. Unfortunately for them, his feet were too alarmed to move.

"Er, yes." Maybe if he didn't move; but even if he wanted to, where would he go? The voice was coming from everywhere!

"Oh, that's a relief," said the voice after another delay, which was just long enough for Sloot's mind to run rampant with how the blood-and-gore-covered demon speaking to him was going to torture him for eternity. "I'll just lock up and be on my way."

"All right," Sloot replied, daring to hope that he might not be flayed alive, so that thin strips of his skin could be used for tinsel at whatever demonic celebration plays out during the Yuletide season.

More silence. Sloot waited for nearly half an hour before he ran for the door. Disembodied voices were new to him, but he knew himself well enough to correctly predict that he wouldn't sleep very well that night.

※ ※ ※ ※

Standing in the ridiculously long line at Central Bureaucracy had been rated by Achtungfelder's Guide to Salzstadt as "five stars, would give it a sixth if such a thing were possible." There was no definitive proof that threats (having been rebranded as "subtle persuasion") by the jackbooted thugs in the Salzstadt Ministry of Propaganda were responsible for the glowing review; however, anyone who'd ever spent the better part of a week getting a license to use a public toilet might develop suspicions.

As a matter of legal compliance, it is compulsory at this point to direct anyone having developed suspicions regarding the motives and methods of the Ministry of Propaganda to report to the Ministry of Conversation for a cup of tea. Those not familiar with the Ministry of Conversation will note that it was formerly known as the Ministry of Interrogation. It has recently gone through a complete rebranding, courtesy of the Ministry of Propaganda.

Early on in the day, Sloot managed to suppress the memory of the disembodied voice and was feeling nearly chipper. His contentment nearly rivaled his days of obedient, ignorant bliss, which had ended upon learning his mother's secret and subsequently volunteering to be a heretical traitor to his country. Perhaps it was due to his having been through the line at Central Bureaucracy so many times that he felt at home here. It may also have had something to do with his knowing that if one is going to spend a significant amount of time standing—with the occasional shuffle forward—one should spend a little extra at Blinzwalder's on Bittestrasse, where August Blinzwalder makes shoes specifically designed for standing in. They're entirely unsuitable for walking, but one pair of shoes can't do it all.

They were worth it. His feet felt as though they were at home, in their favorite comfy chair with their feet up. It's a bit convoluted as metaphors go, but anyone who owns a pair will agree that it's the best explanation available. Buy a pair of Blinzwalders today!

But despite his general feeling of comfort in his surroundings and his impeccably supported arches, a sense of uneasiness insisted that it had every right to loom over him, and would not be moved. He initially thought that it must have been the doom that awaited him on the road to Nordheim, but he'd spent most of the night worrying about that. That particular dread was practically an old friend. No, this was something new. And it was coming from behind him.

The ability to feel the gaze of another upon one's person has been attributed to a number of possible causes: an undiscovered sense that people possess, heightened situational awareness, or invisible goblins who pull the hairs on the back of one's neck until they stand on end. All are equally credible, and all equally fail to take into account the training manual for the Union of Queue Position Engineers.

The members of the UQPE, quietly referred to as "placeholders" by people smart enough not to refer to them as such within their earshot, have a well-documented history of politely and amicably working with members of the local community to provide queue position engineering services at a fair price, without a hint of coercion or a single lawsuit involving city-wide riots.

It is worth noting that the UQPE, like the Ministry of Conversation, has availed itself of the rebranding services offered by the Ministry of Propaganda.

In the old days, it was rumored that engineers belonging to the union would receive training on intimidation tactics, including—but not limited to—making non-union members feel particular discomfort by staring at the backs of their necks in such a way as to make their hairs stand on end. According to the well-documented history of the union, such things were certainly not transpiring in the line at Central Bureaucracy today; nevertheless, Sloot turned around.

"Oh, hello," he said to the sneer given human form in line behind him.

"What's that you've got there?"

"My papers? Er, permit applications."

"Permit applications? Why would you need those for standing in line?"

"It's the other way around," said Sloot. He imagined that the bureaucrats would have a lot of questions regarding his need for permits to go to Nordheim, so he'd taken the liberty of filling out several additional forms. It could never hurt to have a Requisition for Foreign Mockery or a Writ of Obeisance handy.

"You're standing in line to file your own permit applications?"

"That's right."

From the way that everyone nearby turned to stare at him, Sloot reckoned that he must have slipped into that dream where he was standing naked in line at Central Bureaucracy. It's an unusual feeling, looking down and being surprised to see one's self fully clothed.

"That's a nice pair of Blinzwalders," said the man.

"Thanks," said Sloot. "They're my first, I've always wanted some."

"Stand in line a lot, do you?"

"Only when I come here. I've always heard that a good pair of Blinzwalders makes all the difference, and until today I never—"

"I don't suppose you have a union card, do you?"

"Sorry, which union?" Either the room had just grown a bit darker of its own accord, or the people standing nearby were looming over him with a fair degree of menace.

"Queue Position Engineers, Salzstadt local. We overlook the average citizen, but a fellow comes in here in a brand new pair of Blinzwalder Buckskin Standers, wing tips and everything, and we start to wonder what he's got against the industrious union workers queueing up here on the daily."

"I don't understand," said Sloot. "I work hard, and I'm queueing up. Should I be here more often?"

"You should have a union card! Especially if you've got the coin for a pair of shoes like that!"

"Or he should have the decency to hire bona fide union labor to do his standing for him!" shouted a scrappy young line engineer with his cap pulled down low, who should definitely be nicknamed "The Salzstadt Kid," if he wasn't already.

"Yeah," said a pile of muscles who could start moonlighting as a librarian, if he knew his way around a warhammer. "Scab like that could find hisself blacklisted at the door." The man's fingers were the size of Sloot's arm, and therefore had no difficulty in plucking the papers from his grasp.

"Please," said Sloot, "I need those—"

"Hapsgalt!" roared the shaved gorilla. "He's working for Lord Hapsgalt!"

"Yes, but not the—"

"Are you putting me on?" asked the human sneer who'd originally started in on him. His fists went to his hips, and the chorus of angry grumbling around them grew in volume and intensity. "Lord Moneypiles himself is too cheap to squeeze out the silver to support a working man at his trade!"

"I'm sorry," said Sloot, "I knew you could hire someone to stand in line for you, but I didn't know there was a union!"

"It's exactly this sort of disregard for the honest salt that's made it so hard to scrape by these days! Makes me mad enough to say every swear word I know, even make up a few. I'm headed out to the crags tonight, lads! Anybody else want to pop off a few?"

"I'll be there," said the Salzstadt Kid. "What do we do with him?"

"Get him out of here!" shouted the sneer. "And then I need to talk to my union rep."

"With pleasure," said the pile of muscles, who waved to the queue monitors and pointed at Sloot. "Now, what did you want to talk to me about?"

※ ⊼ ※ ⊼ ※ ⊼ ※ ⊼

Among the other firsts for the day was Sloot's having failed to secure their travel permits at Central Bureaucracy. He'd always prided himself on his ability to make it all the way up to the counter without being deterred, and now his perfect record had been blemished. And for what? A nice pair of standing shoes.

He'd somehow lost his walking shoes in the process of being ejected from Central Bureaucracy, so his walk back to Whitewood had been accompanied by the clamorous "clop, clop" of his Blinzwalders. The soles would need a good sanding down if they were to be useful again for their intended purpose. The cobblestones had wrought havoc on them, but it was better on balance than having gone barefoot. Well, probably. The streets were rather empty at night, so there was no way of knowing for sure whether roaming congresses of goblins were defiling them with their noxious bodily fluids. The safe bet was assuming they were.

"And Roman will be none too pleased that I didn't manage the permits," said Sloot.

"The valet?" Myrtle looked up from mending a torn sleeve on Sloot's coat with a quizzical expression. "Why would his opinion matter?"

"Right," said Sloot, "because I'm his boss, aren't I?"

"Right. Assertiveness doesn't sit well with you, does it?"

"I suppose it doesn't."

"That's all right," said Myrtle, turning her attention back to her stitching. "I can help, just let me know if he gives you any trouble."

"How did you get so good at assertiveness?"

"I HELPED HER."

"What?"

"Sorry, that was Arthur. He's right, despite his lack of modesty."

"Is he listening all the time?"

"MORE OR LESS, THOUGH I ONLY CHIME IN WHEN MY CHERISHED WISDOM IS PARTICULARLY ESSENTIAL."

"I see." Sloot noticed that Myrtle enunciated more clearly when it was Arthur doing the talking. Sloot knew that trick. It was a favorite among those who needed to seem smart, whether they were or not.

"YOU SHOULD PRACTICE ASSERTIVENESS WITH THE VALET. EVEN YOU SHOULD BE ABLE TO MANAGE IT WITH SOMEONE WHO WORKS FOR YOU."

"Thanks for that, Arthur," said Sloot, "but I don't think—"

"IT'S DR. WIDDERSHINS, PLEASE. I'LL LET YOU KNOW WHEN WE'RE ON A FIRST-NAME BASIS."

"Sorry," said Myrtle. "A bit tetchy about getting all the mileage they can from their degrees, doctors. I only get to call him Arthur on account of the free rent I'm providing."

"Degrees still count once you're dead, then?"

"OF COURSE THEY DO!" Myrtle rolled her eyes. "May as well for philosophy," she said. "Not like you could write prescriptions or anything."

Sloot and Myrtle chatted about nothing in particular, which galled Dr. Widdershins to no end. Philosophers tend to disapprove of any discussion not relevant to "what's it all mean," or discourses on trees falling in unattended forests. In the absence of meaningful talks, they opt for pondering in silence. That's where the best epiphanies come from; besides, silent pondrances are far better for a philosopher's image than saying something that might be seen as lacking depth.

"SAY SOMETHING DEEP, OR SOMETHING CONDESCENDING, OR NOTHING AT ALL." That's the philosophers' credo.

Sloot was enjoying himself immensely. He generally wasn't one for idle chit-chat either, but Myrtle had a strange way of making it seem far more interesting than it should.

"All finished," she said at last. While the coat had technically been mended, it had not been done in a way that anyone might have referred to as *well*. No one who'd ever worn—or seen—clothing, anyway. The faded black wool was all bunched up where the rip had been, and the mended sleeve was several inches shorter than its counterpart. But she was beaming at him, and her smile was making him feel all warm in a way that quickly turned troubling.

"Er, thank you." Sloot stood up abruptly and took a step backward. He was her boss! He was committing enough moral turpitude as it was. This was dangerously close to flirting! Any more of this and a congress of goblins would likely name themselves The Sloots, get it embroidered onto jackets and everything.

"What's the matter? Is there a problem with the stitching?"

"Not at all," said Sloot, followed by a very loud cough to cover up the sound of a goblin popping in. Goblins like lies, especially polite ones meant to spare feelings. Lies masquerading as etiquette are particularly dastardly in their opinion.

Myrtle exhaled sharply and frowned a bit.

"OH, STOP IT," mumbled Myrtle in a very Arthur sort of way. "IF YOU GET ALL MOONY, IT COULD VERY WELL INTERFERE WITH MY PONDERING, AND I WON'T STAND FOR IT."

Myrtle's eyes went wide and turned toward Sloot. Her cheeks went so deeply scarlet as to resemble a crime scene that needed mopping.

"I'll just be off to bed then," she quavered, then turned and nearly ran down the hall.

"No good can come of that," said Roman.

Sloot jumped. "How long have you been there?"

"Wouldn't you like to know? Not to worry, once you've completed your spy training, I'll never be able to sneak up on you again. Anyway, you're a lucky lad."

"How do you figure?"

Roman nodded down the hallway in the direction Myrtle had run. "She fancies you. Walk with me for a moment." They headed down a different hallway.

"But you said no good can come of it! And you're right. I'm her boss after all."

Roman shrugged. "Just because it's a bad idea doesn't mean you shouldn't do it. Some of my best ideas have been bad ones."

"That doesn't make any sense."

"Listen to yourself," said Roman, pushing Sloot into a sitting room and closing the door behind them. "Why do you put so much stock in good ideas that make sense? What good have they ever done for you?"

"I'd say I've done all right for myself."

Roman said one of a lower tier of swear words that goblins considered too tame to warrant their attention. It rhymed with "crabapple" and, when delivered mockingly, conveyed very mild derision.

"You're the least relaxed person I've ever met! You're hiding acts of high treason, a crazy old bat with a broom, and who knows what else?" Roman poured them each a brandy from a glass decanter. "You're charged with making a man out of a stuffed shirt, and the most dangerous woman in Salzstadt is eager to see you fail. That's what sensibility has gotten you."

"I get it," said Sloot, gripping his drink with both hands to stop from shaking. "If I don't go after Myrtle now I'll regret it for the rest of my life, is that it?"

Roman chuckled. "You and I are too young to start looking at women and wondering 'will she be the one that got away?' No, my pupil. You've got it all wrong."

"Then I shouldn't pursue her? I was right all along, and you're just … I don't know, testing me?"

"The point is that if you don't get to dabble in bad ideas every once in a while, all of the sensible ones have been for nothing. It's your reward, don't you see?"

"Yes," replied Sloot, who had no idea what Roman was talking about. Sloot loved the rules and all the security that they offered. The straight-and-narrow had never steered him wrong before, and he was now more convinced than ever that his current predicaments were nothing more than a string of very unfortunate coincidences; and yet, the way Myrtle had blushed before had stirred something in him.

"Something happened last night," said Sloot, desperate to change the subject. "I heard a voice in the trophy room."

"What'd it say?"

"Just asked if the goblins were all gone."

"I thought that was obvious."

"I did, too, but I don't think whoever was asking was really there."

"Where?"

"There, in the room with me."

"Someone down the hall, then."

"No," said Sloot, "it was coming from inside the room. From *everywhere* in the room!"

"Oh." Roman gave a dismissive wave. "Probably just a ghost."

"A ... ghost."

"I'll bet the place is full of them," said Roman. "Oh, by the way, how'd it go with the permits?"

## ⫷⫸PHILOSOPHICAL AFFLICTION⫷⫸

Despite Roman's insistence, Sloot had no confidence that the matter of the permits would work itself out, *wink, wink*. He ultimately agreed to let Roman work it out through back channels, though he'd much rather have just paid the fines that the UQPE alone referred to as "reasonable" and then contract with them for services.

Sloot was actually relieved to have the permits off his plate for the time being. He had other things on his mind. The world was still spinning on its axis, much to the chagrin of the fire-and-brimstone soothsayers peddling prophecies on Proclamation Street. Many of them had predicted the end of the entire ball of wax several times over, including one cult that only wore red and insisted that the world was, in fact, a ball of wax.

Not only were any recently-foiled lunatics forced to revisit their sacred texts, any financiers similarly still drawing breath would have their end-of-week balance sheets due for their lords' perusal. Therefore, Sloot was as near to giddy as any self-respecting mathematician could manage at the prospect of balancing the accounts.

Aberfoyle's Theorem states that the time required to complete a task is inversely proportional to one's skill with the matter at hand. So it was that the ledgers were balanced and double-checked (not that Sloot's work needed even single-checking) in a matter of minutes.

Sloot sighed. He was disappointed in the way that only the flawless performance of duty could make him.

Perhaps a walk would lift his spirits. He'd been so busy lately with committing treason and heresy that he'd neglected to see how the staff were getting on with sprucing up Whitewood. He'd seen about half the inside of the place, but very little of the grounds.

Mr. Dirtsmith had done some truly magnificent work with the trellises lining the back garden. The roses would be coming in any time now, or perhaps not—Sloot knew as much about gardening as anyone who graduated with his accounting class at the University of Salzstadt, which was to say that he knew absolutely nothing about gardening.

It didn't matter. Sloot knew pretty when he saw it, and that's what the trellises were. In fact, he was almost convinced that he was using the word "trellises" correctly.

Speaking of pretty, there was Myrtle. He'd been so intently focused on the trellises—or "big walls with roses on," if "trellises" really meant something else—that he'd nearly tripped over her, sitting on one of the little stone benches in the garden.

"Well hello, Mister Peril," she said. "Fine day for a walk. OR FOR A PONDERANCE. OR AT LEAST IT WAS UNTIL YOU CAME ALONG. Arthur! Terribly sorry, Mister Peril."

"Er, sorry," said Sloot. "I'll just leave you to it then."

"No, please stay! Sit, there's plenty of room."

Myrtle shifted to one side of the little bench and patted the other, smiling up at him. Sloot sat. Between his natural impulse to obey anything that sounds remotely like an order and the way Myrtle's lips curled when she smiled, it was the inevitable outcome. Not even the presence of her undead philosopher chaperone could have dissuaded him.

If history were any indicator, disaster was imminent. Sloot knew all of the warning signs, most of which were a pretty girl sitting anywhere near him. It was only a matter of time before some combination of profuse sweating, nervous vomiting, high-pitched laughter, and/or fainting dead away brought the occasion to a close. She'd be polite to him after that, but she'd never give him *that* smile again. The sincere one that curled up at the ends.

But then, something genuinely worrisome happened, or rather didn't. Sloot neither vomited, nor did he faint or sweat through his clothes. He even managed to keep his laughter in the tenor octaves, though experience had taught him that he was a serviceable soprano when his insecurities demanded it.

Their conversation was pleasant. She was easy to talk to, even going so far as to ask him about his day, *and* sound remotely interested in hearing the answer.

"Ask me a question." She was still smiling at him.

"Oh. I'd rather not."

"Really? You're not curious about me?" Her smile faded.

"It's not that," Sloot replied, "it's just that I'll ask the wrong thing."

"No, you won't. I won't let you."

"I can't see how that would work unless you're going to ask the question for me."

"I can't do that, but I can promise to consider whatever you ask to be exactly the question I feel like answering."

"That would require seeing into the future."

"Yes, but not very far. Just the sort of thing that women's intuition was invented for."

Sloot had heard of women's intuition before and regarded it with an abundance of skepticism. He didn't like to believe in things that he couldn't experience first-hand. He only placed faith in things like mathematics, gravity, and the infallibility of the Domnitor, long may he reign.

"OH, GET ON WITH IT. SHE WON'T LEAVE IT ALONE UNTIL YOU DO."

She smiled again and batted her eyelashes. Sloot wasn't able to resist that, not even long enough to think before he blurted out the first question that came to mind.

"How'd you get possessed?"

"Oh," said Myrtle. "Getting right to it, I see."

"I'm terribly sorry, I just—"

"No, no," said Myrtle, who may or may not have wished at that moment that she was not honor-bound to uphold the mystery of women's intuition. "There's not much to it, really. Do you remember the Philosophers' Rebellion? GLORIOUS DAYS! WE REALLY GAVE THEM WHAT FOR!"

"A bit," said Sloot. "I was just a boy when it happened."

"Me too. A child, I mean. I was a girl though."

"That adds up," said Sloot. He realized too late that she might not get how funny that was, not being an accountant.

"Anyway, the headmistress was walking us back to the orphanage after our shift in the salt mines. It was right after they'd squashed the rebellion, and they were hanging some of the upstarts in the square. REVOLUTIONARIES, YOU MEAN! THE VERY SOUL OF THE PROLE-TARIAT, CRYING OUT FOR JUSTICE!"

Sloot bristled. Though the Philosophers' Rebellion was barely a footnote in history, the state-issued textbooks left no doubt that it was the worst sort of heresy against the Domnitor, long may he reign.

"We stopped to watch," Myrtle continued. "Entertainment was hard to come by in the orphanage, and the headmistress had a severe allergy to exercise. She needed to catch her breath.

"I was looking right into the eyes of this skinny, bespectacled man with enormous sideburns when the guillotine came down on him. One moment, he was yelling at the top of his lungs about who owned farm implements or something—THE OWNERSHIP OF THE MEANS OF PRO-DUCTION BY THE PROLETARIAT!—right, that; and then I could still hear him over the cheering of the crowd, even though his head was off. MORE LIKE JEERING OF THE CROWD. TELL HIM HOW THEY RUSHED THE STAGE IN PROTEST! Sorry, I don't remember that. Anyway, Arthur has been with me ever since."

"Funny," said Sloot. "Of all the executions I've seen in my day, you're the first person I've met to have been possessed as a result."

"NOT SURPRISING. MOST PEOPLE AREN'T WELL-VERSED IN PLUCKY THE DITHERING'S LAWS REGARDING THE DUAL STATES OF CONSCIOUSNESS."

"You sound like you're from Stagralla."

"I might be, I don't remember anything from before the orphanage."

"I'm sorry, I meant Arthur."

"I'M ORIGINALLY— Now don't you start!" Jumping to her feet, Myrtle set her finger about the business of a very severe waggle. "I'm not Arthur, so don't talk to my face as though I were!"

"Oh, I'm terribly sorry," said Sloot. "I don't have a lot of practice with people afflicted with philosophy."

"It's just—" Myrtle shook her fists in frustration, then exhaled sharply. "I didn't ask for this, you know?"

"I know," said Sloot, who was glad to hear that she didn't willingly truck with former heretics. "I won't do it again, I promise."

"WHAT ABOUT ME? NO ONE CAN SPEAK TO ME DIRECTLY JUST BECAUSE I DON'T HAVE A BODY OF MY OWN? Yes, that's exactly what that means! You should count yourself lucky that I don't spend my time figuring out how to exorcise you! OH, THAT'S NICE."

"It must have been strange," Sloot remarked, "growing up possessed."

"It was a lot of work," said Myrtle. "Arthur helped me convince the courts to emancipate me from the orphanage because of inheriting destiny, or something like that—THE STRICTURES ON DESTINY INHERENT IN STATE-IMPOSED WELFARE!—Right, that. He was good at that bit, but then I didn't have a place to live or anyone feeding me. He was less helpful with that."

"Not a lot of opportunities for young urchins outside the state welfare system, I imagine."

"You imagine correctly. We did all right busking for arguments at the University of Salzstadt. Not many people expected to lose to a little girl. AHEM. Well, they didn't know I was possessed, did they? If they'd known they were losing to the undead, we might have had different problems!"

Myrtle went on to describe, with frequent interruptions from Arthur, how she brought herself up on the streets of Salzstadt with no formal education. Philosophers are notoriously lazy, so it was entirely up to her to find something to use as a table and put food on it. Arthur argued in his defense that he didn't need to eat, being dead and all, so that was Myrtle's business anyway.

"At least I learned to read from him."

"He taught you how to read?"

"Oh no," said Myrtle. "He just insisted that I stare at the pages of books so that *he* could read. But I can sort of hear his thoughts, so I started recognizing the letters over time, and I picked it up."

"That's clever," said Sloot. "The benefits of a university education without having to matriculate."

"I don't know anyone who would resort to *that* just to go to university. 'MATRICULATE' MEANS 'TO GO TO UNIVERSITY.' Oh." Myrtle blushed. "So I hear you're going to Nordheim?"

## ❧A FINE WELCOME HOME❧

Nordheim was unique in that the gods of the Vikings lived there among them, as opposed to everyone else's gods who respected the way things were supposed to be done. Other gods had the decency to show themselves infrequently (if at all), speak to their constituencies through a select group of devotees (thus adding jobs to the economy), and let their followers work things out for themselves based on signs and innuendos.

The Vikings were not so fortunate. They saw their gods every day, hurling thunderbolts on a whim and riding golden chariots across the sky. The Vikings never get to tell tales of the might of their gods, because they're always showing off.

"Settle down, children, and I'll tell you about the time that Heimdall ripped a tree out of the ground, roots and all!"

"No thanks, Granddad, we were there. It was yesterday."

They were no help at all with calming unruly children, the gods of the Vikings. It was no wonder they had so many berserkers in Nordheim.

If you've seen one deity drink up the sea or pulverize a mountain with a single hammer blow, repeat performances are less impressive and more worrisome—especially if you happen to be a fisherman or a miner.

Perhaps the most challenging part of negotiating with Vikings is the fact that they trust nothing and no one. They have one god in particular who's known for being a trickster, but in truth, they're all at least mildly mischievous from time to time. Walking with one's gods means one is always surrounded by a fog of myth and reality intertwined. Discerning truth from some trick of a bored god trying to spice up eternity can be problematic at best.

"Still," said Willie, "they sold it to me, didn't they? They didn't want to, but I'm a shrewd negotiator."

The journey to Nordheim had only taken a couple of weeks. Thanks to Roman's familiarity with the mountain passes between the Old Country and Carpathia, they'd managed to skirt the border with no trouble at all.

"They were all too happy to sell it," said Sloot, "once they'd decided that we weren't part of an elaborate prank from their gods."

"But there was that part, wasn't there?" Willie said a swear word with an impish grin. Sloot heard a *pop* a few feet away, and then the sound of a goblin cackling and rustling around in the brush.

"We're back in the Old Country," Roman told him.

"That's enough, Willie." Nan had insisted on going along with them and complained the entire way. "You'll make a habit of swearing, and the house will fill up with goblins!"

"I suppose you're right," said Willie. "I'm a famous explorer now, better tune up my dignity a bit."

"Famous explorer," mumbled Roman, just loud enough for Sloot to hear. "More like a rube who can follow someone who can follow a map. What's he going to do with that thing, anyway?"

The journey home had taken more than a month thanks to Willie's prize, which the horses had to pull the entire way. It was an enormous wooly mammoth, or had been at one time. More accurately, it was a dead and taxidermied mammoth, poised on a plinth in the *rampant* position, with its two front hooves raised into the air as if having its portrait painted mid-battle. There were wheels on the plinth, which must have been designed to spend great deals of time stuck in ruts of their own construction, because they did just that. The fact that they'd gotten the thing within sight of Salzstadt at all was impressive on its own.

"Dunno," said Sloot, whose stomach had been tied in knots since the moment they'd left Salzstadt in the first place. "The better question is how we're going to get the thing into the city. Better still, how are *we* going to get into the city? We never got permits!"

"Same way we got out," said Roman. "Winking Bob."

In the official record—from which all history books in the Old Country are written—there is no such thing as a black market in Salzstadt. The overwhelming majority of history books are purchased by academics, the second poorest profession including panhandlers, who come in twelfth; therefore, a bit of extra fiscal engineering is needed to make them affordable. To that end, most history books in Salzstadt have "fallen off of wagons" and are purchased on the black market.

The title of Poorest Profession in the Old Country is held by the lawyers. They're not actually poor, of course, but they make sure that they appear that way on paper. The title comes with some hefty tax breaks.

Many salts make an honest living in the sales trade, not a one of whom was Winking Bob. When Sloot had failed to secure permits for their excursion in a timely fashion, Roman had promised to handle it.

Despite Sloot's largely unblemished record of staunch patriotism and devotion to the Domnitor, long may he reign, he'd heard of Winking Bob before. It was a name whispered in pubs, a phantom capable of delivering anything for a price.

Before this excursion, no temptation could have lured him away from the straight-and-narrow; except for his having joined up with Carpathian Intelligence, which was probably a lot worse than buying foreign sausages and whiskey without a tax stamp. Sloot sighed. He was already a heretic and a traitor, what would some illicit dealings with his fellow criminals add to his sentence if he were caught?

It was supposed to be springtime, but tell that to the snow drifts piled up on the sides of the road. Sloot would have loved to have made it closer to the city before nightfall, but they couldn't bring Willie's prize within sight of the gates before the sun went down.

"Soon enough," said Roman. He swept the snow from a spot on a stone wall, sat, and busied himself with packing tobacco into his pipe. Nan had lit a small fire to heat up Willie's dinner.

"Should we be doing that?" asked Sloot.

"Doing what?"

"Lighting fires, smoking pipes! Won't it give away our position or something?"

"I could light a dozen pipes and draw less attention than a thirty-foot mammoth."

"Fair point."

Roman looked to make sure that they were out of earshot of Willie, who was singly focused on proving to Nan that he was perfectly capable of cutting up his own meat. It was evident that he was not.

"Your mum really never told you anything about the spy business?"

Sloot sighed. "No. I never knew anything about it until I'd been conscripted."

"Job well done," said Roman with a grin.

"What do you mean?"

"Well you're our secret weapon, aren't you? Sladia raised you knowing nothing of your true heritage so that you'd blend in. Look at you! There's as much salt in you as anyone in the city. It's the perfect cover!"

"It's not a cover," said Sloot, "I'm a real salt, through and through! A loyal subject of the Domnitor, long may he reign!"

"No need to lay it on that thick, it's only us here."

"I'm not— Oh, forget it."

They sat there in silence for a while, which is one of the worst things that a person in the midst of an existential crisis can do. A good brain, a loyal one, knows to keep itself distracted; otherwise, it starts to think, and thinking inevitably results in ideas.

Most ideas end up as recipes for soups that don't work out. Some ideas turn out well, and we get useful things like agriculture, or the metric system, or recipes for soup that *do* work out. The rest fester and turn into terrible things that people go to war over, like greed, wrath, or the metric system.

"Wait," said Sloot, "what did you mean, 'our secret weapon'?"

Roman coughed on his pipe, sending a tiny cloud of smoke slinking uncomfortably away as his enormous eyes focused on something in the distance.

"Well, er … what?"

"That's what you said. Mum kept me in the dark about my Carpathian heritage, and I'm your secret weapon."

"I'm sure I didn't say that," said Roman.

"What are you two talking about back here?" Willie had wandered into their midst, still wearing his bib.

"Nothing," Sloot replied. Roman gave an exasperated sigh.

"Oh, go on," said Willie. He took a seat beside Roman on the stone wall and leaned in so that he could whisper. "I'm just one of the lads out here in the wild. No time for lords and servants with danger around every corner, right? Come on, you have to tell me! I am your *lord*, you know."

Sloot and Roman glanced at each other.

"Actually," said Roman, "we were just discussing your birthday."

"My birthday! I love my birthday. There will be cake, I imagine."

Roman nodded. "Probably."

"What do you mean, 'probably'? There has to be cake, or it's not a birthday! I think there's a law. If not, there should be. I'll talk to my father, he'll—"

"That is to say," Roman began, "that while there will *almost certainly* be a cake, there are certain rules about keeping secrets."

"I know that," said Willie. "I'm very good at keeping secrets."

"But not from yourself … and it's *your* birthday we're discussing, after all."

Willie's face wore an expression that insinuated offense, then faded to perplexity, and finally to realization.

"You're planning me a surprise birthday party!"

"That's a possibility," said Roman. "And assuming that were true, we couldn't give you any of the details, could we?"

Willie's expression returned to perplexity.

"Because then it wouldn't be a surprise," said Sloot.

"Obviously," said Willie. "That was a test. Well done, the pair of you. Just one thing, though."

"Yes?"

Willie hesitated. "Well. I've made my feelings about cake very clear, haven't I?"

"Perfectly clear," answered Roman with a wink.

"All right." Willie gave a satisfied nod. "I'll leave you to it, then." He stood, smiled, turned, and wandered back in Nan's direction.

"*Nothing!*" Roman hissed at Sloot. "Really? Have you learned nothing at all about being a spy?"

"No," said Sloot, "I haven't! What do you mean, 'nothing'?"

"That's what you said when Willie asked what we were talking about! Everyone knows that when someone asks 'what were you talking about,' saying 'nothing' can only mean 'definitely something, but we don't like you enough to include you in it'!"

"Fine, what should I have said?"

"Just get him talking about something he likes. Works on just about anybody."

"Clever," said Sloot. "But don't think I've forgotten about that whole 'secret weapon' business. You owe me an explanation."

"And you shall have one. But first, tell me about Myrtle! How are things going between the two of you?"

The cloudy grey afternoon wore into a darker grey evening, then ended up greying itself so thoroughly as to end up inky black. Roman passed the time by giving Sloot a master class in evading difficult questions, whether he realized it or not. Then, under cover of night, the four horses, their riders, and one enormous taxidermied mammoth made their way through one of the bigger supply gates in the wall surrounding Salzstadt.

Bribery made Sloot uncomfortable. Neatly kept books meant that not a penny went unaccounted, squarely notated in perpetuity. Sure, he could quite easily pad another line item or make up some clever code. He could file it under "poultry research." But what happens when an auditor's brother is a chicken farmer, and she wants to wax philosophical about feather fungus?

The bright side was that Sloot had these thoughts to keep him occupied on the way through the wall, down the streets, and into Whitewood. He'd just let Roman do all of the talking.

It worked! Merely being an accessory to Felonious Excursions and Importation of Questionable Art had been far simpler than carrying them out himself. Sloot had made it past panic and was well on his way back down to his base level of worry when he did his nerves the disservice of walking inside the house.

"Oh, Mister Peril! It was simply awful!"

Sloot struggled to remain conscious in the face of so many conflicting demands on his composure. In addition to the panic he was already nursing, he was startled by Myrtle's sudden rush toward him, concerned for her trembling as she threw her arms around him, pleasantly wobbly in the knees for the same, and utterly perplexed to see not a stick of furniture in the living room.

"His Lordship's been burgled!" exclaimed Roman.

"Burgled?" asked Willie, with his usual degree of latent bewilderment. "Doesn't that mean I've won an award?"

"Oh, my sweet Willikins! Don't look!" Nan pressed Willie's head ferociously against her bosom. "It's going to be all right! Mister Roman, go and wake up all of the shopkeepers! Willie's going to need new things until we can hunt down the culprit!"

"New things?" Willie's voice was muffled. He struggled to extract himself from Nan's comforting embrace. "That sounds like fun! The stuff I had was weeks old. What colors go with my trophy? It is a trophy, isn't it? Redecorating for a plaque seems ... I dunno, excessive."

Sloot reluctantly pulled away from Myrtle so that he could meet her gaze.

"What happened?" he asked.

"It was this morning," said Myrtle. "I awoke to the sound of Mister Dirtsmith shouting in the garden."

"He does that a lot," remarked Sloot.

"Yes, but this was beyond his usual threats to the weeds. His flowers had been trodden upon, and he was furious! When I left my room to calm him down, that's when I saw. They'd taken *everything*!"

"Good thing," said Willie. "Though I'm surprised that *none* of it matched the trophy."

"None of the servants' quarters were burgled," said Myrtle. "Probably the Burglars' Union. It's in their rules, servants are out of bounds."

"Willie gets cranky when he's tired," said Nan. "I'll just go put him down in your bed, Mister Peril. You'll not be needing it, as I'm sure you'll not rest until this injustice has been settled?"

"Of course," said Sloot, who hadn't had a decent night's sleep since inheriting his mother's spying duties. He and Roman walked through the house with Myrtle and confirmed that whoever had done this had been incredibly thorough.

They'd taken the curtains. They'd taken the rods upon which the curtains had hung. They'd taken the little sashes that the maids used to tie back the curtains in the morning to let the light in.

"That's not the most disturbing part," said Roman. He and Sloot had found the bottom of Roman's flask, and took no time in deliberating whether they should relocate their commiseration to the pub.

"I know," said Sloot, placing one of his two beers under his chair. "They absolutely cleaned out the vault. Every copper. Gone."

"Well of course they did," Roman replied with an agitated wave. "They're burglars, aren't they? The money's always the first thing to go."

"At least it will be easy to fit into the ledger. A single line: *burgled.*"

"They took the garbage," said Roman.

"The what?"

"The garbage," Roman repeated, "the rubbish from the bins in the kitchens. They took it. The bins, too."

"Why would they do that?"

"It's a message," said Roman. "Smash-and-grabs don't go in for curtains, no matter how nice they are, and they certainly don't see a bin full of table scraps and go for it. No, someone wanted to send Willie a message."

"Why? What was the message?"

Roman said a phrase involving a swear word that implied that Willie, being the target, was the sort of pig who ate his acorns twice. It was a swear word so vile that three goblins popped in under the table, cackling like mad.

"Careful," exclaimed Sloot, "goblins!"

"It's only the Old Country," said Roman with a shrug. "Horrible place is full of them anyway."

Sloot restrained the impulse to call for the guards like one is supposed to do at the first sign of heresy. He wondered if he'd been a heretic long enough for the interrogators to be able to tell just by looking at him.

"Well, what do we do now?" Sloot was wringing his hands with a precision that would distract other worriers. This was why he was no longer welcome at their regular meetings.

"I'll ask around," said Roman. "Whitewood getting cleaned out while we were away, while the servants slept, and even the trash being taken? Too many coincidences. I don't like it."

"But who would want to send Willie a message? And who would benefit from that message being 'I have all of your things'?"

"Exactly," said Roman. "If that were the message, it would be a regular burglary, and they'd have left the garbage."

"And the curtains."

Roman said another swear word. *Pop, cackle.* "Forget about the curtains, will you? This is serious!"

"I know it's serious!" Sloot had half a mind to say a swear word, too; perhaps the culinary one whose noun and verb forms contradict each other. "Were you not listening when I said that the vault is completely empty?"

"Why should that matter? The insanely wealthy don't keep all of their money in their vault, Sloot."

"They don't?"

"Of course not! It's a sizeable chunk, sure, but they spread it around just in case— Wait, what do you mean, 'they don't'?"

"It's a common phrase," said Sloot.

"I know what it means! Are you trying to tell me that *all* of Willie's money was in the vault?"

"Well, I hadn't had a chance to spread it around yet! We'd only just moved into Whitewood before the trip to Nordheim, and—"

Roman exploded into a string of profanity that got the two of them expelled from the pub. They wandered the streets aimlessly for a while, neither of them speaking.

"Willie gets an allowance," said Sloot after a while, when they paused atop a footbridge over the river that ran through the city. "It's not enough to do much more than pay the servants, but at least there's that."

"That's good," Roman grumbled. "We've got to fix this. If Willie's poor, then the whole plan just sort of turns to—" He looked over his shoulder and, seeing no one, swore another phrase aloud that applied literally to what people do in canoes during rainstorms, but was figuratively taken to mean that everything was doomed to fail.

*Pop, splash! Pop, splash!* There was a coalition in the city who opposed goblin cruelty, and they'd have had a lot to say if they'd known that Roman was conjuring them over the river bridge. Said people also had rough words for bathing, which they seemed to take as an affront to artistic license. Fortunately, they were too poor to afford a commune in this part of the city.

"So the secret plan hinges on Willie's money?"

"Probably," said Roman. "I haven't figured out that much yet, but why else would he be important?"

"No idea."

Roman shrugged. "Me either. That's why we've got to fix it."

"You're asking me to take a lot on faith, you know."

"That's the spy business. We don't often have much more to go on than that. It's hunches and gut feelings most of the time."

"But there's got to be something! I've spent my whole life dealing with facts. The only thing worse than committing heresy by simply continuing to breathe is having nothing to confess at my eventual torturing!"

"Plausible deniability." Roman pressed one finger on the side of his nose. "It's part of what makes you the perfect spy, Peril! Don't you see?

Even under pain of death, you'll give 'em nothing! Blood and honor! That's sticking it to 'em."

"No it isn't," groaned Sloot. It didn't matter, he was tired of arguing. Moreover, he was simply tired. "Forget it, let's go sleep it off at my place."

"I've a better idea," said Roman. "Let's start your spy training."

"Really? Now?" Sloot was still terribly worried over the whole heresy thing, but he was just curious enough to want to know what spy training entailed.

"Now. A spy must be ready to spring into action at a moment's notice! He doesn't always have the luxury of a good night's sleep and the chance to digest his breakfast before intrigue throws herself at him, like the tramp she is."

"All right," said Sloot. "I'm already exhausted and still a bit drunk. Where do we start?"

"Another pub," said Roman. "Follow me."

❧⚗❧⚗❧⚗❧⚗

Sloot decided almost immediately that "fog" would be the wrong word to use to describe the events of the night before. War often borrows the word from meteorology to convey the dearth of information available in the thick of it. Soldiers don't really know if their side is winning or losing. It's all bloody gurgling from that fellow who's just been stabbed through the chest, an arm flying across one's field of vision, the disappointing realization that it was one's own arm, etc.

Sloot's night of spy training had differed from fog in that he remembered every detail, it just lacked the passage of time. It was as if someone had filmed it, cut each frame out, and stacked them all on top of each other.

"I knew I could expect great things from you," said Roman. He was holding his head in his hands, sitting against a wall in the dirtiest alley that Sloot had seen in his life, and trying to make both of his enormous eyes focus on any single thing.

"My ability to get blackout drunk counts as greatness in Carpathia? My teachers were right, you're all barbarians."

"Easy," warned Roman. "I didn't expect you to manage it on your first try, but you've surprised me."

Sloot desperately wanted to stand up and get out of the stinking muck where he'd awoken, but was hesitant with regard to his legs' ability to support him.

"I just don't know if I can separate all of the bits," said Sloot. He decided it was better to concentrate on standing before thinking in any depth. Managing both at once was unfathomable in his state.

"You can do it. It's the spy training. In order to be perfectly aware of our surroundings, we learn how to ingurgitate. You let everything flood into your mind, and you cram it into a single flash of memory. You remember the color of the door from the third pub we went to last night, for instance."

"It was red, but that—"

"And the name of the barmaid who brought you your eighth pint?"

"Griselda," answered Sloot, with a bewildered lilt.

"And how many people in the fourth pub were taking odds against that fellow stabbing the table between his fingers?"

"Fourteen."

"And how much money you won?"

"Eight silver."

"And how much we spent on booze?"

"Seven silver between six pubs. Six?"

"Yep. The proof is in your vest pocket."

Sloot used one hand to guide the other to his pocket. There was a single silver coin tucked inside it.

"Ingurgitating," said Roman with a wink. "I imagine your years in the counting house were a great help with the mathematical bits. Oh, and when they try to get you to talk, just do what you know. Got it?"

"Got it. Wait, what?"

It dawned on Sloot a bit late that Roman was looking over his shoulder with a measure of apprehension. As the bag slipped over his head and everything went black, he couldn't help wondering if there were a point in the spy training when one learned to detect people sneaking up behind you. He considered how nice it would have been to have learned that first.

## UPPANCE COMETH

Having a bag thrown over one's head does not, in the overwhelming majority of cases, end well. For that matter, nothing that happens during the beginning or middle of the experience tends to go very well either.

After the sheer panic surrounding the business of "expletive redacted, impending doom is upon me!" has settled in, the next sensation that many people experience is nausea. The inability to focus while bouncing along on the shoulder of some brute has parted many a lunch from its respective stomach.

Sloot had managed not being sick in his head bag, and he deserved a measure of credit for that. He was naturally susceptible to motion sickness, and the rough ride was an unfortunate pairing for his hangover. Had he been given the chance to coordinate his own abduction, he'd have done it quite differently indeed.

He also could have done without the unceremonious drop from atop his brute onto a cold and wet stone floor, to say nothing of the hour or so he then waited in silence, hands and feet tightly bound, before he heard footsteps coming toward him.

The footsteps sounded ominous, not that that was unusual. Under the circumstances, just about anything would. The bag was pulled roughly from his head, the stinking burlap chafing his ear on the way past. His eyes adjusted to the dim torchlight of what was evidently some sort of dungeon.

"We meet again, Mister Peril." Amusement and malice conspired a leering grin across Mrs. Knife's face.

"Mrs. Knife," said Sloot. "I don't—"

Mrs. Knife interrupted Sloot with a slap across the face that had no doubt taken lessons in both speed and power, and graduated at the top of its class.

"Ow." Sloot tasted blood.

"You should thank me for doing you a favor," said Mrs. Knife.

"Thank you?"

"You're welcome. You seemed dangerously close to pretending at innocence, and I'd have had to punish that by simply slitting your throat and finding a new financier for Willie."

The threat was more than simple intimidation. Sloot didn't need any advanced spy training to know that she was serious. She'd said it as leisurely as she might have asked a stranger if he had the time, but with the subtext of murdering everyone said stranger loved.

Sloot said nothing. It was a survival tactic he'd picked up for dealing with bullies on the schoolyard, and he'd gotten quite good at it.

Mrs. Knife smirked. "I'll get right to the point. Willie's valet has already told me everything. I just need to hear it from you before I decide the severity of your punishments."

*Do what you know,* Roman had said. Sloot had the distinct impression that there was no time to think, so he relied on his memories of old Mrs. Milchabschreckung, his kindergarten teacher, who'd been given the job due to her tireless suspicion of young people. Sloot had been too great a worrier to risk breaking any rules, but she relentlessly tried to catch him in the act anyway; in fact, Sloot often wondered if he never broke the rules *because* Mrs. Milchabschreckung was always there. Always watching.

"I already know everything," she'd say. "It'll be easier for you if you come clean now."

"I haven't done anything, Mrs. Milchabschreckung," he'd always reply, and his face would wear an urgent veneer of terror-stricken sincerity that would occasionally convince her to direct her inquisition elsewhere. For now.

But that wouldn't do for Mrs. Knife. He'd have to give her something. In the midst of all the heresy that had ensnared him of late, there was only one actual crime that he'd committed, and he was reasonably sure the punishment would be less than death. Besides, there was little in the house at the moment aside from Willie's mammoth, and Mrs. Knife was bound to hear about that eventually.

"I'm sorry," said Sloot, mustering up every ounce of simpering dread he could, which was quite a lot, and really no trouble. "I didn't get the permits to leave the city, but we went anyway! It was all my idea, Willie didn't know!"

"What else?"

What else? Sloot thought a swear word. He didn't have any other crimes to confess, but Mrs. Knife was plainly far from appeased.

"The mammoth," he said. "We bought a mammoth from Nordheim, a stuffed one!"

"What else?"

"I don't have a tax stamp for it!"

"What else?"

"I may have used an outdated currency exchange rate for the transaction!"

"What else?"

"I wasn't sure how long I'd been sitting here with the bag on my head, so I recited the Loyalist Oath a hundred times just to be on the safe side, but I'm afraid it wasn't enough, and I'm terrified of you, and I want to go home, and I don't have anything else to confess, oh please don't slit my throat!"

His voice had steadily climbed to a shrill soprano by the end, and then he caught his first lucky break. He'd felt the call of nature, and answered it with gusto. They'd been his favorite trousers, and now they'd never be the same.

Mrs. Knife wrinkled her nose and took a step back. Her gaze shot daggers at Sloot, which further improved his situation by compelling him into a fit of wheezing sobs.

Mrs. Knife grinned with delight.

"I'll refrain from killing you for now, Mister Peril. Just remember that while Willie may be your employer, you will always answer to me."

"Yes, Mrs. Knife."

"Willie doesn't leave the city again. He'll become an explorer over your dead body. Do I make myself clear?"

"Yes, Mrs. Knife."

"Good. Just a standard beating, boys."

The laws that determine the fundamental truths of the universe are hardly laws at all, but rather loose-knit tribes of guidelines, which are roughly as decisive as married couples stuck in a loop of "I don't know, what do *you* want for dinner?"

That conversation, if not resolved in a reasonable amount of time, tends to resolve in nature's solution for cleaning out pantries: stew.

There is no recipe for stew. Any cookbook claiming such is describing something else entirely. It nearly always means "soup," or possibly "casserole." But then there's the very rare case of horrifying lunatics plumbing the depths of madness, and actually trying to codify stew. Said lunatics usually end their days strapped to gurneys, or working in municipal governments.

A proper stew is the amalgamation of small amounts of food that haven't quite gone bad yet, known to every gran in the world as "perfectly good food." It is an interesting characteristic of food in general, that it is only ever referred to as "perfectly good" when put to the question of whether it is "still good" or not. It is generally agreed among culinary scholars that stew was invented by spectacularly tightfisted people as a means of pinching pennies, mostly because none of said scholars care enough to seek out evidence to the contrary.

Culinary scholars have no love for stew.

Sloot was no culinary scholar, and on most days would give his opinion of stew as "firmly indifferent." Thriftiness was a virtue according to the Domnitor, long may he reign. After all, there was a cold war on, so a loyal subject should smile on any attempt to save a penny for the war effort.

The bowl of stew in front of Sloot had a history. It had quite a bit of chowder in it as well, an observation which could be made of most of the people who frequented the docks. It would never have been his first choice for a meal, but given that he had no money in his pockets and felt as though he hadn't eaten in days, he counted himself lucky for it.

"That's when I seen 'im," said the gnarled old sailor in the raincoat. He held his arms out to his sides. "Massive 'e was! Nearly six feet long, if I've a hair on my chin."

"Looks about five-and-a-half feet from here," said another sailor, who had enormous mutton chop sideburns connected via moustache. He squinted at Sloot. "Maybe five seven."

"Like I said, nearly six feet! I'd watch that tongue if I were ye." The first sailor's fists went to his hips.

"I ain't afeared of a kick from your peg leg," said mutton chops with a laugh.

"Ah, the leg that I lost to the Kraken, now there was a leg! Thick as a whiskey barrel, would've kicked that bleedin' Kraken to death! Only he was a sneaky bugger."

"Don't get him started about his leg," said the barkeep. He'd extended a free bowl of stew to Sloot on hearing that he worked for Lord Hapsgalt. Sloot was relieved not to have been asked which one.

"But I'm an old salt o' the sea, me! I'd no need o' that leg to bring in this one here. Half dead he was, lyin' on the dock."

"Which dock?" asked a man sitting on a stool, who was fingering an old concertina but not actually playing it.

The old sailor leaned in close to his tiny circle of hangers-on. His eyes went wide and his hands went up in front of him, heralding the *coup de grace*.

"Dock three west!" he gasped and recoiled, but thunder failed to punctuate the gesture. The weather in the Old Country was not renowned for its participation in the telling of a good fish story.

"How did I get there?" Sloot wondered aloud.

"Beats me," said the sailor. "A good tale don't go all the way back to the beginning, lad. It starts at the good part, when the handsome hero saves the day."

Sloot choked down the rest of his stew, which tasted less like the sum of its parts and more like a warning to anyone zany enough to ask what those parts might have been. He just hoped it stayed down. He offered his thanks to the sailor and the barkeep and slumped toward the door.

As he limped the long road toward his apartment, his worry gnawed on something that Mrs. Knife had said. "Willie's valet has already told me everything." He doubted Roman had spilled his guts about the permits and ruined his trousers, which meant that she'd lied just to get him to talk. Nothing surprising there, she was a sinister figure after all; but what *had* happened to Roman? Mrs. Knife's thugs *had* taken the both of them, hadn't they? What would it mean if they hadn't? If Roman didn't have any bruises when next they met, Sloot would seriously have to consider how best to phrase a request for answers without being too brusque about it.

"Blood and honor, there he is!" Roman was sitting on one of the chairs at the little table in Sloot's apartment, not a scratch on him. "You look awful, my boy. Your first interrogation, yeah?"

"I don't want to talk about it," said Sloot. He winced as he started slowly pulling off the torn remnants of his clothing.

"Sorry, Sloot, I need to know what you told them. Who was it that got you?"

"Mrs. Knife," said Sloot. "They left you alone, I see."

"Left me alone!" Roman's eyes went wider than usual, and he clutched his heart with both hands. "If only that were true! They stuck a knife in my face, said I'd keep quiet if I knew what was good for me!"

There it was. Sloot had always suspected that there was a darkness lurking within him somewhere, and it was starting to rear its ugly head. Never in his life had he been so tempted to resort to sarcasm, nor could he recall ever having been given a more fitting occasion.

Oh, the barbs he could have quipped! But he didn't. He took a deep breath, thought of the Domnitor, long may he reign, and made a mental note to tell Roman one day how close he'd come to getting a real earful just then.

"What'd you tell her?"

Sloot sighed. "The permits. I told her we'd left the city without them."

"What else?"

"The mammoth."

"No great harm there," said Roman. "I imagine I'd have given up a few things if they'd roughed me up half as bad as you."

"That was before," said Sloot.

"Before?"

"Before the roughing up. They didn't lay a hand on me until after I'd spilled my guts."

"Oh." Roman made his card-playing face. It might have passed for stony and unreadable if he'd been alone in a dark room; but even if Sloot had never seen Roman try to bluff before, he'd know the "oh" of disappointment anywhere. He'd heard it often enough—many times, in fact, since the one and only time his mother had asked him to move her armoire.

"Well that's all right," said Roman. "Was there anything else?"

"No." Sloot washed his face gingerly in the basin on the dresser. "I just started crying about how afraid I was. Some spy I am."

"Oh, now don't talk like that. You didn't say anything about our operation, did you?"

"Of course not," said Sloot. "You think I want to hang for treason?"

"Well, there you go! Not exactly courage, but you kept it together when it counted! That's a start. I told you, I'm an excellent judge of character. We'll make a proper spy of you yet."

Sloot sighed. It wasn't exactly the encouragement that he wanted to hear, but it was something.

"Well that's a shame," said Roman.

"What?" Sloot followed Roman's gaze to the floor beside his foot, and there was his mother's watch. It hadn't been in peak condition for many years, but it certainly didn't look this bad before the beating. The plate that covers the face was only just hanging on by the mangled hinge. The glass was shattered, and the *clank, clank* was more labored than ever. It seemed ready to give out altogether at any moment.

"No, no, no, no, no, no, no, no, no," cried Sloot. He snatched it up and wound it with whatever passed for athleticism in that regard.

"Take a deep breath," said Roman. "I know just the thing for it."

## ⊱⊰ THE GIFT OF CLARITY ⊱⊰

The front of the clockmaker's shop looked very much like all of the other street-level storefronts in the city, which was as it should be. Despite his involvement in enemy intelligence, Sloot had a healthy appreciation for things that resisted the dissident urge to stand out. Individuality is a statement, a worrisome one that says "being *one of us* isn't good enough for me. For now, having this enormous feather in my cap might be good enough, but at some point, I might feel the need to be one of *them.*"

So it was that Sloot felt very much at peace as he walked into the shop, secure in the knowledge that, unlike Roman and himself, nothing about the place was embroiled in intrigue or divergence.

"You're an over-winder," said the woman sitting behind the counter. She didn't look up from what appeared to be a surgical procedure on a well-illuminated pocket watch in an advanced state of disassembly. She was surrounded by lenses, some large ones on stands, a few strapped to her head by a brown leather band, and several lined up in front of her eyes.

"I assure you I'm not," said Sloot. He gave it an extra twist for good measure here and there, but anything in excess ends in hedonism on a long enough scale. That includes brushing one's teeth, salting one's breakfast, and even winding one's watch.

"That's a Kovalcek Mark Eight ticking in your pocket," said the woman, "or at least trying to. Don't see many of them anymore. They used tin for the main spring in that model because it was the middle of the war, and the army needed the steel. Tin stretches like crazy if wound too tightly, and yours is probably twice as long now as it was when it was first made. I'm surprised it hasn't snapped already."

"How would you know all of that?"

"Because it's her job to know," said Roman. "She's the clockmaker, right? Either that, or she's doing a bang-up impression. Use your head, Peril."

"Wait," said the clockmaker, "did you say Peril?"

"That's right," said Sloot.

"Not *Sloot* Peril, is it?"

Had they met before? No, it couldn't be. Sloot took great pains to remember everyone he met because he disliked awkward moments. Especially the ones in which he couldn't decide whether he had a good reason for feeling awkward.

"Yes," Sloot eventually responded. "I'm sorry, I—"

"You're Wilhelm Hapsgalt's financier, aren't you?"

"I should think so." He hadn't been dismissed yet, but in light of everything that had happened of late, he was worried that it was only a matter of time.

"Lock the door, would you?" She got up from her work and started turning the lights off. Roman turned the lock on the door, and the two of them followed her into the back room of the shop. The walls were lined with clocks in various states of repair. There were tools and contraptions that held no meaning for anyone outside the field of clockmaking—or for Sloot, in any case—and shelves with stacks of springs, gears, and other little bits of machinery that he assumed were all a part of her trade.

There were also dozens of vases of flowers resting among the professional detritus. Sloot barely had a moment to wonder why they were there before she was standing uncomfortably close to him.

"I need you to tell me what he's said about me," she said.

"Who, Willie?"

"Wilhelm. Willie, yes. Whatever. I'm afraid I've done something to give him the wrong impression, and he won't leave me alone!"

"I'm very sorry," said Sloot, "but I can't seem to remember where we've met."

"We haven't," said the woman. "Or rather, we just have."

"You knew my name."

"Wilhelm ... *Willie* has mentioned it. One doesn't easily forget a name like 'Sloot Peril.' Sounds sort of Carpathian."

"It's not," said Sloot, who would love to have been named something less remarkable. Anonymity was big with worriers. "So I'm not supposed to know who you are?"

The woman seemed surprised. "He's in here so often that I assumed he would have mentioned me before."

"And you are?"

"Greta Urmacher," Roman interjected. "Her name's on the door, you know. Have you forgotten how to ingurgitate already?"

"Oh! You're the clockmaker's daughter."

Greta rolled her eyes. "I *was* the clockmaker's daughter, now I'm the clockmaker. My father is dead."

"I'm sorry," said Sloot.

"It was years ago," said Greta with a shrug. "If you want to be sorry for something, be sorry for assuming that the person sitting behind the desk—who was clearly repairing a watch—was someone other than the clockmaker! Honestly, who repairs clocks in your tiny village, the blacksmith?"

"I'm from Salzstadt."

"Then I repair the clocks where you're from!"

"I'm sorry," said Sloot. "This is the first time I've needed clock repair, I didn't know. It's only that I heard you mentioned as 'the clockmaker's daughter,' so I—"

"Never mind," interrupted Greta, squinting in frustration and waving her hands. "It's fine, it just happens a lot. Can't you get Willie to leave me alone?"

"You want your fiancé to leave you alone?" asked Roman.

"Fiancé! You must be joking, who said anything about the two of us being engaged?"

"Er, well, Lord Hapsgalt for one. For two, actually. Both of the Lords Hapsgalt. Willie and his father."

"This isn't happening." Greta buried her face in her hands and started pacing around the room. "I've had to rebuff suitors before, but this is getting out of hand!"

"So you're not engaged to Willie?" asked Sloot.

"Of course not! You've seen him, he's ridiculous!"

Sloot and Roman exchanged a look. She was right of course. If Sloot doubled his estimation of Willie's mental capacity, he'd still only be half as smart as his wardrobe.

"Look," said Roman, "Miss Urmacher, I'm not sure what's transpired between the two of you, but Willie seems certain that the two of you are headed toward marriage."

"I complimented his shoes." Greta slumped into a chair and sighed heavily.

"His shoes?"

"I'm afraid so."

"It's quite a leap from 'nice shoes' to 'until death do us part,' Miss Urmacher."

"I thought so, too," said Greta. "I'm glad to hear someone else say it as well. Unfortunately, Willie doesn't seem to recognize the distance between the two."

"I'm sure other people have complimented his shoes before." said Sloot. "He spends an awful lot of money on them, I've seen it in the ledgers. But I've not heard the subject of nuptials come up, except with you."

"I can't account for anyone else," said Greta. "I only know that I said exactly four words to him, and the flowers started turning up the very same day. 'I like your shoes,' I said. Then I kept walking."

"That can't be it," said Sloot. "You must have given him a wink or something, or said it in a sultry sort of way, perhaps?"

She was on her feet and pointing a threatening finger in his face with alarming speed. It was the warning finger, not the vulgar one that would have invited a goblin or two to join them.

"I know what I said," snapped Greta, "and I know how I said it! If you know anything at all about your *Willie*, you know that I don't have to be some sort of floozy for him to misunderstand a situation!"

"You're right," said Sloot. "I'm terribly sorry for implying, I only thought—"

"Thought what? That Willie was capable of thinking like a sensible person?"

"It sounds ridiculous when you say it."

"That's because Willie Hapsgalt is a ridiculous person!" Greta took a step away from Sloot and breathed slowly and deeply, calming herself down. "I'll repair your Kovalcek Mark Eight. I'll make it as good as new, no charge. But you've got to help me fix this!"

"I don't know what I could possibly do to—"

"You should give him a chance," Roman remarked, interrupting Sloot.

"What?" Greta shouted, her fists on her hips. Her voice was like a cat box: low, and full of gravel. Sloot took a step back.

"Hear me out," said Roman. "He presents himself as a dim-witted idiot, but there are … *things* at work here. Things I can't tell you about. It's a very complicated situation."

"Complicated situation? Your lord has convinced himself that he and I are engaged to be married. We are not engaged to be married. That is the very length and breadth of an entirely uncomplicated story, as far as I'm concerned!"

"Oh, but there's so much more to it than that! The entire predicament revolves around Willie's secret, doesn't it?" Roman nudged Sloot with an elbow.

"Of course," said Sloot, pretending he had the foggiest clue what was happening. "It would, wouldn't it?"

"Secret?" Greta's fists were still at her hips, meaning that she'd not yet been convinced that a good kicking wasn't in order. "What secret?"

"I can't say," said Roman. "Willie decides who to bring into his confidence and when to do it."

"I fear we've already said too much," said Sloot, trying to keep his stomach from spilling its contents. He tended to develop nausea during the act of deceit.

"This is ridiculous," said Greta. "There *is* no secret, is there? Your lord is simply a nitwit who's incapable of treating women like people, and you're a pair of toadies too afraid of his displeasure!"

"On the contrary," Sloot retorted, "I've delivered far worse news to far scarier people!"

"Name one," said Greta.

"Well, you, for example."

"You're more afraid of me than your lord?"

"At the moment, yes!"

"What he means to say," said Roman, "is that Lord Hapsgalt—Willie—is a very benevolent and decent fellow, who would never rebuke honesty. Not even if such were vexing."

"He's not benevolent, he's an idiot! I was the target of more effective wooings in kindergarten, by boys whose most inventive flirtations involved mud in my hair. At least they had the nerve to shout 'do you love me, yes or no?' Your lord just sends me things like this!"

Greta stormed off through the back door of the shop. Roman and Sloot glanced at each other, shrugged, and followed.

They ended up in a courtyard ringed by the backs of several neighboring buildings. It was nearly entirely occupied by a taxidermied mammoth rampant.

"It came with a note. The note said 'Hi,' and had badly drawn hearts all over it."

"So that's what he wanted it for," said Sloot.

"What? You knew about this?"

"Of course we did," said Roman. "Well, part of it, anyway. Lord Hapsgalt brought us with him on his expedition to Nordheim, where he negotiated most vigorously with the Vikings for it."

"He went all the way to Nordheim for a stuffed mammoth?"

"He went all the way to Nordheim for *you*," said Roman.

It almost worked. Greta's scowl disappeared for an instant as she looked up at the wooly monstrosity, then she shook her head. Her scowl resumed its position.

"That doesn't make anything better. I've told you, we've barely ever spoken! I complimented his shoes, and now he's invading my courtyard with the preserved remains of prehistoric monsters!"

"I know it seems that way," said Roman, "but Lord Hapsgalt is actually a very cunning fellow."

"That's right," said Sloot. "He has his secret to protect, and so he must give the impression that he's a complete imbecile."

"That doesn't make any sense!"

"It does," said Roman, "but only once you know his secret! I know it's a lot to ask, but if you'll only give Willie a chance, all will be revealed."

Greta looked down, her scowl taking on all the hallmarks of utter confusion. She turned to Sloot.

"Is this true?"

There was the nausea. Sloot knew that there was no secret, but he could see Roman giving him that wide-eyed 'just go along with it' look. Greta was a nice person who only wanted to be left alone. It seemed unnecessarily cruel to subject her to Willie's lunacy, but Sloot felt as though he had too many loyalties to take on another.

"Every word of it," Sloot answered, fighting to keep his bile down.

"Let's say I believe you," said Greta, her hands finally falling from her hips. "What happens now?"

"Come to Carpathia with us," said Roman.

"What?" exclaimed Greta and Sloot in unity.

Had Roman taken leave of his senses? What good were Carpathian Intelligence agents in Carpathia? Sloot's heart threatened to palpitate its last. It had one foot out the door already. There were plenty of other chests it could go live in, chests that would appreciate it!

"Don't worry," said Roman, "you'll be perfectly safe!"

"Are you mad?" asked Greta, her fists moving hips-wise again. "We can't go to Carpathia, it's full of cannibals!"

"That's mostly propaganda," said Roman. "Ours and theirs, actually. It's really quite nice, I've been there before."

"Has Lord Hapsgalt?"

"Not yet," Roman replied, "but he's got essential business there. The Hapsgalts are very involved in national security, you know. He's going on the Domnitor's orders, long may he reign!"

"The Domnitor?" Greta asked. Roman nodded. "Long may he reign. But why would he want me to go along with him?"

Sloot held up a timid hand. "I don't know that he—"

"He wouldn't tell me why," said Roman. "It pains him to be so secretive, and it's vexing at times, but I can tell you that His Lordship has never failed to reveal his purpose in the end, and every time it's made perfect sense! In the end."

"I don't know," she said.

"If it's any enticement," said Roman, "we'll be going up into the clock tower in Ulfhaven."

"Really?" Greta's suspicious brow-furrowing abandoned its post to make room for a look of curious wonder.

Roman nodded. "Really. One of the oldest and grandest clocks on the continent."

"I've heard stories," said Greta. "I just imagined that Carpathian savages would have set fire to it during one of their blood orgies or something."

"More propaganda," said Roman. "Here's the thing: that clock stopped working ages ago, and none of the clockmakers in Carpathia have been able to figure out why."

"Really?"

"It's an unusual clock, or so I'm told. Doesn't work like most clocks do. I can't tell you anything more about it, knowing nothing about clocks, like I ... don't. You'll have to see for yourself."

Greta looked up at the mammoth. Sloot envied what he saw in her: courage. He knew it when he saw it, but it was a slippery thing in his experience. Sure, he'd been all the way to Nordheim, survived severe beatings, had stood in the presence of Mrs. Knife, and was so deep undercover in service to the most reviled enemy of the Domnitor, long may he reign, that he barely knew who he was anymore. But courage never had anything to do with it. He'd always been driven by a medley of fear, loyalty and a sincere desire to avoid drawing attention to himself.

"When do we leave?"

❧⚜❧⚜❧⚜❧⚜

Sloot fired a multitude of questions on the way back to Whitewood, all of which Roman countered by walking very quickly.

"Not here!" was all he'd say. While Sloot understood the need for discretion, he had needs of his own. Needs that would be met by things like answers, assurances, and simple pleasures like never having to leave Salzstadt again, and certainly not for trips to Carpathia!

"You've got to learn to keep a cool head," said Roman when they were finally alone in the parlor. He thrust a tumbler of whiskey into Sloot's hand. "Drink that, it'll help."

"No, thank you!" said Sloot very firmly, his discomfort starting to boil over. He was very likely feeling something very close to anger just then. He'd always known the day would come, but nothing could have prepared him for it.

"What are you so afraid of? A Carpathian in Carpathia, what could be more natural than that?"

"Probably nothing," said Sloot, "but you seem to forget that I'm not a Carpathian!"

"It's in your blood. Your instincts will take over."

"I doubt my instincts to cower and run will be very helpful the first time a cannibal wearing the skin of his breakfast offers me a flagon of blood."

"Propaganda! They've got you all believing it, poor wretches."

"Sorry I'm late," said Myrtle. She closed the door behind her. Sloot sat up a bit straighter and wished he'd thought to bring a fistful of lilacs, or some chocolates or something. He remembered reading somewhere that pretty girls like those sorts of things and was curious to test the theory. "What's the topic of conversation?"

"Propaganda," said Roman. "Sloot's head is bloated with it."

"So was Myrtle's," said, well, *Myrtle,* "before I explained the subtle and insidious barrage of oppression that the ruling class constantly inflicts upon the unsophisticated proletariat."

"Come again?"

"And that's the sort of talk that got you beheaded, isn't it, Arthur?" said Myrtle. "Which only serves to prove my point! Knowledge is power, and those in power will do anything they can to silence the most educated citizens, should they dare to speak truth to their brethren! And sistren, of course."

"What's Arthur on about?" asked Sloot.

"Any chance he gets," Myrtle mumbled, casting her eyes to the ceiling with an apologetic sigh. "He seems to think that the Domnitor, long may he reign, is somehow mistreating his subjects."

"Long may he reign," echoed Sloot. "That's ridiculous! What would have given him that idea?"

"Philosophy," answered Myrtle with a shrug. No one needed to tell a salt that thinking too deeply inevitably turns up seditious thoughts. The Ministry of Propaganda had spent decades making sure they were all well aware.

"He's got a point," said Roman. "You'll see when we get to Carpathia."

"We're going to Carpathia?" asked Myrtle, her eyes going wide.

"He's only joking!" Sloot stared daggers at Roman and jerked his head tersely in Myrtle's direction. For a spymaster, he was being rather careless with sensitive information.

"It's all right," said Roman. "She knows."

"She knows?"

"Blood and honor," said Myrtle, her hand raising in a half-hearted salute.

"What? How did— Why did—"

"What can I say?" said Roman with a shrug. "I'm an excellent judge of character. She seemed like she'd be good for the cause."

"He doesn't seem happy about it," said Myrtle.

"No, he doesn't. What's the matter, Sloot?"

What was the matter? This from the man conducting the orchestra playing the fugue of his inevitable demise! It was bad enough that he and Sloot's mother had conspired to ruin him utterly, apparently since before his birth, but to drag the woman that he liked into it as well? Atrocity! Unthinkable atrocity! Sloot didn't know any swear words that could accurately describe the depths of his dismay with all of this, but if he did, he'd have half a mind to say them out loud.

He wouldn't, of course, but he'd think about it.

"It's nothing," Sloot replied, "just … why?"

"Why what?"

"You know, join up! It's treason!"

"You did it."

"That was different! I didn't have any choice."

"Of course you did," said Roman. "You could have refused to take your mother's post, but you didn't. You had a choice, and you made it!"

"You took over for your mother?" Myrtle looked genuinely surprised. "She was a spy?"

"My entire life, apparently. Not much of a choice there, she said it was the only way that she could retire. But what about you?"

"My reasons are my own," Myrtle replied. "Let's just leave it at that. I thought you'd be happy that we were in it together."

Sloot hadn't thought of it that way. To be fair, this was the first time that he'd been in the position of having to think of things in terms of how they fit with someone else. If she were ever convinced to return his affections, wouldn't he eventually have had to tell her that he was living a highly treasonous double life?

People in love tell each other things. He was sure he'd read that.

"It's not that," said Sloot, wondering what muscle one should flex to suppress blushing, "I just don't want to see you get hurt."

Myrtle also failed to suppress her blush reflex. She stared at the floor, grinning from ear to ear and fidgeting like mad.

"All right you two," said Roman, reminding them that he was still in the room before that fact became awkward. "We need to get down to business."

"Oh," said Myrtle, "you're not going to tell him about the other thing, are you?"

"What other thing?"

"Oh, that." Roman gave Myrtle a very pointed sidelong stare. "I don't think that's worth Mister Peril's attention at the moment."

"What's not worth my attention?"

"Nothing worth telling you about," said Roman.

"OH, DID YOU MEAN THE THING ABOUT THE BURGLARY?" Myrtle clamped her hands over her mouth and ran from the room.

"It's nothing," said Roman with a nervous chuckle. "You're management now, Sloot. Got to let your minions worry about some of these things for you!"

"Well, I suppose—"

"That's the spirit!" Roman clapped Sloot on the back, sending him into a coughing fit. "Now, you should head home and get a good night's sleep. We've got Willie's next expedition to prepare for tomorrow."

"Do you really think that taking Willie to Carpathia is a good idea?"

"Sloot, the plan is finally starting to take shape! I can see how more of the pieces fit together now. Once we've proven Willie's worth to old Constantin, everybody wins! Just trust me, this is all going to work out."

## ☙⟿THE PRICE OF PROFANITY☙⟿

Sloot was hoping to talk to Myrtle the following morning, but she was nowhere to be found.

"Well, I ain't seen her," said Nan. She was sitting at the little table in the kitchen, knitting a scarf. She did that a lot. Grans of the Old Country seemed certain that young people were in constant danger of freezing to death, and took up knitting so they could stare death in the face and say, "Not today. Not on my watch."

Sloot was concerned about what Myrtle, or more probably Arthur, had said the night before, just before she'd fled the room. Did one of them know something about the robbery?

"What's this room?" asked Willie, who must have wandered in by accident.

"It's the kitchen, Willikins. How on earth did you get in here?"

"I'm an explorer now, Nan, remember?"

"Of course you are, dear, you've been all the way to Nordheim!"

"Just keeping my skills sharp until the next expedition. When is Sloot coming back? He plans the expeditions, I think."

"He's just there," replied Nan, nodding in Sloot's direction without taking her eyes off her knitting. Willie regarded Sloot with suspicion, then with apparent remembrance.

"Sloot!" Willie exclaimed. "I'm glad you're here. What do you think of these boots?"

"Very nice, m'lord." Sloot silently congratulated himself on a lie well-told. It was a horrible pair of boots by any standard. If you were the sort of dandy who paraded around the city's fashionable haunts in high heels, you'd want to know why they were so brown and rugged-looking. If you were Sir Wallace Scoffington, you'd probably wonder what cobbler put high heels on a perfectly good pair of expedition boots, and assume that he or she was in the pocket of whatever lobby represented tassels and wing tips.

Lying wasn't Sloot's strong suit, which was fine. With the exception of mathematics, it was a weak wardrobe all around.

"Where are we going next?"

"Er, well," said Sloot, who'd never begun a sentence with a self-assured air in his life, "I'm not sure that the estate can, er, *afford* another expedition at present, m'lord."

"I don't understand."

"Well, Whitewood was the victim of a substantial burgling."

"Right, I remember hearing something about that. Did I read it in the Herald?"

"It— Maybe? It happened while we were away. We found out about it when we returned from Nordheim, remember?"

"Of course," said Willie, with a flourish of the cape that Nan had given up asking him not to wear in the house. It was far too long and knocked something from its proper place every time he flourished with it, which was about every ten minutes. This time it was a pair of tea-cups, which crashed to the ground and released their contents into the brave world to seek their fortunes.

"Bad luck, that." Willie checked his cape, relieved to see that it bore no evidence of the incident. "Anyway, yes, I remember. That was around the same time that they took everything from the house that didn't match my award, wasn't it?"

"Very good, Willikins!" Nan ruffled his hair and handed him a sweet roll. Grinning, Willie bobbed his head from side to side, feeling very pleased with himself.

"Not to worry Sloot," he said, sending sweet roll crumbs flying from his mouth. "We'll get to the bottom of this. One question though, if I may?"

Sloot hastened to answer but was interrupted by the fact that Willie had never intended to pause.

"What does 'afford' mean?"

"Er, well … expeditions cost money, you see."

"Yes, right. So we must pay for the expedition. You're the money man, aren't you?"

"Yes, thank you, m'lord. We must pay for expeditions, and we also must pay to refurnish the house, given that it's been burgled. Your allowance is enough to keep us all in food and lodging, but the vault's been cleared out."

Willie blinked. Twice. It was a very deliberate sort of blink, from a man who was not accustomed to having to respond to information by understanding it.

"The cost of the expedition exceeds the cash we have on hand," Sloot stated.

"So," said Willie. "We … *need money?*"

"That's right."

"So we can … *afford.*"

"Afford *things,* m'lord."

"So money affords things?"

"Something like that, m'lord."

"Then it's a good thing you're here," said Willie, who seemed relieved.

"What?"

"Well, you're the money man! That's who you talk to when you want money." Willie performed a scoff-and-eye-roll maneuver that invited Sloot to give thinking a try before he bothered the vastly wealthy with stupid questions.

Sloot took a deep breath and used the moment it spanned to reflect fondly on simpler times, before he'd found himself leading a double life. No, probably at least triple at this point. It seemed ages ago that he was an unassuming clerk in a counting house, nestled snugly among the ledgers, and dreaming of nothing loftier than a promotion to senior clerk in the very same counting house. He hadn't realized at the time that those had been the halcyon days, or that his future would be fraught with adventure and plagued with being meant for greater things.

Willie was an entirely ridiculous person, but thanks to Sloot's time in the counting house, he had a fundamental understanding of what was happening beneath his freshly-powdered wig. He'd balanced enough accounts of the children of wealthy families, and he could read Willie like a ledger.

Willie was an idiot, but it wasn't his fault. When one has never had to consider that their pile of money must have a bottom, it leaves certain parts of the brain at leisure to avoid developing themselves.

"I'll tell you what," said Sloot, who was entirely exhausted at the effort of continuing the conversation with Willie, "why don't you go to your club and tell everyone about the mammoth? I'll have a look at the ledgers and work out whether we can afford another expedition."

"*Whether* we can afford?" The expression of confusion that came over Willie's face carried a banner that identified it as a herald for a much more sinister threat. An army of all-out panic. The sort of panic that made for very interesting rampages, if one were the sort of person who enjoyed reading about the handful of survivors later on.

"Oh, hey, *hey* there, Willie!" Roman's stroll into the room erupted into a sprint. He put his hands on Willie's cheeks and shook him gently, causing his powdered wig to go askew. "What's old Sloot been joking with you about then, eh?"

"I was just telling him that we can't afford—"

Willie groaned in anguish. He tried his best to collapse to the floor, the opening number of what promised to be the tantrum of the season.

"Oh, butter and cheese," wailed Nan, "it's going to be a big one!"

"Hey, ah! Hoo hoo!" Sloot had never heard Roman babble distractions before, but he knew gibberish when he heard it. He held his tongue.

"What did the money man mean," choked Willie in sobs, "about the affording?"

"Oh, ha! Ha, ha, haaa! Quite the joke he played there, Willie!"

"Joke?" said Sloot, followed by a pointed look from Roman. "Oh, the joke! Right. I love to joke about money and affording. It's sort of a money man thing. I think. Right?"

"Right!" Roman was still wrestling with Willie, only barely keeping him from a kicking fit on the ground. "And they sometimes forget that exceptionally clever boys don't need to waste their time with stupid *affording*, do they?"

"Of course not," said Sloot. "That's dull stuff for money men! I forgot that Willie's far too rich to worry about money … things."

Willie was thrashing a bit less. It seemed to be working.

"I think you owe Willie an apology," said Roman. He worked Willie into half a headlock.

"Yeah," said Willie, panting for breath. "And a pony for Snugglewatch!"

"Er, all right. Sorry, Willie."

"That's okay." Willie relaxed at last.

"That's our big boy," said Nan. "And if you can be good until Snugglewatch, I'm sure Sloot will get you that pony. *Won't* you, Mister Peril?"

"I'm not sure how we'll aff— Er, right. Of course."

"Right then," said Willie, getting to his feet after a long and uncomfortable silence. "I'm off to my club to tell Nipsy and the boys about my mammoth. You'll work out the expedition then, Sloot?"

"I will, m'lord."

"Shall I accompany you to the club, m'lord?" asked Roman.

"No thanks. I don't think they allow valets in."

"I understand, sir. Have a good time then." Roman made a good show of looking disappointed but did a less than thorough job of telling Willie about the dingy room where the valets all waited for their gentlemen to get too bored or too drunk to continue complimenting themselves. Roman had frequented that room on a few occasions, while he was undercover working for dandies who lived charmed lives, if not long ones. None of the other valets ever wanted to play cards or anything. They just sat around, wearing expressions that suggested they'd only thought about their lots in life for the first time when they got there.

It took Willie a few tries to find his way out of the kitchen, but the second that he managed it—with Nan's help—Roman did not hold back in savaging Sloot with the obvious.

"What's the matter with you? Telling rich people about how money works! Are you trying to give the poor boy a heart attack?"

"Better him than me," said Sloot, shocking even himself with his utter lack of self-effacement. "Oh, and why not? I'm simply to put on a brave face, and then what? When the money actually runs out, what happens then? I'm not a secret millionaire myself, you know! I can't finance his outrageous lifestyle on my solid grasp of mathematics alone."

"Money never runs out for his sort," said Roman. "Keep it together! If not for his sake, then for the Motherland!"

"Motherland," echoed Sloot. Every patriotic impulse within him strained to say it derisively, but he couldn't manage it. It came out completely deadpan, as though he were trying it on for size. Really, properly trying it on.

And why not? Profanity redacted, what good had his loyalty to the Domnitor, long may he reign, ever done for him, really? Aside from making him believe in something greater than himself, giving him assurance that there was order to be found in chaos, meaning to it all, and a language and culture that had been the very soul of his identity for as long as he could remember? Nothing, that's what.

A chill crept up Sloot's spine. His first genuinely heretical thought! Until now, he'd merely been paying lip service to Carpathian Intelligence, doing his duty to his mother until the opportunity presented itself to break away; but what now? Was it true, that this had been his inevitable fate all along? Perhaps he truly did have veins full of barbaric Carpathian blood.

"I wish we had time for you to fully embrace this existential crisis," said Roman. "Alas, we do not."

"Oh, I'm sorry," said Sloot, suddenly embracing a wellspring of sarcasm he'd never known was within him, "is my inner turmoil inconvenient for you, Roman? Perhaps I should simply stuff my mouth full of the babies of my enemies, like a proper Motherland cannibal!"

He managed some proper derision on the word "Motherland" that time. That made him feel a bit less heretical, but who was this brash ne'er-do-well, who so liberally befouled the air with mockery and contempt? Not Sloot Peril, that's for sure.

"I've already cooed to one crying child today, I'll not do the same for you. Come on, let's handle this like men."

Sloot huffed and grumbled as he followed Roman through the house and out behind the stables. The lawns were lush and green, so much so that Sloot sort of felt they were showing off. The only point of exception was a circle behind the stables, about three feet larger than the blackened barrel that sat in its center.

"What is that?" asked Sloot.

"It's blood brandy from … well, from *up north*, if you catch my drift."

"It's a very subtle code, but I'll try to keep up."

"You've got sarcasm now! I can't say I approve. If I was your dad—"

"Blood brandy?"

"Bear's blood, traditionally fermented in hollowed-out oak trees. You know it's ready when the tree slumps over and dies."

"That's filthy!"

"Careful now," said Roman, "that's your culture you're demeaning! Did you know that there are no goblins up north? Only in the Old Country. I'd remember that when comparing nations, my boy."

Roman unhooked an old wooden mug from his belt. He placed it under the spigot near the bottom of the barrel and turned it. A black liquid slowly started to ooze from it in sickly glops.

"Does Mister Dirtsmith know you've got this back here?"

"He does," answered Roman. "And he never fails to mention that he does. It's why he's always grumpy with me."

"I thought he was just generally unpleasant."

"Oh, he is, but I think he appreciates having a reason; though I can tell you, nobody *up north* would object to having a barrel of this lying around!"

"Let's talk about something other than *up north*," said Sloot. "Little Lord Hapsgalt is in a lot of trouble at the moment, which means that we're in trouble. How are we going to refill his coffers?"

"Can't talk about that without talking about *up north,*" Roman replied. The slow drip from the spigot had finally managed to fill the mug. Roman took a sip, closed his eyes, and made a sort of contorted grimace that reminded Sloot of a dog sneezing. He passed it to Sloot, who took a sip as well and instantly regretted it.

He'd never tasted anything so malicious in his life. It was the sort of flavor you'd expect from rat poison, but only if the poison really wanted the rats to suffer. It tasted like a swineherd's bare feet on a hot day.

Sloot resisted the urge to vomit. He didn't want to taste it again, though the addition of his stomach bile would probably improve it.

He was nearly ready to give up booze altogether. Then again, he *was* having the worst week of his life. Perhaps not the best time to stop drinking.

"Don't tell me you enjoy the taste of that."

"It's an acquired taste," said Roman. He took another sip, and his jaw attempted to retreat upward into his brain. "Had you been raised *up north,* your parents would have forced you to acquire it as well."

"And what does *up north* have to do with Willie's money?"

"Plans are already in motion. That reminds me, we've got to go see Winking Bob."

"Winking Bob? So we're regularly cavorting with the criminal underworld now? And since when are plans set in motion without my knowing about them?"

"Since I became your spymaster," said Roman. "Your accounting skills aren't going to get us out of this one, Sloot. We've got to rely on other means."

"Oh, right. And just how many of Lord Hapsgalt's staff have you involved in your *northern* schemes? Is it just Myrtle and myself, or can we speak freely around the stable boys as well?"

"Drink." Roman shoved the cup back into Sloot's hand. He did so without thinking, then coughed and cursed his own talent for obedience. "Just you and Myrtle. That's all we needed. Blood and honor!"

"Blood and honor," mumbled Sloot. "Where is Myrtle, anyway?"

"Have another drink."

Sloot obeyed. Fortune smiled on him, robbing him of his sense of taste. He started seeing double.

"Where is Myrtle?"

"Gone."

"Gone? What do you mean, *gone?*"

"You're not going to like it."

"I haven't liked anything else that's happened today," said Sloot, punctuating the thought by handing the virulent mug of viscous unpleasantness back to Roman.

"The robbery ..." Roman took a sip from the mug, winced, and exhaled heavily. "It was her doing."

Sloot said a swear word, and he said it with gusto. A pair of goblins popped into existence, congratulated each other, then ran off cackling.

"Rein it in, my boy," said Roman. He'd taken another sip of the blood brandy and was starting to wobble.

"You take it back!" Sloot spoke more slowly than usual, slower even than he would have if he'd spent most of the night in a pub.

"Won't change anything if I do." Roman's speech was slowing as well, though he had the benefit of experience when it came to fermented bear's blood.

"You're a liar!" shouted Sloot, in the particular way that seriously inebriated people are wont to do. They're generally unable to tell when someone is lying to them, and this is their means of tricking sneaky liars into revealing themselves. At least that's what psychiatrists have concluded, and then billed by the hour for having done.

"I am not! You've come unhinged and started shouting at dashing older gentlemen! You think I'm going to take this from an accountant?"

"I do! And you are!"

That, as they say, tore it. In a single maneuver lacking wisdom and grace in equal measure, Roman lunged at Sloot with a haymaker so poorly aimed it got lost on the way over. Even Sloot had time to dodge it, or he may have gotten woozy and fallen out of its path. Either way, it still counted as a punch. Enough goblins to field a decent game of boulderchuck popped in, and ran cackling toward the house.

"Oh, that's bad," said Roman.

"Not as bad as ... as your ... stupid ..." Sloot trailed off, as so many drunks nowhere near the verge of a really biting insult have done before him.

"That's it," said Roman through clenched teeth. "Tuck your shirt back in and follow me."

"Where are we going?" Sloot was following out of habit. It was what he did when it was implied with authority that he should.

"To the crags."

"Oh," said Sloot, a chill running down his spine. "I've never been to there before."

"Well, it's high time you did. We've got precious little time, and we can't waste it squabbling. Besides, if I punch you again, it could kill you."

The crags were a rocky outcropping on the southwestern coast of the Old Country, where the great wall that kept Salzstadt secure against the hordes of foreign invaders ended. If one were to listen to the Ministry of Propaganda, one would know that everyone north of the Old Country was a member of some foreign horde or another, all of whom passed the time from birth until death by salivating over the tender organs of those living south of the wall.

On the other hand, if one were to *not* listen to the Ministry of Propaganda, they'd know about it. The Ministry, that is. One's file would then be turned over to the Ministry of Scrutiny, which everyone knows is simply a middle-man who, in turn, turns files over to the Ministry of Comeuppance, who had received new appropriations for dungeons that year.

The crags were the only place in the Old Country where goblins dared not go. No one had ever found a reason why, but then the practice of asking lots of questions was discouraged by the Ministry of Information Defense, who likewise referred files to the Ministry of Scrutiny.

So it was that the crags were a favorite place among the residents for airing their grievances. One could snarl any number of swear words without fear of bringing down a congress to infest it.

People did, however, tend to refrain from using the one that rhymes with "doorknob" and suggested what one's mother might be doing in the company of lawyers behind a church. They still had to look their own mothers in the eye, and it's a well-known fact that mothers know everything their children have ever done and said.

Sloot and Roman arrived at sunset, and fortunately, there wasn't much of a line. Nary a kick was thrown while they were in the most heated parts of it, but they must have been determined to wear out all of the worst swear words they knew.

In the end, if anyone had been keeping score, they'd have reported that Sloot favored the one that literally meant "Carpathian banjo player," and was an allegory for people who tickle their attractive cousins at family reunions for so long it gets weird.

Roman, on the other hand, was all over the place. He used several that Sloot had never heard before, including the one that means the same as eating beans in a canoe, the one that implies Sloot has hairy feet from sleeping in a barn too often, and the one that means the same thing coming and going.

"Do we have a deal?" Roman was lying on the ground, out of breath and covered in sweat.

"O-okay," stuttered Sloot, who'd only just stopped crying.

"Good. You're promoted to Agent Ninth Class in Carpathian Intelligence. It's still not a paid position, but I can share a bit more information with you."

"All right." Sloot wiped his nose on his sleeve. "Now tell me what happened with Myrtle."

"On yer own time!"

Sloot looked to see that a line had formed in their wake. He could only make out their silhouettes because the rising sun was behind them, but all of them had their hands on their hips. They were angry.

"We've been at it all night," said Sloot.

"We know!" yelled the angry shadow at the head of the line. "Now do yer makin' up elsewhere, my wife's been waiting for hours to give me what for!"

"Sorry, folks," said Roman. He motioned to Sloot, and the two of them started walking toward the seashore.

"Oh, Myrtle," Sloot cried, his face in his hands.

"Tough luck, that."

"I really liked her, Roman."

"I know."

"How could she do that to us?"

"Try not to think about it."

But it was all that he could think about. His career was destined for ruin, but he'd been worried about his career since he could remember. He'd never been this fond of a woman before, and he'd not even had a chance to fret over his deficiencies as a lover, or his incapacity to say the word "love" with intent. Their romance had been snuffed out before he'd had a chance to ruin it.

"You said you had a good feeling about the two of us," said Sloot.

"That's the funny thing," replied Roman. "I still do. And I'm never wrong about these things."

"You can't possibly be right about this one though. Can you?"

Roman shrugged. "Time will tell, or it won't. All we can do is get on with it. Come on, it's time you got your hands dirty."

## ❧⟶ALLEGED HYPOTHETICALS❧⟶

Sloot was rapidly running out of preconceived notions. This one in particular, in which the black market was a metaphor for the platform upon which illicit items were exchanged—not an actual market with handcarts and everything—was one which he'd felt very certain he'd gotten right; however, one secret knock on a door he'd have missed entirely if Roman hadn't pointed it out, a mumbled passphrase he didn't quite catch, and there they were.

"Not a bad price on molotovs," said Roman as they walked down an aisle with improvised incendiaries on one side and a variety of stilettos and blackjacks on the other. One prominent display implied that Sloot's manhood might be seriously called into question if he were to strangle a person with anything other than genuine Malstruchen Garotte Wire, owing its quality to its "specially patented strand weaving technique" which was "preferred by nine of eleven professional assassins."

There were stages where dubious-looking characters employed all manner of showmanship, from dancing monkeys to scantily-clad ladies who didn't seem to mind being narrowly missed by knives. There was a man in a top hat festooned with black feathers selling a sickly green ichor in glass bottles from a brightly painted wagon. He was next to a desk where a woman was selling goblin insurance.

"It's the same people in line to buy insurance every day," said Roman. "Everybody walks into a crowded line. Works like a charm with the rubes."

"I can't imagine the UQPE is pleased about them."

"Who?"

"The queuers' union."

"Oh. They've probably blackballed every one of this lot, standards and all. Still, everybody's got to work, right?"

The entire black market was housed in what appeared to be a cavernous confluence of sewer tunnels, which were thankfully free of the gallons of flowing excrement one might expect to find in such a place.

"How is this place here?" asked Sloot, as they walked past bargain bins filled with three-for-a-silver brass knuckles, complete sets of lock picks, bags of caltrops, and other implements of assorted treachery to give one the edge in the course of less-than-savory pursuits.

"I'm no philosopher," said Roman. Sloot's heart sank a bit as he thought of Arthur—Doctor Widdershins, rather—which, of course, made him think of Myrtle. He wished he could talk to her, ask her why she'd done it; then again, that sounded awfully like engaging conflict head-on, and he was more of an avoider in that arena. He pushed it out of his mind to focus on the market.

"I mean it seems like a permanent arrangement," said Sloot.

"It's well-hidden," Roman replied.

"Yes, but with Uncle on the prowl for places like this, you'd think they'd eventually—"

"You'd think," interrupted Roman, "and yet here we are."

"And yet here we are. I'll bet you could get a really decent belt down here."

"Stop staring at the ceiling with your mouth open." Roman nudged his shoulder. "That's practically an invitation for every hoodlum within fifty feet to pick your pockets clean and sell you to a fellow they know down by the docks."

Sloot's mouth snapped shut and, in a fit of improvisational genius, he adopted a scowl with one eye squinting and the other wide open.

"Eh, better. But really, a belt? All the utensils of skullduggery at your disposal, at very competitive prices, I might add, and the first thing you'd think to buy is a belt?"

"A nice leather one," said Sloot. "Schlegelmann's on Prancing Row is the only shop that's got permits to sell them to civilians, so they cost five times what they should, and their craftsmanship is horrid. I've had wool belts my whole life because I won't give in to their highway robbery. I'd really love a nice leather one, though."

"We'll see what we can do," said Roman. Sloot followed him through a low archway, past the palest woman he'd ever seen in his life, who was selling an assortment of bones that he convinced himself belonged to animals who'd died of natural causes. Next to her was a steel door with a wheel in the center. Roman picked up a hammer lying next to the door and gave it three solid *thunks.*

"Wossat?" The voice belonged to the bloodshot pair of eyes lurking behind the little panel in the door that slid open. Sloot imagined that there must be a mouth below them to which the voice actually belonged, but the way his week was going, he wasn't quite ready to risk one of his endangered preconceived notions.

"We seek an audience." Roman patted a pouch on his belt that made a meek little jingling noise.

"With who?"

"With *whom*," said Sloot.

The little portal slammed shut.

"What'd you do that for?" asked Roman.

"Because it was correct!"

"If you're done being smug, there's more at stake down here than proper grammar!"

"Sorry," said Sloot. He then silently retracted the apology. A gentleman should never apologize for defending the Domnitor's rules on grammar, long may he reign.

Then again, as Roman repeated his hammering on the door, the peculiar realization dawned on Sloot that wielding his grammatical prowess had never won him a single friend. It was awfully lonely, being right all the time.

"You again?"

"Pardon the professor," Roman apologized. "We seek an audience."

"Having trouble hearing you."

Roman sighed and glared at Sloot. He moved a handful of silver coins from a different pouch to the one he'd jingled before, then held it up and shook it with reluctant vigor.

"With ... with *what person?*"

"With Auntie, if she's not gone to bed."

The little panel slammed shut.

"I thought we were here to see—"

"My auntie, that's right!" said Roman. "Probably best if you let me do all of the talking then, all right?"

After a series of clanks and rattles, the great steel door eventually opened. They were waved through by a man who must've been half-ogre. The other half was some sort of scientific experiment, likely an attempt to answer the question "how many muscles are too many?" He snarled at Sloot as he passed, his throat thundering a grumble that dared Sloot to correct its tense. Sloot refrained.

The sizes of both the door and the doorman had given Sloot the impression that there would be a lot more behind it, yet there they were, inching and shouldering their way around the little table that occupied most of the room. Calling it a "room" was generous. It made the closet in Sloot's apartment seem palatial by comparison.

Roman and Sloot sat on two of the three wooden stools around the little table just as a knock came from the identical steel door on the wall opposite the one they'd used.

"Pardon me." The ogre reached across to the other door with an arm that was so severely overpopulated with muscles it qualified as a humanitarian crisis. It showed no sign of exertion in spinning the big wheel in the door and pulling it open.

"Hello boys," said an older woman, who only could have been Winking Bob. She nodded to the ogre and took the final seat at the table. The ogre pushed the door closed behind her, then folded his arms and stared off into space, which the room lacked entirely.

"Will he be staying?" Roman made a tiny nod toward the ogre.

"Don't worry about Edmund," said Bob. "He's just here in case voices are raised. Not that he's technically *here*, mind you. None of us are, as far as anything outside this room—which may or may not exist—is concerned. Agreed?"

"Insofar as there is anything to agree *to*, yes," Roman replied. He and Bob smiled at each other with their mouths, but it didn't appear that their eyes were joining in the festivities.

Bob wore a simple yet elegant black dress with a corset that defied even the smallest of meals. She looked to be about as old as Roman, though in terms of his abject failure to age with a shred of grace, the two could not have been more different. She flashed Sloot the same dead-eyed smile, both alluring and unnerving.

"I don't believe we've met," said Bob, "not that it's happening now, of course."

"Of course," said Sloot.

"This is Sloot Peril," said Roman. "Financier to Lord Wilhelm Hapsgalt. Sloot, if you were meeting anyone at the moment, there's a chance that she might be Winking Bob."

"How do you do?" asked Sloot.

"Busy," said Bob, "I'm always busy. Too busy to be here, of course, which is why I've got a rock-solid alibi that places me across town. What can I do for you gentlemen, in theory?"

"We'd like to discuss the burgling of Whitewood," answered Roman.

"The *alleged* burgling, don't you mean?"

"Oh, the burgling is a matter of fact," stated Roman. "The alleging has to do with what person or persons, who may or may not be in this very room at the moment, may or may not have been involved in such."

Sloot was bewildered. Wasn't Myrtle responsible for the burglary? She wasn't in the room, was she? He looked under the table but saw nothing but an arrangement of knees.

"A matter of fact? Then there's a report on file with the constabulary?"

"You know perfectly well there isn't," said Roman. "People as wealthy as the Hapsgalts don't go running to constables when they're burgled. It would be a scandal, a sign of weakness! 'Just wait a few weeks until we've trucked a few new piles of money into the vault,' you may as well shout to the local villains, 'and do bring your own sacks, ours have been burgled!'"

"Of course," said Bob. "Forgive my *naïveté* in these matters, I'm completely at sea when it comes to thievery."

"Of course," said Roman with a smirk.

"So sorry to hear of Lord Hapsgalt's misfortune, though. Edmund?"

"Any use of the word 'sorry' by any persons or absences of persons in this or any past, present, or future context shall not be construed as an admission of guilt or wrongdoing, and is inadmissible in any court of law."

Bob gave Edmund a satisfied nod.

"Thanks," said Roman. "There's still the matter of the involvement of parties who shall remain nameless for the moment. I don't like to use words like 'evidence' or 'corroborating witnesses' in polite conversation. I'd prefer to rely on your good graces to obviate the need."

Bob *tsked*. "Roman, if I didn't know any better, I'd think you were harboring suspicions. Edmund?"

"Any use of the word 'know' shall not be interpreted as an acknowledgment of prior awareness to any event or events that may or may not have preceded this event, which may or may not be happening, and thus may or may not be possible to precede."

"Oh, come on," said Roman. "Remember when we used to just *talk*, Bob? We've been through a lot together, you and I. We go way back!"

Edmund took in a breath, to which Bob held up a hand.

"Assuming for a moment that was true, it simply doesn't change the fact that business is business," Bob countered. "I'd honestly like to help you out, Roman, but my hands are tied. Edmund?"

"Use of the word 'honestly' shall not be taken to imply dishonesty in any other statements made by the person or persons, present or otherwise, having allegedly used said word."

"There's always a way," interjected Sloot.

"Don't mind him." Roman gave a nervous chuckle and shot a dirty look in Sloot's direction.

"Business is business, isn't that right, Bob?"

"Speaking in hypothetical generalities, yes." Bob regarded Sloot with a curious smirk.

"Best if I do the talking," said Roman through clenched teeth.

"Not so fast," said Bob. "Mister Peril is the financier, is he not?"

"That's right," answered Sloot.

"But he's not a negotiator," said Roman. "Didn't you say you were looking for a belt, Sloot? Perhaps you could go and—"

"Nonsense," interrupted Bob. "Tell me, Mister Peril, if that is indeed your real name—which you need neither confirm nor deny at this juncture—what sort of business would you like to discuss?"

"The sort that puts enough gold back into Willie's treasury to keep up appearances," Sloot replied. "I know I can't convince you to give back what you stole from Whitewood—"

"Objection!" said Edmund.

"Withdrawn," said Sloot. "Look, we could go to the elder Lord Hapsgalt and have the money replaced in a heartbeat, but we'd be a laughing stock! Willie would never—"

"Live it down!" shouted Roman, drawing a sidelong glance from Edmund. "You're right about that, he'd definitely be deeply embarrassed by that, having to crawl to his father."

"Er, right," muttered Sloot.

"No, no," said Bob, "please do go on, Mister Peril. No more interruptions please, Roman."

"You seem like a reasonable person, Bob."

"If, in fact, that is my real name."

"Sure," said Sloot, "and I have no doubt that you understand our predicament. Surely, we can come to some sort of mutually beneficial arrangement?"

"Well," said Bob, "I could offer you a contract for services if you'd be amenable."

"Sloot, don't—"

"What sort of contract?"

Giving a forlorn groan, Roman hung his head.

"What's the matter?" asked Sloot. Roman said nothing.

"We've entered a negotiation," said Bob. "You didn't specify that Roman should be party to it, so you'll be the sole delegate for your contingent. You are empowered to enter into financial contracts on behalf of Lord Wilhelm Hapsgalt, are you not?"

"Well, yes, but—"

"Let the record—which may or may not exist—reflect that the contract allegedly being negotiated is between Roberta Golubkin on behalf of The Four Bells Trading Company, and Sloot Peril on behalf of Lord Wilhelm Hapsgalt."

"So noted," said Edmund, "hypothetically speaking, of course."

"Mister Peril," Bob continued, "we are prepared to offer you a sum in the amount of one-tenth of the value of all property allegedly burgled from Whitewood at the time purported, said value to be based on wild conjecture on the part of the Four Bells' accountants, and certainly not on a detailed accounting that could never be performed, given that neither the Four Bells nor any of its agents or subsidiaries were involved in said burglary."

Sloot said nothing, making that the smartest thing he'd said since having entered the room.

"In return for said one-tenth of the aforementioned alleged burglary, Lord Wilhelm Hapsgalt and his agents will be held accountable for ten individual services to The Four Bells, deliverable on a schedule to be determined by the same."

"Ten for a tenth? That's larceny!"

"Allegedly," said Bob.

What Sloot lacked in the ability to recognize when he was in over his head, he made up for in stubborn persistence. He was first and foremost an accountant, after all—if he couldn't walk away from a services contract negotiation with vaguely favorable terms, he'd be honor-bound to return his diploma to the University of Salzstadt.

There was no way to tell time in the little room, but Sloot would have guessed that they'd been at it for nearly three hours when they finally came to terms that took on the outer shape of adequacy.

"What do you say to that?" asked Sloot. He'd removed his shirt half an hour prior and was dripping with sweat.

"A quarter of the conjectured value of the alleged burglary," said Bob, who glistened but showed no real signs of exhaustion, "in return for two services to be specified in advance."

"And the answer to one question," began Sloot, "to be asked by me and answered by you, once the rest of the business is settled."

"Very well."

"Name your services," said Sloot.

"The first is the installation of an item in the old clock tower in the Ulfhaven town square."

"That's the capital of Carpathia!" exclaimed Sloot.

"Please don't interrupt," said Bob. "The second service will require the gentleman to sign this confession. Edmund?"

Edmund produced a single sheet of paper folded into thirds and handed it to Sloot.

"Confession? To what?"

"Oh, nothing yet," said Bob. "It's just the last page."

Sloot read the paper. It was indeed the last page of a confession, though it mentioned no specific crime or heresy. It started with "I, the undersigned, do hereby firmly attest in very flowery language that I was the heinous perpetrator of whatever atrocities just happen to be pinned atop this paper," or something very close to that.

"This is diabolical," said Sloot.

"This is how we do business. Edmund?"

"The use of the term 'we' does not affirm any association—"

"Right, whatever." Sloot signed the paper while Edmund droned on with his disclaimer. He handed it back to Edmund, who stamped it with a notary seal and placed it in a satchel, which resembled a purse in his enormous hands.

"Oh, good," said Bob with one of those mouth-only smiles that unnerved Sloot so much. "Look on the bright side, you've fulfilled half your end of the bargain already!"

"What do you intend to do with that?"

"Probably nothing," said Bob. "It's a fairly standard practice, I've got dozens of them." She paused. "Or do I?"

"So you're not planning on pinning some crime on me?" asked Sloot, who was trying to decide if being jailed for a crime he didn't commit—while going unpunished for the ones he did—counted as irony.

"Not yet," said Bob. "As long as I'm pleased with the status of our association, it's altogether possible that that paper will never see the light of day."

"Would it be possible to repurchase it from you someday?"

"Everything is for sale," said Bob, "but try not to think about that. Edmund?"

Bracing himself for another disclaimer, Sloot wondered whether Edmund had been the burliest lawyer in his class at the university, or simply a savant in the area of rote recitation; but the droning legality never came. Instead, he produced from his satchel a weathered black box, which he handed to Roman. Roman opened the box.

"Is that what I think it is?" asked Roman.

"Objection," said Edmund. "Conjecture."

"Ugh," groaned Roman, "sustained. It's a blood star, isn't it?"

"It's perfectly harmless to you," said Bob. "Best not to think about it, yes? Better still to refrain from asking questions, especially now that you're committed."

"What's a blood star?" asked Sloot.

"We've concluded our negotiation, Mister Peril. Is that the question you want me to answer?"

"No it isn't," said Sloot, "and no we haven't. We haven't shaken on it."

"That's ceremonial." Bob lifted one shoulder in a halfhearted shrug. "I've got your signature."

"On a fabricated confession. That was a part of the deal, and a fabricated confession doesn't constitute a contract ... unless, of course, you'd like to use it to frame me for having agreed to close the negotiation."

"Oh, very well." Bob donned a scowl in an earnest attempt to be annoyed, but she couldn't repress a grin. "Well played, Mister Peril."

She extended her hand, and Sloot shook it. He thought her grip was surprisingly firm, then chastised himself for thinking that it would have been otherwise just because she's a woman.

"Now, then, what's your question?"

Sloot cleared his throat. "Who is Myrtle Pastry?"

Bob smiled. A real one, with her whole face—not the dead-eyed, burn-a-hole-into-your-psyche sort she'd been practicing up to that point.

"You're cleverer than I thought," she said. "You like her, don't you?"

"I just need answers."

"Very well, a deal's a deal."

"Allegedly," stated Edmund.

"Right," said Bob. "Myrtle came to work for me a long time ago. When the opportunity came along to place someone in little Lord Hapsgalt's service, I thought she'd do nicely. It was just supposed to be a bit of pilfering here and there, nothing that would be noticed; but then she told me she wanted out, wouldn't say why. The burglary was the price."

※ 常 ※ 常 ※ 常 ※ 常

"You've really stepped in it," said Roman as they were leaving the black market. "If you'd let me do all of the talking, neither of us would have signed one of her awful confessions!"

"You didn't have to do it," said Sloot. "Besides, she said it'll probably never see the light of day."

"Right. Keep repeating that to yourself while you're trying to sleep tonight."

Sloot wasn't going to get any sleep anyway. He'd be up all night trying to fit all of the pieces together. Bob said she'd placed Myrtle in Whitewood, but that was impossible. It had been Mrs. Knife who insisted she be hired. How were they connected?

"What's a blood star?" asked Sloot, confused on that point as well.

"Keep your voice down!" Roman hissed. He looked over his shoulder to make sure no one was following them, then leaned in close to Sloot.

"Necromancer stuff," he whispered. "Very nasty. I don't know exactly what it does, and I don't want to know."

"Necromancer?"

"Wizard who trucks with the dead."

"Wizards? There are no such things!"

"Well, that's a relief. And I suppose that we should pay no mind that we've just been offered a quarter of a Hapsgalt's fortune to place one of their trinkets in a tower!"

"A tower in Carp— *up north*," said Sloot, "no easy feat, is it? Plus the confession."

"Oh, yes! I forgot all about the accountant who signed a piece of paper! Quite the coup, that. She's a criminal mastermind, isn't she?"

Roman was right. Given the difficulty of the journey, why make it just to hang a trinket in a tower? It was obviously worth a lot of money to Bob to get it done, unless Sloot's signature really was worth that much.

"So wizards are real?"

Roman nodded. Sloot said a swear word. There was a pop and a cackle behind them.

"It's nearly lunchtime," remarked Roman.

Sloot yawned. They'd been up all night at the crags and then down in the black market, so he hadn't slept.

"We should be getting back to Whitewood," said Roman. "Got to maintain our cover, after all."

"Right you are. Plus, we need to convince Willie that he needs to go *up north,* and I doubt old Nan will be too keen on that."

## ❧A BIT OF SKULKING❧

Among the things on Sloot's desk, or rather the stack of apple crates that was filling in since the proper desk had been burgled, was a package wrapped in plain brown paper.

"That's not a good sign," said Roman. "Never open a package you weren't expecting."

"Is that—" Sloot paused to look over each shoulder, making sure they were alone. "Is that part of the spy training?"

"It's common sense! Could be anything in there, right? What if it's … I dunno, poison or something?"

"It's from Greta."

"It *says* it's from Greta."

"Right, on the return address. It's probably just my watch."

"Repaired so quickly? Doesn't that seem suspicious to you?"

Sloot had no idea how long it took to repair a watch.

"What else would she send me?"

"You're assuming it's from her."

"It's not assuming if it's written on the package."

"You're assuming she wrote it!"

"It's ticking," said Sloot. He was holding the package to his ear.

"It could be a bomb!"

"A bomb that ticks? Don't be ridiculous. It would have to have a— what do you call it—burning bit of string?"

"A fuse."

"If you say so." Sloot had only ever seen a bomb once, and it had had a burning bit of string coming out of the top. It was on a poster that the Ministry of Propaganda had plastered up on every wall that wasn't already occupied by something with an official stamp of higher priority.

Thinking of the poster gave Sloot a chuckle. The bomb was dressed up like a baby on a plate, being handed to some unsuspecting Carpathian cannibals by a pair of clever soldiers. "Giving The Enemy What For!" read the caption. Solid patriotic humor.

Sloot tugged at the string, which both opened the package and sent Roman diving behind a different configuration of apple crates that was serving as a sofa. As Sloot had suspected, Greta had delivered his watch.

It was merely ticking now, a faint whisper of its former violent clanking.

"She must have been right about the overwinding," said Sloot.

"You got lucky." Roman was back on his feet and dusting off his coat.

"I just opened a package."

"Mark my words, one day you'll open the wrong package, and BOOM! No more Sloot. You'll wish you'd listened to me then."

"Won't I be dead?"

Roman's eyes narrowed, and a snarl of disapproval took root in his upper lip. "That's dangerously close to insubordination, Peril."

"Sorry."

Sloot was relieved to have the watch back and resolved to thank Greta properly. He didn't know what women liked, but he could get to know her a bit on the trip to Carpathia—that should help him think of something.

That's when the guilt started sinking in, over adding Reckless Endangerment of a Loyal Subject of the Domnitor—long may he reign—to his list of atrocities.

"Why did you convince Greta to come up north with us?"

"It's all part of the plan," said Roman.

"Which plan? The plan to get Willie's finances in order? Since when does it involve dragging innocent hostages along?"

"No, that plan is just one part of *the* plan! I told you, it's starting to take shape. The fact that she and Willie aren't actually engaged makes it interesting."

"I'll say. When Constantin finds out, he'll be furious! We've got to think of something, or we'll be out on the streets before we know it."

"If only that were the worst of it." Roman glanced over his shoulder. "You don't understand men like old Constantin. He doesn't abide disappointment. He's been far too rich for far too long to let a simple thing like the free will of other people get in the way of how he's decided things are going to be."

"So that's it then? We convince Greta that she's in love with an expensive suit filled with ridiculously wealthy cretin, and off into the sunset they ride?"

"What if it is? There are far worse fates befalling far nicer people every day. Marrying an innocent dimwit for a healthy profit is far from cruel, as fates go."

"It's not fair, that's all I'm saying."

"Like you'd know fair if it bit you in the face! Which it won't, because fairness has got no teeth. Don't worry about Greta. Leave it to me, it's all part of the plan."

Sloot didn't really trust Roman any more than Roman trusted packages wrapped in brown paper, but some shred of pragmatism deep within him knew that there was no sense in worrying about it just then. Had that shred not been vastly outnumbered by his preternatural talents for worrying, it might have been able to slow the growth of his latest ulcer by a day or so.

"Fine," said Sloot. "Let's go and find Willie."

They found him in the courtyard. He was standing atop the stone bench where Sloot had once sat to hire the staff. He was dressed all in khaki, the explorer outfit he'd copied from his hero.

"Is that Sir Wallace Scoffington, come to visit?" asked Roman.

"What? Where?" Willie jerked his head around, then leapt into a sort of martial pose with his fists swaying clumsily over his head. Any sparrows in the neighborhood might have thought twice about flying low near him, but probably not.

"Oh, no," said Roman. "That's Willie! Forgive me, m'lord, you looked just like Sir Wallace there."

"I forgive you," Willie replied, looking puzzled.

"You look quite dapper in your explorer's get-up," said Sloot.

"Thanks." Willie cracked what must have hoped to be a dashing grin when it grew up. "It's called a *kit,* actually. My tailor said that's what all of the explorers call their outfits. I told him that we'd been to Nordheim, and I told him about the mammoth."

"That's nice," said Roman. "And I see that you've given the mammoth to Greta as a gift."

"That's right. Wait, have you seen her? Did she like it? She's my fiancée!"

"That's right," said Roman, "she is. She liked the mammoth very much, your fiancée. In fact, she's asked if she can come along on our next expedition."

"Really? Wait, I thought the women were supposed to stay at home while the men went out into the wild frontier."

"So we should leave Nan at home?"

Willie's eyes narrowed, as though that would help him see through whatever trick was being played on him. He moved into a slight crouch, a sort of warning pose for the danger which was all around him.

"I don't like that idea," said Willie. "Nan knows how I like my sandwiches cut, and I'm not allowed a knife."

"Well, that settles it." Roman shrugged. "We'll be allowing women on the trip. That was truly cunning insight, m'lord."

"Happy to help." Willie puffed up his chest. "So, where's the next expedition?"

"This will be your best one yet," said Roman. "In a few days, we leave for Carpathia!"

"Carpathia? But won't that be dangerous?"

"It will most certainly have the appearance of danger," Roman answered, "but we've taken precautions to ensure that it's quite safe."

"You're sure?"

"Of course! It will have all of the hallmarks of danger. In fact, you'll probably feel as though you're standing on the precipice the entire time we're there!"

"I don't know," said Willie. "Why don't we go to Stagralla instead?"

"Well, we can plan a trip to Stagralla in the autumn if you like, but we can't have an expedition there."

"Why not? I like Stagralla."

"Everyone likes Stagralla," said Sloot. "It's the capital of Sothumbria, one of the greatest allies of the Old Country. We can't have an expedition there!"

"Why not?"

"In order for a trip to be an expedition," said Roman, "you've got to go to either an uncivilized place or a hostile one. Preferably both. Stagralla is very civilized, and the only hostility you're likely to encounter there will be at the bakery counters."

"They do take their pastries very seriously," said Willie. "But what about Nan? I don't think she'll be very keen on letting me go to Carpathia."

"It shouldn't be up to her to *let* you do anything, Willie. You're Lord Hapsgalt now! You're a field-hardened explorer, all staunch and brazen! Don't you just feel the call of adventure beckoning to you?"

"I have to admit that I do." Willie stuck his chin up and gazed off toward the horizon, as though he were modeling for a statue. "I suppose I'll just have to remind Nan that I'm a big boy now and that this is my profession ... nay, my calling! Make ready, men, for soon we ride!"

Sloot astonished himself by giving a "whoop!" and throwing his fists into the air. Inspiration of that sort was rarely, or rather never, employed in the counting house. He wondered whether settling up accounts would have been more rousing if the lead financier had riled them up every so often. "We'll not give the sums an inch of ground until the quarterly reports are ready for independent review! Eat a big lunch lads, for tonight we collate monthly summaries!"

Perhaps not.

❧⚞❧⚞❧⚞❧⚞

Individually, words hold little power. They become powerful when they collude together in gangs. When enough of the wrong words throw in together and get their dander up, you can bet they'll end up vandalizing unattended walls or harassing old grans.

Less rebellious phrases may end not in vandalism, but in magic, and contrary to what old wizards in robes with stars all over them will insist, one does not have to spend years and years in a magical college in order to tap into the power of words. People without pointy hats are perfectly capable of unleashing the vast energies of the universe by uttering the right phrases at the right times.

A simple incantation like "I'd like to see you try," for example, can compel a person to attempt just about anything, provided they've had enough to drink.

"Santa will only come if you're asleep," when uttered on the right night of the year, will send even the most willful youth running for his or her bed.

Sloot knew that he'd never convince Nan to approve of Willie's going to Carpathia. According to Roman, he didn't have to. The trick wasn't saying the right thing, it was getting Nan to say it. They'd have to be subtle about it, but all they needed from her were two simple words.

"Oh, yeah?"

Roman suppressed a grin, but poorly.

"Sorry, Nan," said Sloot, "but we've been through every possible scenario. We simply can't have you along on this expedition."

Nan was fuming. Her fists trembled as they made their way toward her hips. Sloot sensed danger and started to think slightly less of their clever approach.

"If you think for one minute," started Nan, "that you're going to take a little boy like my Willikins out into the wild without his Nan—"

"It's already been decided," Sloot interrupted. "I'm sorry, Nan, but we're worried that you'll be a bit too—"

"Oh, I see! Too what, too *old?* Is that it? Or maybe you think I'm too *frail* to go along! What a load of rotten cabbage. Who drove an entire stinking congress out of Whitewood, eh? Answer me!"

"Why, you did, of course. Look, I'm not trying to upset you."

"I'm not upset! If there were any chance you'd be able to keep me from going on this expedition, I might be upset. But you don't. Where are we going?"

"I'm afraid I can't tell you that," said Sloot. "I'm under strict orders from the lady who's funding the expedition not to breathe a word of it to anyone."

"It's a lady, is it?"

"I've already said too much."

"Talk, Peril! How will I know how much underwear to pack for Willie?"

"He can pack his own underwear," said Sloot, knowing that it was a lie. His stomach started to churn. He was comfortable enough with this particular fib, he just knew that he wasn't any good at telling them in general.

"There are only so many ladies who would fund an expedition," said Nan, trying to out-maneuver him. "I know a few of the widows in the High Tea Knitting Circle, I'm sure I could ask around."

"Please don't!" Sloot stepped closer, and nearly put a hand on her shoulder for emphasis, but decided in the end that there were some lines not worth crossing. "Please, is there anything that I can do to convince you to sit this one out?"

"Absolutely not."

"Fine." Sloot let his shoulders slump into a show of dejection. That he managed with some skill, practice making perfect and all. "You can come, but I really can't tell you where we're going. The success of the mission depends on it!"

"And why is that?"

"It will all make sense in the end," said Roman. He'd let Sloot carry the farce that far, but closing it required more finesse than he had to offer. "Now, why don't you tell me all about which knots are gentlest on Willie's shoelaces?"

Sloot excused himself after dinner, promising to return before sunrise to make an accurate accounting of all the apple crates currently in operation as furniture. No one responded with the enthusiasm he'd anticipated, but that was the least of his worries.

There was a chill in the air, which Sloot marked as particularly unremarkable. It was that time of year, after all. Had it been warm, now that would have been something worth noting.

That was as far as he got.

Sloot used to be able to bury his head in unremarkable tedium for hours before realizing he was doing it. The realization made it impossible to continue, so now there was nothing for it but to engage in the ponderance of difficult questions.

Why did Myrtle burgle Whitewood? That much was easy enough. She was secretly working for Winking Bob, and she wanted out. But what did that mean? Did she just want out of her contract, or did she want out of Whitewood altogether? She stayed around for awhile after, but was that only for appearances?

He turned down the street that led to his apartment. Mrs. Knife had instructed him to hire Myrtle. He'd assumed she was her niece or something, but that didn't add up. It was really Bob who wanted her working there, wasn't it? Mrs. Knife just made sure it happened. Were the two of them working together? That didn't make sense! The Four Bells had to be cutting into The Three Bells' profits with all of their black-marketry, which makes them natural enemies. Why would they ever cooperate?

Sloot couldn't get Mrs. Knife out of his head. He pictured her in harrowing detail, that being one of the principal ways in which worriers torture themselves. He could see her steel grey eyes burning with soulless indifference for his continued drawing of breath. Her severe black dress, the wicked-looking knife on her belt, the silver ring on her left forefinger…

Perhaps there was something there. How many of those rings had he seen that night at the elder Lord Hapsgalt's table, on the Feast of St. Bertha? Easily a dozen. Two silver snakes coiled around a black stone. He didn't know the fabulously wealthy to follow such specific trends. In fact, he'd once seen a scuffle start up between a pair of women who'd worn lilac gowns to the opera on the same night. That much matching jewelry in the same place should have ended in a bloodbath! What was the significance? Were they in some sort of club?

Winking Bob hadn't worn one during their negotiation, but then she struck Sloot as very careful never to give anything away. If there was some sort of secret behind the rings, it was a very well-kept one. The answers weren't going to walk up and introduce themselves.

Up the hill, through the door, up the stairs, and into his apartment. There was only a bit of moonlight in the room, scarcely enough to see anything. At least it served to reassure him that he hadn't gone suddenly blind, a fear that even he had to admit plagued him far more frequently than it should.

He undressed and got into bed, though his brain still was buzzing with questions. Full of bees, he was. There was a terrifying thought, though not so terrifying that it distracted him from the matter at hand for long. Of all the nights that he'd been able to stare up into the darkness and worry about grisly deaths that would never come to pass, this was the first time he could remember wishing that the gruesome fantasy hadn't been so easy to dismiss.

He couldn't tell how much time had gone by, but it had been an hour at least. He needed to do something, anything, or he'd never get to sleep.

But what? He was an accountant, not a detective! What could he do? What talents did he possess that might compel secrets that didn't want to be discovered to … well, be discovered?

The money. That was it. He could follow the money. He practically leapt from his bed and got dressed.

Whatever Mrs. Knife and the other silver ring wearers—who probably called themselves something much cooler, like the "Really Wicked Spiders"—were up to, he had little doubt that there was a paper trail that would give them away. They were all wealthy to one degree or another, and Sloot knew that the wealthier one was, the more accurate and detailed their ledgers would be.

It was a sort of defense mechanism. The more money a wealthy man has, the more likely the people who work for him will be to think "he won't miss this little bit right here." Shine lights on all of your pennies and no one will risk stealing them.

So it stood to reason that if several wealthy people were in financial cahoots with one another, they'd need to keep each other honest, in addition to their employees! Given that Mrs. Knife and both of the Lords Hapsgalt worked most of their interests through The Three Bells, the counting house would be the best place to start.

Sloot was proud of working all of that out on his own, making him practically giddy as he walked to his former place of employment. It wasn't until he reached the main gate in Salzstadt's north wall that he realized he'd fallen quite naturally into his old morning routine. Did he even know the way to the counting house from his own front door?

As long as he was thinking about what the Really Wicked Spiders might be up to, he was fine. So, of course, his mind wandered away from that with great haste, and he was left to spend his walk considering the potential dangers of what he was doing.

He was committing a crime! Well, not yet, but that was the intent, wasn't it? Was skulking through darkened streets toward the scene of a crime not part of the act itself? Crime wasn't heresy *per se*, but it wasn't far off.

What if he was caught? Sloot wasn't cut out for *not* answering questions. He only knew of one way to deal with authority figures, and that was to do precisely as he was told. A simple "what are you doing out so late?" from a passing constable was as likely to end in a full confession of every crime to which he could possibly be linked as a casual "just taking in the air, Constable."

Fortunately for Sloot, constables on the night shift are far more fastidious in seeking out criminal activity in Salzstadt's many pubs than anywhere else. Further fortune provided an unlatched window on the alley side of the counting house, and Sloot only *nearly* broke his nose shuffling through it.

The counting house! He'd forgotten the smell of the ink-stained desks and mouldering paper; the sound of the creaking floorboards, upon which he'd been so sure that he'd one day keel over and expire. It was like coming home.

The door to the supervisor's office had been left open. He'd so often fantasized about the promotion that would win him that sad, window-less closet, which was barely larger than the sad little desk inside it. He lit a candle, pulled a few ledgers from the shelves, and got to work.

Most of this sort of thing is exactly as dull as one might think, meaning that Sloot found it utterly riveting. A few missing pennies in one column often turned out to be the product of sloppy work, the in-evitable conclusion of well-meaning parents telling their children "we don't care if you *like* it, accounting is a steady career! It's either this or the army, you decide."

Sloot had been lucky. When he'd told his mother that his dream was to become an accountant, she'd given him her blessing. If all parents were so supportive, all accountants would love their work, the ledgers would be far more accurate, and Sloot would have had far fewer dead ends to chase down before finding the one clever deception that brought the whole facade tumbling down.

Well, not tumbling down, *per se*. In truth, it did little more than point out that a facade did, in fact, exist. What had been made to look like massive quantities of rope being purchased at prices that would make professional extortionists balk was actually ... well, something else. It was hard to say for sure without having a look at some land deeds and partnership contracts, but he was sure it couldn't have been rope. Sloot himself had started clerking for the rope division when he was new on the counting floor, and knew from experience that all the ships in the entire Three Bells fleet couldn't have needed that much rope; in fact, they didn't even have enough ships to carry that much rope.

*Strange they tried to hide whatever they're doing as bulk rope purchases,* thought Sloot. *I'd have expected something a little bit less scintillating, more low-key!*

The signature on the log sheet was the genuinely cunning part of the cover-up. Vasily Pritygud's name had very nearly made Sloot overlook it without a second thought. Why would anyone ever consider that an error by that twit was anything but carelessness?

*Very clever indeed*, he thought, just as he caught a glint of light in the corner of his eye. He'd only lit the one candle … sunlight! It was coming through the window where he'd gotten in. He'd been there all night!

He'd only just started to clean up after himself when he heard a click in the lock on the front door. Someone was coming! Luckily, Sloot Peril lived in a constant state of panic. It would take a lot more than the possibility of being caught in the commission of a crime to freeze him in his tracks. Unfortunately, his ability to keep moving through the panic was not joined by any shrewd instincts for self-preservation. His solution was to sit back down and continue digging through the ledgers.

The front door creaked open, and someone stepped inside. Sloot's back was turned to the door, so he had no idea who it was.

"Who's there?" said whoever it was. It was a woman's voice, but he couldn't place it.

"Hmm? Oh, hello," replied a calm and care-free voice that sounded remarkably like Sloot's, and even seemed to come from his mouth. It couldn't have been Sloot though, he was too busy losing his composure and falling into tiny pieces. Apparently, there *was* a level of panic above his resting rate that could freeze him up! The voice that had spoken was entirely calm.

"You're not supposed to be in there," said the woman's voice, "come out at once!"

"I'm nearly finished," said the mysterious Sloot Peril impersonator. The real Sloot wondered—between attempts to stop hyperventilating—how and when this interloper had managed to invade his mind and take over. Perhaps he could ask Myrtle if this was possession.

He remembered then that Myrtle was gone, and that cut his panic with sadness. He couldn't tell if that was good or bad, but he decided to hold off on lamenting that he'd been possessed, at least for the time being.

"I'm going to call for the constables if you don't come out of there this— Sloot?"

"That's right." He turned around. It was Beatrice, one of his former coworkers.

"You don't work here anymore," said Beatrice. "What were you doing in my office?"

Sloot waited for whoever had possessed him to step in, but nothing happened. Perhaps he hadn't been possessed at all. Had his mouth simply launched into the rote recitation of simple phrases while his brain caught up?

"Well?" Beatrice's fists were on her hips.

"Ahem, sorry," said Sloot. "Just ... you know, checking on things."

"Checking on things?"

"No. Yes? That is—"

"Look, Sloot, I don't want to get you in trouble or anything, but this—"

"Congratulations!"

"What?"

"The promotion!"

"Oh. Thanks, but—"

"Well, I've got to go."

A nice walking panic. That was what Sloot needed, and that was what he got. He was doomed! Not in the general spirit of inevitability sort of way, well and properly doomed! He and Beatrice had got along as well as any two competent accountants might, under the standard tacit agreement not to involve themselves in each others' business, or really learn anything about each other, or socialize at all, but could he trust her to keep her mouth shut?

Not likely. She'd still been shouting questions at him when he fled the counting house, and none of them had been very cordial. He walked as quickly as he could toward Whitewood. He needed Roman's counsel on this one.

※ 🡒 ※ 🡒 ※ 🡒 ※ 🡒

"That's the problem with my job," said Roman. "No one ever comes to me before they launch their zany capers, only when things have gone horribly awry."

"Sorry for that," said Sloot. "I had the idea and I just, I don't know, went for it."

"That's a first for you."

"It's a last for me. What was I thinking?"

"You weren't. Bravo! How old are you?"

"Thirty-six," answered Sloot. He could have been far more specific, but people didn't usually appreciate that.

"Far past due for an inadvisable rush to action!"

"What?"

"I'm torn." Roman's comically large eyes darted about the room as he stroked his chin.

"Between?"

"On the one hand, in my role as spymaster for the Salzstadt office of Carpathian Intelligence, I'm compelled to reprimand your recklessness. What were you thinking? You can't approve your own stealth missions, not at your pay grade!"

"And on the other hand?"

"I feel as though I've become something of a father figure to you, Sloot." Having never known his father, Sloot resolved to take Roman's word for it. "It's a father's duty to keep his son on the straight-and-narrow, but not to excess. Boys are supposed to make some mistakes! Bloody noses, hands in the cookie jar, all that. Have you ever been reprimanded for something like this before?"

"No." Sloot had never done anything worthy of a reprimand, not before he committed treason and fell under the guidance of his self-proclaimed father figure, at least.

"Well, blood and honor, then! Get out of here, you scamp!" Roman ruffled Sloot's hair.

"Stop that! What am I going to do about Beatrice?"

"Can you trust her to keep her mouth shut?"

"Am I the first accountant you've ever met?"

"No."

"Well, there's your answer. We do things by the book, accountants."

"I see," said Roman. "And what does this book compel you to do in this situation?"

"Say something," replied Sloot. Roman should have known about that one. Even though he was entirely unaware that Sloot was, in fact, referring to the Three Bells employee manual, there were the posters. The Ministry of Propaganda had spent a great deal of time and effort on their *Suspect Something, Say Something* campaign.

"Leave it to me," said Roman. "Just make yourself scarce for the rest of the day."

"What are you going to do?"

"What I do best. Subterfuge."

It was no counting house, but the library was still one of Sloot's favorite places in the world. It had been since he was a child. He'd often thought that if accounting hadn't been the only logical career choice for him, he'd have become a librarian. He never really regretted the missed opportunity—ledgers were clearly superior to books, after all—but he'd always fantasized about what might lie beyond the steel-reinforced door to the restricted section. Although he didn't fancy himself a dreamer, he'd never wholly given up the thought that he might see it one day.

Today would not be that day, of course. Today, he had but two things on his mind: to keep out of sight, and to figure out what was going on with the mysterious transactions he'd uncovered.

Oh, and the Really Wicked Spiders. Three things, then.

He couldn't help thinking of Myrtle. Arthur was fond of alcoves, as they were good for ponderances. The library was absolutely silly with alcoves. It was a wonder she'd ever managed to drag herself—themselves?—away from it.

Beyond the alcoves, there were books. It was a library, after all. The shelves on the first floor were mostly devoted to nationalist propaganda, of course. Most of the good people of Salzstadt had no need of the rest of the building.

The second floor was fiction. Bah. Fiction was dangerous, as far as Sloot was concerned. Things that *happened,* now that was worth reading! Works of fiction were the product of fussy debutantes who couldn't stomach reality. Three cheers for Imelda Lillellien, librarian extraordinaire, for exiling it all to the second floor where it could moulder and rot in obscurity!

The third floor. Now there was where things got interesting! Mind you, land records were no economic theories—you'd have to continue up the stairs to the fifth floor for those—but they had real stories to tell. *True* stories. Tales of who owned what parcel of land, operated what sort of business, and sold it to whoever else since the founding of Salzstadt. Heady stuff, if you're an accountant. The stuff dreams are made of.

Anyone preferring "the stuff of which dreams are made" should bugger off to the second floor where they belong.

"How can I help you?" The third-floor librarian's long white beard continued to jiggle for a moment after his lips stopped moving.

"That's all right," said Sloot. "I know what I need, if I might just—"

"You might *not,*" interrupted the librarian, bristling at the offense. "That's not the way we do things around here! This is the third floor. Deeds and titles. You're free to roam the stacks downstairs, but it's trained hands only up here."

"Really? I've gotten my own things here before."

"Things have changed," said the librarian. "You can tell me what you need, you can leave of the power of your own two feet, or I can ring this bell and have Thorgrim escort you out."

Sloot didn't imagine that he and anyone named "Thorgrim" would agree on the specifics of what an "escort" would entail, so he didn't push the issue. He didn't want to leave empty-handed either, so that only left one choice. He needed to know more about a few fishy-sounding companies and addresses that he'd read in the counting house, so he wrote the names on a scrap of paper and handed it over.

It was a good thing that Sloot wasn't in a hurry. The librarian had several tries at holding the scrap of paper at various distances with one hand, while peering at it through different monocles held in the other. Sloot had time to wonder how awful it must be for a librarian to have so much difficulty reading. He felt sorry for the old man.

"You have the penmanship of a child," remarked the librarian. "The wild animal who taught you should be put down at once!"

"I'm sorry," Sloot replied, feeling slightly less charitable. "I could try again if you like. I've got some more paper just here—"

"No, it's fine," said the librarian, drawing out "no" and "fine" in a very musical way that implied it was anything but. He was holding a stack of three monocles now and had lit another pair of candles. He moved the paper closer ... closer ... and he stiffened.

"What do you want with these?"

"Just doing some fact-checking for Lord Hapsgalt." Sloot refrained from mentioning *which* Lord Hapsgalt. It was the same strategy he'd suggested to the kitchen staff when talking to the grocer.

"For ... Lord Hapsgalt?"

"That's right."

"And you ... know what these are?"

"Of course," said Sloot, who'd only just noticed the ring on the librarian's finger. Two silver snakes coiled around a black stone.

"Then why are you wasting my time? These will be down below."

"Down below?"

"I thought you said you'd been here before." The librarian was squinting at Sloot, which could have been suspicion, or perhaps he was just trying to focus. He had a fistful of monocles that were throwing off Sloot's perception.

"So you'd have me go down below on my own, then?" It stood to reason that the old man would be just as unreasonable about that, and he was right. He was the sort of man who, if on fire, would have precise criteria for men bearing buckets of water. As such, he insisted on personally marching Sloot down to a part of the library he'd never visited before. It was two floors below the ground, and the stone walls had a very "dungeony" aesthetic that filled Sloot with dread, whether they were designed for that purpose or not. They almost certainly were.

"Hello Susan," the old curmudgeon said to the hammer-wielding librarian posted outside a steel door with wicked gargoyles etched into it.

"Hello Stan!" shouted Susan. The veins in her neck bulged at the effort, though she had very little neck showing through the entourage of muscles surrounding it.

"For the last time, I'm not deaf! Here, he needs to go inside." The old man jerked a thumb toward Sloot, then started walking back up the stairs without another word.

*He has the sort of interpersonal skills that would have taken him far as a bureaucrat,* Sloot thought.

"Name?"

Sloot hadn't been prepared for that. He was supposed to be lying low! Roman hadn't taught him anything about subterfuge or secret identities yet, but he was reasonably sure that giving one's real name would poorly service the effort.

"Bannister," answered Sloot, blurting out the first thing he saw. "Er, Roger Bannister. Ma'am."

"Papers." Susan held out a hand so rough there might have been a few loose coins lodged between the calluses.

"Well," said Sloot, who lacked papers with the name "Roger Bannister" on them, "I don't exactly—"

"Papers."

Susan's monotone insistence on the point implied that she was the sort of person who didn't ask for things a third time. Some bestial, primordial part of Sloot that knows only instinct sprang into action. Unfortunately for Sloot, the instinct that drew itself up from within him was obedience. He handed over his papers.

"Wait here." Susan lumbered through a smaller door in the wall opposite the big scary ones, and Sloot was left alone to panic.

What had he done? He'd given a fake name! He'd handed over his real papers! He didn't like his chances that there was someone older than Stan looking them over just then, who'd run out of monocles and decided "no one would be stupid enough to come down here if they didn't belong, much less give a fake name. Let him through, and offer him some tea, would you?"

He should run. There were real instincts at work now, older and simpler than the ones that govern things like obedience and hygiene. They'd know he was guilty if he ran, but so what? They were about to realize he was guilty anyway! He was as skilled a runner as most newborns, but at least when they caught him he'd not have to ask himself why he stood there, stock still, waiting for death like a—

"Mr. Bannister, is it?"

"Yes! No. What?"

"Imagine my surprise," said Imelda Lillellien, the head librarian in a hushed voice, "when Susan told me that the most notorious assassin in the ranks of our order was waiting outside the sanctum door!"

Sloot said nothing. Either this was a bizarre mind game, or the fake name he'd given—by some stroke of outrageous fortune—had some fortuitous significance among The Really Wicked Spiders that just might result in his blood remaining inside his body, whizzing around a full set of intact bones!

"Forgive me," said Imelda, "I don't mean to pry, it's just that … well, have you *ever* given your name outside the Shadow Chamber?"

"It's a long story," said Sloot.

"Never mind." Imelda waved her hands. "We shouldn't be talking out here, anyway. Please, allow me. Susan?"

Susan put her shoulder to the door and heaved. The steel hinges groaned, and the door opened into the darkness beyond it. Sloot followed Imelda inside, and his heart sank into his chest as Susan pulled the door closed behind them with a grunt. The darkness enveloped them.

"Have you ever entered this way before?" asked Imelda.

"I haven't," answered Sloot. It felt good, telling the truth.

"Your eyes will adjust in a moment," she said. "While we wait, do you mind if I ask … Sloot Peril?"

"Yes?"

"Well, in addition to being a superb set of fake papers, that name happens to belong to one of the pawns that Mrs. Knife has placed in the game."

"Is it?"

"Financier to the younger Lord Hapsgalt. Of course, you must have known that already! But why take an alias of someone in the public eye? And a name that sounds so *Carpathian.* Aren't you afraid it will give you away?"

"Er, hiding in plain sight." Sloot didn't know what sort of game in which he was a pawn, but it didn't sound good. He blinked a few times, and a greenish glow started to flood into what turned out to be the very long hallway in which they were standing.

"Marvelous." Imelda's silhouette was handing him the silhouette of his papers, which he took and shoved into his coat. "This way."

Imelda led him toward what only could have been his grisly death, and he could not but follow. He couldn't tell where the green light was coming from. It just sort of oozed in from between the stones in the walls, casting a glow of despair on all of the nothing around them. It was precisely the sort of ambiance one might expect from a place perfectly embodying the absence of hope, warmth, and cheer. Well done, if that's what they were after.

They made several turns and passed several doors on either side of the hallway. The ghastly green light was far brighter through the cracks in most of them, except for the one that was entirely dark. That's not to say that there was simply no light within it — it was *entirely* dark. It gave Sloot the impression that no light could survive within it, not even the metaphorical sort that lived in the hearts of children and kittens. He wasn't monster enough to even wonder how a kitten might fare in a room like that.

"Here we are," said Imelda at last, her silhouette motioning toward a door that had ghastly green light within it, thankfully. "Please take as long as you like, and give Lord Hapsgalt my compliments. I assume you can show yourself out?"

"Er, yes, thanks."

"The pleasure is mine! If you leave the way we came in, just bang on the door and Susan will open it for you."

Imelda took a key from her belt, unlocked the door, and opened it. Then she gave a little bow, backed into the shadows, and was gone.

It was just what Sloot would have expected from the subterranean archive of a clandestine society whose nefarious ends he couldn't begin to fathom. Why wouldn't there be smoke roiling from within that book next to some perfectly normal land records? There was a book on the shelf below it that gave a constant, baleful moan, as though it desperately wished someone would end its life, wedged between two volumes of romantic poetry. It didn't seem out of place at all when one considered the vaguely human-shaped lump under the bloodstained sheet on the floor that twitched every so often.

Honestly, if the sourceless green glow that illuminated the room had failed to send Sloot screaming from it as fast as his legs would carry him, why should a few malevolent terrors succeed in its stead?

Context. Why should any of these horrible things inspire any more dread than the place itself? Sloot suppressed his palpable urge to scream at the top of his lungs, mustered up all of the context he could in lieu of courage, and set to work.

He found the records he sought, and they told him exactly what he thought they would: Mrs. Knife and all of the other Really Wicked Spiders were part of a secret society calling itself The Serpents of the Earth, and the Hapsgalts and The Three Bells made up its black and odious core.

While Sloot thought his name for them was better, he really hadn't anticipated just how nefarious they were. They held a lot of sway in Salzstadt and beyond, and their membership included just about everybody who could afford a street named after them (that is to say, those who can afford the *street,* not just the name).

It did nothing to soothe Sloot's nerves to find several mentions of assassinations performed by one Mr. Roger Bannister, whose face is known to no one else in the society.

Until today. Sort of.

He rifled through several other books and found a passage that mentioned how the Serpents of the Earth handle changes in leadership. Constantin had told Willie that he'd have to render proof of his worth to inherit the Three Bells, and here was the same phrase: "Whomsoever

Woulde Rule o'er The Serpentes of the Earthe Neede Render Proofe ov Their Worthe." Just how tightly were the Three Bells and the Serpents of the Earth linked?

He didn't find anything specific with regard to the connection between Mrs. Knife and Myrtle, but he wanted to leave as quickly as possible before someone more discerning figured out that he wasn't who he was pretending to be.

He wondered, hopefully, if lacking an innate sense of direction was grounds for dismissal from the spy business, because he left the room and was immediately lost. The most natural thing to do would be to leave the way he'd come in, but he had about the same odds of retracing his steps as building a ship and sailing it out.

Wait … had he ingurgitated it? There had been a lot going on, but perhaps he could rely on what little spy training he'd received so far.

"Think, Peril," he said to himself, then wondered if that had ever worked for anybody.

He relaxed his mind, thought back. It was all there! Every twist and turn! Bless Roman, he was going to be able to do it!

He started to the right, then turned left, left, and right again. It was no good, none of it was looking familiar.

What Roman had failed to tell Sloot was the role that trust plays in ingurgitation. If you start questioning whether this bit or that bit actually happened the way you remember, the whole thing just sort of falls apart. That's how Sloot ended up at a dead end, where he was sure there should have been an intersection.

Could he retrace his steps to the horrible library and try again? Not if he questioned the second ingurgitation he compiled while trying to follow the first one. After a few minutes, he found himself wandering the hallways in sickly green near-darkness, as far from anywhere as he was from where he stood.

The only thing that he could do then was to start walking, abandon all pretense of making educated guesses, and hope that he eventually came to an exit. He assumed a walking posture that said he knew exactly where he was, which turned out to be a passable imitation of the then-fashionable strut called The Great Ghost of Derry Bottom, though Sloot didn't know it at the time.

He tried a few doors. Some were locked. Some opened into inky blackness. The contents of one caused Sloot to scream out a swear word that sent a pair of goblins scampering back the way he'd come, or at least the way he thought he'd come.

At last, he opened a door and daylight blinded him. He was in an alley between a couple of buildings, and thankfully, no one was around. He closed the door behind him and walked away as quickly as he felt he could without attracting any attention.

How long had he been down there? It was mid-morning when he'd arrived at the library. He looked at his watch. The sun would set soon.

There was a pub nearby, one he'd never been in before. That should be good for lying low, he reckoned. He'd have a few pints and wait for nightfall. Yeah, that sounded like what a spy on the lam might do.

※〒※〒※〒※〒

Between not having slept for nearly two days and the strength of the pints at his new favorite pub, it was all that Sloot could do to stumble back across town to his apartment. Sure, he was supposed to be lying low, but wouldn't anyone looking for him assume that he'd be living at Whitewood? It was just that sort of thinking that left him entirely at a loss for what to say to Mrs. Knife when he found her sitting at his table in the darkness.

"Well, well, well," said Mrs. Knife in a passable imitation of pleasantry, "you were slightly more difficult to track down than I would have thought, Mister Peril … or should I say, *Mister Bannister?*"

The game was up. Overthinking his response wasn't going to get the job done, so in a wanton fit of improvisation, Sloot decided to do the opposite and *underthink* it. He put on his most affable smile and was walking toward the kitchen before he had a chance to wonder what he'd do when he got there.

"Coffee, Mrs. Knife?"

"No," she growled. "Sit down, Peril. We have things to discuss, you and I."

"I'd rather not." Sloot opened the cupboards and spied the coffee on the top shelf. As he reached for it, he heard a noise that was barely a whisper, like a breeze stirring up leaves. He was distracted from his inability to think of how he might get out of this when he suddenly found himself falling.

There was a swift and sudden impact with the floorboards. That was unpleasant on its own, but there was something else too. Something on the left side of his body, very near his heart.

"What you'd rather," said Mrs. Knife, suddenly close enough for Sloot to feel the heat of her breath and smell the onions on it, "will make a fitting epitaph for you, Mister Peril. You know too much, and you refuse to listen to reason. I'm afraid there's only one proper way to address this situation."

"I'm sure there's been some kind of misunderstanding," Sloot would have said, and did in fact try, though all he managed was a gurgle and cough that produced an alarming amount of blood.

"I'd tell you to save your strength," Mrs. Knife continued, "but you have no need of it." She chuckled, amused at her own wit. "I really thought I'd coaxed the whole truth out of you the other day, Peril. I must say, I'm impressed! I never thought a sniveling weakling like you could accomplish so much, but then I heard you'd been snooping around in the counting house. And *then* I had the most interesting conversation with Imelda Lillellien."

Sloot tried to take a breath, but his lungs were filling with blood.

"Pity all of that blood going to waste. I've got no talent with blood magic myself, should have brought Gregor along. Oh, well." She took Sloot's favorite dish towel from the rod by the sink and used it to clean her bloody knife. "I imagine Roger Bannister will change his name when he hears about this. Really, kudos on that one!"

Sloot gurgled again.

"And to think, I thought you were secretly working for Carpathian Intelligence! You hired their spymaster as Willie's valet, did you know that? You're either incredibly smart or incredibly stupid. In either case, the last words you're ever going to hear have been redacted due to their filthiness."

Except instead of that last bit, Mrs. Knife clearly enunciated a vile phrase that alluded to some very antiquated ideas about foreigners, which would only ever be repeated by the most despicable sort of villain. Sloot was sure that he heard the sound of corn popping in an oily skillet, which was followed by the cackling of an entire congress of goblins.

It was freezing in his apartment, except for the warm, wet spot very near his heart where Mrs. Knife's knife had been. The room was going dark, which was an odd thing to occur so early in the morning. He heard, in a very muffled sort of way that sounded like someone had stuffed wool into his ears, what sounded like a box of matches falling to the ground.

Goblins cackled, matches flared bright, and Mrs. Knife smiled cruelly back at him as her shoes went *clack, clack, clack* toward the door.

## ❧⚜CALAMITY HO!⚜❧

"Mr. Peril?"

"Ugh," said Sloot. The effort burned his throat like he imagined gargling poison and broken glass would. His eyes were closed, and he was afraid to open them. "Am I dead?"

"You got closer than the Ministry of Health advises," replied a breathy, musical voice that Sloot wanted to curl up into and sleep forever. "Can you open your eyes?"

He gave it a go, relieved that he was still in control of the muscles involved in the maneuver, at any rate. Once his eyes adjusted to the very bright light in the entirely white room, he found that he was sitting in an overstuffed chair and facing a very lovely blonde woman in a white dress. She was smiling at him.

It struck Sloot as funny that he's never known what to do when beautiful women smile at him, funnier still that he was more concerned with that than how he came to be neither bled nor burnt to death in his apartment.

"Ow," said Sloot, having become aware of his body.

"We've sewn you up as best we could," said the woman. "You'll need time to heal. It's a pity you've got to set out for Carpathia right away."

The sole benefit of his near-death experience had been snuffing out his resting rate of dread altogether; he hadn't even noticed until the mention of the word "Carpathia" sent it from nothing to full frenzied terror in an instant.

"What? No! Who are you? I don't—"

"It's all right," she said. "My name is Flavia, and I'm here to help!" She smiled at him again, the sort of warm and caring smile that used her whole face. Her eyes twinkled a bit, in a way that Sloot didn't imagine they could if the brain behind them were plotting something grisly. He relaxed at that, but only insofar as he was capable of forgetting that he was helpless. He hovered around what medical professionals would call "the verge of hysterics."

"I can tell you're a gentle sort of person," said Flavia. "I was right about you."

"Right about me? In what way?"

"I think you're just the sort of person we need working with us."

"And who are you? In the plural sense, I mean."

"Uncle."

Having recently been stabbed so close to his heart, Sloot wasn't altogether sure that he should get it up and racing at that speed. A man came into the room, set a bucket at Sloot's feet, and left.

"You mean … *Uncle,* Uncle?"

"That's right."

This felt much more real than his usual nightmare about Uncle knowing that he was involved with Carpathian Intelligence. Everything was more vivid. Aside from that, the only real differences were that he had a stab wound and that he wasn't naked.

Sloot vomited. It was the only reaction anyone could have expected under the circumstances, and in fact, they had. The bucket was taken away as Sloot wondered how they knew about Carpathia, and how *much* they knew.

"I—"

"Don't," she said with a gentle smile. "If you deny that you've been recruited as an enemy agent, I'll have to assume that you're more dedicated to their cause than ours, and things will take a turn for the worse."

"Oh," said Sloot. "I mean, I wasn't going to—"

"Yes, you were. Your instinct for self-preservation would naturally compel you. I can't fault that, but there are rules, you see. Those rules have robbed us of dozens of would-be agents over the years, so we'd be ever so grateful if you kept your defenses to yourself for now."

"Would-be agents? So you want me to join up with Uncle?"

"Precisely."

Sloot's face lit up like he was five years old, and he'd just awoken on the first day of Snugglewatch. This was a dream come true! He'd gotten in over his head with foreign intrigue, and he was being offered absolution!

"Oh, thank you!" he exclaimed, unable to hold back his tears. "I promise I'll be vigilant day and night. I'll be the most dedicated Uncle you've ever had!"

"I have no doubt," said Flavia.

"What happens next? Do I get a sword? I'll need to learn to use one, I'd imagine. I'll practice—"

"No, no, no." Flavia shook her head. "You're already exactly what we need you to be! Just get back to Whitewood, and don't let Mrs. Knife find out you're still alive. We need to keep that a secret for as long as possible."

"But I thought—"

"That we'd give you a secret mission? Have you assassinate someone?"

"Something like that, yes."

"You're an inside man, Mister Peril. We just need you to be who you are. Do you think you can manage that?"

"Probably. I'm not entirely sure what that means."

"You don't know what it means to be yourself?"

"I did a few weeks ago."

"What happened a few weeks ago?"

"Vasily Pritygud wrote a report."

"You're lucky," said Roman.

"Lucky? I was stabbed!"

"And you lived to tell the tale! I've been stitched up in Salzstadt's miserable excuse for a hospital before. I wouldn't trust most of those 'doctors' to lace up a boot properly."

Sloot had been sparse with the details of his near-death experience. People don't question a hazy memory when you've got a nice stab wound to go with it. He wasn't looking forward to riding a horse with a chest full of stitches, but he supposed he should have thought of that before he went and got himself stabbed.

"Sunset," said Roman. "Everything's arranged, we've just got to get Greta on the way out."

"Where are the permits?"

"Didn't need them for Nordheim, did we? I told you, it's all arranged! Come on, let's get moving."

Sloot groaned. He still hated the idea of breaking the law, though getting out of Salzstadt was starting to sound like a good idea. It would be difficult for him to explain why he wasn't dead if anyone were to ask.

*Some Carpathian I am,* he mused. A real Carpathian wouldn't have any trouble with sneaking out of Salzstadt without a signed form, would they? According to his elementary school teacher, they wouldn't have any objections to eating babies or spitting on sidewalks either.

Did Carpathians even pretend to adhere to a moral code, or were posts on their Council of Etiquette handed out to whichever of their battle lords had collected the most ears and noses, along with a mandate to do nothing so long as they were in office?

Sunsets in Salzstadt were unpredictable mélanges of purples, oranges, and the occasional green that most of the city's grans insisted meant goblins. The city council had a long-standing committee for sunset reform, but they'd not yet been able to force any sort of order upon it.

They walked under a purpling sky. The brisk pace caused some uncomfortable tugging at Sloot's stitches. Fortunately (or unfortunately, depending on your perspective), Sloot was far too preoccupied with the lack of permits to pay it much notice.

"What's the name of the guard we're supposed to bribe?"

"Better just let me handle it," said Roman. "You maintain some of that plausible deniability, it might come in handy."

"Nobody said anything about bribery," said Nan, who'd crept closer than Sloot realized. "What are you involving Willie in, anyway? He's a Hapsgalt, by the Domnitor's eyes! There's going to be a scandal!"

"Long may he reign," Sloot mumbled out of habit.

"Hello," said Willie, slowing down to join the conversation, now that it seemed to be about him. "I heard my name. It's true, I am a Hapsgalt. I don't like to brag, but there it is."

"Yes, Willie," said Roman, "we know. Are you sure that neckerchief goes with that cape?"

"You might not think so at first glance," Willie gave a wink and a waggle of his finger, "but there's a little-known principle about cost ratios, and how they allow you to break all the known rules of fashion. Technically, this neckerchief is expensive enough to go with anything."

"That should keep him busy," said Roman, loud enough to be heard but soft enough to avoid interrupting Willie's droning on about how little the very, very rich are accountable for understanding things.

"Look you," Roman continued, waggling a finger at Nan, "do you want Willie to inherit the Three Bells or not? We're trying to satisfy old Constantin's demands here, and Mrs. Knife stands to inherit in his place if we fail. She'd never sign a permit for Willie!"

"Just so," said Nan, "Willie can't be caught breaking the law. He's too young for jail! Do they make jails for little boys?"

"The constabulary cells have never seen a highborn heir in all of Salzstadt's history, and that's not going to change over a permit. Constantin won't let it."

"Greta's house is this way," said Sloot.

"Greta," said Nan, "you mean that cradle-robbing hussy is coming, too?"

"She's nearly ten years younger than Willie," replied Sloot.

"What? That's ridiculous! She must be thirty!"

"She's more important to this expedition than you are," said Roman.

"Remember, you're being allowed to tag along because you pleaded with Mister Peril. Are you going to be nice?"

"All's I'm saying—"

"Hey, isn't this the way to Greta's house?" Willie must have finished his treatise on the bearing of wealth on fashion and started paying attention to where he was walking.

"It is," answered Sloot, who thought they'd have more time before he realized.

"We have to go back home," said Willie.

"What? Why?"

Willie rolled his eyes and stomped his foot. "Haven't you been listening? These are *expedition* shoes! I can't very well turn up at my fiancée's house in them. There are very specific heel heights that are appropriate for unannounced trysts, and two-and-a-quarter inches is not among them!"

"This isn't a tryst," said Roman. "Your fiancée is coming along on the expedition."

"Really? Well, then we *definitely* have to go back home, I've got a whole series of cravats—"

"Don't worry," said Roman. "Nan knew all about it, and she's packed for you accordingly. Haven't you, Nan?" The question was delivered with all the subtlety of a clay pot filled with hornets aimed directly at her face.

"Oh, fine." Nan slumped into a competition-grade sulk.

"Oh good," said Willie. "Now, where's the best lighting?"

"What?"

"I need to be standing in favorable light when you knock! Honestly, have you never courted a woman?"

"Have *you*?" asked Sloot.

"I beg your pardon?" Willie's hands were on his hips in a flash. All the years he'd spent in prep school practicing his *well-I-never* expressions had really paid off.

"Er, I mean, have *I*? Sorry, I was just clarifying who you were talking to."

An expression of confusion carried out a very successful coup to supplant Willie's outrage and seized control of his face.

"The gaslamp across the street," said Roman.

"Thank you, Roman," said Willie. "Was that so hard?"

Sloot waited several minutes until Willie had decided on the pose that best suited his cape length. He ultimately went with a modified Dimples on a Daffodil, leaning gently against the lamp pole, but not so much as to seem haughty about it.

*Knock, knock.* The door swung open immediately.

"I was wondering how long it was going to take him to get that pose just right," said Greta. "I'll give him credit though, it comes off a lot less haughty than I'd have expected. Who's this?"

"This is Nan," Sloot replied. "Nan is Willie's—"

"Seamstress," interrupted Roman.

"Seamstress? Why would Willie need a seamstress for a trip to Carp—"

"Fishing!" exclaimed Sloot. "Carp fishing can be very hard on the linens, am I right?"

"Carp fishing?" Nan questioned. "This time of year?"

"Why don't you go help Willie?" said Roman. "That was a very complex pose, and he seems to be having some trouble on the dismount."

"Coming, Willie!"

"Not so loud about our destination *up north*," said Sloot after Nan was out of earshot. "You never know who's listening!"

"I'm sure I'd know if Uncle was within earshot," said Greta. Sloot Peril, newly-enlisted agent of Uncle, tried very hard to act naturally and failed into a fit of tittering. Luckily, people expect accountants to be a bit off.

"All the same," said Roman, "better to avoid mentioning it to Nan at all."

"Won't she figure it out eventually?"

"We'll worry about that when it happens."

Greta shrugged. "She'll be upset about having lugged the fishing gear all the way to— *up north*, but I guess that's your problem. Let's get this over with."

Greta shouldered a canvas travel bag and locked the door behind her. Nan brought Willie over. He was grinning like an idiot. To be fair, that was the only way he knew how.

"You two behave yourselves," Nan scowled. "I'll be watching you every minute, so there will be no hanky-panky. Am I clear?"

"Fine," said Willie.

"Thank you," said Greta with a broad smile.

※ ♪ ※ ♪ ※ ♪ ※ ♪

They made it to the east gate with no trouble, and Roman managed the bribery with an ease that suggested it wasn't his first time. That didn't surprise Sloot, though it also didn't do anything to quell the maelstrom in his stomach. He was openly consorting with people who dealt with bribery! What would his mother think?

He'd forgotten for a moment that his mother had been a Carpathian Intelligencier as well. He couldn't bring himself to wonder in horror at what the Domnitor, long may he reign, would have thought.

"Have you ever been outside the city, Greta?" asked Willie.

"No," she replied.

"I have." Willie smoothed down his pencil-thin moustache. "We went to Nordheim not too long ago. That's where I bought that mammoth you love so much."

"I see." Greta kept her eyes fixed on the ground in front of her.

"You're learning quickly," said Willie. "No cobbles on the streets in the wilderness, good to watch where you're— *Oof.*"

"Where you're oof?"

"Just testing my reflexes," said Willie as he picked himself off and brushed the dirt from his cape. "Fraught with danger, the wilderness. I thought I'd practice falling down just there, measure my recovery time. Er, Sloot, how'd I do?"

"Very well, m'lord."

"That was just *perfect*, Willie!" Nan ruffled his hair. Greta narrowly suppressed a chortle.

The road was dark, with only a thin crescent of the moon to guide them. They set up a little camp once they'd made it out of sight of the torches atop the city wall.

They started walking again in the morning, stopped briefly for lunch, and came eventually to a remote farmstead where Roman said Bob would leave them horses and provisions.

"Yer them salties what m'lady said would come," said the filth-encrusted yokel who greeted them at the gate, if you could call it a greeting. Or a gate.

An entire life in the city had exposed Sloot to a panoply of different greetings, ranging from tips of the hat with intricate flourishes that would only be fashionable for a week or so, all the way down to ill-rehearsed sneers that demanded whatever coin he had on him at knifepoint. This, by contrast, was little more than an acknowledgment of their presence. On their trip to Nordheim and back, Sloot had learned that country people tended to stick to facts. They had little interest in interpretations thereof, and reserved flowery displays of affection, such as handshakes, to immediate family, and then only on their birthdays.

"I'm Roman, and this is—"

"That's fine," said the yokel, rolling his eyes and walking toward a barn. Roman looked to Sloot and shrugged, and they all followed along.

The rest of the journey to Carpathia was relatively uneventful, with the exception of Willie's occasional yelps of surprise at seeing yet *more grass*.

"You just never get used to it," he kept saying. While it was true that there was rarely more than a few square feet of the stuff to be found in any one place inside the city, Sloot felt that he'd acclimated to the abundance of it with ease.

Then, after nearly a week of riding, the plenitude of grass started to wane.

"We're nearly there," said Roman, a hint of excitement in his voice. Sloot wondered how long it had been since he'd been home.

Grassy hills rolled into stony, barren fields. This was starting to look like the Carpathia that Sloot had been taught about as a boy. His hyper-vigilant sense of worry began to see danger lurking behind every boulder, death over every steep incline on the horizon.

By the time that the last of the grass disappeared, the afternoon had given way to evening and an ominous red sky. This was *definitely* the Carpathia he'd learned about as a boy, and he started hyperventilating as his oldest fears gripped him.

*Was* a cannibal lurking behind that boulder, sharpening his long knife in anticipation of gutting Sloot and making a turban of his intestines? Would he have an extra row of teeth like in the pictures, and stink lines coming off his head, and would he be waving a flag made of human skin that says "The Domnitor Is A Ninny" like in his nightmares?

By the time the sun was nearly down and the ominous shadow of Castle Ulfhaven loomed into view, Sloot was having trouble deciding whether he was relieved that there had been no cannibals, or unsettled by the possibility that nothing he knew about Carpathia might be true.

## ⋙⋙HEART OF CARPATHIA⋘⋘

The first bloodthirsty savages they encountered were at a farmstead not unlike the one just outside Salzstadt where they'd gotten the horses. The proprietors here were also yokels by trade, and equally disinterested in conversation that deviated from simple facts. The only notable cultural difference was the uniquely Carpathian surname on the gate: *Entrailravager.*

Sloot was still doing his best to come to grips with his recently discovered Carpathian heritage. It helped to see that yokels were more or less the same in both countries, but he still wasn't able to get past the ominous surnames thing. Was he really to believe that the Entrailravager family were as unlikely to consider him for their stew as your run-of-the-mill Old Country yokels?

Old Man Entrailravager led them all into the barn, where Sloot mostly managed to refrain from pleading for his life. The proprietor refrained from reassuring Sloot, owing to the fact that he hadn't seen any proper whimpering in quite a long time, if his gleeful giggle was any measure.

Once Old Man Entrailravager retired to the house, they watered the horses and minimized their packs for the five-mile hike to Ulfhaven. This caused Sloot to wonder if the most challenging part of sneaking into Ulfhaven would be explaining to Willie the concept of *need.*

Convincing him that there would be no parties requiring dancing left him with a hangdog look, as well as thirty pounds lighter for all of the shoes left in the barn. Further convincing him that there would be no parties *at all* nearly left the entire expedition several hundred pounds lighter, to the tune of Willie's remaining gear and Willie himself, but Roman convinced him to stay the course.

Eventually, under cover of darkness, they set out on foot. Sloot jogged ahead to walk with Roman, who'd opted to scout ahead.

"What's your surname, Roman?" he asked.

"Didn't I tell you it's classified?"

"You did," said Sloot, "but I've been promoted since then."

"I've forgotten it."

"You've forgotten your own surname?"

"It's been a long time since I've used it. Anyway, it's probably long since expired."

"Oh, come on," said Sloot. "Surnames don't expire, they outlive us all. It's the way they're designed, isn't it?"

"Fine! I remember it, I just don't want you getting the wrong idea."

"What wrong idea?"

"I know what they teach you in those salt schools," Roman spat. "Everyone from Carpathia is some sort of wild barbarian! We don't pray to the right gods when we offer up blood sacrifices, and we murder people for grammatical infractions. What would it change for you to know my surname, anyway? Have you ever seen me raise a fist in anger?"

"Well, no," said Sloot, who was worried that even talking about fists might cause the ears of any nearby goblins to perk up. "But how am I ever to learn about my mother culture if my mentor won't teach me?"

"Mentor, eh?" That made him grin and swell. "All right, fine ... but don't go telling any of the others, all right? It's still classified."

"My lips are sealed."

"It's Bloodfrenzy."

"Oh, that's lovely." Sloot repressed a shudder. "What's it mean?"

"It comes from an old Middle Carpathian word that describes the gentle elation of—"

"Yes?"

Roman sighed. "Of having blood all over you and going sort of ... very ... *enthusiastic* on the battlefield."

"Right," said Sloot. "That's not so bad, I suppose."

A silence of the uncomfortable variety settled in between them.

"See? This is why I didn't want to tell you."

"What?"

"You know very well, what! You'll be glancing over your shoulder at me now, thinking 'oh look, there's that savage Roman, good thing he hasn't got blood on him, or I might be in for a keelhauling!'"

"I will not," said Sloot. "What's a keelhauling?"

"Enough education for one day!"

They walked the rest of the road in silence. When they finally came close enough to see the great stone wall surrounding Ulfhaven, Sloot couldn't help comparing it to the one that sat along the northern boundary of Salzstadt. He might have mistaken one for the other, if not for the ghastly swarm of gargoyles atop this one. There were lots of rusted steel spikes as well, and the stony ground in front of it was littered with the weathered bones of the long-dead.

But they were both tall and made primarily of stone. In that, they were very similar.

His idle thoughts were inclined to find other similarities between Ulfhaven and Salzstadt, so Sloot elected to stop thinking altogether. Idle thoughts lead to heretical ones. Everybody knows that.

"Here we are," said Roman at last. They'd come to a spiky steel gate at the base of the wall, several hundred feet away from the main gate and obscured by the clever piling of boulders. He produced a rusty key from under his shirt, which was hanging from a length of twine around his neck. He fit it into the lock and gave it a creaking turn that ended in a *click*.

Once inside, Sloot felt the familiar slipperiness of wet cobbles beneath his feet. They inched slowly into inky blackness until there was no hint of light visible from beyond the gate, then Roman paused and lit a torch. They were in a sort of arched tunnel, all stoned in with cobbles underfoot.

"Where are we?" asked Greta.

"The Catacombs of Ulfhaven," answered Roman.

"That's not possible," said Nan. "Those are in Carpathia."

It was at that moment that Sloot realized there was a part of the journey for which he'd neglected to prepare. He stayed quiet, hoping against hope that this would somehow resolve itself.

It seemed that everyone else had the same idea, and the result was one of those deafening silences that could only be made worse by a fight breaking out, which was more or less what happened.

All of a sudden, Nan rushed past Sloot, and he saw the shadow of her foot colliding with Roman's backside. He went sprawling forward, landing hard against the slick cobbles. The torch went clattering into the tunnel ahead of them, ending up in a puddle and fizzling out.

"You curling fletch!" Nan shouted, clearly never having said a swear word in her life, but having decided to take full advantage of the fact that she was out of goblin earshot. "You apple-polishing pair of spectacles! You've lured my Willikins into corking *Carpathia?* I'll wrench down your lying throat and schlepp your reeking guts from your gob!"

There was an impressive scuffle, in the midst of which Sloot was certain he felt an open hand strike him across the mouth. Such incivility! They definitely weren't in Salzstadt anymore.

"That's enough!" The sounds of the scuffle ceased instantly at the boom of Willie's voice, apparently the first time it had done so. A match flared from behind them, and Willie's torch shed its light over the tangle of arms and legs that had been dragged down fighting with Roman and Nan.

"Willie," said Nan, "where'd you get matches? You know you're not allowed—"

"This is *my expedition*," he said with a thunder Sloot didn't think he had in him. "I'm scared of Carpathia, too, but Mister Roman says it'll be safe, and I believe him! He also said that we couldn't tell you where we were going, Nan, or that something like this would happen. I believe him on that one too, because look what happened!"

"Willie—"

"No!" Willie stamped his foot. Though he'd taken that tone with Sloot on several occasions before, it was impressive to see him using it to stand up to Nan. "I say we're going to Carpathia! I'm Wilhelm Hapsgalt, intrepid explorer, and I've got to have something to talk to Sir Wallace about when I invite him over for an explorers' lunch!"

While the content of Willie's newfound assertiveness was cringeworthy, Sloot cringed the hardest at the possibility of a squadron of guards overhearing all of the shouting. Of all the series of events he'd ever worried might end with him rotting in a Carpathian dungeon, Nan's swearing and Willie's standing up for himself had never crossed his mind.

Fortunately, during the stunned silence that followed Willie's righteous tantrum, Sloot noticed two things: a complete absence of jackbooted footsteps coming their way, and Greta looking up at Willie from her recumbent position in the pile, her face a mixture of curiosity and admiration.

Roman seemed sure that a proper romance between Willie and Greta would be helpful in securing Willie's inheritance. Was this why he wanted her to come to Carpathia with them? He fancied himself a good judge of character, perhaps he knew that Willie would rise to the occasion, and that Greta would respond to that sort of thing?

Then, unbidden from some cockle of his heart, Sloot thought of Myrtle. He hadn't seen or heard from her since the unpleasantness at Whitewood. If Roman was such an excellent judge of character, why had that business gone so poorly?

"Get up," demanded Willie, "all of you. I'm going into Carpathia with Mister Roman. Who's coming with us?"

"I suppose I must," said Sloot.

"I've come this far," said Greta.

"Nan?"

"Oh, all right," Nan muttered. "I can't very well let you go in there without your Nan, can I? Who'll cut your sandwiches the way you like?"

After winding their way through a seemingly infinite maze of passageways, they emerged from the catacombs through a grate and walked out onto the cobbled streets of Ulfhaven. There were torches here instead of gaslamps, but it was otherwise very similar to the streets of Salzstadt. Fewer people though. None, to be precise.

The torches were all set in fixtures that were made to look like skulls. They may have *been* skulls, but that would have required contributions from lots and lots of people, or those who had formerly been. Sloot preferred to believe that it was the clever work of highly skilled stonemasons. That was obviously true of the gargoyles that loomed from the top of everything, so it wasn't stretching the imagination in a way that would require yoga.

Suddenly curious to test a theory, Sloot uttered a curse word. One of the bad ones. He listened carefully.

Roman was right! No goblins in Carpathia. Not so much as a single pop-and-cackle. He might have felt bad if Roman had been wrong, but not terribly. A few goblins would serve them right, the stinking barbarians.

"Careful," warned Roman. "We'd do best to steer clear of the watch, you know."

They shuffled from shadow to shadow, most of them cast by torchlight in the shape of a gargoyle. They saw and heard no one at all as they wound their way through the narrow streets.

Salzstadt had some narrow ones, too, closer to the city center. The buildings that lined them had been built over a thousand years prior when people were smaller, and before they had a Domnitor to enforce nutrition standards, long may he reign.

"Shhh." Roman put a hand up as he came to the edge of a building, then turned around and beckoned them all to gather in closer.

"We're here," he whispered. A chill ran up Sloot's back. "This is the city square. The clock is just on the other side, so we'll have to make our way 'round. Quietly, now."

They backtracked a few paces, and Roman led them down an alley that seemed to have been designed for the singular purpose of giving constables a place to discover murder victims.

They ducked under a low arch, climbed a narrow staircase flanked by snarling stone wolves, walked across a makeshift bridge over a canal, and tiptoed through a little garden between the backs of two tenement buildings.

"Be quiet through the garden," Roman had warned them. "Fairies live in nearly all of the gardens in the city, and they can be more dangerous than the goblins in Salzstadt."

"Humbug," said Willie. "I'll give you odds on your fairies any day! Is there a betting arena where we can settle this?"

"Now's not the time for civic pride," said Greta. "Let's keep going, I want to see the clock."

"Clock? What clock?"

"The big one in the square," replied Roman. "The one you wanted to show Greta, remember?"

Willie wore an expression that clearly showed he remembered no such thing.

"The reason she agreed to come along in the first place?"

Still nothing.

"Such a gesture would go a long way in showing your *fiancée* the depth of your affection for her," said Sloot.

"Oh," Willie exclaimed, "right! Well, what are we waiting for? Let's show the lady a clock! Who cares how boring that is if it's what she wants?"

Through the garden they went, then came another series of alleys, arches, an access tunnel under a building that seemed to be abandoned, and a tight passage between a hedgerow and the back of some sort of memorial wall that had names etched into the front of it. All of the names were "Vlad."

Sloot was impressed with Roman's knowledge of the city, especially given that he'd spent so much of his life in Salzstadt. He could have a promising career as a tour guide in either city if the intelligence game dried up; or in both, if the Domnitor and Vlad the Invader decided to stop burying the hatchet in each other.

Through all of it, they encountered not a single person. Between the late hour and having kept off the main streets, it wasn't that surprising. Sloot wondered if there was some sort of curfew though, as Salzstadt would have provided at least one angry drunk, hard at work, cursing the stars for twinkling too brightly or somesuch. He could only assume that Ulfhaven drunks held themselves to a lesser work ethic.

And then, as though it had managed to sneak up on them, there it was. The Great Clock Tower of Ulfhaven. Still, dark and quiet, and festooned with more gargoyles than eyes on a fly.

"It's gorgeous," said Greta.

"I knew you'd think so," said Willie. "I picked it out especially for you."

"What?"

"He's just nervous," said Roman.

They hurried over to a little door in the side of the tower, where Roman used a key to open the lock.

"Was that the same key you used at the catacomb gate?" Sloot asked once they were safely inside.

"Of course," Roman replied. "It's my key to the city. You'll need to be an Intelligencier for another ten years or so, but you can earn one, too, if you play your cards right!"

"Great," said Sloot. In they went, Willie and Nan following Greta up the little spiral staircase. The bottom floor was bare except for a few crates. One of them was open, and Sloot saw a few gears and levers—replacement parts, probably—packed in straw. There was also a family of mice who'd made their home there. Sloot gave them a wide berth, his innate fear of all things Carpathian warning him that they were as likely to leap for his jugular as make cute little preening gestures with their human-like hands.

As Sloot climbed the spiral stair with Roman in tow, he heard Greta exploring the inner workings of the clock with delight.

"I'm not sure what that lever does—no, Willie, don't touch it—it probably engages the main gear configuration. Oh, look! I've never seen a system of counterweights set up like this before! Well, they would be, wouldn't they? If you stacked your cogs in sequence like that."

"She keeps going on about these weird metal things," said Willie. "They're boring. You're not allowed to play with any of them! I don't see the point."

"These are what make the clock work," Sloot explained.

"I doubt it," said Willie. "All a clock needs are a pair of arms and a bunch of numbers. Sometimes there's a third arm, a little one that gets to run around while the other ones have to stand still."

"I see ..." Sloot tried to draw Willie away from Greta.

Roman was missing. *Where could he have gone?* Of all the people to go missing while they were in dangerous territory, Roman was the one Sloot worried about the most. He shuddered at the thought of leaving anyone behind in this lair of heresy and violence, but without Roman, he'd have no way to find his way back to Salzstadt to spend the rest of his life swallowing the guilt of having left Nan—or whomever—to the wolves.

Sloot looked up into the darkness of the tower, which was occasionally broken by little shards of moonlight from the diamond-paned windows running up the back wall. It really was a magnificent machine, though Sloot couldn't begin to fathom why most of the bits were there. Greta, on the other hand, had been fathoming since she'd come up the stairs.

Fathoming will only take you so far, though, so Greta had moved on. She was now working levers and working big chunks of metal over with a hammer. Sloot admired both her expertise and her courage, and was more than a little bit envious of the forceful way that she could swing a hammer.

Sloot saw something in the shadows above, a flicker of movement. He hoped that it was just another swinging block, a part of the machine only occasionally called upon to put forth some effort in the clock's machinations, and not some hellish bat-cousin of the mice below that lusted for his blood.

Whatever it was, it was descending. It was coming closer! Just before Sloot drew in a breath in preparation for a high-pitched shriek, he realized that it was Roman.

"What were you doing up there?" Sloot whispered, once Roman had made his way over to them.

"Getting our payday," answered Roman. "You remember, the one you agreed to when we had our little chat with Auntie?"

Sloot had entirely forgotten about the blood star that Winking Bob had given them to hang in the tower.

"How will she know whether we've done it? We could have just thrown it in the box with the devil mice."

"With what?"

"Never mind."

"She'll know," said Roman. "I told you, those things are bad magic. Better we do our part and not ask any questions, got it?"

"Got it," said Sloot. "Can we get out of here now?"

"Give it a minute," said Roman. "If Greta actually manages to repair the clock, she'll be a national hero!"

"She's a foreigner! Are foreign heroes given medals when they're hung in the square?"

"Fine way for an Intelligencier to talk," said Roman. "Those under our protection have no need to fear ... especially not in the heart of our home city. If she can't manage it, we'll be back in the catacombs before dawn. We've got hours yet. Relax!"

Greta spent the next couple of hours moving things around, hitting things with hammers, and thoroughly giving the clock what for, if Sloot were any judge of clockmakery, which he wasn't.

Willie spent that time feigning interest in clocks, on Roman's advice. Nan disapproved of everything that was happening. Sloot tried to convince himself that Roman was right, and that they were in no real danger. He spent the last hour or so sitting in a corner, holding his mother's watch to his ear, trying to find some comfort in the now-immaculate whirring and clicking of its insides.

*Clank.*

"That's it!" Greta was covered in sweat and grease, beaming up with an ear-to-ear smile—which, frankly, was a bit too liberal with its use of teeth—at the machinery of the clock, as it started to move on its own.

*Clank. Clank.*

"It's working! Someone had tried to balance the main crankshaft, but it's clearly an unbalanced design! Once I'd figured that out, the rest was easy!"

"We should go," said Roman. "The sun will come up soon. We need to stay ahead of the dawn patrols."

"No, no," said Greta in a monotone voice that probably had a knife in its pocket, "don't waste so much time congratulating me. All I've done is unravel the mystery of this bizarre machinery in a couple of hours, no big deal really."

"Sorry, Greta," said Roman. "Bang up work you've done there, the people of Ulfhaven owe you a debt."

"There was a reward for fixing the clock?" Willie's eyes went wide. "What's my share?"

Sloot was already down the stairs. He plumbed the depths of his own psyche, hoping to find some magic lurking there that he could use to compel a greater sense of urgency from the rest of them, but found little more than the perfect environment in which one might foster a malignant heart condition.

"Right," said Roman, his hand on the door. "Across the alley, down the steps, and we'll work our way back around to the drainage grate. Ready? Behind me now, last one out closes the door!"

Roman eased the door open and stepped out onto the street. He made it a few steps before stopping dead in his tracks, turning to the left, and throwing his hands into the air.

"No trouble here! Just fixing the clock, all by myself. You're welcome!"

"Hey!" exclaimed Greta.

"That? That was just the *hey spring*," said Roman in a fit of improvisational brilliance. "It may do that a few more times until the spindle gets warmed up. All's well, no need to look inside!"

"Hide!" Sloot hissed at the rest of them. They all ran up the stairs and found places to conceal themselves within the workings of the clock. Sloot ran for the network of ladders that Roman had used to hang the blood star high among the rafters, and made it up several of them before his fear of heights prevented him from climbing any further.

"Wait a minute," said Willie from below. "Why should we be hiding? This is an expedition!"

"Willie, don't!" Sloot scurried down one of the ladders a bit. "It's not—"

"No need to be afraid," Willie shouted. "We're from the Old Country, just exploring your primitive culture! We mean no harm, you bloodthirsty savages!"

The jig was up. Figuring there was nothing to be gained by staying up his ladder, aside from the possibility of being lassoed and pulled down, Sloot made his way to the floor. If there was one thing he'd learned from the bullies at school, if you didn't put up a fight, they tended to go easier on you. The guards came in brandishing pikes, the "guards" in this case being a bunch of very old people who moved surprisingly swiftly. One of them grabbed Willie with an utter lack of tenderness and shoved him against a wall.

"You take your hands off him!" Perhaps Nan hadn't been bullied in school. She obviously didn't know about getting bullies to go easy, as she relieved an old man of his helmet with a sudden upstroke of her broom.

"Kill that one!" shouted a woman armed with a whistle, who had what looked like sergeant's stripes on her sleeve.

"Stop!" came a commanding shout from somewhere near Willie. No one moved. "Do you know who I am?" the voice shouted again. It took Sloot a moment to realize that it had come from Willie himself. He couldn't help but pay it heed. Probably an inherent trait of the ridiculously rich, the ability to insinuate the size of one's piles of money with one's voice.

"Er, no," said the guard who'd managed to force Willie's arm into a textbook pincher hold.

"He's my cousin," said Roman, from his pinned-to-the-cobbles-with-a-boot-on-his-neck vantage.

"You'd be so lucky," said Willie. "I am Lord—"

"—ing your thick, luscious hair over all of us," said Greta, "I know! It's lovely, but—"

"No!" boomed Willie, doing the thing again. "I am Lord Wilhelm Hapsgalt of Salzstadt, and I insist that you release me at once!"

"Good one," said Roman, "and I'm the king of Niflheim! Don't mind him, officers, we're just having a laugh!"

"What y' think, Sarge?" asked one of the guards.

"Dunno," said the woman with the whistle. "He sounds important, doesn't he?"

"Yeah," said another woman with impressively thick spectacles. "Probably is a lord, but not from around here."

"I demand to speak to your superior officer!" shouted Willie. "When my dad finds out what you've done—"

"Yep, he's a lord, all right. Let's bring 'em all in."

※↝※↝※↝※↝

Sloot awoke sometime later, on the damp stone floor in the dungeons under Castle Ulfhaven. There wasn't a sign or anything, but the piles of skulls in the corners meant that it hardly could have been anywhere else.

"What happened?"

"You fainted," said Roman, "when the watch handed us over to the Lebendervlad."

"Who?"

"The ghosts wearing suits of armor. Don't you remember?"

Sloot realized that he was actively trying to suppress that particular memory. They'd been marched through a gargoyle-infested courtyard to an old gate. The gate opened, and a pair of ghostly horrors descended upon them. Then everything went black. Why did ghosts need suits of armor?

They were all sitting with their backs to the wall. Sloot was in the middle, with Roman next to him, then Greta on the end. Willie was on the other end, huddled up in Nan's lap.

Willie, as it turns out, was an ugly crier. His face rolled through a series of contortions, each more pitiful than the last, as though he were making a run at some sort of record for homeliest man-child. He never seemed to pause his high-pitched wail of despair to take a breath.

"That's an impressive performance," said Roman. "He must be breathing through his ears!"

"Leave him alone," commanded Nan in her sternest tone. "He's only a little boy! You'd be crying too if you were only six years old."

"What?" Greta's look of incredulity could moonlight as a reaction to having seen a pig ask for bacon.

"Leave him alone!"

"Are you mad? He's easily forty!"

"Lying to yourself to justify your cradle robbing? Oh, that's low!"

"Cradle robbing? I don't— You just— *What?*"

"She's under some sort of spell," said Roman. "Best just leave it."

Willie did a sort of choke-and-sniffle thing that interrupted his wailing for one blessed second, but was back at the helm of the SS Annoyance without delay.

"I've already had quite enough advice from you two," snapped Greta, her forefinger venting its agitation at Roman and Sloot. "Come to Carpathia, you said! There's a neat old clock! It'll only cost you your freedom!"

"This is a temporary setback," said Roman. "I'm sure—"

"You were *sure* that we'd be perfectly safe! You were *sure* that I'd grow fond of Willie if I gave him a chance!"

"And did you?" asked Willie, pausing his wailing in the blink of an eye.

"No!"

The wailing resumed.

They'd relieved Sloot of his mother's watch when they arrested him, along with everything else that they'd been carrying, so Sloot had no idea how much time had passed. He'd gotten a bit of sleep though, one of very few benefits extended to those prone to fainting. There was only a bit of torchlight in the dungeons, and no windows.

"Impressive," said Roman, with a nod in Willie's direction. "I mean, I could go the rest of my life without hearing that racket, but you've got to acknowledge talent, haven't you?"

"Leave me alone," said Sloot.

"Oh, come on." Roman. inched over into whispering range. "Relax, would you? This is all going according to plan!"

"You got us thrown in here on purpose?" Sloot hissed.

"Calm down," said Roman, oblivious to the fact that that phrase is universally guaranteed not to work. "I've planned all of this down to the letter. Just play along, and we'll all be out of here in a jiffy."

Sloot groaned. He couldn't tell if that made him feel any better or not. They were both in the Carpathian Intelligence game, but that fact didn't place them any less in a damp and musty dungeon full of skull piles. He was sure he could also hear something enormous and terrible growling beneath the floor.

All of a sudden, Sloot could hear a high-pitched ringing in his ears that blocked out everything else in the room. Everything, that is, except for the beating of his own heart, which seemed to have moved into the space normally occupied by his brain for a spot of thunderous pounding.

*Yep,* he thought, *I know what this is. This is panic.*

How did he know that Roman was indeed *in* Carpathian Intelligence? He trusted his mother, sure, but Roman had never shown him papers, or a badge, or anything. What if he was just some old lunatic who'd decided to involve Sloot in his ridiculous fantasy?

His heart was beating faster, faster. His chest went tight. He breathed in frenzied gulps, and stars began flooding his vision.

*Wait, no,* he thought, *he had the key! He knew how to get into the city through the catacombs. How could he have faked that?* His heartbeat felt like it was starting to slow down a bit. The tightness in his chest subsided. *That's better. I'm sure the panic will pass back into the usual fretting in a moment, and I'll be able to hear Willie's sobbing again.*

While a regular person would take no comfort in that, Sloot was a worrier. To a worrier, fretting is a tame, even desirable state of affairs.

It's the teacher's equivalent of students quietly passing notes during a lesson, but at least they're trying to hide it.

"On your feet, foreign devils!" shouted a misshapen hunchback. He was dragging a bad leg as he limped along, and was accompanied by two of the ghostly suits of armor that had caused Sloot to faint before.

The hunchback carried a large ring of keys. Sloot had to help Nan drag Willie to his feet while the guard tried several of them in the lock without success.

"We demand a trial!" shouted Greta. "You can't just keep us here like this!"

"You don't make demands! I dunno how they do things down in Salzstadt, but you're in Carpathia now. The only person here doing any demanding is Vlad the Invader, and I wouldn't talk to her like that if I were you!"

"Oh my stars," said Nan, pulling Willie closer to her bosom. "Did he say Vlad the Invader?"

"That's right." The hunchback finally found the right key, and after a few creaking twists, the bolt clanked open. "I hope you've made your peace with whatever heathen gods you southerners pray to, because Vlad wants to see you."

## ⊱⊰ COURT OF THE INVADER ⊱⊰

The Carpathians didn't stop at terrifying surnames when it came to striking fear into the hearts of their enemies. Or their friends, for that matter, or casual acquaintances, or people delivering packages. Everything in the castle, as far as Sloot had seen, was engineered specially to culminate in a heart attack.

All of the walls in the castle proper were constructed of red stone. It wasn't the same reddish-brown of the clay bricks that one would see used for building houses in the countryside in the Old Country, these were *blood* red.

Carpathians were renowned hunters, and the walls were festooned with the heads and skins of horrible beasts, the likes of which Sloot had never seen, even in books. Many of the grisly trophies had weapons mounted alongside them, perhaps the swords and lances that had felled the wicked monsters, or maybe they felt the presence of deadly steel simply helped to inflate the general threat level of the place.

And fire! Everything was on fire! Not just torches here and there, but great roaring braziers made of spiky steel, hearths with more animal heads mounted all over them, and chandeliers so overloaded with candles that Sloot didn't imagine there was a living fire marshal anywhere near the castle. Or if there was, his corruption knew no bounds. Columns of black smoke roiled up from the multitude of flames, blackening the vaulted ceilings above.

They came at last into a vast chamber that the Great Cathedral of Salzstadt would have fit into, with room for an art gallery besides. Torches and braziers burned, wicked-looking animal heads sneered, and pairs of crossed axes looked very cross indeed. Red and black stained glass windows cast a bloody pallor over the fifty-or-so soldiers standing before a dais, their little horde split down the middle by an aisle. Upon the dais was a throne of red marble, carved to look like a pair of dragons fighting each other.

Upon the throne, resplendent in a wickedly spiked and fluted suit of steel armor, was Vlad the Invader.

*She's pretty,* thought Sloot. The thought surprised him. There he was, scared out of his mind, and the first observation to strike him was how beautiful the steel-clad tyrant was, with her cold, black embers of hate where a normal person might have eyes. She sat there on her throne, waiting to drain them of blood, perhaps.

He stood by it, though. Strip away the armor, the hateful eyes, the predatory posturing, the sword resting across her lap that seemed to be permanently stained with blood, the hordes of faceless soldiers before her, the fact that their lives were dependent on her whim, the malevolent scowl, and the bubbling fonts behind her that could have been blood (hard to tell with all the red light), and she was very pretty indeed.

The horde of soldiers were more of the *Lebendervlad*. There was smoke all around them, as though they'd just finished stamping out a campfire, and it was still smoldering at their feet.

If only that had been the case; alas, there was no fire. They were actually a bunch of soldiers in wicked-looking armor *made of* smoke. The ghastly things turned to look at them as they passed, and Sloot confirmed that there was nothing human about them. Where their eyes should be were a pair of dim red embers, which flared at a tempo not unlike a beating heart.

"Kneel," Vlad's voice rumbled. It wasn't a request. The laws of probability did not bother calculating odds on what might have happened had they refused. Inevitability came to pass.

"All hail General Vladimyra Defenestratia," shouted a cleric in red robes with the hood drawn up, "Commander of the Armies of Carpathia, Conqueror of the Eastern Marches, and Thirty-Seventh of her Name!"

"Hail!" cried all of the soldiers in unison, their voices somehow declining to echo in the great hall. "Hail, Hail!"

"You snuck into my city," said Vlad. "Why?"

"Mighty Vlad," Roman began, kneeling as lowly as possible and spreading his arms out before him, "we sought only to—"

"Hold your tongue, wretched cur! Generals do not parlay with your filth. I will hear the words of your lord."

"I don't want to," said Willie. He started crying again.

"You what?"

"He said he doesn't want to talk to you!" Nan snapped, rising to her feet.

"On your knees, hag!" Vlad lifted the wicked sword from her lap, reversed the grip, and buried the tip in the stone at her feet. "One more word, and I'll have your head."

"You'll not harm a hair on—"

The ease and fluid grace of the stroke had come from practicing it hundreds of thousands of times. Vlad's face was placid, her form was perfect. Nan's head stayed where it had always been for just a moment before gravity pulled it to a place it felt would be more sensible. A torrent of blood began to gush from her neck, and her body slumped in the direction of her head.

Willie's mouth dropped open. Sloot vomited. Greta blinked.

Before they'd even come up from the dungeon, Sloot had been fairly certain that death was imminent. He'd already more or less made peace with it, and that was the only reason he hadn't fainted.

Nan's eyes were still open. She stared lifelessly at Sloot, her face frozen in the scowl she used for telling people off. She'd often told Sloot that she would die for Willie, and now it appeared that she had been right.

Vlad moved to stand in front of Greta, staring down at her. Greta stared back, but not in fear as Sloot was sure he'd have done. Sloot didn't recognize the expression, but it was something like wonderment.

"Do you have a name?"

"I do."

"I had heard that they do not give names to women in the Old Country."

"They do."

"Tell me."

"Greta."

"You're not afraid of me, I think."

Greta blushed. Vlad's lip twitched as though it would sneer, but it wasn't that. It may have been the Carpathian equivalent of a smile.

"You do not look like thieves to me," said Vlad. She strolled over to Roman and looked down at him. Roman averted his gaze toward the commingling pools of Nan's blood and Sloot's sick.

"Yet you *are* thieves," she continued. "You trespass where you have no right. What have you come here to steal?"

"Nothing, Your Dominance," answered Roman.

"I'm told your lord had a bag with a lot of shoes in it. A suspicious number of shoes. You came to Ulfhaven to steal shoes?"

"Certainly not," said Willie. "Those are mine! My spare skulking shoes, some dancing heels in case there was a party—"

"Silence!"

Willie, probably for the first time in his life, hushed himself when he was told. If Sloot was granted a dying wish, he resolved to ask Vlad how she'd managed that.

"Not thieves then," said Vlad. "Not *only* thieves. In Carpathia, a person is all of the things that they are."

*Isn't that true everywhere?* Sloot wondered.

"You," said Vlad to Roman. "What else are you, that is not a thief?"

"I'm a valet, Your Dominance. A servant to that man there." He nodded to Willie, who seemed to forget what was happening for a moment and puffed up his chest.

"So I was right," Vlad looked at Willie, "you're a lord as well as a thief."

"Right you are," said Willie, flashing what must have been intended as a charming smile. "Although I'm not a thief, I have far too much money for that to be worth my while."

*Oh dear,* thought Sloot.

Vlad snorted in disdain. "Lords are the greatest thieves of them all. The greatest fools as well, incapable of knowing when to hold their tongues."

"Now see here—" Willie started. He was interrupted by what must have been laughter coming from the platoon of spectral soldiers, though it was a chilling, uneasy laughter that made Sloot's blood run cold.

"You prove me right," said Vlad. Her face made another of those bemused sneers, though rather more sneery than the one Greta had received. "You're a hostage, then. That's what your wealth affords you here."

She nodded toward the ghostly soldiers. Two of them lifted Willie to his feet and started leading him away.

"Wait," said Willie, "where are we going? Is Mister Roman coming, too? Someone has to run my bath. Is Nan going to be okay?" He kept talking but was soon too far away to be understood.

"And you, valet. I suppose that you'll want to look after your master now that his wet nurse understands the price of defiance?"

"As it pleases Your Dominance," Roman replied, still staring at the floor. Another nod, and Roman was led away as well.

"You've been quiet, thief." Sloot's heart started beating a lot faster as Vlad moved to stand in front of him. What should he say? He couldn't reveal that he was an Intelligencier, not with Greta still there. Was he allowed to talk about it in front of the ghost soldiers?

"You're still quiet, I see. Aside from that whining noise." Sloot hadn't noticed that the back of his throat was giving a pained little howl. He stopped immediately. "What else are you?"

"I'm an accountant," Sloot squeaked. "A financier, actually."

"I see," said Vlad. "Here to tell your lord what's worth stealing, are you?" Her blade was inches from his face, still dripping with Nan's blood. As though this state of affairs wasn't terrifying enough, Sloot noticed that the drips of blood never made it to the floor; instead, they floated up and away like horrible little birds.

"N-no, Your Dominance," said Sloot. "I just— I was—"

"Out with it!"

"I don't know! It doesn't make any sense to bring your accountant along on this sort of mission! I just want to go home!"

Sloot lost what remained of his composure and was wracked with sobs that would not be silent. Vlad only had herself to blame, really. Proper heroes would have had trouble remaining calm in his place, and they learn that sort of thing in school. School had taught Sloot nothing that he could use in situations like this. Sure, he could have taken elective courses in Remaining Calm in the Face of Certain Death, but what were the odds that they'd ever come in handy?

He'd taken statistics instead. That's how he knew that this eventuality was referred to as an "outlier." He shut his eyes and braced himself for the stroke of Vlad's sword.

"There may be penance for you, thief." Vlad did another sort of sneer that went with a roll of her eyes. Sloot's bawling probably had something to do with that.

Sloot flinched when he felt hands grabbing him roughly, and opened his eyes when he realized he'd not been cut down. He was being led away by a pair of spectral warriors. The pool of blood surrounding Nan's corpse had started to float upward in tiny drops, like a gentle rain in a nightmare that Sloot kept having. At least he had clothes on this time. A couple of the red-robed clerics that flanked Vlad's throne had noticed as well, and looked as though they were trying to follow it. Studying the migratory pattern of blood would be a terrifying field, though rife with grants if the phenomenon became more frequent.

"So," Sloot heard Vlad saying when he was nearly out of earshot, "what will we do with Greta the thief?"

He didn't hear the response. The specters took him back into the dungeon and pushed him into a small cell, nearly long enough in one direction for him to lie down, but not quite. He might have managed it by sticking his legs out through the bars, but he feared for his ankles. Inadequate lighting in the dungeon, and his captors didn't seem as though they'd be courteous enough to look where they were stomping about.

That's statistics. He settled for slumping into the corner that had the fewest skulls in it and curling into a ball.

"On your feet, Mister Peril."

When had he fallen asleep? Such a feat was difficult at best on a damp stone floor, but it seemed he'd managed it. He was so stiff and cramped that he couldn't decide whether moving or staying still was a greater source of agony. Doing as he was told was historically least likely to result in a beating, so the choice wasn't that hard.

"Good morning," said Sloot.

"It's nearly suppertime," said the young woman before him. She was apparently some sort of wizard, or at least very fond of dressing like one; or rather, dressing like a wizard who thought that standard wizard attire was far too drab, and had applied a garish array of multicolored stars to her robes and pointy hat.

"You're young for a wizard," Sloot said, much louder than he'd intended. Trying to shout over her outfit, he supposed. He tried not to stare at the cacophony of stars on her robes, which were shooting around quickly enough to tickle his motion sickness.

"And you're filthy for an Intelligencier."

"You know who I am! Can you get me out of here?"

She nodded. "As soon as you to stand up. The door opens inward."

Sloot stood and moved into the corner. Half an hour later he'd washed and changed into a suit that had fallen out of fashion in Salzstadt when he was a boy. It fit him well though, and was more formal than anything he'd ever owned before. He waited in the little changing room, wondering what was coming next and trying not to roll into a little ball and hyperventilate.

"Come out when you're ready," came the voice of the woman who'd opened his cell earlier.

Sloot took a breath and opened the door. There she was again, nauseating stars and all.

"Not bad," she said. "A little drab, but you wear it well."

"Thanks," said Sloot. "Er, could you tell me your name, please?"

"Nicoleta Goremonger," said Nicoleta. "I'm Her Dominance's court wizard."

"Pleased to meet you, Nicoleta. Is this— I'm sorry, but are you rescuing me?"

She laughed with her mouth open.

"From the dungeon, I suppose. Wow, you've lived your entire life in the Old Country! Tell me, what's it like? Do you really have to take turns feeding the Domnitor? Does he really weigh a thousand pounds?"

"What? No!"

"Oh. The feeding or the weight?"

"Neither!"

"Huh. I've always heard he was a glutton and a tyrant, that you're not free like we are here."

"We've got freedom," said Sloot with a shrug. "Maybe not as much as some. As long as we follow all of the rules and don't forget to say the Loyalist Oath at least once a day, we do more or less as we please."

"Loyalist Oath?"

"Yeah," said Sloot, suddenly remembering that it had been a while since he'd recited it. *Perhaps later,* he thought, *might be bad form in front of the Carpathians.* "It's basically allegiance to the Domnitor—long may he reign—the Old Country, good hygiene, that sort of thing."

"That's funny." Nicoleta laughed aloud again.

Sloot wondered what it would be like to enjoy things that much, but reasoned that he'd have to break several dozen rules of etiquette in the process. He resolved to avoid it.

"If you're not rescuing me, what happens next?"

"We're going to dinner." Nicoleta's eyes narrowed, and she studied him with disbelief. "Do you think you're a prisoner?"

"Well, the cell …"

"That was to protect your cover! Did Roman fill you in on the plan at all?"

"Well no," said Sloot. "He said it was above my pay grade, even after I was raised to Agent Ninth Class."

Nicoleta doubled over laughing, going red in the face.

"You ... he said ... ninth class!" She was gasping for breath.

"I'm sorry," said Sloot. "I don't know what's funny."

"I probably shouldn't say." A modicum of restraint was vying for control of Nicoleta's face, but it wasn't faring well. Her maniacal glee had the high ground.

"Oh," said Sloot. "Okay."

"It's just probably above my *pay grade*," she said with a snicker. "Look, I'm sure Roman has his reasons for keeping you in the dark about ... *things*. Just know that you're not a prisoner. You're home."

Perhaps even more than watching Nan's bloody execution, the thought of Carpathia as *home* terrified him. Like all loyal subjects of the Domnitor—which Sloot may or may not still be at this point—Sloot believed in inevitability. The sun rises in the east, swearing causes goblins, and the Old Country is the center of the world. He'd never considered living anywhere other than Salzstadt, and why would he? Everything he'd ever known was there.

Besides, he wasn't really a Carpathian Intelligencier, he worked for Uncle! He'd gotten so wrapped up in his cover that he'd nearly forgotten about Flavia recruiting him. That was real, wasn't it? He'd been a bit woozy, what with the stabbing and all. He hadn't dreamt it, had he?

Of course not! Sloot was the most loyal salt in the Domnitor's service, of course he'd want Sloot working for him! Wouldn't he, long may he reign?

Was this some sort of test? His mother had left Carpathia to spy on the Old Country, was he supposed to do the same in reverse? That would be poetic, not that Sloot approved of poetry. Washing away the sins of the father—or, in this case, mother.

The Domnitor, long may he reign, had a plan, after all—who was Sloot to question whether that plan had led him to this point?

He followed Nicoleta to dinner and tried very hard to stop thinking about the Domnitor, long may he reign. He needed to pretend to be as

Carpathian as possible, to preserve his secret identity. To that end, he resolved to spit somewhere inappropriate as soon as the opportunity presented itself.

Sometimes it's difficult to see the grand scheme of things, and sometimes it's hard to have faith; but sometimes things seem to align the way they're supposed to, and that was just what seemed to happen when Myrtle appeared beside the chair across from Sloot and smiled at him.

For a moment, Sloot had difficulty in deciding how to react. His heart raced in his chest, and he was overjoyed to see her, but he simply gave her a polite smile and a nod. Emotions are guests within the jurisdiction of etiquette, after all.

She was breathtaking. Even allowing for the fact that he'd been moping about her for weeks, she was stunning by any measure. Not only that, she was beaming at him in that way that women typically reserve for men with a surplus of pectoral muscles; chin models who speak octaves below the range of ordinary men.

Sloot had never been on the receiving end of a look like that and was at a loss for what to do. He made a sort of flustered chortle, grinned from ear to ear, and stared at his feet while his shoulders pivoted wildly. He blushed forcefully enough to start sweating.

Roman walked in next, followed shortly by Greta. They'd both gotten cleaned up as well, in ancient-looking get-ups similar to Sloot's. Carpathia, like every grandparent the world has ever known, had decided upon its retirement—apparently some thirty years hence—that everything in its closet was as modern as it would ever need to be.

They all remained standing until Vlad came in. She'd eschewed her frightful suit of platemail in favor of a simple yet elegant red robe of raw silk. She wore a smaller sword than the one she'd used to behead Nan. She took the seat at the head of the table.

"Sit," she said, and they did.

Then Vlad stood back up and drew her sword. Everyone else stood as well.

"I told you to sit!" she yelled. They all sat again, much more quickly this time. Sloot felt the familiar rush of panic and, as was his custom, braced for death. Fortunately, Vlad's attention was focused at the far end of the dining room. Sloot turned to see one of the shadowy guards standing there, its great sword drawn.

"Who gave you leave to take my seat?" it asked in his hollow, lifeless voice.

"This is my seat," said Vlad, sounding more bored than threatened. "I am Vlad now. Must we go through this every night?"

"You'll not live to see the sunrise, infidel!"

Vlad sighed. With her free hand, she used her thumb to twist a ring on her forefinger. In a burst that resembled the cloud that appears when an inkwell is tipped into a bucket of water, a smoking shadow coalesced around Vlad, taking on the shape of the fluted platemail she wore when Sloot saw her for the first time. She kicked her chair backward, jumped atop the table, and started running at the shadow.

"It's Vlad the Thirteenth," said Nicoleta. "He took too many hammer blows to the helmet in his day. She'll only be a moment."

Their swords clanged together, her real one and his ethereal one. Block, parry, kick—the departed Vlad went flying backward but managed to recover and parry as the living one descended upon him.

"Not fast enough," he said. He threw a punch with his off hand that sent Vlad sailing through the air. She managed to twist and land in a crouch.

This went on for several minutes, the two gaining and losing the advantage until the living Vlad's sword severed the dead one's shadowy helmet from its shoulders. A shower of purple sparks erupted from the ghostly wound, and the corpse disappeared in a puff of smoke.

Vlad sheathed her sword and twisted her ring. Her armor evaporated from her in a puff of smoke, and she retook her seat.

"The Hapsgalt lord tells me that you are his fiancée," said Vlad to Greta. "Is that true?"

"Er," Greta blinked several times, "he believes that it is." She looked at Vlad with *that* look, the chin model one. Sloot had never seen her look at Willie that way, though he was also sure that Willie had never defeated a spectral warrior in a savage duel.

"Good," said Vlad. She wasn't even breathing hard. She reached for her goblet and savored a swallow of wine.

"So it's true," said Myrtle. "The shadow warriors are your forefathers."

"And foremothers, yes," said Nicoleta. "They are the spirits of the departed Vlads the Invader."

Nicoleta went on to explain that the former Vlads the Invader, who referred to themselves collectively as the *Lebendervlad*, still roam the halls of Castle Ulfhaven thanks to several magical totems throughout the castle known as Black Smilers. They're made from the charred skulls of vanquished enemies, stuffed with demonic larva, mounted on spears and enchanted so that they glow a sickly yellow.

"The glowing isn't the point of the enchantment," Nicoleta had felt the need to point out, "just a side effect. It's an effective deterrent though. People tend to leave them alone."

"So they just wander around thinking they're still Vlad, challenging people for chairs?" asked Greta.

"Just Vlad the Thirteenth," replied Nicoleta.

"Seems more trouble than it's worth."

"Not at all! It's nice having all the Vlads around. Her Dominance trains with them regularly, and they do all of the guarding around the castle now that—" She stopped speaking and stared down at her plate. Vlad was glaring at her.

"Now that what?" asked Greta, causing Sloot to breathe a silent sigh of relief. He didn't want to ask himself, but the silence had started to grow beyond his standard resting rate of discomfort.

"The curse," Vlad murmured. She drained her cup of wine, refilled it, and settled into a brooding stare. You had to be flush with gravitas to brood like that. "You may as well tell them," she said with a wave in Nicoleta's direction, who treated them all to a history lesson.

※ ※ ※ ※ ※ ※ ※ ※

Sloot had always been told that the first Vlad the Invader was just one of many clan chieftains in the Badlands, the lawless wastes north of what was becoming the Old Country, in the time just before the Year of Reckoning. That was the proper name given to the first year in modern counting, when the wise men and women of all the world's nations gathered at Blåsigtopp and reckoned that it was as good a time as any to start up a common counting of the passage of time. Not long after that, according to the official state textbooks issued in Old Country elementary schools, the first Vlad the Invader rose to power over all of the other chieftains by proving that he could eat all of the least desirable parts of a cow while using the wrong fork, having not first washed his hands, and then leaving the table without asking to be excused. He followed this by saying all of the worst swear words, then immediately going for a swim.

It turns out that the truth, in this case, had been judiciously mitigated by the Ministry of Propaganda, though Sloot wouldn't be so foolish as to point that out. The penalty for finding fault in the logic published by the Ministry of Propaganda was being immediately referred to the Ministry of Conversation.

Before the Year of Reckoning, what is now the sovereign nation of Carpathia was known as the Badlands, a highly disputed territory whose primary export was unadulterated violence. It boasted a one hundred percent employment rate among berserkers, blood riders, and war criminals in exile. Despite the flourishing economy of violence that they enjoyed at the time, Vlad the Bloodthirsty figured that they could do better. He put together a warband of slaves and former slaves, which was rather huge, as nearly everyone who'd spent any time in the Badlands had been a slave at some point, and marched on Ulfhaven.

Before the mighty fortress in which Sloot was presently dining had been built, Ulfhaven had been a small collection of crude stone towers, where the clans gathered to conspire against each other. It was run by a plutocrat who had been given a seat of power for promising all of the clan chieftains that he'd make them rich. Vlad's warband met little resistance, and before the sun had risen so high in the sky that the daily tradition of asking "I don't know, what do you want for breakfast?" had begun, Vlad had thrown the plutocrat from the tower. He would thenceforth be known as Vlad Defenestratia, and set himself about the business of invading neighboring holds that had the audacity not to recognize his authority.

Over the course of the next few generations, Vlad and his children and grandchildren who inherited his name subjugated all but one of the clans, one by one. The berserker battle lords advised attacking them all at once and having a really good blood frenzy—one of whom was a distant ancestor of Roman's, hence the name—but the Vlad at that time knew that sort of thing would make for an economy that was entirely too bullish.

There was one clan that Vlad the Fourth left to its own devices. They were called the Virag, and their chieftain, a gruesome-looking wizard named Ashkar, was rumored to be over a thousand years old. They would not swear fealty to anyone, but offered Vlad a bargain: in exchange for Ashkar's blood oath that the Virag would never use their magic to the detriment of the kingdom, Vlad would grant them immunity from reality.

The Virag believed that fealty was just another tether to reality, and such tethers limited their ability to peer beyond the veil that separates the realms of the living and the dead. They wanted to explore the mysteries of the ether, not be tied down to constraints of mortality that were, in their words, "Heavy, man."

Vlad the Fourth saw no glory in cleaving the clan of skinny nomads, having not a single sword among them, so she granted their request. They would be allowed to roam the undesirable lands in the outskirts of the kingdom, occasionally trading with the Carpathian people, but otherwise stay out of their business.

Time went on, and the Virag kept their word. They stayed out of Carpathian affairs, lived in the hinterlands, and occasionally threw music festivals that would last for days at a time.

Nothing changed for centuries until Vlad the Thirty-Fifth, grandfather of the present Vlad, decided it had been too long since Carpathia had invaded anybody. The war with the Old Country had been waging for years and looked as though it might run cold. He couldn't invade

Nordheim due to a peace that Vlad the Twenty-Ninth had sworn with their king on Odin's spear, *Gungnir*. The only other place that shared a border with Carpathia was Blåsigtopp, which wasn't really a nation but rather a monastery where the Blessed Few spent their lives contemplating the mysteries of the universe. It stood at the top of a steep and treacherous pass, and everyone knew that invading it was bad luck, though no one could remember who'd figured that out. Probably the Abbot of the Blessed Few.

That left the Virag. Vlad the Thirty-Fifth donned his most threatening suit of armor and rode out into the hinterlands with two hundred thousand soldiers behind him. He knew he didn't need that many to subjugate a tiny clan, but he could hardly say "no" to them—it had been a long time since they'd had a good war march, and they agreed to do it *pro bono*.

Whether the leader of the Virag was the same man or, like the Vlads, it was a hereditary name, the wizard Ashkar refused to swear fealty to Vlad. He demanded that the pact be honored. The Carpathian army slaughtered the rest of the Virag and tied Ashkar to a pyre. As he burned alive, Ashkar laughed in a shrill, blood-curdling sort of way that only the worst of villains are able to manage. He laid a curse upon the Carpathian army, declaring that so long as the line of Defenestratia sat at the front of it, not a single soldier more would join their ranks. Vlad laughed and spat and drank and celebrated his victory, as he was wont to do.

In the years that followed, there was a strange drop in the rate of new enlistments for which the army recruiters could not account. They were under strict orders to disavow any magical interference in the day-to-day operations of the army, so the official forms on the matter, which have been heavily redacted, offer no explanation.

According to Carpathian law, all citizens are compelled to serve in the army from the ages of fifteen to fifty. When the day came in a young person's life when he or she should have been turning fifteen and putting on their first oversized uniform (they'd grow into it), they instead gave in to the urge to wander off into the hinterlands and beyond, or found themselves missing a leg and were therefore ineligible, or spontaneously turned sixteen and were turned away by orientation specialists who didn't know what to do with them.

"By the time Vlad's father passed the throne to her," said Nicoleta, "all of the soldiers had retired or passed away."

For a long time, everyone at the table was silent. That was the Old Country thing to do, since voicing an opinion about the culture was frowned upon, to say the least. It could land one in a complicated and uncomfortable steel harness in the belly of the Ministry of Conversation, to say the most. The silence lasted until they'd all finished the simple spread of bread and cold chicken that the kitchen staff had brought out, and then washed it down with a nice Carpathian red. It should come as no surprise to learn that Carpathian vineyards do not produce white wines.

"Have you thought about stepping aside?" asked Greta.

The incredulity with which Vlad answered Greta was orchestrated in three parts. The stage was set in the first part by a horrified grimace. It reached a crescendo with a stream of ill-tempered swearing in the second, followed thirdly by Vlad sending her chair crashing to one side by means of a denouement, and then storming away before the curtain call.

"I didn't mean to offend," said Greta, who'd turned bright red.

"Her line has ruled Carpathia for a thousand years!" shouted Nicoleta. She stood in haste. "I'm sorry," she whispered, "but it's really expected of me to storm out, too!" And storm she did, with a few fireworks from the point of her hat punctuating the maneuver.

Sloot remained in his chair, for want of a place to which he might storm off. He felt compelled to show deference to his host but thought it would have looked ridiculous to stand up and storm around the table in a circle. Instead, he sat in silence until Roman offered to show Greta back to her rooms, which she accepted. That's when the tension became the most palpable, as he was now alone with Myrtle for the first time since she'd left Whitewood.

"You're here," he said. The impulse to speak had offered Sloot every assurance on its way up that it was going to say something debonaire, or at least witty. Still, he hadn't vomited. That was something.

"You say so," said Myrtle in Arthur' ridiculous Stagrallan drawl, "ergo you're here as well."

"Oh," said Sloot, having forgotten about the interloping philosopher. "I should go."

"No, wait," said Myrtle. "Arthur, could you give us a minute? Fine, why would anyone want to have a fully qualified philosopher in their conversation? No matter, I have some eternity to contemplate anyway. Just pretend I'm not here."

They sat together in silence long enough to feel as though they could reasonably pretend that Arthur had left the room and gone to bed or something.

"I just wanted to say that I'm sorry again," said Myrtle.

"That's all right. It hardly seems to matter now. We'll most likely meet our doom here."

"What do you mean? I really like it here."

Sloot gave Myrtle a look of surprise. Had he heard her correctly? That kind of talk was treason! Well, not in Carpathia, he supposed. Still, it triggered his instinct to drag her out into the street by her hair and proclaim her a traitor, the way one supposed to do when heresy is spoken in earshot.

Then again, he was with Uncle now. Was he supposed to be more subtle about it? Or possibly just murder her on the spot with one of the crossed swords above the hearth? He wouldn't have wanted to do that to anyone, let alone Myrtle.

"You ... *like* it."

"It's a lot nicer than you'd think! Plus I'm rich now, which makes just about anything better."

"Rich? From robbing Whitewood?"

Myrtle blushed. "I'm afraid so. I wanted to give the money back, but Roman told me not to! He told me to take it and run to Ulfhaven, to present myself to Vlad as an Intelligencier."

"Roman!" Sloot stood up abruptly, which seemed the thing to do in Carpathia when one is upset, based on the events of the evening up to that point.

Myrtle explained that she'd really wanted to stay, but Roman had convinced her that she wouldn't be safe in Salzstadt if she were discovered. She'd received one percent of the haul from burgling Whitewood, which was a small fortune by any standard.

"I suppose that makes sense, but why were you here tonight? At dinner?"

Myrtle blushed again, a much deeper shade of scarlet this time.

"Her Dominance," said Myrtle. "She thought that you'd be happy to see me."

"Oh?" Sloot felt himself blushing as well. "I didn't think she'd care about something like that."

Myrtle shrugged. "And are you?"

"H-happy to see you, you mean?"

Myrtle nodded. Sloot nodded. Myrtle smiled.

"OH, THIS IS RIDICULOUS," said Myrtle. "You said you'd give us a moment! IT'S BEEN A MOMENT. SEVERAL, IN FACT. Well, then take the night off!"

Sloot sighed. He was burning with embarrassment for having floundered so inartfully through a quasi-romantic encounter, and Arthur was making it unbearable.

"I suppose I should—"

"Would you walk me home?" blurted Myrtle, rather more forcefully than she might have intended.

"Oh, umm ... do you think I'm allowed?"

"You were Vlad's dinner guest," said Myrtle. "You're also an Intelligencier. You're not being guarded by one of the Lebendervlad, so it stands to reason that you'd be free to leave the castle."

## ❧⇀ULFHAVEN BY MOONLIGHT❧⇀

Myrtle was right. Sloot was free to leave the castle. He wasn't a prisoner, but he was free to walk Myrtle home, and that was nearly as bad. At least he had experience being a prisoner.

This was the sort of anxiety that should have confined itself to his awkward teenage years. Sloot wished that it hadn't extended so far into his awkward adulthood, despite the fact that not a single wish he'd ever made had come true. At what point does optimism become gullibility?

There they were, strolling across the cobbles in the dim light of skull-mounted torches and half the moon. Myrtle had hooked her hand through the crook of his arm once they'd walked through the castle's spiky portcullis.

Did that mean she'd done this sort of thing before? If so, she had him at a disadvantage. Walking ladies home at night was something he'd always seen himself doing someday, but had never quite gotten around to it, like spending time abroad. He'd just gotten started with *that,* in fact. He couldn't be expected to take on too much at once.

So had she? Had she been walked home on another gentleman's arm before tonight? He considered demanding an answer. He worked for Uncle now, after all, and one can't withhold things from Uncle! Then again, he couldn't be sure, but interrogation through official capacity didn't seem like the best way to woo a lady. He decided against it.

The old buildings that lined the streets of Ulfhaven were very different from the ones in Salzstadt. They were considerably farther north, and almost certain to be full of people who'd jump at the chance to be disloyal to the Domnitor, long may he reign. They also looked a lot older. You didn't see wicked, snarling gargoyles on new buildings, and the rooftops of Ulfhaven were absolutely silly with gargoyles. Though Salzstadt was technically older by a century or so, it was home to an ever-increasing population of architects, which are considered an invasive species of pest by the Salzstadt Historical Preservation Society. They're absolutely terrible for old buildings.

They walked across a little stone bridge over a canal, then past a little pub where some old men were having an animated discussion that was completely unintelligible.

"They're speaking Olde Carpathian," said Myrtle. "You don't hear it much anymore, except from really old people. They like to complain that no one speaks it anymore."

"So they don't teach it in schools?"

"No, the old people won't hear of it. They *like* to complain that no one speaks it anymore."

Myrtle pointed out the library as they walked past. It was smaller than the one in Salzstadt, probably due to its lack of funding by the wealthy families of Salzstadt. Score one for the Old Country! Sloot asked if they had both sorts of librarians there, but Myrtle had never been inside.

"Well, this is me," said Myrtle as they stopped in front of a big iron gate. A pair of gargoyles snarled down at them, but then, of course, they would. The absence of gargoyles would have been suspicious. Myrtle opened the gate, hesitated, and then took a step to stand very, very close to Sloot.

"Thank you for walking me home." She looked up at him with a little smile. "Would you like to come in?"

Even Old Country accountants have instincts, though they do everything in their power to avoid relying on them. Instincts are base, wicked things that are fine for savages like the Carpathians, but a good salt knows better than to let them run willy-nilly. So when the part of

Sloot's brain that was ruled solely by instinct was figuring out how to say "yes" in a way that seemed casual, the very Old Country part of his brain leapt into action.

"I shouldn't."

Myrtle sighed. "All right then. Good night."

She tilted her head upward and leaned in, her lips pursed. All that Sloot had to do was lower his face by an inch, and he'd finally have a love life! Some proof that he was a gentleman, for having kissed and not told! He thought about that almost exclusively on the long walk back to the castle and cursed himself for being the coward he'd always been. He couldn't even take consolation in the surprising firmness of the handshake he'd managed instead, as it couldn't have come off as confidence. Not when paired with the high-pitched warbling noise he made, and definitely not when followed by his sprint back in the direction they'd come.

When he told Roman about it over breakfast the following morning, he'd been as stone-faced as Sloot had ever seen the bug-eyed old man.

"Bad luck," said Roman. "Not to worry though, it sounds like she really fancies you. You're just a late bloomer, that's all."

"I wish that were true." Sloot heaped an unidentifiable brown mash onto his plate that he'd been told was the traditional Carpathian breakfast. It was tasty, but he lacked the courage to ask what it was. He was having trouble finding a courage he didn't lack, in fact.

"Of course it is," said Roman. "I told you I'm an excellent judge of character, didn't I? She likes you, and you're just having trouble working up your nerve."

"It's more than that. Nothing makes sense anymore! Everything was fine, then I corrected that stupid report and got promoted to Willie's financier. Every waking moment since then has been a steady decline into the unknown."

"That's just life, that is."

"But I can't live this way! Before I suddenly found myself in the Carpathian Intelligence service, I could have told you what pair of socks I'd be wearing every day for the rest of the fiscal quarter. I don't even know if I'll be wearing socks by the end of breakfast now! Do they even have fiscal quarters in Carpathia? When do they do their taxes?"

"Easy, easy," said Roman. "I know things are different, but—"

"But how do I know if I want to pursue a romance with Myrtle if I don't have my quarterly socks projections worked out?" Sloot was on his feet and shouting in his voice's highest register. His chest was going tight, and he was having trouble breathing.

Roman had no confidence in the curative powers of breathing into paper bags, so he opted for a nice hard slap instead. Sloot's eyes did a little acrobatic routine to regain their focus. He regarded Roman with shock for a moment, then returned to his seat.

"One thing at a time," said Roman. "Are you wearing socks right now?"

"Yes," replied Sloot.

"Then you'll probably still be wearing them by the end of breakfast. Have you neglected to wear socks since you've been capable of dressing yourself?"

"Not once."

"Then you'll most likely manage them tomorrow as well, and the day after that, and the day after that."

"Of course you're right." Sloot was surprised by how much better he felt. "Thanks."

"Don't mention it. And as far as Myrtle's concerned, who said anything about pursuing a romance?"

"She tried to kiss me."

"So, nobody," said Roman. "If the last few months have taught you anything, shouldn't it be that everything can change, no matter how well you've planned things out?"

"I suppose."

"When somebody you like tries to kiss you, you kiss them back. It's not honeymoons and broom makers yet, and it may never be. You just kiss her back, and see where that goes."

"Good advice," said Vlad, who was surprisingly light on her feet, even in a gleaming suit of steel armor.

"Thank you, Your Dominance," said Roman, who jumped out of his chair and gave a bow. Sloot did the same. Vlad waved a hand, and they all sat.

"Roman tells me this is your first time in Carpathia," said Vlad. A servant crept in and made an impressive pile of breakfast on her plate. "How do you find our city?"

"Quite, er, nice, Your Dominance."

"You are surprised."

"He's been raised as a true salt, Your Dominance," Roman explained. "He didn't even know he was a Carpathian until this year, when he took his mother's post."

"Really?" asked Vlad.

Sloot nodded, his mouth full of breakfast. It was delicious despite its appearance, and learning what was in it could only take away from his enjoyment. Salts are very good at refusing to learn things not bearing the Domnitor's seal of approval, long may he reign, so he could expect it to remain delicious in perpetuity.

"You'll be a great asset to our cause," said Vlad between enormous mouthfuls of breakfast. "You just need some time to warm up to your true heritage. You'll stay for a month here in the castle, free to explore the city as you will."

Sloot choked on his breakfast in surprise. "A month?"

"And then you'll bring the ransom to the elder Lord Hapsgalt."

"But they'll be looking for him," exclaimed Sloot. "For us!"

"Building suspense," said Roman. "Don't worry, they'll rough us up good! Make it look like we barely escaped with our lives."

"What?"

"No broken bones or anything. Well, maybe a finger or two. Have to make it look convincing, don't we?"

Sloot tried to take comfort in the fact that he now knew what he'd be doing for the next month, but it was no good. He started to panic. He tried to do it quietly.

"I'm going to practice." Vlad rose from her chair. Her plate was empty. Sloot and Roman stood and bowed as she strode from the room.

"I love to watch her eat," said Roman in a confidential tone, once he was sure she was out of earshot. "She was raised by wolves, you know."

"Raised by wolves? The thirty-seventh of a royal family?"

"Tradition," said Roman. "All the Vlads were raised by wolves. She's spent her whole life fighting something or someone. That's where she's going now, to fight with the Lebendervlad."

Vlad spent most of her waking hours fighting her departed forebears in the courtyard. Sloot spent several hours watching her from the battlements one day, dispatching the shadowy warriors one by one in puffs of black smoke. They'd coalesce anew from one of the nearby Black Smilers and come at her again.

She changed weapons frequently. Nicoleta told him that the chaos of the battlefield requires constant improvisation, and swords tend to slip from bloody hands, especially when the battle's run long and the corpses are waist-high.

Sloot's first order of business had been to establish a daily routine for himself. He knew he could only rely upon it to keep him sane for a month or so, but who knew? There just might be the vestiges of an old routine waiting for him in Salzstadt when he returned. So long as he wasn't dismissed by the elder Lord Hapsgalt and blackballed from working in the financial sector for the rest of his life, he just might be able to forget that most of this had ever happened.

He started each morning by staring out his window at the Carpathian flag. A red eagle flanked by white wolves on a field of black. There was no paper reproduction of the Old Country flag on his wall, and it didn't seem right to recite the Loyalist Oath to the Carpathian one, so he just stood there in silence and stared at it. It was a shadow of his customary observance, but it was something.

Then there was breakfast. It was the one part of Carpathian culture that he felt he'd genuinely miss once he'd returned to Salzstadt, and he looked forward to avoiding learning what was in it every morning.

As luck would have it, the city was surrounded by a massive wall, and it had a massive southern gate that never opened. If it did, it would open onto the great road that led eventually to the main gate of

Salzstadt. He passed it on his after-breakfast walk, placed his hand on it, and while it didn't make him feel as secure as the one back home, the crows picking the soft bits from the caged corpses along the top of the wall certainly loaned it a sense of foreboding that would keep attackers away. Who would be insane enough to invade Vlad the Invader, anyway?

He wound his watch. It was still keeping impeccable time thanks to Greta. She'd done an equally impressive job with the clock in the square, which ticked along in perfect synchronization with his watch, day after day. He looked for her a couple of times to thank her, but she spent so much time with Vlad that he never saw her.

"The two of them are getting awfully cozy," said Roman with a wink and a pair of eyebrow raises.

"Wait," said Sloot, "you don't mean ..."

"I thought they might hit it off," said Roman. "I told you, I'm an excellent judge of character."

"I can't imagine that Willie's very happy."

"Oh, he's fine. He's got one of the nice suites that were designed just for high-ranking hostages. Fresh linens, locks on the outsides of the doors."

"Not that! Greta is supposed to be Willie's fiancée."

"That was never going to work out," said Roman. "Even setting aside the fact that he's a china set and three guests short of a tea party, it's just not meant to be. I'm an excellent judge of character, you know."

"So you keep telling me. But Greta and Vlad?"

"You wouldn't think it," Roman shrugged, "but there you are. The warlord and the clockmaker. Stranger things have happened."

People are good at coping with strangeness in small doses, but not at the outer limits. Perhaps Roman was worried that someone in the trades becoming romantically involved with the ruler of a warlike nation would be enough to send Sloot careening headlong into madness. If that were the case, sending him to the wizard's tower was a curious move.

Everything in the place was a candidate for the strangest thing that Sloot had ever seen, starting with the door.

"All right now," it said when Sloot knocked on it. "Try that again, and you'll draw back a stump!"

"You can talk!"

"And you assault first and state the obvious later."

"I knocked on the door, that's all."

"He said as though I weren't here," said the door.

"I'm sorry, that's just … well, it's what you do."

"'What you do' indeed! You're one of them, then."

"I'm sorry, who?"

"Peopleists," replied the door. "If it's not people, it's not worth talking to, is that right?"

"Well, it's just—"

"Spare me. How'd you like it if one of my boards lashed out and walloped your front surface every time I wanted something from you?"

"I wouldn't like it. I wouldn't like it at all!" Sloot had never been reprimanded by a door. He was fairly certain that this particular door was unique, but he couldn't help wondering if it wasn't. He was going to lose a measure of sleep while indoors for a while, just to be on the safe side.

There was a rattle, and the door swung inward.

"I thought I heard somebody," said Nicoleta. "Come in!"

"I just … I'm terribly sorry."

"Oh, come on," said Nicoleta. She pulled Sloot through the door and slammed it shut.

"Easy!" said the door, its voice rather muffled now.

"Pay him no mind," said Nicoleta.

"I didn't mean—"

"It's the downside of being a wizard," said Nicoleta. "The confluence of magical energies just sort of saturates things over time." She leaned over his shoulder and shouted, "And if the door has a problem doing its job, I can melt down its fittings and use it for kindling!"

Silence.

"That's better," said Nicoleta. "Now, into the box with you."

She led Sloot past a row of bookshelves and a table littered with glassware in ridiculous shapes and configurations. Strange colored liquids bubbled in some, churned in others, and in one case seemed to be learning to make obscene gestures.

Standing next to a brazier of purple flame was a roughly human-sized box, which Sloot was failing to refrain from comparing to a coffin. He would have been relieved about the lack of a corpse inside when Nicoleta opened it, but he was too busy cowering from the tentacles that lunged out from it.

"Oops." Nicoleta produced a wand from the folds of her garish green robes and started shooting sparks into the box. "Don't let them touch you!"

Sloot ducked, dodged, and scampered away from the box as deftly as he could. Only one of the tentacles was more persistent than his instinct for self-preservation and managed to grab him by the ankle.

"I said *don't* let them touch you!"

"Sorry!" said Sloot. The tentacle hoisted him into the air and waved him around like an insane toddler conducting its first symphony. Sloot was sure that he was supposed to panic at this, but he didn't; nor did he try curling into a ball, wriggling free, or even grabbing onto any of the furnishings that he was being bounced so inartfully among.

"This seems about right," he said. He was probably going to die, and he felt … well, nothing. It was a simple matter of fact, as immutable as gravity having selected "down" as its signature maneuver.

"Got it!" Nicoleta exclaimed. With one final shower of sparks from her wand, the tentacle that was wagging Sloot popped out of existence.

Sloot wondered, as he collided with the ground, whether the same thing happened to goblins before they were called to answer breaches of etiquette back home.

"Sorry about that," said Nicoleta as she helped Sloot to his feet. "Anything broken?"

"Only hope, for all time." Sloot wondered why he'd said it, but not enough to spend any effort pursuing the thought, or ever doing anything else again.

"Yeah, that'll wear off soon," said Nicoleta. "Tentacles of Doom. I thought I'd reset the box already, sorry."

"Okay." Sloot shrugged, though it hardly seemed worth the trouble. He watched as Nicoleta mumbled and waggled her wand at the box. He felt as though he should have been at least marginally curious as to what was going on, but what did it really matter, considering the eventual heat death of the universe in a few trillion years?

"That's done it," said Nicoleta with a satisfied grin and a nod. "Tentacle-free, cross my heart. In you go."

"What's it do? Never mind." When set against asking scary questions, getting into the box seemed like the lesser hassle, so in he went. Some ancient vestige of self-preservation screamed at him that he normally wouldn't put himself into a box that had recently been overflowing with Tentacles of Doom, or any sort of tentacles for that matter, but he was beyond listening to that kind of noise now. There wasn't any point to it.

The lid was closed, and the absence of tentacles was replaced with an abundance of Sloot. Every bit of Sloot that there was, in fact; that is to say, every instant of Sloot that had ever been was playing out inside the box at once. It was a master class in ingurgitation, and it was giving Sloot a headache.

"Everything all right in there?" asked Nicoleta.

"No," said Sloot. "My youth is directly proportional to my disappointment with my achievements as an adult. Not that it matters. Nothing does."

"It sounds like the box is set properly. Cheer up, the dooms should wear off soon."

"I doubt that very much."

"Try not to talk, it'll take the box longer to get a good reading."

Sloot attempted pondering on his utter disinterest in what that meant but decided it was too boring. Silence it was, then. At least he'd be able to wait for death in peace.

"I'm sorry to barge in here like this," came a voice from outside the box.

"Better than knocking," said Nicoleta. "You've met the door."

"Right. Do you have a minute?"

"Of course. What's on your mind, Greta?"

Sloot hadn't realized that the two of them were friends. Then again, he didn't tend to understand how friendships between women worked. There didn't seem to be any sort of spectrum dividing fierce loyalties from blood feuds.

To be fair, Sloot had few enough friendships of any variety to count them on his fingers without running out. His five-year-old self had been so sure that he'd have made loads of friends when he was really old. In fact, there were very nearly forty Sloots looking to him for an explanation on that score.

"Nothing interesting, I'm afraid," said Greta. "That's the problem. I'm afraid I'm going a bit stir crazy."

"Carpathia not to your liking?"

"Oh, on the contrary! It's a fascinating place, as far as I can tell from the castle. I like the gargoyles especially."

"Why not go out into the city? Vlad's not keeping you locked away, is she?"

"Oh no," answered Greta. "I'm as free to roam as anyone else in Carpathia, she's told me that on several occasions. I just don't want to."

"You just said you were going stir crazy."

"I just miss my shop. You're lucky, you know … this tower is just amazing! I'll bet you could spend weeks in here without getting bored."

"You're welcome to come up anytime," said Nicoleta. "Just don't touch anything, unless you know exactly what it is. Even then, it could be a faerie masquerading as what you think it is."

"Faeries?"

"Like goblins, only with wings. And without the sense of humor. And they have a flair for the dramatic. Never met a faerie who could let a spotlight go un-stood-in."

"I wouldn't know what to do with any of this stuff anyway," said Greta. "The clocks in my shop, on the other hand—I could fiddle with them all day. That's what I'd be doing right now if I were back at home."

Sloot knew a thing or two about intellectual curiosity. In fact, at that very moment, his nine-year-old self was reminding him of the time he'd experimented with the rapid displacement of tablecloths, much to the detriment of his mother's stemware. That was when he abandoned the pursuit of a career in magic, and had logically moved toward accounting instead.

"There are clocks here, you know," said Nicoleta. "I'm sure people would line up at the castle gates if they knew you were repairing clocks. In fact, Vlad might appreciate it if you did."

"Ugh, that's hardly an enticement." There was a pause. "No, nothing like that, everything's fine. It's just that I don't have anything here that's my own, you know? It's like I'm expected to have breakfast with Vlad, then sit around looking pretty until she's done practicing swords with her dead ancestors, then we have dinner together, and then … well, you know."

Nicoleta giggled. Greta blushed, not that Sloot could see it. He was too busy recalling the worst of his crackly-voice-and-acne years.

"I'm sure that there are other clocks in the castle that could use your attention."

"It doesn't have to be clocks," said Greta. "I'm just tired of feeling that I'm nothing more than my ability to wear a dress well and grace Her Dominance's bedchamber."

"Both of which you do with aplomb, no doubt," said Nicoleta with another giggle.

"Oh, don't you start, too!"

"Sorry. You did a great job on the old clock in the square though. I was glad I didn't have to resort to magic to get it working."

"Really?"

"Magic is great and all, but sometimes it just seems like cheating. That clock's historic. It was nice to get it running the proper way."

"No use romanticizing old clocks to me, wizard. I'm spoken for."

"Don't flatter yourself. Anyway, if you need any tools that you can't find here, Myrtle says she's got a connection in Salzstadt that can smuggle things in."

"Myrtle. She's the one infected with philosophy, isn't she?"

"Possessed," said Nicoleta, "but you're not far off. Philosophy is technically magic, but it's the lowest form. Worthless, really. *Why are we here?*" She said that last bit in a quavering voice usually employed by people who have never spoken with a ghost, trying to sound as if they knew what one would sound like.

"I'll think about the clock."

They chatted for another hour or so. By the time Greta left, Sloot's case of the dooms had indeed worn off. Once he'd decided that there was, in fact, good in the world, and that he had reasons to go on living, he started to panic over his cramped conditions. If the box were any smaller, he wouldn't have been lying in it, but rather wearing it.

He had to keep silent. Nicoleta hadn't given him any instructions to that effect, but once he'd been unintentionally eavesdropping on their conversation for ten minutes or so, it couldn't be undone. Be silent, or be some sort of pervert. Those were his choices.

"All done," said Nicoleta as she opened the lid.

"That's good news. I hope I won't have to do that again."

"Poor dear, I know it's cramped in there. But no, you won't. Unless you're accused of treason, in which case you will."

Sloot thought back to the Tentacles of Doom. He shivered. "I'd have a trial to see if I was guilty, I hope."

"Of course! That's what the box is for."

"How's that?"

"That's why you were in there," explained Nicoleta, "to verify your loyalty! You see that sigil on the lid of the box?"

"There's a glowing orange squiggly. It looks like two bees fighting over a loaf of bread."

"That's the one. In most cases, it should be blue; however, given your lifetime of indoctrination in Old Country oppression, we figured you'd need to be graded on a curve. Orange is fine."

"And if I'd failed?"

"I don't want to worry you, but ... well, do you remember the tentacles that were in the box before?"

Myrtle was avoiding Sloot. He couldn't say that he blamed her. The skill with which he'd botched their romantic moonlight walk must have left her wondering if he'd taken lessons. A regular person would simply march right up to her and apologize, but that was the sort of thing that required a modicum of courage. Sloot, as it turned out, was utterly bereft of modica.

Roman chided Sloot for moping about it, and Sloot took offense at the insinuation. He was clearly *sulking*, after all.

A sulk differs from a mope largely in terms of decorum. Moping is the favorite pastime of teenagers, especially those who've not yet decided what perceived injustice they want to rebel against. It consists primarily of a great deal of sighing, wearing trousers with holes in the knees, and derision toward anything other than the two things they think are cool at the time.

Sulking, on the other hand, is most commonly undertaken by adults who have come to grips with the fact that they're not rebelling against anything. Regardless of their mood, they've still got to dress nicely, smile at their coworkers, and say "that sounds great" when they'd really like to say "shut your face, or I'll shut it for you."

He went for a walk. Walking often helped to break a sulk, but the only other time he'd gone walking in Ulfhaven thus far had been with Myrtle. He sulked about that until his feet had taken him to the one place they remembered: the gate in front of her house. Panicking, he ran back the way he'd come to avoid discovery, only to realize once he was several blocks away that she'd seen him from the balcony. And made eye contact. And waved at him to come up.

All the forces of nature seemed to be working together to put Sloot and Myrtle together. Perhaps something in Sloot's subconscious was suspicious. Why were the forces of nature so interested? Luckily, he possessed a specific blend of smarts and cowardice to ensure he didn't fall for it.

The sky was a gloomy grey, very nearly the same shade as the buildings and cobblestone streets of the city. There was a steady drizzle. It was heavy enough to make him wish he'd brought a cloak to keep it off him, but light enough to make him wish the clouds would just open up and get on with it, already. Gargoyles sat on every rooftop, scowling down at him.

He'd just managed to get his clothes saturated to the point of miserable shivering when he returned to the castle. Just as he started smiling at the prospect of a dry pair of socks, he saw Roman and Nicoleta walking out toward him. Her outfit was a more savage assault on the senses than usual. Roman wasn't quite as garish but was bundled up in an orange and yellow cloak, waving a pennant to match.

"Hey, it's Sloot!" said Roman. "You're just in time! The Gore Flayers are playing the Boiling Blood, let's go!"

"The who, and the what?"

"Boulderchuck," Nicoleta replied. "It's our national sport! You have to come, we'll buy you a scarf or a rusty axe or something!"

"Er, thanks," said Sloot. "I know you're just trying to cheer me up, but—"

"Did you need cheering up?" asked Nicoleta.

"Oh, well probably. But no, thank you."

"I mean, isn't that just the way he looks?" she asked Roman.

"No," he answered, "that's his sulking face. The difference is subtle, but you pick up on it after a while. He sulks a lot."

"I see what you mean," said Nicoleta. "Come to think of it, you *do* seem more down than usual."

"It's Myrtle," said Roman. "I told you, remember?"

"Did you?" asked Sloot. "Thanks for that, no sense keeping secrets or anything."

"She outranks you." Roman jerked a thumb toward Nicoleta. "Besides, you'll thank me for that later."

"Yes you will," said Nicoleta. "I'm working on something special for you."

"Oh, you shouldn't," said Sloot, who was as fond of surprises as he was of extensive dental work.

"After the game. It'll be ready by the time we get back, come on!"

Sloot had never developed a knack for resisting peer pressure—or charity bell ringers, or marginally persistent salesmen, or the urge to say "what?" in response to "ablitheringidiotsayswhat"—so off to the game he went. It was played in a huge arena encircled with stone benches, on a ruined field of dirt and rock. It was littered with chunks of stone, some of which would require more than one person to lift.

Two teams of a dozen heavily armored players each took the field, eliciting all manner of cacophony from the stands. People blew horns, shouted, threw entrails, and generally made a spectacle of themselves in anticipation of the carnage to come.

"They're not wearing any weapons," said Sloot.

"Why would they?" asked Roman. "It's *boulderchuck,* they chuck boulders at each other."

"Swords might make it more interesting though," remarked Nicoleta. "Can you imagine?"

"I'm not sure how," said Roman. "It's the most exciting thing I can think of already!"

"How's it played?" asked Sloot.

"I told you. They chuck boulders at each other!"

As simple as the rules (or rather, "rule") of boulderchuck were (or rather, "was"), keeping track of the chaos that ensued was anything but. The players mostly went solo, in pairs, or in trios, and set about the task of filling the sky with the assortment of stones available on the field. Blood and teeth flew. Limbs dangled from their sockets at unnatural angles. Screams were met with cheers, "smashing" and "bashing" were considered entirely separate concepts, and Sloot was forced to drink more beer than he'd ever done in a single sitting.

Roman and Nicoleta were Gore Flayers supporters, as were all of the other fans in orange and yellow on that side of the arena. They cheered when one of the red-on-red Boiling Blood players failed to get out of the path of a flying chunk of rock, and cried "foul!" every time the same thing happened to one of the Gore Flayers.

Sloot was aware of the concept of fouls from hearing people talk about other sports. They were illegal actions that should have punishments associated with them; unfortunately, the duty of enforcing said punishments was left to people called "referees," who traditionally had severe vision and hearing impairments. As there were no referees in boulderchuck, it was just something you shouted now and again.

"The blood's doing that thing again," said Nicoleta.

Roman nodded, his brow furrowed. "I noticed that."

Sloot looked down onto the pitch and saw tiny drops of blood floating away from what had been a massive pool of blood only moments ago. The people sitting in front of him had been very excited to be close enough to catch some of the spray from Algernon Snappingbone, left splatter for the Boiling Blood. Their faces were clean again.

"Has it got anything to do with the bloodless murders back in Salzstadt?" Sloot wondered aloud.

"We'll know soon enough," said Nicoleta. "We've got some clerics following the FOUL! Pull out his spine and feed it back to him, Gurm! Woo woo!" she screamed.

Nicoleta was particularly fond of a Gore Flayer by the name of Gurm Deathcrush. He was a massive brute who would do well in the library if he decided that boulderchuck wasn't his true calling. His performance in this game made Sloot doubt that very much.

"I almost hope he doesn't score anymore," said Nicoleta, who'd celebrated every one of Gurm's chucks that found its mark with an impressive show of fireworks. "I've only got a couple of volleys left!"

In the end, Gurm only managed to score one more time. After the judges had counted the number of teeth each team still possessed, the Gore Flayers had narrowly trounced the Boiling Blood, whose doctors were busy with hand tools cutting their irreparably smashed armor away from them. The side of the arena on which they were sitting erupted in applause, fist fights, and a few small fires that forced them to leave through the exit on the far side.

※.⫪※.⫪※.⫪※.⫪

Sloot awoke close to noon the following day. He couldn't remember how he got home, though his violent dry heaving was explanation enough for the fuzzy memory. There was also the matter of his brain having transmuted itself into a fiendish torture implement, the sort that red-robed zealots might use to coerce people into taking lifelong vows of sobriety.

"Good morning!" shouted Nicoleta, striding into Sloot's bedroom in the manic fashion of a motivational speaker who *still can't hear you!* Sloot screamed feebly and threw his hands over his ears.

"Oh my," said Nicoleta. Then she giggled. "Someone needs to work on his tolerance, either for booze or for pain."

"Please go away," whined Sloot. "I'm dying, and I'd like to do it in peace."

"You're not dying. But by the looks of it, I've arrived just in the nick of time." She was holding a glass bottle filled with a dark blue liquid. She set it on his nightstand.

"Hangover cure?"

"Better. Roman told me about your troubles with Myrtle and asked me to brew it for you."

"What is it?"

"It's a hero's potion." Nicoleta beamed with pride. "All you need is a little sip, and you'll have all the pluck and courage you need to face your sweet lady."

"Thanks," said Sloot. "That's the nicest thing that anyone's ever done for me. I'll take a sip as soon as my eyes can focus."

"Do it now, it'll help! I promise!"

"It cures hangovers, too?"

"Not exactly. Just trust me."

Trust. Sloot would have laughed, had he not been absolutely certain that doing so would cause a rupture in what was left of his brain, or worse. Still, he had to acknowledge that Nicoleta had been completely upfront with him thus far, and the worst the potion could do was kill him. That would be a pyrrhic victory in terms of hangover cures, but it would do the job.

He uncorked it. It smelled like oiled leather and victory. He took a sip, and without blinking decided that it was time to get up off the floor and bend something to his will.

Nicoleta was right. It didn't cure his hangover. It was still as robust as it had ever been, and in fact may have gotten a bit worse, but he found that he simply didn't care. The entire concept of a hangover seemed insignificant, a thing that wasn't worth crying over if you were a day over two years old.

"There," said Nicoleta as Sloot stood up, "feeling more like yourself?"

"Well, yes. More like myself than I've ever felt, in fact! How long does it last?" His voice had dropped to a velvety baritone.

"Your first sip will last a day or so. You'll build up a tolerance to it, so try to use it sparingly. Oh, hello!"

Sloot glanced down to find that he was naked. He'd started getting changed without regard for the fact that he had company. And why shouldn't he? This was his room after all, and she could go along with the program or find herself elsewhere!

"See anything you like?" asked Sloot, nearly startled at his own boldness, but that was the sort of reaction that sissy men went in for, with a glass of warm milk and something called a "good cry."

"That was a particularly strong batch," she said with a giggle. "Do try not to fight anyone, will you?"

"I can't make any promises." He'd felt an urge to promise he wouldn't, but lying is the comfort food of the weak! The only thing he was serving up was lean, rare steaks of truth.

"Fine, just remember that punching isn't frowned upon here. Roman's told me all about salts and their kicking."

Freshly shaven and feeling like he could take on all of Carpathia, Sloot strode from the castle more boldly than he'd ever strode in his life. The sky was still grey, but it seemed a more promising shade of drab than it had the day before.

Straight to Myrtle's house, then. Why had it been so hard for him that night? It was perfectly simple! She'd wanted a kiss, and he'd wanted to give her one.

Something had prevented him. What was it? And why did he never let his chin jut like it was doing just then? His stride was longer than usual, owing no doubt to the fact that he was keeping his shoulders back. Posture! He was practically marching through the streets now, a warning to any lowlifes within striking distance, and a "you're welcome" to any appreciative onlookers.

There was her gate. He'd been terrified of that gate! Why? It baffled the imagination. He marched through it now, up the stone steps and knocked on the door.

A man answered the door, but said, "Can I help you, sir?" with such deference that he could only have been a butler, and not another suitor to challenge him. A pity! Sloot would have easily thrashed him within an inch of his life.

"Sloot Peril," he said in a forceful baritone. "I'm here to see Lady Myrtle, and I take my whiskey neat!"

Unfortunately, Myrtle was out of the house. The butler, whose name Sloot didn't bother to learn, didn't know when she would return. He made Sloot very comfortable in the sitting room with a large quantity of sausages and a decanter of whiskey. His instincts, which were now speaking to him very forcefully, advised that it would be just the thing for forcing his hangover, mild as it was, into submission. Lesser Sloots might have asked what role whiskey played in a hangover cure, but did well to keep quiet.

As the hours rolled past, he contented himself to leaf through a book on one of the shelves, the title having caught his eye: *Carpathian Invasion Theory*.

According to the book, several hundred years earlier, the nineteenth Vlad the Invader had found her horns locked so ferociously with King Oskar of Nordheim that the father of the gods of Nordheim had to intervene. Impressive!

Unfortunately, the intervention closed on an oath being sworn on *Gungnir*, Odin's spear, by Oskar and Vlad. Odin's spear is enchanted with deep magic, and an oath sworn upon it is unbreakable. The oath brought an end to nearly two centuries of war between Carpathia and Nordheim. A shame, but Sloot supposed all wars must end eventually.

It seemed that Odin had finally become unsure of a Viking victory over the bloodthirsty Carpathians. He wasn't usually one to intercede in such matters, feeling that the Vikings shouldn't get into wars they couldn't win on their own; however, the gods hadn't managed a single good night's sleep since the war began, and enough was enough.

The Vikings were sad to see the end of such a well-balanced war, as were the Carpathians. Vlad was sad for the same reason, but she paid an even higher price.

To continue calling herself "the Invader," she had to have at least one rival worth invading. Aside from Nordheim, the only nation that bordered Carpathia was the Old Country in the south. Nordheim was technically an ally now, as the oath sworn on Gungnir constituted a treaty.

To be sure, the world was full of other nations, all of which could use a good invading; but aside from Nordheim and the Old Country, invading would require boats.

Carpathians are not a seafaring people. They don't like being in places that cannot be conquered, and the sea is singularly unsuited to the planting of flags, the garrisoning of troops, and the building of castles. Furthermore, it is utterly bereft of tracts of land to dole out to the generals who expect that sort of thing when wars come to an end.

Sloot kept reading until the light grey sky turned purple and then black. Eventually, his eyelids grew heavy, and then someone was shaking him gently.

"Wake up, Sloot."

"Hello," said Sloot. His voice had gone tenor again.

"I have to say that I was confused," said Myrtle. "When Gustav told me that there was a Mister Peril in the sitting room who'd challenged him to wrestle, I wondered if you had a relative here."

"Right." Sloot shook the fog of sleep from his mind. "Sorry about that." Oh, no! *Sorry about that?* The potion must have worn off!

"It's no problem," said Myrtle. "Carpathian men always talk to each other like that. Gustav would probably have taken you up on it if I hadn't specifically forbidden wrestling in the house."

"Did you?"

"Well, Carpathians are fond of wrestling, and I— HANG ON, DON'T FORGET THAT YOU'RE MAD AT HIM. Oh, right! What's with you, Peril?"

*Yes*, thought Sloot, *the potion has definitely worn off, and I've left the bottle in the castle. I'll just open my mouth and see where the conversation goes then, shall I?*

"I was afraid of you," answered Sloot, then instantly regretted it. What would the heroic version of himself had said? Not that, in any case.

"Afraid of me? Why, because I tried to kiss you?"

"Well … yes?"

Myrtle's hands were on her hips. She squinted at him with her mouth open, her upper lip occasionally jerking up in a sort of sneer. Disbelief and something bordering on amusement were trying to negotiate terms of peaceful coexistence.

"THAT DEFIES LOGIC ENTIRELY," said Myrtle, sort of. "IN MY PROFESSIONAL OPINION, HE'S NOT WORTH THE EFFORT. I didn't ask for your professional opinion, did I? PERHAPS YOU SHOULD! YOU'VE BEEN HAVING SOME PARTICULARLY SCANDALOUS DAY-DREAMS ABOUT HIM LATELY, AND I DON'T KNOW IF HE'S CAPABLE OF— Would you please stop talking!?"

Sloot's face felt hot. He could hear his blood rushing in his ears. He was likely as red in the face as Myrtle was at that moment, but he had the distinct impression that she was still entirely in control of the situation.

His mind raced to unlock the secret of that heroic version of himself that spoke in a deep voice and knew things about posture. He'd been summoned via magic, but he'd felt so genuine! Was he still inside Sloot somewhere, standing by to take control of this madness with practiced grace and the leathery hands of a man who knows how to make a bow and arrow if he found himself stranded in the wilderness?

If he was still in there somewhere, what would he do?

Whatever he wanted. Without bothering to think through all of the pros and cons first.

"Right," said Sloot. The next thing he knew, his lips were on Myrtle's, and they were kissing. His arms were around her and everything. In fact, he thought there was a very good chance that he'd done it himself, no hero potion involved.

Myrtle wrapped her arms around Sloot and kissed him back. He felt her lips smiling against his, and couldn't suppress a smile of his own.

## ⇛THE WITCHWOOD⇚

I t was nearly dawn when Sloot returned to the castle. His hangover had not yet entirely left him, but he didn't really care. He was a man in love, and that's just the sort of thing that could convince even the most seasoned of worriers that all was right with the world.

Maybe not. Real worriers are renowned for their lurking senses of dread, which are unflappable even in the face of the greatest strokes of luck.

"Nice pile of money you've just found," Sloot's lurking sense of dread might say under the right circumstances. "It would be a shame if it were to, I don't know, push you up into a new tax bracket."

Most things were right with the world, then. Well, that would require knowing most of the things in the world. Sloot didn't want to take on the liability that goes along with blind optimism being interpreted as a guarantee.

Several things, then. There were several things right with the world.

Even with the chill of the castle's drafty halls biting into him because his more heroic self had gone off without a cloak, he didn't care. Even when one of the Lebendervlad seemed to be giving him a judgy look, he didn't care. Sloot Peril was a man without a care in the world.

Without a care in his immediate vicinity, at least.

There was a note pinned to his door. He'd been summoned to breakfast with Vlad, a few hours hence.

His room had been untouched since he left. Clothes were strewn about in the style of a hero with a singular sartorial focus, who had neither time to clean up after himself, nor regard for his mother having raised him better.

The hero's potion was still on the little table where he'd left it. Truly, that was a treasure that needed protecting! He squirreled it away beneath the clothes in his bottom drawer, then thought better of it. Wouldn't that be the first place that a thief would look? He moved it instead to a high shelf behind some books. Poor people who needed to steal things were generally illiterate, according to the Domnitor, long may he reign, and likely to fear books for their seditious content, having been warned to that effect by the Domnitor. Long may he reign.

He then kicked off his boots and fell into bed, feeling as though he'd earned a bit of sleep before breakfast. Giddy with the prospect of new romance, he dreamed of very few things that wanted to either kill him or smear all of the really good numbers in his ledgers.

Roman and Nicoleta were already helping themselves to steaming piles of breakfast when Sloot entered the dining room with a spring in his step.

"You look awfully chipper this morning," said Roman.

Sloot grinned like he was being paid to do it.

"I'd say the hero's potion did its job," said Nicoleta.

"What's this about a hero's potion?" inquired the one voice that Sloot longed to hear above any other. He turned and smiled at Myrtle. She smiled back, but with a side of suspicion.

"Nicoleta brewed one for me," Sloot explained.

"Oh," said Myrtle, looking crestfallen.

"It had worn off by the time you returned," Sloot hastened to add.

"Really?" said Myrtle, imploring it to be the truth.

"Really," said Sloot. "Believe me, I've never been more terrified in my life than when I kissed you!"

"THAT'S THE SORT OF ROMANCE YOU CAN EXPECT FROM AN ACCOUNTANT. Arthur! WHAT? HE'S AS CHARMING AS THE WAX I USED IN MY MOUSTACHE WHEN I WAS ALIVE."

"Do you hear that, Sloot?" asked Greta, who'd just entered the room with Vlad. "I think Arthur is jealous."

"Hardly. And I'll thank you for addressing me as Doctor Widdershins."

"Don't hold your breath."

Greta was wearing a very elaborate dress in the Carpathian fashion, which meant that it had lots of studded leather and steel plates on it, and came with a matching sword at her hip and wolf pelt draped over her shoulders. Vlad was wearing steel on steel, and a hint of a grin that was the smarmy Carpathian equivalent of Sloot's goonish one.

"Good, you're all here," said Vlad, as she and Greta sat. Her tone wasn't exactly welcoming, given its association with her wandering stare that implied there would have been trouble otherwise.

Roman stood. "Her Dominance has asked for a formal briefing on the latest affairs in Salzstadt. I believe that everyone here has the proper intelligence clearance?"

It was commonly understood in every kingdom of the world that the court wizard was entrusted with enough royal secrets that her presence in an intelligence briefing would not be out of place. All eyes turned to Greta then, as she was the only other non-Vlad person in the room who Roman hadn't recruited into the ranks of Carpathian Intelligence.

"Greta swore allegiance to my banners last night," said Vlad.

"I did a lot of swearing last night," murmured Greta, whose cheeks went a bit pink upon realizing how softly she'd failed to whisper.

"Get on with it," said Nicoleta to Roman, with a shooing motion.

"Right," said Roman. "Then let the record reflect that all in attendance are properly cleared to be … in attendance."

"Is someone taking a record?" asked Myrtle.

"Of course not," said Roman. "You can't leave an official record of an intelligence briefing lying around! What if an Old Country spy got his hands on it?"

"But you just said—"

"I was observing traditions! There's another one about interrupting the spymaster during a briefing, you know!"

"Perhaps if there were some sort of a written record of these traditions—"

"Do be quiet!"

Roman went on to explain, in agonizing detail, just how little things had changed in Salzstadt since his last report, which had been nearly a decade prior. That report had been made to the current Vlad's father though, so Roman took great pains in elucidating those references, regardless of how relevant they weren't.

Sloot, Myrtle, and Greta were occasionally called upon to corroborate or give further details. Yes, the same families who had been insanely wealthy at the time of the last report were still insanely wealthy now. Most of them were considerably richer, in fact, owing in large part to the fact that the city's poor were significantly poorer now. If there was one thing that the Domnitor—long may he reign—seemed to appreciate, it was a nice, stark contrast between the classes in his city. On the off chance that he decided to walk among them, it would help to ensure that he didn't accidentally acknowledge the wrong sort of person.

The Hapsgalts were still chief among the wealthiest families, of course, given that there was not an industry or venture within the ken of any of the other wealthy families that didn't rely on the shipping monopoly held by The Three Bells. Furthermore, Roman was sure that the Hapsgalts were very influential within the Serpents of the Earth.

"Don't start on that," said Nicoleta. "Where's your evidence that they exist?"

"They're very good at not leaving any evidence," replied Roman.

"I don't waste time grasping at wisps of smoke," said Vlad. "Give me an enemy I can see, and I will tear out his heart."

Greta's eyelashes fluttered at Vlad. Who'd've thought a clockmaker would go in for that sort of thing? Roman, as it turned out.

"They're very real," said Roman, "and they're at the center of every nasty conspiracy that goes on in the south."

"Then they're a southern problem," said Vlad. "The enemy of my enemy is my friend, is it not?"

"This isn't the sort of enemy that would meet you in the field and try to stab you in the face," said Roman. "They'd sneak up on you when you weren't expecting it and stab you in the back."

"They can try!" Vlad pounded the table with her fist. "I've been training with the Lebendervlad since I was a little girl. No one can sneak up on me on the battlefield!"

"They wouldn't do it on the battlefield," said Roman. "They'd do it when your guard was down, possibly while you're sleeping."

Vlad's brow wrinkled. Her eyes flashed around the table, as though trying to ascertain whether they were all playing a joke on her.

"They would wake me up for a fight?"

"No," said Roman, "they wouldn't. They'd just sneak into your bedroom and cut your throat or something."

"Impossible." Vlad shook her head. "My hearing is too keen, no one can walk quietly enough."

"That's not the point."

"Plus there's the Lebendervlad. One of them watches over me always, and they do not sleep."

"That's true," said Greta, with a pointed look at Vlad. "It's creepy."

"That's not the point!" Roman exclaimed. "The point is that they work in shadow, and enemy of your enemy or not, you cannot call them a friend. They can't be trusted, and they won't meet you on the field of battle. They'll attack in secret, and by the time they've done their worst, it will be too late."

"What sort of cowards won't take the battlefield?" Vlad laughed. "If they won't show their faces, we have nothing to fear from them."

It was becoming apparent to Sloot that Carpathians didn't truck with things like stealth and subterfuge. It was a wonder they had an intelligence service at all. Trying to kill someone without telling them first seemed as ridiculous to Vlad as telling Vlad you wanted to kill her would seem to anyone else.

"I will hear no more of these cowards until you can prove that they exist," said Vlad.

"I've seen proof," interjected Sloot.

"What? Really?" Roman's mouth was hanging open as he stared at

Sloot. Hearing that Sloot knew anything about the Serpents of the Earth may have been the cause of his shock, or it may have been that Sloot had just made himself the center of attention. On purpose.

"Well, yes," said Sloot, just realizing his folly himself.

"What proof?" asked Vlad. "Show me."

"Well, it was in the library."

"Ha!" Vlad rolled her eyes. "In a story book, no doubt."

"All books tell stories," Sloot responded, "though some have to be read more closely than others to find the truth."

"Be that as it may," said Vlad, "I will hear no more of these Serpents of the Earth until someone can show me some real proof. Now, tell me about this Lord Hapsgalt that all of my servants want to murder so slowly."

Luckily for Sloot, Vlad found his input very valuable on the matter of Willie's ransom. Vlad wanted to demand a high price for her hostage, one that would hurt the Hapsgalt coffers, but not so severely that old Constantin might decide he could just churn out a new heir instead. Sloot wasn't able to give any sort of accurate accounting of their wealth, but he'd seen enough ledgers between his time in the counting house and as Willie's financier to make some estimates regarding the number and height of piles of cash they had available.

The conversation then turned to settlements close to the Carpathia/Old Country border, and Sloot noticed that Myrtle was trying to hide a pained expression.

"What's wrong?" Sloot whispered.

"It's nothing," Myrtle whispered back. "It's just taking all of my concentration to keep Arthur from dissertating aloud about the superiority of socialism, and whether A RIGHTEOUS ASSEMBLY OF THE PROLETARIAT SHOULD RISE UP AGAINST THEIR OPPRESSORS AND— Stop it! Sorry, he's leaking out a bit."

Sloot was suppressing his own urges, namely the ones compelling him to report Arthur's heresy to Uncle. Simply speaking to Vlad about the height of the money piles of a subject of the Domnitor, long may he reign, made him want to turn himself in. Would this ever get any easier?

"Lord Wilhelm will write his ransom letter," said Vlad, "assuming he knows how to write." She looked at Roman and Sloot.

"I couldn't say," said Sloot. "The wealthy of Salzstadt are usually well-educated, but I've never actually seen him do it."

"I'll take care of it," said Roman. "I know how ransom letters go, anyway. I'll make sure it has the right hint of desperation." He stood, bowed to Vlad, and left.

In a peculiar lapse in standard Carpathian meteorology, the clouds parted in the early afternoon and a glorious sunny day slipped past them. Everyone else was otherwise occupied, so Sloot and Myrtle took the opportunity to visit The Witchwood.

Long before Carpathia and the Old Country had erected enormous walls, invented taxation and generally complicated the concept of human existence, there were witcheries all over the place. Wherever a witch makes a circle of stones and starts yelling at other people to leave her alone is a witchery. There are very few of them around now, or at least very few that most people are able to find without doing a bit of scrying, or maybe having a cousin who knows someone. Witches are, among other things, professional introverts. They usually throw up wards to interfere with people's ability to see their witcheries when they become too popular. The bar is often set and met at the appearance of their first customer.

This makes the Witchwood something of a rarity. It's the oldest—and only—known witchery in Carpathia, having been in continuous operation since before the Year of Reckoning. Upon completing their apprenticeships, witches who take over operation of the Witchwood are those rare gregarious ones who enjoy things like making eye contact with people and engaging them in conversation. Beyond that anomaly, the Witchwood had everything that one would expect to see in such an enchanted place: talismans of feather and bone hanging from the trees, otherworldly fog clinging to the ground, ethereal flashes of eyes and teeth in the corners of one's vision.

Nicoleta had mentioned that the witch who currently ran the place was named Agather. There was no one else there, so Sloot assumed she was the old crone with the pointy black hat.

"Don't be shy, dearies," said Agather, not taking her attention off the cauldron she was stirring. Sloot hesitated. He hadn't thought he'd come across as shy, but had he? Perhaps something about his regular walk betrayed an innate hesitation. He'd always thought that Willie affected silly walks because the ridiculously wealthy had nothing better to do with their time, but maybe there was something else?

"I said *don't* be shy."

"Sorry," said Sloot. He caught up to Myrtle.

"And what brings ye to The Witchwood, Sloot Peril?"

"How did you know my name?"

"I didn't," said Agather. "Not really, until just now."

"A very clever guess, then."

"A witch never guesses," said Agather. It was a lie, of course, but Agather had guessed that Sloot wouldn't know that. "The future becomes clearer the closer it gets. This morning, I knew someone would come. After breakfast, I knew it would be two of ye. A minute ago, I knew it would be ye in particular, and just before my mouth started to make the shape of your name, it was made clear to me."

"THAT'S INCREDIBLE," said Myrtle.

"Thank you, Arthur. Unusual name for a woman, isn't it?"

"My name's Myrtle."

"Nice try," said Agather. "Ye're too young to be a Myrtle. Plus, yer name's Arthur."

"NO, MY NAME'S ARTHUR."

"Ah, I see. Bad luck that. Hard to sleep when ye're possessed by a philosopher. Wait, ye really are named Myrtle!"

"That's the part you find surprising?"

"That's a reserved name for the elderly! I just renamed a 'Lily' to 'Pearl' last month, and a 'Timmy' to 'Murray' the month before that. Can't get on with being old if yer named 'Timmy,' can ye?"

"I suppose not."

"Yer parents were frugal, I'll give them credit for that, but witches have to eat, you know."

"Sorry," said Myrtle. "I'll bring you any hexes I need done, shall I?"

"There's a good girl," replied Agather with a smile. "So what'll it be? I can do fortunes if ye believe in that sort of thing. Also dentistry, midwifery, livestock exorcisms, and there's a special on talismans if ye've prebottled yer own blood."

"Do you sell brooms?" asked Myrtle.

"Of course I do," said Agather. "Ye're a tall one, what are ye, a number seven?"

"W-what?" Sloot's look of abject terror coaxed a cruel sort of grin from Myrtle, the likes of which one would expect to see on that strange kid who lives a few houses down and has an alarming collection of fireworks.

"Relax," she said. "Anyone can buy a broom in Carpathia, or so I'm told."

"Truth," said Agather. "Oh, then ye must be from the Old Country! How fortunate that ye've managed to defect."

"Defect? Never!" Sloot wasn't about to add defection to the list of heresies he'd committed against what may or may not still be his mother country. He was still considering his next move and had not yet removed his finger from the piece.

"Ye poor dear," said Agather, "I imagine that after living in a cage for most of yer life, all of this freedom must seem rather frightful. That tree over there's got a hollow in it that ye'd just fit into, if ye need to collect yerself."

"The Old Country isn't as bad as all that." Myrtle shrugged. "Though I must say it's refreshing, not having people follow you around taking notes."

It seemed to Sloot that Carpathians were very fond of telling lies to their children about the Old Country. He hadn't really expected anything less, not from a culture where etiquette is only taught so that people can intentionally use the wrong forks when eating their murder victims raw.

Agather wasn't all bad, though. She took a few measurements from Myrtle, stripped a nice oak branch, and started making her a broom. It was a slow day, what with Carpathian witches doing nothing to abate the common belief that direct sunlight causes them to burst into flames. Witches don't like having to resort to magic for every little thing, so when superstition offers to do the heavy lifting, they don't argue.

"There ye are." Agather smiled at the gold coins in her hand. "Keep that handy if ye find yerself back in the Old Country. Yer goblins won't stand a chance."

"It just isn't right," muttered Sloot.

"Well ye wouldn't think so, would ye? All that brainwashing they do to ye poor sods."

"It's just … brooms are supposed to be for weddings! It makes them less special if anyone can just go and buy one."

"A broom is a wonderful thing," said Agather. "Why would it bother someone that someone else has one?"

"It just *does*," Sloot replied.

"That's no reason to keep someone else from having one," said Agather with a shrug.

"I heard witches can fly on brooms," said Myrtle.

"Oh yes," said Agather, who was taken at her word. "But that's years of practice and lessons, not for a fledgling sweep such as yerself."

"No," blushing, Myrtle gave a wave, "I wouldn't even presume to try." After a pause, she made her *although* face.

"But won't it cause goblins," questioned Sloot, "giving a broom to an unwed woman?"

"Not in Carpathia, it won't," said Agather. "Tell me, has it ever done so down south?"

"As far as I know, it's never been attempted. Why risk the goblins?"

"The better question would be why *not* risk the goblins? Think about it! If goblins are such an affront to yer Domnitor, why not put a broom in the hands of every man, woman, and child? Even if doing so causes a few goblins to turn up, everyone is armed!"

Sloot opened his mouth to accuse Agather of blasphemy, but was blasphemy supposed to make so much sense? Anyone in Carpathia can buy a broom, and there are no goblins in Carpathia.

Sloot said a swear word.

"Sloot!" Myrtle raised her broom high, looking all around for goblins, but none appeared.

Agather laughed. "For a silver, I can teach ye much better cussing than that."

They spent the rest of the day walking through the streets of Ulfhaven. Myrtle kept her broom over her shoulder, strutting around like one of the Salzstadt city watchmen with their long pikes. The afternoon sun eventually got bored and wandered off, and they returned to the castle. Myrtle seemed singularly interested in seeing Sloot's apartment, for reasons that Sloot's complete lack of experience with women failed to make clear to him.

She started kissing him the moment the door closed behind them, then stopped abruptly and gave a groan of disapproval.

"It's the cost of freeloading in the mind of a woman," said Myrtle in agitation, while staring at the ceiling. "No, you haven't got rights! Those are for the living! Sorry, Sloot, give me a minute?"

Sloot nodded, at once disappointed and grateful for the momentary reprieve. He was worried that the kissing before may have been a one-time thing, yet it seemed to be about to happen again! The only problem was his unrelenting certainty that he was sure to fail at it somehow, either by not knowing what to do with his hands, or perhaps his lips would spontaneously become ticklish.

The potion! While Myrtle was giving Arthur what for, he could sneak a sip. He'd be sure to not miss her face with his!

He walked over to the bookshelf in a way that he thought would seem casual, worrying the entire time that he would instead look as though he were trying very hard to seem casual. This was exactly the sort of reason he needed the potion!

He reached behind the books, felt around, and ... nothing.

Gone! The potion was gone! Myrtle had just finished yelling something at Arthur about exorcisms, and then she was smiling at Sloot. He felt the familiar grip of panic at his throat.

There was a knock at the door.

"Sloot! Are you there?" came a woman's voice, muffled by the thick wood of the door.

"Yes!" shouted Sloot, a bit too eagerly. He didn't know if that was why Myrtle was wrinkling her brow at him, or if it was just that another woman was knocking on his door unannounced. He could not fathom how he was going to survive whatever was about to happen.

The door opened, and Nicoleta burst in. Her cape sent up a shower of sparks.

"Thank goodness you're here!" Nicoleta stopped and gaped at Myrtle. "And you, too, Myrtle!" She shook her head to chase off the scandalous grin.

"What's going on?" asked Sloot.

"You both need to come with me," said Nicoleta. "It's Roman! He's fine, but we've got big trouble!"

## ❧FLIGHT OF THE DANDY❧

Sloot had been dragged into dungeons twice in his life: once by Mrs. Knife's goons, and again by the Lebendervlad. Historically speaking, they had not been happy visits. He had a sinking feeling that this time would be no exception, but followed Nicoleta and Myrtle down the dark stairwell nonetheless.

"This way," said Nicoleta, "Roman's waiting."

Why would Roman be waiting for them in the dungeon? Sloot racked his brain for a sensible answer but came up empty. He'd have to settle for the old-fashioned practice of waiting for things to happen in due course, the bane of the worrier's existence.

"Took you long enough," said Roman from up ahead, in the vicinity of a torchlit glow. Sloot wondered how he'd known it was them, somehow having forgotten that he was following the most flamboyant wizard in Carpathia. She was wearing her comet robes, which bore a sufficient rating to warn ships away from craggy outcroppings on moderately foggy nights.

"What happened to you?" asked Myrtle. One of Roman's eyes was swollen shut, and the side of his face was all purple.

"Willie happened," said Roman. "When I went to get his signature on the ransom note, he blindsided me with a chair leg! When I woke up, I was locked in his rooms, and he was gone."

"Willie hit you?" exclaimed Sloot. "I wouldn't think he'd even know how! It's not fashionable to fight your own battles, not with his crowd."

"He didn't seem himself." Roman sneered at Sloot. "If I didn't know any better, I'd have said he seemed rather more *heroic* than usual."

Sloot's eyes went wide. The hero's potion!

"But how would Willie have gotten it from my room? He was locked up, wasn't he?"

"I don't know," said Roman, "you tell me! Been up to visit him? Maybe you had it with you, just in case you got nervous?"

"I didn't! Honestly, I don't even know where Willie's room is! I haven't seen him since the throne room."

Roman shifted his gaze to Nicoleta.

"Don't look at me," she said. "I only made the one potion, and Sloot had it last."

"Never mind," said Roman. "We'll figure it out later, now we've just got to find him."

"Oh, that's nice," said Myrtle. "It couldn't possibly have been the exceedingly clever philosopher, the brains of the bunch. Why would he have motives the likes of which no one could foresee?"

"You got something to confess?" asked Roman.

"Sorry," said a distinctly more Myrtle-ish Myrtle. "He feels left out."

"I've got to go," interjected Nicoleta. "I'll stall Vlad for as long as I can, but she's going to go berserk when she finds out. Possibly literally, she minored in berserking in college."

"Really?" asked Myrtle. "I mean, I know she'll be miffed about losing her hostage, but—"

"He's got Greta," said Roman.

"What? Are you sure?"

"We can't find her anywhere," said Nicoleta. "A sip of hero's potion and I wouldn't put it past Willie to knock a few heads, grab the girl he thinks he loves, and head south as fast as possible."

"Oh dear," said Sloot. "When Vlad finds out—"

"She won't," said Nicoleta. "She mustn't! She's grown quite fond of Greta, and I have no doubt she'd ride south on her own to rescue her."

"She's the only warrior in Ulfhaven! Other than the Lebendervlad, I mean, but they can't leave the castle. She can't go to war with Salzstadt on her own!"

"She can," said Nicoleta, "and she will. She fights a dozen of the Lebendervlad at a time! There's no greater warrior in the world. If you don't get Greta back, thousands will die!"

Sloot had heard hyperbole before, and didn't care for it; but even if Nicoleta's opinion of Vlad were higher than it should be, it probably wasn't by much, and he didn't want to see even one person killed because Greta had been abducted by a vacuous idiot.

"What can we do?" asked Sloot.

"We can find Willie," Roman answered.

"But he's all hopped up on hero's potion!"

"It doesn't give you unnatural powers or anything," explained Nicoleta, "just confidence. Extreme *if-I-can-think-it-I-can-do-it* confidence. You just have to believe in yourself!"

"I don't suppose you have time to brew up another potion, do you?"

"No!" said Nicoleta, who then turned and ran back the way they came.

"It's down to us," said Roman. "If we can rescue Greta before Her Dominance finds out and takes up her sword, we can prevent a war. This is what the intelligence game is all about! Are you with me?"

⁂

Down the catacombs, through the grate, and quickly along the road they went. They made it to the Entrailravager farm when the sun had nearly set, where the proprietor confirmed that Willie and his bound-and-gagged lady friend had stopped for a horse that morning.

"Great," said Sloot. "He's got nearly a full day's head start! We'll have to leave at first light."

"We leave now," said Roman.

"But I'm exhausted!"

"And he's got most of a hero's potion to keep him going," said Roman. "The moon is nearly full, we'll have to make the best of it."

"I'm exhausted, too," said Myrtle. "What? Why would you be

exhausted? You're dead! AND THAT MEANS I CAN'T GET TIRED? I THOUGHT YOU, OF ALL PEOPLE, WOULD BE MORE TOLERANT OF THE NON-LIVING."

Old Man Entrailravager watched Myrtle's argument with the somber amusement of a man who'd have preferred to have gone without amusement altogether. Country life was a lot busier than city folk realized. The distance wasn't going to stare blankly into itself, after all.

Well, just the once, if we're being entirely literal; but that will be right at the end of eternity, so there won't be anyone available afterward to say "oh, now I get it" when it comes to pass, so it's hardly worth mentioning.

They rode hard for several days, only stopping when the horses firmly refused to take another step until they'd been fed and brushed. Roman cursed them for being smarter than southern horses, who'd allow themselves to be run to death. Sloot was glad for the respite, sincerely wishing that he could turn off all sensation in the lower half of his body.

Eventually, Salzstadt came into view on the horizon.

"We're too late," Sloot groaned.

"Not yet," said Roman. "As long as we get Greta out of Salzstadt before Vlad smashes her way in, we can avert a war."

"And how are we supposed to do that?"

"I don't know yet."

"You don't *know*?"

"I don't know *yet*."

"Then how can you be sure it's a good idea for us to go into Salzstadt after Greta?"

"Oh, it's not."

"Then why are we doing it?"

"Because it's less bad than all the other ideas I've had thus far."

"And that's the intelligence game, is it?"

"Congratulations, Peril!" Roman shouted, while invading Sloot's facial airspace with a very stern finger. It was the pointing one, not the rude one. They were back in the Old Country, after all. "You've discovered the limits of my patience! For your own safety, I am revoking your right to speak until we've made it back into the city. And to answer your question, yes—this is the intelligence game, and it's one that I've been playing for decades now. Now shut your whining trap, and let's get moving!"

They rode the rest of the way to the east gate in silence.

Smugglers the world over love a flagging economy because it drives the rates of bribery down; unfortunately, the market was bullish at the time. Entrance to the city cost them nearly all the gold they had on them. The guards had eyed Myrtle's broom as part of their price until she brandished it at them with surprising ferocity.

"I still don't think it was a good idea to bring it along," said Sloot as they hurried through the streets. "It's not legal! What if you get arrested for it?"

"No one stops a woman to ask about her broom," countered Myrtle. "It's not proper. Besides, we may need it. We have no idea what's waiting for us in Whitewood."

Sound though her logic may have been, Sloot wasn't the sort of person to take risks. At the age of seven, he reported one of his classmates on suspicion that she might have used a swear word, just in case someone had noticed him partially overhearing her on the schoolyard and was watching to see if he'd do the right thing.

*Snitches Get Riches.* That was the catchphrase of a very successful leaflet campaign that the Ministry of Propaganda had been carrying out at the time.

"It's fine, Sloot," said Roman. "If she's stopped in the next few blocks and questioned, just keep your mouth shut. She can say she's holding it for a friend."

They turned the corner, and Sloot was distracted from his work on what would certainly grow up to be a massive ulcer someday. He wasn't sure what he thought he'd see when Whitewood came into view, but dozens of white-gloved servants running around the place hadn't been a leading contender.

"Wow," said Roman as they walked into the courtyard. "They certainly work quickly, don't they?"

"What's going on?" asked Sloot. "It's like they're getting the house ready for—"

"For the reception," said a woman dressed in a black dress so well-starched it would double as armor.

"Olga ..." Sloot remembered her from his dinner at Gildedhearth when she'd served as his mannerist. His hands darted behind his back to hide his knuckles.

"Mr. Peril," she replied. "I must say, you and Willie's valet have gone to a great deal of effort to make an explorer of him. Frankly, I figured you'd just pay off the newspapers to write some glamorous reviews, while you spent a few weeks in Stagralla or something."

"Er, yes," said Sloot, turning a pointed look to Roman. "That would have been much easier, wouldn't it?"

"Just the one then, ma'am?"

Sloot jumped. He hadn't been expecting anything in particular, and he certainly hadn't been expecting the ghoulish figure in the black robes and pointy hat who was suddenly standing next to him. He hadn't made a sound, but rather abruptly began existing uncomfortably close to Sloot in a particularly ripe-smelling way.

"That's all I know of. How about it, Mr. Peril? Any more ghosts in the house?"

"Ghosts?"

"There was Millford," said Olga. "He was the butler when the goblins first infested the place. He was charged with locking up after everyone else had fled, never made it out."

"I talked to him," said Sloot. "He asked me if the goblins were all gone."

"It takes more than a conversation to exorcise a ghost on the haunt. Just the one then, Milgrew. Thank you for your services."

Milgrew nodded, then turned to Sloot and flashed a butter-yellow row of teeth the way that coyotes smile at rabbits, before slinking away to whatever crypt he was squatting in.

"Anyway," said Olga, "Willie brought his poor, traumatized fiancée to Gildedhearth yesterday, and we got started on the arrangements at once. There are some things that need your signature."

Olga held out the master ledger to Sloot. Sloot, being himself, started to panic. Surely she'd seen that there was no money in the coffers! They hadn't had a chance to get their payment from Winking Bob for the Carpathia job.

"Yes, right." Sloot took the ledger and opened it. Instead of bursting into flames as he'd expected, the totals came up to far more than had ever been there before. Not only that, but the zero and less-than-zero figures he'd entered before were missing entirely.

"What is the meaning of this?" yelled Sloot. He'd been angry before, but he now found himself boiling with a rage unlike any he'd ever felt. He had never expressed rage before and decided that he didn't care for it. He wished he'd known that it was coming so he could have prepared for it better.

"Lower your voice," said Olga. She still had her wand, which was now pointing in Sloot's face.

"I will not! The numbers in here are— Ow!" Olga's wand smacked firmly against his forehead. "Stop that! I said the numbers in here are—"

Her wand did not find its mark the second time, thanks to the intervention of Myrtle's broom.

"That's enough now," she said to both of them. "Why don't we go inside and have a little chat?"

Sloot and Olga wore scowls as the four of them moved past decorators, tailors, bakers, and a burly woman with a chisel who was turning a colossal block of ice into what looked like Willie fighting a pack of lions with one hand, his other busy holding a fainting Greta about the waist.

"It's not finished yet!" she barked, when she saw Roman's sidelong glance at her work.

They moved into the study, where Olga shut the doors behind them.

"I'm parched," said Roman, who started pouring himself a brandy from a crystal decanter. "Anyone else?"

"This is all of Willie's stuff," said Sloot.

"Of course it is," said Olga. "What else would it be?"

"But it was stolen!"

"*Ahem.*" Roman opened his eyes wide and jerked his head toward Olga.

"Give it up, Roman," said Sloot. "It *was* stolen, and it's back now. I'm sure that's no secret to Olga."

"You are correct," replied Olga. "I was one of the first to know that this one was likely to steal from you." She pointed at Myrtle with her wand. "However, I must admit I didn't expect that she'd utterly clean you out! I apologize for underestimating you."

"That's complicated," said Myrtle, "and besides—"

"What about the ledger?" demanded Sloot.

"What about it?"

"You know very well. The numbers! I kept a very accurate accounting of every penny in and out, including the bit about the robbery, but that's gone. All gone!"

"Is that really what's bothering you? Come now, Mr. Peril. You know how things work, you've spent most of your adult life in the Three Bells counting house! In all of that time, have you ever had cause to use red ink?"

"Only here," said Sloot. "Only when Whitewood was robbed, and—"

"Exactly. I wonder where you even got it. Please don't answer, it wasn't a question. The point is that you work for the Hapsgalts now, and the Hapsgalts are wealthy beyond measure. You never speak to them about money, and you certainly never record temporary truths in their ledgers!"

"Temporary truths?"

"Where did you get it into your head that Willie was going to be allowed to go broke? Sure, Lord Constantin likes to talk tough, but those of us who see to his interests would never let something as simple as not having any money turn a Hapsgalt into a poor person!"

"So you ..." Sloot stumbled about in the dark of his vocabulary, unable to find the words. "Just like that?"

"Just like that."

"And the furniture?"

"Everybody knows Winking Bob, Mr. Peril. Now if you please, you're all three expected at Gildedhearth for dinner, and so help me if you're not wearing something more expensive than the horse farm where you've undoubtedly slept for the last month, I'll shove you into the closet and swear through the keyhole until you're smothered in goblins."

Credit had been extended to them at Olgropp and Delancey's, a tailor so grotesquely posh that they had to go see a slightly lesser tailor first, just so they could meet the dress code to get past the surly man at the velvet rope who was all nostrils and no breath mints. Sloot was not so much offended as curious as to how someone whose job seemed to consist entirely of asking, "Do you 'ave an appointment?" and competition-level scoffing could afford the dress code himself.

Truly top-notch tailoring, it seemed, involved a detailed set of measurements that Sloot doubted could have been useful. He was posed, stretched, and prodded by a team of seamsters in ways that would have made him blush with abandon even if he'd been allowed to remain in his undergarments.

"And *why* must I remove them?" he'd asked at the outset.

"Oh, right," said a seamstress brandishing a measuring tape like she knew how to murder him with it, "because we're all a bunch of perverts who'd rather look at *that* than not."

"I just don't understand what it's got to do with tailoring!"

A very tall seamster with double recurve moustaches stepped close enough to Sloot that he nearly fell over backward trying to look up at him. Given Sloot's relative state of undress, this made him even more uncomfortable than it would have otherwise.

"Every one of us spent years studying tailoring at the University of Salzstadt to harness the mysteries of double-stitching, gussets, and buffeted lapels. You need to attend a wedding rehearsal dinner in the home of Lord Constantin Hapsgalt in a matter of hours. I have time to either explain to you what this has to do with tailoring or to put my years of study to work. Now strip, hold your arms out, and pray that our gossip moves on to something more salacious than your paler regions within the week!"

The immensely capable staff at Olgropp and Delancey's finished their challenge with minutes to spare, and the impeccably festooned three of them were whisked away by carriage to Gildedhearth.

"I've never been dressed this well in my life," said Myrtle, as the carriage rumbled over the cobbled streets. "IT'S JUST THE SORT OF ABSURD CARICATURE OF HUMAN EXPERIENCE THAT THE PRIVILEGED RULING CLASS USES TO BOLSTER THEIR DIVINE RIGHT TO SUBJUGATE THEIR COUNTRYMEN. Will you shut up and let me have this?"

"I hope you can keep him under control tonight," said Roman.

"NICE TALK," said Myrtle. "DID THAT AIR OF SUPERIORITY COME WITH THE SUIT? Arthur! Sorry, Roman."

"Just you remember that people have rotted away in dungeons for speaking truth to the wealthy. I'm not sure what happens to those who possess those who rot in dungeons, but it can't be pleasant."

Myrtle looked up and to the left. Up and to the right. "That seems to have done it," she said after a moment.

"How about you, Sloot?"

"I don't like this," said Sloot.

"What, the suit?" asked Myrtle. "I think you look rather dashing in it."

"Thanks, but I meant *this*. We put Willie in mortal danger, and he escaped despite our not lifting a finger to help him. Now we're being invited to dinner at Gildedhearth?"

"It'll all be fine, trust me," said Roman.

"How do you know that?"

"Don't worry about it!"

For all of Roman's apparent worldliness and purported ability to judge the character of others, he had a blind spot for one simple fact: telling a worrier not to worry is as likely to be successful as telling any living person to *calm down*. When they finally arrived, Sloot was worrying so ferociously that he could hear nothing more than a high-pitched whine and his heartbeat. Myrtle held his arm tightly as they walked, in case he toppled.

Sloot was dressed well enough to get past the butler without filling out an application this time. He even got a curt little bow out of him. "The clothes make the man," as the old saying goes. That had only been true in a literal sense once in recorded history, and the resulting chaos was harrowing enough that wizards were henceforth forbidden from summoning laundry golems in every civilized nation worth visiting.

The last time he'd seen the dining hall, it had been tastefully decorated with a few paintings of wealthy Hapsgalt ancestors, cherubic statues, and hunting trophies. Now it looked as though a wedding cake's nightmare had projectile vomited on every surface, and goblins had attempted to clean it up by showering it with tinsel. There were white silks draped over everything, pearloid baubles gathered in conspiratorial cliques, and every stick of furniture was gold-leafed within an inch of its life.

"You're just in time," said Olga. She appeared abruptly, startling Sloot. "Those are your seats, and these are your mannerists." A pair of black-clad young men stepped to her sides from behind a pillar, each holding a wand similar to Olga's.

"Your protégés?" asked Roman.

Olga nodded.

"And you'll be 'helping' me again, I presume," said Sloot.

Olga nodded again. She seemed to be having a hard time suppressing a truculent little grin that begged Sloot to give her a reason.

The hairs on the back of Sloot's neck stood up, but it wasn't in anticipation of the dinner thrashing that awaited him. He looked toward the head of the table and saw Mrs. Knife and Gregor sitting in the same seats as before, sneering at him with all of the malice that old house cats employ in welcoming a new puppy.

"There they are," said Willie, beaming in the goofy way that only he could, "my sidekicks! So glad that you made it out of Carpathia alive. I was worried. I had to resort to heroics to manage it myself."

"Good to see you well, m'lord," said Roman.

"Thank you, m'lord," said Sloot, immediately following the first *whack* of Olga's wand for the evening.

"Yes," said Constantin as he entered and everyone rose, "welcome back, Mr. Peril. I'd never imagined in a hundred years that you'd have the intestinal fortitude to brave the Carpathian capital, much less convince my Willie to do the same. Yet here you are!"

Constantin sat, then Willie, Mrs. Knife, Gregor, and everyone else with respect to their relative importance at the table. There was a round of toasts primarily directed at Willie, though Sloot and Roman were mentioned once or twice. At Olga's prodding, Sloot dutifully insisted that all of the credit went to Willie, and that he'd never have made it out alive without Willie's heroism. It was his day after all.

"Tell me about that," Constantin said to Willie, as the servants laid out a course that had all the trappings of soup, but came with a hammer and a knife. "You returned a full day ahead of the rest of them—"

"Through the *east gate*," interrupted Mrs. Knife, "and without any permits! You're not above the law, Willie."

The whole table broke into laughter. Gregor supported Mrs. Knife in a grimace.

"I admit it," said Willie, "it was a dashing bit of daring-do that got us out of there. Roman was very concerned about Greta—"

"Where *is* Greta?" asked Roman. His mannerist gave him a firm *whack*. "Please forgive the interruption, m'lord, I just assumed she'd be here with us."

"Miss Urmacher is recovering from her ordeal," said Mrs. Knife. "The poor thing is hysterical, has trouble remembering that Willie is her fiancé."

"Trauma!" said Constantin, a bit louder than expected, causing everyone to jump. "It happens to many people behind enemy lines, but not my Willie! It was his cool head and bare-knuckled gumption that saw them through it, wasn't it, Willie?"

"Right you are, Father. Oh, and Roman's potion, too."

"Potion?" asked Constantin. "What potion?"

"I think—" began Roman, who then succumbed to a *whack* across the throat that was forceful enough to throw him into a coughing fit.

"The blue one," said Willie. "He brought it to me, unlocked my door, and told me where Greta was. I took a sip, ran down to the gardens where she was walking alone, threw her over my shoulder, and made for the stables."

Sloot stared at Roman with his mouth open, which earned him a *whack* on the chin.

"Greta kept fighting to get away, so I had to tie her to the saddle. The poor thing—she seemed to think that she was in love with Vlad, and was trying to go back to her!"

"Not Vlad the Invader!" exclaimed Sir Dennis Frumpton, who was all moustache. His monocle dropped into his soup.

"That's right." Willie turned to the side and leaned an elbow on the table. It was a maneuver that Sloot had seen him practicing on a few occasions, something called the Softly Now, Dolly. Wait, no—if paired with the smile that Willie was also doing, it was the Long Cool Sunday. If he'd been glaring instead, it would have been called the Long Cold Fish.

"Elbows off the table," whispered a smiling mannerist standing behind Willie's chair, "if you please, Lord Hapsgalt."

"What do you think of that?" said Constantin. "My boy gave Vlad the Invader what for!"

"He endangered the lives of Old Country citizens," said Mrs. Knife. "He left the city without permits, his crossing of the Carpathian border could be considered an act of war, and he consorted with a known criminal to plan the venture!"

"Permits," scoffed Constantin. "Willie's a Hapsgalt! Did you think something like that would make a Hapsgalt man pack it in? He used his gumption! I'd have expected nothing less."

Roman was avoiding Sloot's gaze. Sloot was doing his best to place trust in the spymaster, but he'd lied! Willie hadn't overpowered him and escaped, Roman had all but sent him home in a carriage!

The next course was brought out. It looked like a leafy tower with feathers on top. Sloot considered it with caution and picked up a fork, which was summarily *whacked* from his hand.

"This one's just for smelling," said Olga. "You can't eat it, it's poisonous."

"It's a glorious day," said Constantin. "My son, the explorer! A very respectable accomplishment. I believe that he has indeed rendered proof of his worth!"

The sound of dozens of rings clinking against stemware filled the room. Sloot wasn't quite fast enough in remembering which spoon was the glass-clinking one, and received no fewer than three gleeful *whacks* before he worked it out.

"People have been to Carpathia before," said Mrs. Knife. "It's hardly exploratory if you're on roads and cobbles the entire time."

"He went into hostile territory," said Constantin, "for the benefit of … well, for our benefit. Isn't that right, Gregor?"

"Yes and no," said the pasty old wizard. "I'd have sworn it yesterday, but now I do not … have the proof, if you will."

"What do you mean?" asked Willie.

Everyone went silent. Sloot and Myrtle exchanged worried glances. Roman continued to avoid eye contact. Constantin gave a little wave to one of his butlers, who approached so the old man could whisper in his ear.

"Ladies and gentlemen," said the butler, "Lord Constantin thanks you for joining his table on this joyous occasion, and wishes you a pleasant evening."

No one appeared upset about the prospect of missing dessert. The malnourished look was all the rage in those days, and people who dressed in ensembles that had financial portfolios of their own tended to grow despondent when their cheekbones fell into subtlety.

Sloot tried to stand up because everyone else was doing it, and the very idea of not following a trend made him uneasy, but Olga's hand was surprisingly firm on his shoulder.

"Where's everyone gone?" asked Willie. "They must have been bored, too. I told you I should have brought my sword with me, I could have shown them some moves."

"You said you'd handle it." Constantin was glaring at Mrs. Knife. He had a way of making eye contact with a person that left them cursing themselves for not having died sooner.

"I did," she replied. "Gregor had the connection yesterday, didn't you, Gregor?"

Gregor seemed to have nodded, though it was a clumsy maneuver that may have been his neck attempting to rot out from beneath his head. He was greener than the first time Sloot had seen him, thinner too.

"Oh, is this secret business?" Willie looked positively delighted, like he'd just been told that Snugglewatch would fall on his birthday this year. "Can I invite my friends into the club?"

"It's not a club, Willie." Constantin's eyes closed, and he pinched the bridge of his nose.

Fate rarely goes fishing. It's got quite a lot to do, and simply can't spare the time; but every once in a while, it dangles a line in the face of the unsuspecting. And like a fish, people rarely have the good sense to ignore it and find something less risky to do.

"What's he talking about?" asked Sloot, who would shortly regret having done so.

"We've already said too much," said Mrs. Knife.

"About what?" asked Willie. "Do you mean the Serpents of the Earth?"

"Curse you, boy!" said Gregor, spittle flying from his mouth.

"Of course," said Roman, "it all makes perfect sense! It was your blood star, wasn't it?"

"How did you know what it was?" asked Gregor, looking genuinely surprised.

"You handled a blood star for the Serpents of the Earth?" said Myrtle, gaping at Roman.

"You know about all of this?" Sloot gaped at Myrtle.

"I'm as surprised as the rest of you," said Willie, who wasn't, but didn't want to feel left out.

"Silence!" shouted Constantin. You have to practice to get that good at shouting. Even Mrs. Knife flinched.

"Yes," Constantin continued, after pausing for dramatic effect, "we sent a blood star with you into Carpathia, and by 'we' I mean the Serpents of the Earth. Of course, now that you know about it, we must determine whether you can be allowed to leave this place alive."

"Please don't say anything else," said Sloot. "I don't know anything about the Serpents of the Earth, and I'd be happy to refrain from re-membering anything about this conversation."

"That's a lie!" snarled Mrs. Knife. "He was the fool who imperson-ated Roger Bannister to gain access to the archives!"

"You, Peril?" Constantin appeared to be surprised, possibly for the first time in his life.

"It's a secret club," said Willie. "All of my friends are in it. Well, not you. Hey, Dad! Can Sloot and Roman and Myrtle join the club? Please?"

Mrs. Knife exhaled in disgust.

"Curse you again, boy," said Gregor. "You're a legacy! Don't you know what you've done?"

"I just asked if my friends can be in the club. They're really nice, they helped me escape from Carpathia! Not that I needed the help, I was just about to break out on my own before Roman—"

"That's enough, Willie," said Constantin. "By the Book of Black Law, you've just invited these initiates into our court for proving."

"What? Oh no, I couldn't." Sloot flinched, then remembered that Olga had left the room.

"Nor should you, Mr. Peril," said Mrs. Knife. "You see, Constantin? He'd rather die. I can see to it." She slid her knife from its sheath, causing Sloot to whimper.

"Oh, can you?" Constantin crossed his arms. "If that were the case, would he not be dead already? Oh, don't look so surprised, Mrs. Knife. I *am* the Eye of the Serpent, after all. I know about a great many things you think you're hiding from me."

Constantin was staring daggers at Mrs. Knife. Even Sloot avoided his eye, on the off chance that looks really could kill.

"He knows too much," croaked Gregor. His voice was so dry and cracked that taking up smoking might have improved it. "If he won't join us, he'll have to be murdered and imprisoned."

"SHOULDN'T THAT BE THE OTHER WAY AROUND?" asked Myrtle, or rather, Arthur.

"You might think so," Gregor replied, "if the sum of your accomplishments in the afterlife totaled the possession of one girl. Honestly, did you even bother peering beyond the veil, seeing what fates lurk beyond it?"

"How did you know about Arthur?" asked Roman.

"That's something you'll find out soon enough, if you fail the initiation rites."

"This is fantastic!" said Willie. "You can all be in my cabal. I've never had a cabal before! I'm not really sure what they do."

"Willie!" shouted Mrs. Knife.

"That will be all," said Constantin. "Leave me, all of you."

"LOOKS LIKE HE NEEDS A PONDERANCE," said Arthur, probably.

"What do we do with them?" asked Mrs. Knife.

"Those two are free to go," said Constantin, pointing to Sloot and Roman. "She can be Greta's maid of honor. She'll be our guest."

"Free to go?" croaked Gregor. "But sire—"

"They've got work to do at Whitewood," said Constantin, the edge in his voice waving around at the throats of any further back-talk. "And Peril wouldn't think to try anything, with his lover under our protection and our eyes everywhere."

## ⚜ SCHEMING CONSPIRACIES ⚜

**W**e have to talk," said Sloot, for about the hundredth time that evening.

"We are talking!" said Roman. "Glenn here was just telling me about how the boys are going on strike next week, and there's nothing anybody can do about it! Am I right, boys?"

A cheer went up. Sloot had never seen that many people in his regular pub at once. No mystery there, it wasn't a very nice pub. But Roman was steadfast in his resolve to avoid talking about why he'd betrayed Vlad, and he was using the Union of Queue Position Engineers as a shield.

The UQPE had a list of grievances as long as the lines at Central Bureaucracy, and Roman's distraction spared no detail in dressing down everyone from The Establishment to Those Pencil-Pushing Nitwits over a seemingly endless supply of pints.

Sloot felt a bit strange about not putting a pint under his chair for every one he drank, but the goblins had long since passed out. This was a relief for the bartender, who was able to slow down to a pace that did not dangerously resemble exercise. That was just the sort of thing they tricked you into. One minute you're getting people drunk, and the next you're wearing leotards and using phrases like "feel the burn" and lifting heavy things for fun. They have a word for that sort of thing in bartending: hypocrisy.

"Central Bureaucracy won't know what hit 'em!" shouted a slender man with a pronounced underbite. He punched the air, and so did a bunch of other people who shouted "Yeah!" in response.

"The fools!" shouted a young woman standing on a table. "What do they think will happen with no one standing in the lines? The gears of regulatory commerce will come grinding to a halt!"

"Yeah!" shouted the chorus.

This went on for several hours. Someone would yell something about injustice, or the common man, and everyone else would punch the air and yell "Yeah!"

Disaster nearly struck when the pub ran out of beer. Fortunately for the bartender, who had just taken up fearing for his life—which was still preferable to exercise, mind you—the first rays of dawn cut through the room at about the same time, using their natural talents to find their ways directly into the eyes of each and every reveler. Rays of sunlight are real redacted swear words that way.

Instead of turning their collective frustration against the bartender, they all succumbed to the inevitability that sunlight inflicts upon a pub, paid their tabs, and left.

"Not here," said Roman as they walked toward Whitewood. "We can't discuss *you know what* business out in the open. I'll tell you what, I promise to come clean as soon as we get back to the house, okay? Now, who wants to find another pub?"

Sloot blinked. Unable to find the words to convey the depth of his frustration with Roman's stonewalling, he had nearly reached the end of his tether.

*That's it,* he thought. *As soon as I come up with a string of swear words vile enough to shock the truth out of this old geezer, I'm not holding back.* Unfortunately, Sloot didn't have a lot of experience with really vile swear words, so the work was slow-going. Before he finished, everything went black.

"There's our boy," came a sing-songy voice like sunshine that gave Sloot the impression it was the sort of Sunday to be spent in his pajamas. He was only able to open his eyes to a squint, seeing nothing but very bright light.

"Am I dead?"

"No, though we were wondering the same for a while."

His eyes finally adjusted enough for Flavia to come into focus. She was wearing the same white dress as before and smiling sweetly at him.

"You thought I was dead? Wait a minute, how did I get here? Did you poison me?"

"No, nothing like that. Well, actually yes, in a manner of speaking, but not enough to kill you. We'd never do that, silly! Unless ... oh, never mind. How are you?"

"My head hurts," said Sloot, "and I appear to be tied to a chair."

"I'll get you some water." Flavia snapped her fingers. A man brought him a glass of water and left. "You're not tied to the chair, by the way. Perhaps you're just not feeling well."

Sloot looked down. She was right. It was even quite comfortable, the chair to which he was not bound. So comfortable that he had no desire to leave it. Tied there by his own desire for leisure, then. Clever.

"Oh. All right then. Wait, why were you wondering if I was dead?"

"You were in Carpathia for a very long time," said Flavia. "We heard no news from you past old man Entrailravager saying that you were headed in via the catacombs."

"Entrailravager is an informant? That yokel?"

"Now, now," Flavia wagged her finger, "yokels are a vital asset for the intelligence community. One can't bury bodies in well-lit places with easy access, you know."

"I know," said Sloot, who'd never buried a body anywhere. He took a sip of his water. It tasted soapy.

"So tell me, what happened while you were there?"

While they'd been in Ulfhaven, Sloot had felt that he could trust Roman. He'd never have considered turning him over to Uncle, but he refused to provide any explanation for betraying his homeland. Could a person like that be trusted at all?

"Oh Sloot," said Flavia. "Poor Sloot! You've been through so much in these past few months. Being a double agent is simply dreadful, I know. It's so hard to know who to trust, isn't it?"

Without warning or explanation, Sloot started crying. It wasn't the reserved act of shedding a single tear, which true stoics reserve for their mothers' funerals, amputations of their own limbs, and their boulder-chuck teams' championship losses. It was the wheezing, heaving, wet with drool, every facial muscle contorted in agony variety, replete with a limp slide to the floor and flailing arms. Even toddlers take a moment to stare at their newly-acquired boo-boos in abject horror before descending into this, the most petulant performance of self-pity; but not Sloot. The belief-defying speed of his declension into conniptions was enough to put any other hopefuls off taking it up as a professional sport. They knew in their hearts they'd never achieve his greatness.

It was a traumatic half hour or so before Sloot's breathing returned from hysterics, and he realized that Flavia was cradling him in her lap. He sat up slowly and wiped enough partially crusted mucus onto his sleeve to ensure that his shirt could never be worn again.

"I know what will make you feel better," said Flavia. "The truth."

Sloot was silent. He wanted to unburden himself, to be cleansed of all this deceit, to go back to the counting house and say the Loyalist Oath every morning to the paper flag on the wall of his tiny apartment. He drew in a very deep breath, and every word that came out with his exhalation was the truth. The unpolished, unedited, dash-out-the-door-to-get-the-paper-in-a-very-thin-robe-on-a-very-windy-day sort of truth, which left absolutely nothing to the imagination.

Flavia was right. He did feel better, but then he started feeling woozy.

"I'm so proud of you," she said, smiling at him. She sounded as though she were speaking in echoes. Then everything went black again.

※ 🎐 ※ 🎐 ※ 🎐 ※ 🎐

Before any of this madness had upheaved Sloot's life, he'd woken up alone every single morning. He missed that, and as Roman's bug-eyed gaze came into focus, he wondered if he'd ever get to do it again.

"How'd it go?"

"How'd what go?"

"Your meeting with Uncle, of course! Did my name come up?"

Sloot froze. He'd given Roman up! Where was a good distraction when you needed one?

"Not so fast," he said, relieved for the inspiration and surprised that his brain was able to move so quickly upon waking, "you still owe me an explanation! You betrayed *you know who* back in *you know where!* What good could it possibly—"

"Yes, yes," said Roman, "I couldn't tell you about that before, but it was all part of the plan! Now, I know how good Uncle is at getting things out of people, so don't hold out on me."

"Why shouldn't I? You're holding out on me."

"Fair point," Roman replied, "but horribly inconvenient for me. Look, I promise I'll tell you everything, but I really need to hear yours first."

"Then we are at an impasse."

"Flip a coin for it?"

"Ugh, fine," said Sloot, "I'll just go first." He'd never won a coin toss in his life, and his luck of late hinted that he wasn't about to start now. He told Roman about Flavia, the white room, the crying, everything—including how Roman had been Carpathian Intelligence all along, and how he betrayed Vlad in the end.

"Sorry," he said in the end.

"Don't worry about it," said Roman, who was grinning from ear to ear. "I'd counted on that happening. It was all part of the plan."

"Oh, well that's— What?"

※ ☆ ※ ☆ ※ ☆ ※ ☆

Everyone knows about secret societies. They're usually pretty good at keeping their esoteric rites under wraps, but people aren't stupid.

They tend to be observant when there's no effort involved. Go around wearing fancy jewelry and giving people complicated handshakes, and the supporting cast standing in the background of your life will put two and two together. The only thing preserving the "secrets" of most societies is that people don't tend to care, as long as they're left to finish their drinks in peace.

There are a few *truly* secret societies in the world, but you've never heard of them.

The entire *Carpathian Caper,* which no one would ever call it other than Roman this one time, started nearly thirty years earlier when he'd overheard a pair of burly looking fellows discussing how best to be rid of a body.

"Chop him into pieces," suggested the taller of the two. "Dump the pieces in the river."

"That'd be fine," said the other, "if we only had the one to do."

"We *do* only have the one to do."

"That's true at the moment, but how many did we do last week?"

"I dunno, twenty? Twenty-five? That was different though, we had the big hole."

"Yes we did, but the big hole's full up now."

"Good thing we've only got the one body then."

"We've only got the one body *now,* but what happens if there are another twenty next week?"

"That's too many to chop up and throw in the river," said the taller man. "Constables would wonder where the floating piles of meat were coming from."

"So what would we do with them?"

There was a long pause.

"Well, we usually throw them in the hole."

"But the hole's full up now."

"Can't throw them in the river, it'd be too many."

"Correct."

They both stared at the ground in a diligent abeyance, hoping perhaps that one of the cobbles had an answer written on it.

Roman was crouched behind a barrel. He'd been in the middle of slinking away from an entirely unrelated bit of espionage when he'd come across these two. He was developing a cramp and hoping that something would stir the silence so that he could move undetected.

"We *can* chop this one into pieces and dump it in the river, can't we?"

"I suppose," said the shorter man, "but we're going to have to figure something else out soon. The Serpents of the Earth are piling up a lot of bodies these days."

"We could talk to Mrs. Kni—"

"Don't say her name!"

"We could talk to *you know who* about it, see if she's got any ideas."

"She didn't hire a savvy pair of entrepreneurs like us so she could solve our problems. We're expected to deliver results, without a lot of fuss."

"I did some digging after that," said Roman, "and it turns out that The Serpents of the Earth are the real deal."

"The real deal?"

"In terms of secret societies, there are those who employ dark wizards to perform eldritch rites under blood moons and that sort of thing, and then there are those who just wear a lot of black and meet at the library to exchange moody poetry."

"I see," said Sloot.

"Of course, they mostly do their black masses in the library basement. Fairly rare, blood moons."

"Black masses? You mean with human sacrifices and the like?"

"Oh no," said Roman. "I mean yes, they do that kind, too, but they use the basement of the Great Cathedral for human sacrifices. Much better drainage."

Sloot shuddered.

"The point is that the Serpents of the Earth are really bad people doing really bad things. They're pretty good at keeping it under wraps, too."

"Then how do you know about it?"

"Really? I'm the Spymaster of Salzstadt! You'd be a fool to work for me if I didn't know what the Serpents get up to."

"You still haven't explained why you betrayed Vlad," said Sloot.

"I'm coming to that," said Roman. "Another eventuality in the spy game is getting caught. The helpful bit there is that most intelligence outfits engage in games of catch-and-release. You've got to do something really, *really* bad to find yourself hurtling toward the pavement from a very tall window."

"How bad?"

"I mean, killing the Domnitor would do it. Sorry, sorry, long may he reign, and all that. Or maybe burning down the cathedral during the bristling service on the Feast of St. Bertha. There are a handful of swear words that would get it done, but I only know one of them, and I'm not telling. Just mouthing it out has been known to give every goblin within a mile a severe case of the ragies."

"It's pronounced 'rabies'."

"If only it were that," said Roman. He shivered. "Anyway, I got caught by Uncle in the performance of a less-than-savory errand that I was running for one of Mrs. Knife's lieutenants."

"Were you dropping body parts into the river?"

"Nothing like that, but you know how pork chops are banned on the second Thursday of the month?"

Sloot nodded.

"The Serpents love flaunting that one, and I had a rowboat with secret compartments. Anyway, that was when Uncle figured out that I was in the game. They wanted dirt on the Serpents, I had a bit, and so I was on my merry way without much further ado. Things were good for a long time after that, but recently they've decided that they needed to crack down on foreign incursions."

"They were going to push you out of a window?"

"I decided not to find out. That was where you came in. I knew they'd haul you in once you returned from Carpathia, and that you'd sing every truth you knew when they did. If I could get that truth to be that I've turned on Vlad the Invader, they might not think I'm such a threat!"

"So you betrayed Vlad to stay out of trouble."

"Sort of, only I didn't actually betray Vlad. Much."

"Myrtle and Greta are prisoners at Gildedhearth! Willie was worth a fortune to Vlad! You stole my hero's potion and used it to unleash chaos in the castle!"

"I actually had the potion made for Willie. I just thought you could use a little push to get things rolling with Myrtle, so I gave you the first sip." Roman smiled and wiggled his eyebrows.

"Oh." Sloot started blushing. "Well, what about the rest of it?"

"All of those things are true," said Roman with a hang-dog look. "I wish there had been another way, but this was the only thing that I could see working!"

"To do what?"

"To lift the curse on the Carpathian army, and to crush the Serpents of the Earth. Blood and honor!"

"But we're about to be initiated!"

"Is this your first acquaintance with the concept of an inside job? Much easier to get things done this way. Look, we're running out of time. The wedding's at sunset, and someone's got to open the gates for Vlad."

That was why Roman wanted Greta to come to Carpathia! He must have known that Vlad would fall in love with her—excellent judge of character, indeed—and that Vlad would stop at nothing to rescue her, even if it meant single-handedly invading Salzstadt.

"But how will any of this lift the curse on the Carpathian army?"

"That's still dozens of moves away," said Roman. "I'm still putting it together, but it's going to work. You wait and see."

## INVADER AT THE GATES

Someone's got to open the gates for Vlad," Roman had said. Sloot hadn't bothered hoping that "someone" wouldn't turn out to be him. That would have been lucky, which Sloot wasn't.

Sloot was close enough to the great north gate that he should have been able to see the spot where he touched it every morning, but there were far too many soldiers in the way for that now. He might have found that comforting once, but now that he knew a few more things about the way the world works, he knew that the city guard would only make that sort of display of force if it were necessary.

"Who are you?"

Guards liked asking questions, namely open-ended ones that are likely to catch one unawares and get the proverbial guts spilling.

"Peril. Sloot Peril, of Uncle." There, that sounded official. "What's going on here, Sergeant?"

"Official business," said the guard, "and it's Corporal. You got papers, Sloot Peril of Uncle?"

The guard had a clipboard in one hand and a cudgel in the other. A pencil would have made more sense to the uninformed, but far less sense to the guards, most of whom had never bothered learning to read.

According to Guards Union rule 713, "guards are fully within their rights to carry and brandish their cudgels at all times while on duty." Guards are very proud of their union, and generally insist on exercising all of the rights granted to them by the rules to the fullest possible extent; therefore, with unwavering unanimity, all of the guards in Salzstadt have taken this to mean that they *should* carry and brandish their cudgels at all times.

The clipboards were the result of a great deal of lobbying on the part of the Salzstadt Board of Tourism, who thought that it would make them seem less menacing when questioning tourists. To everyone's great surprise, it worked.

"Here you are," said Sloot, handing over his papers. The corporal gave an adequate performance in skimming them, and Sloot might have been convinced that he really had, if only they hadn't been upside down.

"Where's the gold stamp?"

"I beg your pardon?"

"The gold stamp," said the corporal. "They told us that anybody from Uncle would have a gold stamp on their papers."

"Oh. They've done away with those," said Sloot, surprising himself. He'd told a lie! To a guard! He worked for Uncle now, should he turn himself in? To himself?

"Done away?"

"Yes," said Sloot. "Er, too flashy, you know? Hard to go undercover with a gold seal on your papers."

"Right." The guard squinted at Sloot.

"This bit says I'm with Uncle." Sloot pointed to a paragraph in the middle of the page that read "The bearer of this document, if in possession of livestock or a creditor's letter for purchase of same, is eligible to be prescribed one and a half times the standard measure of whiskey as a treatment for ennui, because we all know how boring it can be, staring at cattle all day."

"Sergeant!" shouted the guard, looking over his shoulder. Another guard walked over, clipboard and cudgel at the ready.

"Yes, Corporal?"

"This fella says he's with Uncle, but he's got no gold stamp."

"Is that so?" The sergeant held his clipboard up next to Sloot's face at arm's length, his eyes darting back and forth between them.

"He says they don't do the gold stamp anymore. Too flashy."

"I haven't heard anything about that," said the sergeant.

"And you're not likely to," responded Sloot, who was pinching himself as hard as he could, trying to resist the urge to confess everything and throw himself at the sergeant's mercy. "Look, I just need to go up on the wall for a moment, do I look like I could cause a fuss?"

They both looked him over. The sergeant gave a little snort and a grin.

"You carrying any weapons?"

"Truth is my only weapon."

"So ... yes?"

"No, it's only a metaphor."

The corporal blinked. He looked at his clipboard, blinked a few more times, then looked back at Sloot.

"I don't think those are allowed up there, you'll need to leave it with me."

"It's not ... it's a figure of speech," said Sloot, "I'm not carrying any weapons. I won't cause any trouble, trust me!"

"What do you think, Sarge, can we trust him?"

"I'm with Uncle," said Sloot, "of course you can trust me."

"That checks out," said the sergeant, looking at his clipboard. "All right, go ahead."

Sloot had never been atop the wall before, but it had never seemed so crowded from below. It was standing room only, and everyone was silently watching a lone figure dressed in red just outside the gates. Sloot politely edged his way between a pair of guards who were too enthralled with watching the solitary figure to notice. He looked down as well and gave a little gasp.

"That's Vlad," he said to no one in particular.

"The Invader!" said the guard on his left.

"What does she want?" asked Sloot, knowing full well why she was there, but feeling the question would help him blend in.

"She hasn't said. Don't worry, the Domnitor will sort it all out, long may he reign."

Vlad was standing in the clearing outside the gates, resplendent in her wicked suit of red enameled steel. The recurved horns on her helmet made Sloot's neck hurt at the mere thought of trying to wear it, and the tower shield on her left arm was nearly as tall as she was.

Sloot didn't see a horse or anyone else with her. Had she walked with all of that, all the way from Carpathia?

There was a blaring of trumpets from farther down the wall, just over the main gate. All of the guards stood up in a very rigid way and saluted.

"Pray attend Domnitor Olaf von Donnerhonig, Defender of the Old Country and Hero of the People! Long may he reign!"

"Long may he reign!" said everyone atop the wall in a single voice.

The Domnitor! He was there on the wall, not twenty feet from Sloot! Should he have brought a gift? No, that's ridiculous. Oh dear, did Roman know that this would happen? Did he send Sloot there to assassinate the Domnitor?

"Why have you come here?"

It was a child's voice. Sloot couldn't see for all the steel-plated brutes in the way. Was the Domnitor letting his son address Vlad? A good tactic for embarrassment.

"Wilhelm Hapsgalt," said Vlad. The sunlight danced over the red enameled plates of her armor, casting red light over everything around her.

"And what do you want with him?"

"He has taken that which is most dear to me. Return Greta to me, and I will return to Carpathia with a clean blade!"

The Domnitor's son started mumbling with his retinue. It was hard for Sloot to make out most of it. Most of them seemed to think that "Greta" was a sword or something. Barbaric lunatics always named their swords, according to the state-approved textbooks, so it stood to reason.

"Look, we don't know what you're after, but you should just go home. I'm not about to start taking things from the great families of Salzstadt and giving them to our enemies!"

"I will cut a bloody swath through your city!" shouted Vlad. "Fires will consume your homes before the sun has set! The people of Carpathia will sup on blood red salt until their grandchildren's grandchildren have grandchildren of their own!"

"You see, this is why we can't be friends! There's no 'please' with you people, it's straight to blood every time! Go home, you big bully, we're finished here."

"I demand a war!"

"Well of course you do. You've probably drunk one of those berserker potions I've heard so much about."

"I'll not be denied by a boy," said Vlad.

A *boy*. It occurred to Sloot that he'd never seen the Domnitor before. It was a hereditary title, after all, and he rarely ever left his palace.

"You're being denied by me," the boy shouted back. "I am Domnitor Olaf von Donnerhonig, Defender of the Old Country and Hero of the People!"

So it was true! The Domnitor, long may he reign, was just a boy! Did Roman expect Sloot to murder a child? It hardly seemed sporting, namely for the guards who would need to flex very few of their ample supply of muscles to put a spear through Sloot, as he attempted bare-handed strangulation on an adolescent who—if he were being honest—would probably have the advantage in terms of upper body strength. Sloot Peril was a calculator, not a fighter.

"You have to have an army to have a war. Everybody knows that. You haven't brought one. No army, no war!"

"I don't need an army to take your city."

"Yes, you do. Now go away."

"No, I don't! Open your gates, and I'll show you!"

"That would defeat the purpose of having gates," said the Domnitor. "That's why you'd need an army, to get them open!"

"Then come down here and fight me yourself!"

"Oh, you'd like that, wouldn't you?"

"I would, very much! Please and thank you!"

Sloot was fascinated by the way that the negotiations were shaping up, though he couldn't see how the Domnitor declining more sarcastically and Vlad threatening more politely would ever end up meeting in the middle. Perhaps with a cold war. Was this how they'd arrived at the current one?

All of the books available in Salzstadt that had anything to do with the Carpathian conflict were in agreement. The open warfare had ended in a very embarrassing way for Vlad the Invader (the current Vlad's father), who had tucked tail and run at the head of his army back to Carpathia, never to be seen again in the Old Country. Likewise, the majority of the Domnitor's forces (this being the current Domnitor's father, or possibly grandfather) had been shipped off to retirement in undisclosed tropical locations, and never you mind all of those six-foot bundles that the ships are dumping way out along the horizon.

"Archers!" shouted the Domnitor, who was apparently finished negotiating. Vlad closed the visor on her great horned helm and crouched behind her tower shield.

"Loose!" shouted someone on the Domnitor's behalf, who was ostensibly empowered to do so, and several trees' worth of arrows filled the sky. To the credit of the Old Country's archers, very few of them missed their mark; however, to the credit of Carpathia's blacksmiths, not one of them penetrated Vlad's shield. They succeeded only in staggering her a bit and pushing her several feet backward, her heavy boots digging a pair of trenches in the dirt.

"You'll need a lot of arrows to get me back to Carpathia that way," shouted Vlad.

"Send the Pride!" shouted the Domnitor, causing everyone on the wall to raise their fists and cheer. The Pride was an elite platoon of Old Country warriors, not a one of whom stood under seven feet tall, though some of that might have been the huge suits of platemail that they always wore.

Their bronze helmets looked like the heads of lions, and their presence on the battlefield brought great honor to the people of the Old Country, thus fulfilling a smug double entendre for the word "pride."

They jogged through the wicket gate in a single file, then formed around Vlad in a semicircle. Vlad cast her shield aside, needing both hands to wield the great sword that she wore on her back. It was nearly as tall as she was.

"Oh well, you win some, you lose some," said anyone having placed money on their talking out their differences. This is why those people's spouses usually held onto the money.

Sloot's gaze followed Vlad in a mathematically improbable pattern of retreating and advancing steps. Had he known anything about the grey-breasted thrushes that summer in the eastern steppes of Carpathia, he'd have recognized Vlad's pattern as being loosely based on their courting dance, which was accompanied by a song of whoops and chirps that are the thrush equivalent of "hey baby, is there a place we can talk where your brothers won't try to peck my eyes out?"

But Sloot was a numbers man and had no interest in ornithology. Sticking to the pattern, Vlad had slain all but one of the Pride within about ten minutes.

"Sir Lars!" shouted the Domnitor. "He's my favorite, I've got all his cards! Send a regiment to help him!"

The Domnitor had leaned forward past the edge of the wall just enough for Sloot to catch a glimpse of him. Sure enough, he was just a boy! Sloot stared at him until he remembered that Roman might have sent him there as an assassin. He wasn't feeling any murderous impulses, but he diverted his eyes quickly just in case.

Vlad and Sir Lars ducked and weaved, swinging their swords, attacking and blocking. Swing, stab, flurry and riposte. It gave the guards on the ground time to open the gates for the regiment to march through in their formations and join the fight.

Sloot wasn't sure what to hope for. He'd grown up hearing about the magnificent daring of the Pride, yet there they were; or rather weren't, not in any way that would be verified by existentialists. It's hard to be proud of two dozen corpses, no matter how shiny their armor is. Plus, Vlad was fighting for love, and Myrtle was with Greta. If Vlad were victorious, Myrtle would likely be freed as well!

Having decided how he felt about things, he wasn't disappointed to see Sir Lars' head coaxed from his shoulders by Vlad's sword just before the regiment was nearly there. He was in the wrong bleachers to start cheering, so he contented himself by thinking "nice one, Vlad!" as emphatically as possible.

"*Now!*" shouted Vlad, just as the forward platoon of foot soldiers stepped into striking distance. There was a flash of ghostly red fire over each of the fallen from the Pride, and each of them stood up and turned their swords toward the advancing soldiers (all except Sir Albrecht, whose inconvenient lack of legs hindered him from rising to the occasion).

Even in death, the warriors of the Pride were each worth a dozen standard-issue Old Country soldiers. To Sloot, who had seen only one death before today and only *almost* experienced another, watching Vlad and the undead Pride cutting through dozens of soldiers would have been disturbing enough on its own; but then the ghostly red fires started flashing over the bodies of the soldiers, and they rose and fought against the living soldiers as well.

"Close the gates!" shouted the Domnitor. All of the soldiers atop the wall scattered, many of them running past Sloot, none giving him a second look.

All of a sudden, there he was: the Domnitor! Sloot panicked and started counting the seconds as they passed, grateful for each one during which he didn't take a run at the boy and try to throw him off the wall.

Perhaps Roman hadn't brainwashed him? Sloot thought about thanking him for that later, but decided it might set the bar a bit too low for their friendship if *not programming me to assassinate a child* merited thanks.

*Someone's got to open the gates for Vlad.* That's what Roman had said. Unfortunately, the Domnitor had just ordered them closed. Under normal circumstances, opening the gates without authorization would be frowned upon. Doing so in the face of the Domnitor's orders would probably count as treason. Just about everything else did.

But what could he do? He knew where the levers were that worked the heavy chains that opened the gates, and he didn't imagine that their operation could be too complicated, but he doubted that the guards would just let him have a turn at them because he asked nicely.

"There you are!" said someone, which was disconcerting. Sloot looked around and found himself alone on the wall.

"What? No, I'm not! Are you a ghost?"

"No, it's me, Nicoleta!"

"Where are you?"

Sloot flinched when Nicoleta exploded into existence in front of him, in a great puff of lavender smoke and a hail of hot pink sparks. She said a swear word.

"I meant to do that in front of a bigger audience, it was my grand entrance! What was that popping sound?"

"Goblin," said Sloot, while slowly releasing his white-knuckled grip on his chest.

"Oh right, the swearing! I'd heard rumors. It's really true?"

Sloot nodded. "Only in the Old Country, as far as I know. Hey, that's the blood star!"

"Shiny, isn't it? Horrible bit of necromancy, though. When Roman told me about it, I wanted to bury it in salt and be done with it; but he was right, it turned out to be very useful."

"Useful?"

"You saw all of the soldiers rise and fight again?"

"You don't mean that—"

"Yeah," said Nicoleta. "It gives me the willies, but it gets around the curse. They're not enlisted soldiers. They're not technically people at all."

"You've got to be alive to be a person?"

"Seems that way. Now how do we open the gates?"

"There's a guardhouse down by the gate, I'm pretty sure you just throw the levers inside of it."

"You're pretty sure?"

"I haven't done it myself! The hard part is going to be getting past the guards. The Domnitor's ordered the gates closed, as you can imagine."

"I can handle the gates," said Nicoleta. "Where's the wedding?"

"In the cathedral. It's the big building at the end of the main road with all the cherubs and gold leaf, you can't miss it. It should be starting any time now."

"All right. You go and stall them. Keep them there!"

※ ⚡ ※ ⚡ ※ ⚡ ※ ⚡

On the island nation of Kaldakos, which can be reached by ship from the Port of Salzstadt in just over a week if the weather is fair, one will find a plurality of the greatest athletes the world has to offer. They believe that their gods are very keen on sport, and that phenomenal displays of athleticism convince them not to stir up the volcanoes underneath their feet. Kaldakosi athletes train year round, except for Saturdays, when they lie around on beaches to keep up with their bronzing.

They have several different words for running. There's one for the give-it-everything-you've-got sort of running that sprinters do, one for the make-it-last sort that the long-distance runners do, and even a specific one for spectators who don't want to miss anything but have had too many cold ones to ignore nature's call any longer.

There are dozens more than those, but not one of them fits neatly around whatever it was that Sloot was doing. It was the unrehearsed flailing of an accountant who'd never given serious thought into how he might propel himself quickly from one place to another, recognizable by the spastic employment of all available muscles in what seemed a random order. It was the sort of running you might expect to see if the brain refused to have anything to do with it, and the knees were deemed most capable of filling in.

His steadfast dedication to the avoidance of athleticism would have left him gasping for breath if he had simply run that far, but his artistic interpretation of running required a lot more effort. He collapsed in a sweaty heap on the steps of the cathedral.

"You're very nearly late," said Olga.

"Then I'm on time."

"Don't sass me, Peril. On your feet."

"I need a moment to catch my breath."

"You can do it while we walk."

"No, I can't! I think I'm dying."

If Olga's wand arm was tired from the thrashing she gave Sloot all the way up the steps, she didn't let on. It occurred to Sloot that the sort of upper body strength and endurance she displayed required the sort of training that would distract one from studying higher mathematics. His smugness helped to shield him from the humiliation of the beating. If trigonometry were weaponized, he could have vaporized her with a thought.

The inside of the cathedral looked different from the way that Sloot remembered it. To be fair, he wasn't particularly religious, so it could have been that he'd only been inside on special occasions before. Perhaps the usual workaday decorations were skulls, black candles, chalices filled with blood, and black banners with silver snakes painted on.

The pews were nearly full, and everyone was wearing black robes with hoods drawn up. They were engaged in the susurrus of idle chitchat that traditionally precedes someone important taking the stage and saying, "All right, settle down now, if we don't get started we'll be here all day."

"Put this on," instructed Olga, shoving a black cloak into Sloot's hands. His face was dripping with sweat and hot enough for frying eggs. He gave a little whimper, which only seemed to fuel Olga's enthusiasm for wand whacking. He donned the cloak and concentrated on not keeling over.

"Now follow me," said Olga, "and do try not to vomit on anything."

They walked up the side aisle and onto the dais where the altar stood. Olga put him between two other hooded figures and left without thrashing him any further. He could tell she wanted to, though.

Sloot stood there, feeling miserable. His heart was still thundering in his chest, and he was panting and sweating under the heavy velvet cloak. A groan slipped out of him, one that was half whimper on its father's side.

"Sloot, is that you?" asked the figure on his left.

"Roman?"

"Yes, keep your voice down!"

"How'd you know it was me?"

"I've heard your whimper often enough," whispered Roman. Sloot could hear him smiling in a smug sort of way.

"What happens now?" whispered Sloot.

"We're Willie's wedding party," whispered Roman. "We just stand here and look ominous, I suppose. What happened on the wall?"

"Vlad's here, though I suppose you know that already."

"No, but I figured. Did you talk to her?"

"To Nicoleta. She's opening the gates, she told me to stall."

"How're you going to do that?"

"I don't know!"

"Shhh!"

Just then, the organ started belting out an eerie, discordant tune. Truly awful by any measure, which probably meant that it was art, which probably meant that it was expensive. Everyone stood up from their pews and started singing along in a language that Sloot didn't recognize. The doors of the transepts opened, and a column of black-hooded figures walked out from each of them. They formed a ring around the altar. Then a single figure (also wearing a black cloak with the hood up, to Sloot's lack of surprise) approached the altar, turned to face the audience, and held his hands out above his head. The organ and the singing abruptly ceased.

"We gather now, brothers and sisters, to witness the joining of two of our number in the necessity of matrimony. Bring forth the bridegroom!"

The figure on Sloot's right stepped forward and pulled back his hood. It was Willie, wearing his most pompous smirk.

"Bring forth the bride!" said the officiant.

"That's old Constantin speaking, isn't it?" whispered Sloot to Roman.

Roman nodded.

"According to what I've read, he's the Eye of the Serpent. That's the living leader."

"As opposed to the dead one?"

"Actually yes," whispered Sloot, choosing to ignore Roman's sarcastic tone. "The dead one is the Soul of the Serpent."

"I hope he's not here," said Roman with a shiver.

"She," said Sloot. "Not entirely archaic, these arcane evil types."

Several people were walking toward the altar from the narthex. The one in front was clearly the bride, or possibly a latecomer with a flair for upstaging.

No, it was the bride, followed by several hooded figures. Sloot had heard that wedding gowns were generally uncomfortable, but having her arms bound at her sides and being prodded forward at knifepoint took the trope beyond its usual bounds. Constantin waited until everyone had taken their places at the altar before continuing.

"Honored guests, who shall remain anonymous, we are gathered here today to witness the nuptials of Wilhelm Hapsgalt and Greta Urmacher. So that none may contest their union in perpetuity, attorneys have been appointed to speak for them, provided at no cost by the Three Bells Shipping Company, a completely independent party with no interest in the matter."

A chuckle drifted through the pews.

Constantin droned on at length about the nature of marriage. It's a mandatory tradition, as inevitable as flatulence during lulls in conversation. Even the officiant would rather have a couple of quick "I dos" and get straight to figuring out which uncle would embarrass themselves the most at the open bar, but that's not the way it works.

Sloot may have been the only person in the room who breathed a sigh of relief every time a long pause turned out not to be the end of Constantin's droning, but a break to draw in a breath.

What was that? The ring of steel on steel! It came from outside the church, barely audible beneath Constantin's agitated recitation of the virtues of patience. Even though he was hurrying through it, maybe it would take long enough for Vlad to intercede.

"Bring them forth," said Constantin. Willie stepped toward him, as did Greta at the gentle coaxing of the knife between her shoulders. "Now join hands, and we'll hear opening remarks."

Greta growled from beneath her veils. Her arms were still bound at her sides, so she didn't move. Standing an arm's length from her, Willie bent over at the waist and reached forward to interlock his fingers with hers. It looked uncomfortable, but Sloot had seen some of the poses that Willie had affected in the name of fashion. This was nothing compared to the Funky Egret or the Hotshot Marmot.

"If it pleases the church," said the hooded figure acting as Willie's lawyer, "we would enter into wedlock one Wilhelm Hapsgalt, being of sound mind and, in his own words," he paused and sighed, "devastating handsomeness."

Constantin groaned. "Very well, let the record so reflect."

"Ha!" said Willie. "My devastating handsomeness is official now. Thank you, legal entanglements!"

"Shush, Willie," said Constantin, "don't interrupt. Opening remarks from the bride's counsel, if you please?"

The hooded figure holding the knife to Greta's back entered a similar statement for the official record, which Sloot noticed was being taken down by a hooded stenographer. Also entered into the record were several instructions to disregard the bride's vigorous head-shaking, noting that they were likely the result of a bee having flown under her veils, and couldn't possibly be taken to constitute disagreement with the arguments entered into the record on her behalf. The fact that bees are not native to the Old Country didn't come up.

Sloot was thankful for the time required to set the record straight. The sounds of combat inched nearer the cathedral. Perhaps no stalling would be necessary on his part!

"Duly noted," said Constantin. "We will proceed to the vows."

Greta's lawyer pulled her veils back, revealing that she'd been gagged as well as bound. She was glaring at Willie as though they'd already been married for quite some time and had discussed divorce on multiple occasions. Willie was grinning from ear to ear, his moony gaze handing textbooks a readymade example of the word "oblivious."

"Insofar as he is empowered to do so," Willie's lawyer began, "the groom does hereby vow to provide no less than the minimum acceptable quantities of love and affection, as set down by municipal statutes relevant to same. Any further issuances of emotional gratification are reserved by the groom as at-will gratuities, to be granted at his sole discretion."

He went on to set out various clauses and addendums pertaining mostly to financial matters, droning on with a particular lack of enthusiasm generally reserved for reading standardized documents, whether done for the purpose of torture or otherwise. It was the first time in Sloot's life that he'd actively hoped such a recitation would come with an encore.

"Let the record reflect that none of the aforesaid vows constitute admission of guilt in any capacity," said the lawyer, and then he was silent.

A motion was put forth to forego entering the bride's vows into the record in long form, but was ultimately rejected on the grounds that the underlying reference documents had been certified by different municipal authorities. Sloot, quietly delighted, had a hard time paying attention to Greta's lawyer as the pandemonium of the battle outside grew infinitesimally louder with every passing moment. It made him feel like a real Carpathian to think, *Oh, goody, the battle will be upon us any minute now!*

"Very well," said Constantin. "By the power vested in me by innumerable dark forces, whose names have been redacted to satisfy the Goblin Control Act of 914, I hereby pronounce—"

"Objection!"

"What? Who said that?"

It had been Sloot. He only realized it after Constantin asked. Why had he done that? He'd been told to stall the wedding, of course, but now he was in grave danger!

"Well," said Constantin, "if no one's going to own up to it, I suppose—"

"It was I!" said Sloot, taking a step forward. The hooded assembly all pitched in on a very dramatic gasp. Willie looked very hurt and confused. Greta looked relieved.

"Peril!" shouted Mrs. Knife, who stepped away from the altar to confront him. "I knew you couldn't be trusted. What is the meaning of this?"

"Uh, well," said Sloot in the traditional mode of someone stalling for time, "everyone's got hoods on! Have we bothered to verify that there is a notary present?"

"I'm a notary," said Gregor, sneering as he removed his hood.

"That makes sense," said Sloot, who'd never had a pleasant encounter with a notary in his life.

"If there's nothing further?" boomed Constantin.

"Objections!" said Sloot, causing himself further panic.

"What?"

"You never asked if there were any objections!"

"That didn't stop you from belting one out, did it, Peril?"

"I beg your pardon, m'lord, but marriage is a complicated legal affair, isn't it? You leave one bit out, and a crafty lawyer can do away with the whole thing! There might even be alimony."

There was another gasp from the pews. Even old Constantin, who was red in the face from shouting, blanched slightly.

"Very well," said Constantin. "If anyone objects to the union of these two people, speak up!"

There was a reverberant *boom*, as something from outside collided with the doors. They'd been barred from the inside, so they held.

"How long must we wait for objections?" asked Mrs. Knife.

*Boom.*

"I think that's about long enough," said Willie's lawyer.

*Boom.*

"All right then," said Constantin. "If there's nothing further—"

*Boom.*

"I hereby pronounce you husband—"

*Crash.*

## ⁂SALZSTADT, SHAMBLING SALZSTADT⁂

V lad's army had not so much stormed the cathedral as shambled into it, a lifetime of impeccable queueing skills chucked right out the window by the simple act of having died and been reanimated with a bit of blood magic. The sheer chaos of it coaxed an entire congress of goblins into the balconies, where they cackled and spit and threw whatever they could get their hands on down below. Most of the hooded figures in the pews were laid low by the horde of undead and started to rise back up and join the other side when it all came to a very abrupt halt.

"What's happening?" asked Sloot, who never thought he'd have mixed feelings about a horde of undead ceasing their shambling in his direction.

"It's Gregor!" said Roman.

"Where is it?" said Gregor with a snarl. His hands were held aloft, his fingers twisted into mysterious gestures that could have been construed as vulgar in any country. He was scanning the room for something.

"Gregor's holding them back somehow," said Roman.

"Is that good or bad?" asked Sloot.

"Hard to say. How do you feel about being ripped apart by supernatural evil, but you take down an evil cult in the process?"

"Strike down the wizard!" shouted Vlad. "We can finish this!"

"There!" shouted Gregor, his eyes going wide with bloodshot glee.

He interlocked his fingers in a way that must have required a great deal of yoga, wiggled his thumbs, and Nicoleta blinked into view. Gregor made another gesture, and she started floating toward him, unable to move or speak or resist.

"Clever, cunning little wretch." Gregor's forefinger twitched. The blood star snapped away from the chain around Nicoleta's neck and flew into his grip.

"I'd wondered where this had gotten to," said Gregor. "Its connection was strong when it was first placed in the clock tower in Ulfhaven, and then it disappeared. This insolent churl must have stolen it!"

"Release her," shouted Vlad, "or you'll pay with your life!"

Gregor laughed. "You can't kill what's already dead, Invader! You'll be with your forebears soon enough. When you see your grandfather, tell him Ashkar and the Virag send their regards!"

Gregor's hands closed into fists, and he worked them in circles while Nicoleta twisted in the air and screamed. There was a series of cracking sounds, and she fell lifeless to the floor. Vlad gave a proper berserker roar, raised her sword, and was grappled by the undead horde behind her.

"*My* servants now," said Gregor with a cackle. "Bring her to me! And take them as well!"

Sloot whimpered aloud and hoped for some version of the phrase "taken by a horde of undead" that ended with all of his insides still *inside*. The gods of linguistics must have heard him, as the corpses of Sloot's countrymen held him fast, but didn't go searching his guts for prizes.

"Get off!" shouted Roman. "What're you grabbing me for?"

"You're involved somehow," said Gregor. "I'll find out— Oh, would you *please* subdue the girl already?"

To her credit, Myrtle had yet to be apprehended by the mob. She was swinging her broom with righteous fury, and while the recently deceased might have forgotten queueing etiquette in death, the power of the broom was still enough to keep them at bay.

"I'll fight you until my last breath!" shouted Myrtle.

"Ugh, fine." Gregor made a gesture, and Myrtle's neck went *snap*. She slumped to the floor.

Someone started screaming, and Sloot thought it was weird that the sound hurt his throat more than his ears. Other than that, he felt absolutely nothing. That was weird, given all the chaos and the looming threat of a grisly death. Perhaps this was one of those coping mechanisms that he'd heard so much about. He'd always wanted to try one.

"If you are quite finished!" shouted Constantin, which was startling enough to stop Sloot's screaming. "Thank you. *Ahem*. Husband and wife. Kiss your bride, boy."

Vlad swore curses and foamed at the mouth. Willie went bright red and giggled like an idiot. Greta locked eyes with Vlad and wept.

"Willie!" shouted Constantin.

"Hmm?"

"Kiss her, you dolt! There's more to get through."

Willie blushed and giggled. Constantin sighed.

It took Willie half a dozen shuffling steps to close the three feet that separated him from Greta, who was held firmly in place by a pair of corpses who'd once been constables. He gave her a furtive peck on the cheek and went right back to giggling like a goon.

"There," said Constantin, "that's done. Now, Mrs. Knife, if you please?"

Mrs. Knife clapped her hands, and the hooded figures around the altar started clearing it off. They lifted Constantin to kneel atop it, and Mrs. Knife placed an ornate golden chalice in front of him.

"All right, Willie," said Mrs. Knife, "it's time for the Rite of Ascension."

"Sorry, the what?"

"The pages from the Book of Black Law that I told you to read. You did read them, didn't you?"

"Of course I did! The old Rite of Ascension then, eh? Piece of cake, right? Good, yeah, let's do it then."

"Take your position," said Gregor.

Sloot watched Vlad struggling against the dozen or so undead who had forced her to her knees and piled themselves on top of her. He'd thought about struggling himself, but reasoned that his own meager frame probably wouldn't support that much weight. Live to fight another day, and all that.

"The thing is," said Willie, "I can't really remember the bit at the beginning."

"What?"

"Yeah, maybe you could just give me a hint as to the first bit? I'm sure I'll remember the Rite of ... what was it?"

"Ascension!"

Willie tried on a look of skepticism. "No, that wasn't it. Was it?"

Mrs. Knife said a swear word. *Pop, cackle* went a goblin.

"He didn't read it," said Mrs. Knife. "Gregor, can you wiggle him like a puppet or something?"

"No," said Constantin, "he has to do it of his own free will. Willie! Come up here and stand behind me."

"Right-o," said Willie.

"But only if you want to."

"Oh, then no, thanks."

"Willie, use your free will to get up here *this instant!*"

"Alrighty, then."

Willie attempted an ill-conceived gymnastic maneuver that nearly won him a broken nose.

"Just climb up, you twit!"

"Sorry."

Once he was in position, Mrs. Knife handed him a wicked-looking ceremonial dagger. Jagged steel with a bone handle carved to look like snakes. Just the sort of ghastly thing you'd expect to see used in a horrible ceremony by cultists wearing black hoods.

Willie held the dagger at arm's length and squinted. He nodded, gave it a couple of good swings, and made twirly loops with it the way that no one who knows how to use a dagger would ever do.

"Very nice," said Willie. "I'll just, er, pay for this and be on my way then, yes?"

"No," said Gregor, "you'll use it to drain your father of his last drop of blood!"

"What? No, I won't! Father needs all of his blood inside of him, I'm sure of it!"

"Do as you're told, boy!" shouted Constantin. "But only if you want to. And you'd better want to, or else!"

"Let me do it, Constantin!" Mrs. Knife moved in close and whispered to him.

"Out of the question," he replied. "I have no doubt you'd make a fine Eye, but Willie is my heir! Do it now, boy, claim your destiny and take my life!"

"But why?"

"It'll all make sense in a moment," he said. "Now do it before I lose my patience!"

"But I've never killed anybody," said Willie, fighting back tears. "I love you, Father!"

"Do it now, or I'll tell Mrs. Knife to kill Greta."

"You wouldn't!" shouted Willie.

Vlad shouted some swear words. *Pop, pop, pop.*

"Kill an old man who wants to die," said Constantin. "Obey your father and save your bride. You'll be the hero, Willie!"

Sloot knew the face that Willie was making. He'd made it himself before. It was the face of resignation to fate. All of the choices before him were bad ones, and he'd lost all hope that the clouds would part. Nothing left to do then but let go, and trust that fate would be kind.

Willie drew the knife across Constantin's throat in a stilted, haphazard way that was consistent with wanting neither to do it poorly nor well. The old man's eyes went wide as the blood poured from him. It filled the chalice and kept going, running forth from him in great arterial spurts.

"There's a good boy," said Mrs. Knife. As she took the bloody dagger from his hand, something like a sickly green smoke started to pour upward from Constantin's eyes and mouth. It flowed out from him and into Willie, who gasped and shot upright, staring wide-eyed up to the dome of the cathedral.

"The ascension is at hand," said Willie, whose voice had a very Constantin echo to it. "What has always been shall continue through me."

"That's right," said Mrs. Knife in a very soothing tone, "that's right." With practiced grace, she reached over Willie's shoulder and drew the ceremonial knife across his throat with a single fluid motion.

Willie choked and sputtered, unable to speak. The dagger fell from Mrs. Knife's hand, and she pushed Willie down atop his father. The ghastly green smoke flowed up from Constantin, through Willie, and into Mrs. Knife.

"The power," exclaimed Mrs. Knife, with echoes of Constantin and Willie mixed in. "The power!"

"Yes," Gregor cried, "it's working! The Serpents of the Earth are ours to command!"

The pair of them went into a full-bellied laughing fit, and the hordes of undead began to howl.

"This is really bad," said Roman.

"I suppose it is," said Sloot.

"We've got to get out of here, quickly!"

"I doubt it would help."

"What? Snap out of it, man, our lives are on the line!"

"I know," said Sloot, "but it hardly seems worth the effort."

"Of course it's worth the effort! Literally anything that you do to preserve your own life would be worth the effort! The alternative is *death!*"

But would that be so bad, really? Sure, Sloot's life up to that point had had a few bright spots, but most of it had been overshadowed by the feeling of dread, the lurking sense of fear that comes with being a natural worrier. He didn't believe in any sort of afterlife. He found himself thinking in that very moment that there was exactly one thing he didn't fear, and that was death.

"D'you think I'll get to see Myrtle again?"

"No, I don't," replied Roman. "There's more courage in you than you think, Sloot Peril!"

"There really isn't."

"Nonsense. I'm an excellent judge of character, you know. I'm not wrong about you!"

"Yes, you are."

"Fine," said Roman. "You might not care about your own life, but are you going to let me die?"

"Why not? You dragged me into this mess!"

"Because I'm your friend! Not the most selfless one, perhaps, but I've always been your friend! You may be a mild-mannered bundle of nerves, Peril, but you're the most earnest and loyal bundle of nerves I've ever met."

"Fine! What would you have me do?"

Vlad shouted another string of profanity. Several more goblins went *pop* and started pestering the undead.

"Swear!" shouted Roman. "Swear like your life depended on it!"

What could it hurt now? He said the one that used to mean "sleeping late on Tuesdays," until teenagers made something filthy out of it. *Pop.* He didn't see how it would help, but it was oddly satisfying.

Next, he said the one that sailors yell at young ladies who tend to be the sisters of other sailors, usually causing fights to break out. *Pop, pop.* He said the one that sounds like pulling a boot out of the muck. *Pop.* He said the one that involved a spatula, the one that meant going fishing without a rod, and the one that no one's actually limber enough to manage, outside of a circus anyway. *Pop, pop, pop.*

It was working! The cackling of the goblins started to rise to the volume of the howling undead, and they started going at each other with a savage fury. Sloot was getting kicked and stepped on in the process. He managed to see Vlad get to her feet, then rolled himself into a ball in a vain attempt to protect himself.

"Get up, Sloot, get up!" Roman sounded very far away. It was getting hard to breathe, for all the weight of the goblins-versus-undead brawl that was happening on top of him. The mad screams, the maniacal laughter—it all went sort of muddy, like someone was packing cotton into his ears.

*Like when Mrs. Knife stabbed me that time,* thought Sloot. *Yep, it's a lot like that.*

# ⚡️NO REST FOR THE WORRIED⚡️

Well you were wrong about one thing," said the most reassuring voice that Sloot had ever heard. It seemed to be all around him, which he found very comforting.

"Yes? And what was that?"

"There is an afterlife."

"Oh." Sloot paused. "So I'm dead, then?"

"So to speak," replied the voice, "but there's no need to sound so dour about it."

"Isn't there? My life is over!"

"Well the one, yes. But you'll get to start your new one soon."

"So I'm *not* dead?"

"I wish you'd stop using that word."

"What, dead?"

"Yes, that one."

"But I *am* dead. I find myself in the condition that the word was invented to describe."

"From the point of view of the living, yes; but you've left that realm."

"Well, I'll have to take your word for it. I can't see anything."

"There's not really anything to see. Not yet."

"But there will be?"

"Of course! You'll be in the afterlife soon."

"Oh," said Sloot. "I thought this was it."

"Not just yet. This is the aether, you're not a fully-formed ghost yet."

"And then I'll be ... what? Undead? Afteralive?"

"I wouldn't want to steer you wrong," said the voice. "There will be a word for it, but it keeps changing. I find it hard to keep up. Suffice it to say that 'dead' is kind of ... I dunno, derogatory at the moment."

"All right. Sorry."

"No problem. You did just get here, after all."

After all. That was it, wasn't it? Sloot supposed he should take some comfort in being d- well, not alive anymore, but comfort was a luxury in which undiluted worriers never learned to indulge.

"How long does this take?"

"I couldn't say. Time passes here, but we don't really mark it down or anything."

Sloot nodded, or rather his social instinct to nod lurched in the general direction of his head, which he no longer possessed. He resolved then to sit and wait; or at least to wait, as sitting required appendages that he presently lacked. He settled for thinking about sitting, how he'd have done it if he still had all his what-do-you-call-thems. Legs and such.

Even that proved difficult. He was having a hard time with the concept of the body he'd left behind, recalling which way the elbows bent, how many digits on each of the appendages, whether an exceptionally large nose could fill in for the ears if they went on vacation—that sort of thing.

He sighed, or rather, didn't.

"You must have questions," said the voice.

"What? No one told me!"

"I meant that you're *likely* to have questions."

"Oh. Well yes, but there are too many."

"Just pick one," said the voice.

"All right. Who are you?"

"Oh, that's a popular one! Some of your brothers and sisters have told me about fairy godmothers. Have you heard of those?"

"I have. You're my fairy godmother?"

"Not at all," said the voice, "but it's sort of like that."

"How?"

"Well, I don't grant wishes or anything."

"Then why bring it up at all?"

"Well, I sort of bring you into the world and watch over you."

"Like a mother, then."

"That would be confusing."

"Right," said Sloot, "and we're doing such a good job of avoiding confusion otherwise."

"They don't appreciate sarcasm in the afterlife either, you know. I meant that you've already got a mother."

"The same one?"

"She doesn't stop being your mother over a silly thing like departing the realm of the living."

"Oh. Well, that's nice."

"Isn't it? So I'm not your mother, but the roles overlap a bit."

"What do I call you?"

"Anything you want."

"So I could call you … call you … oh dear, I've forgotten things!"

"What things?"

"All of them!"

"Oh, that," said the voice. "Don't worry, it's part of the process. It'll all come back to you."

"Right." Telling him not to worry, even in his ethereal state, had roughly the same chance of success as asking the cat to help out with the laundry.

"Hauntings," said Sloot.

"Yes?"

"I know about hauntings."

"You see? Coming back already! You'll get the bits relevant to ghosts first, the rest may take awhile."

Sloot thought to ask how long, but knew that there would be no satisfactory answers in that direction.

"Wait, how could it be coming back? I've never known anything about hauntings before."

"Are you sure?"

"The living don't haunt, though the lurking that teenagers do shares a lot of the hallmarks. I'm sure I remember that."

"Not a lot of teenagers in the afterlife."

Well, that was something. Sloot performed the spectral equivalent of a groan. Was this really all that there was to it? The afterlife was just the thing that comes next? That must have been why Arthur was so existential all the time. There's no meaning of life, you're just alive until you're not.

All the time he'd wasted worrying! Who would do Willie's accounts now? Doesn't matter, Willie's dead. Whose accounts would Sloot do? He wasn't sure whether it would be more unsettling to learn that the formerly living have jobs, or that they don't. He always thought he'd retire someday, but not before he'd gotten more mileage from all the math he'd learned.

Math! He remembered math, his old friend; only he didn't really, he just remembered *about* it. It would come back to him, wouldn't it? He was sure he'd have been hyperventilating if he still had a breathing apparatus.

It was too much. He needed to think about something else.

"I'll be able to haunt people then?"

"If you must."

"What if I just want to?"

"You'll only want to if you must."

"I think I want to."

"Then I suppose you must."

"Is everything in the afterlife so hedonistic?"

"It's not hedonism, more like compulsion."

Sloot was silent again, but whether for no time at all, an eternity, or somewhere in between, he couldn't say. He'd liked to have twiddled his what-do-you-call-thems or something, but for lack of corporeal form, he simply *was* instead.

He was, and he thought he could still do that, anyway. He could probably even think about things other than haunting and appearing in mirrors, but he didn't want to. He worried that he was a bit too interested in said ghostly pastimes, and that's when the floodgates opened.

Worrying! Now *that* was familiar! To be comforted by feeling worried was the sort of duality that only a professional philosopher should ever attempt, but it wasn't as though it would kill him. At that, the concept of smug chuckling drifted through his consciousness, but his worries were sufficiently severe to drown it out.

What about Uncle? What about the Domnitor, long may he reign? He always assumed that death would release one from duty, yet here he was, or rather wasn't, feeling perhaps more compelled than ever to get on with things.

Purposes. He'd had so many! There was his position with Lord Hapsgalt, though Willie's death may abrogate the need for accounting; unless the pragmatists were wrong, and you *can* take it with you.

There was also Carpathia. He still had a duty to Vlad, at least until he could ascertain whether she had lost her life as well. But if her death hadn't released her from duty either, he'd probably still have to work for her. What do ghosts do for other ghosts?

Winking Bob. If he'd had blood, it would have run cold when he remembered that she still had his signature on a blank piece of paper!

"You're doing the thing," said the voice.

"What thing?"

"Unfinished business tends to make the former living a bit crazy."

"Well, what am I supposed to—"

"Nothing," said the voice. "Not at the moment. You've just had a nice long life, and you'll be off to the next bit in … well, in a period of time. Why not just enjoy the silence for a bit?"

He'd never tried that. There had never been time. That was still the case, though in a far more literal sense. What could it hurt? Sloot surrendered to the utterly blank emptiness and did his best to avoid his thoughts.

He existed in the absence of everything, and experienced the spiritual equivalent of the color grey for what may or may not have been a length of time. And then, all of a sudden, Sloot received the distinct impression that something was about to happen.

## ABOUT THE AUTHOR

Sam Hooker writes darkly humorous fantasy novels. He lives in California with his wife and son, who he hopes are secretly amused by his howling at the moon with the dog at all hours of the night.

Read more about Sam at http://shooker.co.

**Other Work**
The Winter Riddle, 2016, Howling Hill Publishing

CPSIA information can be obtained
at www.ICGtesting.com
Printed in the USA
BVHW03s0824290518
517493BV00015B/420/P

9 780999 742303